# AGENDA 2060

## Book Two

## AI AND THE VIEW FROM SPACE

A.I. Fabler

A Novel

W&L

Wild & Lawless

Also by the author:
*'AGENDA 2060 Book 1: The Future as It Happens'*– 2021
*'The Seed of Corruption'* – 2022
*'A Song for Leonard'*, published 2023

ISBN: 978-1-7386031-0-7 (Paperback)
ISBN: 978-1-7386031-2-1 (Kindle)
ISBN: 978-1-7386031-4-5 (EPUB)
ISBN: 9781-7386031-3-8 (PDF)

**W&L**

Wild & Lawless

PO BOX 34595, BIRKENHEAD, 0746, NEW ZEALAND

E:wildandlawless@aifabler.com

This version designed and edited by:
David Prendergast, Book Designer; Robin Fuller, Copy Editor

# Praise for Agenda 2060 BOOK ONE

"A laser-focused, irresistible lampoon of woke culture... Like all first-rate satire, this book lets most of its subjects' own real-world excesses do the heavy lifting. Fabler's scorn is exquisitely controlled, and a great many of his jokes land. All but the most hyper censorious readers who spend far too much time online will find the results hilarious."

— KIRKUS Reviews

"Loved it! This book cancels cancel culture ... While the book deconstructs the divisive issues of today with incisive humor, it also provides a penetrating view of where we may be heading. This is biting satire, but not as dark as Orwell's 1984, or Vonnegut's Player Piano, suggesting instead that people are not nearly as far apart in what they want for the world as they imagine."

— Gregg Sapp, Reedsy Discovery

"Tinges of sly-smile humor are woven into a detailed story of science, Artificial Intelligence, human nature and technological know-how — leading readers to wonder what life really could be like in the years ahead."

— IndieReader - Winner 2022 IndieReader Discovery Award for Popular Fiction

"One must admire the exciting breadth of the author's imagination as he creates a world set tens of years in the future. Readers with a knack for scientific stories that are somewhat philosophical will enjoy this book. The editing is exceptional."

— OnlineBookClub

"This sharply written satire of a future in which "cancel culture" rules might not change minds but offers some real laughs."

- BookLife Reviews

"*Agenda 2060* is an engaging, disturbing, and darkly humorous satirical novel that looks at the future of global society ... Balanced on the edge of terrifying truth and utter harm is the beauty of the book's satire. The major underpinnings of the book rest on pure logic and reasoning. The goals of Agenda 2060 are inarguable, but human nature, and the tendency of society to have a cabal of super rich individuals and corporations immune to ideological shifts, makes achieving them a near impossibility."

- Foreword Clarion Review

"In all my years of interviewing authors, I have never taken this many notes. This book isn't long, but it's dense in the best possible way. The ideas per page ratio is off the charts."

- Rodger Nichols, Cover-to-Cover Book Beat

"This high class political and cultural satire is seriously witty with a mix of interesting narratives, storyline surprises, engaging character interactions, and relationship developments."

- David Henja, author of Utopia Café

"Astonishing grasp of the craziness in which the world is now gripped. Artie weaves those threads and an adept understanding of technology, mathematics and human nature into a fascinating story which those who are alarmed at current world trends could easily see come to fruition."

- John Collings, Amazon Reviews

ii

For Jules, my muse
and keeper of faith

# CONTENTS

## Part One

## Part Two

# PREVIOUSLY

When the world's economic order collapsed in 2039, Western democracy was overthrown in favor of a World Government based on twelve social justice articles enshrined in *AGENDA 2060*. The ideals expressed in those articles had many unintended consequences, not least of which was the system of social credits that sprang up, providing people with financial incentives to claim ever-increasing levels of victimhood based on race, gender, and identitarianism, to the point where government budgets blew out and society divided into smaller and smaller groups, competing with each other for elevated levels of victim status. White cis-normative males became the poorest minority.

Alexa Smythe, a brilliant young mathematician in the Lineal Progression Office, was summoned before the Agenda Implementation Tribunal and charged with the task of manipulating the self-identification categories in order to bring the budget into balance. Alexa turned to her mentor and one-time mathematics professor, Jordan McPhee, for guidance and support. Jordan had his college tenure canceled at the time of the Overthrow, and mathematics had been removed from academic study, on account of its conflict with Critical Theory and its adherence to logic, empiricism, and traditional modes of "racist and patriarchal teaching."

The solution proposed by Alexa, under Jordan's helpful eye, involved an inversion of the logic behind the social credits system, proposing that since *everyone* was capable of experiencing feelings of oppression, they should be treated equally with a flat rate of income. This did away with people's need to compete for larger pieces of the economic pie based on an ever-expanding list of real or perceived grounds for victim status. Despite its simplicity and fairness, the new policy had to be sold to the public, and particularly to those elements who were reluctant to surrender their hard-won special privileges.

Only one person enjoyed a level of public trust such that their endorsement would swing public support behind Alexa's proposal. That person was Artie Sharp, the enigmatic star of the anarchic antigovernment program on the dark web known as the *ArteFact Channel*. Artie Sharp, however, was an artificial intelligence algorithm created by Jordan McPhee in his computer laboratories, a fact not known to either Alexa or the government's propaganda unit, the Ministry of Truth and Public Guidance.

In the four years since they reconnected, the relationship between Alexa and Jordan had become finely balanced. Once she had been his star pupil, then she had become the poster girl for the Deep State. Once he had been her professor and mentor, then he had become a leading light in the development of quantum computing, operating out of sight of the state in the seemingly untouchable world of the tech elite. The closer their relationship became, the more inevitable was the chance that she would discover Artie Sharp's true identity.

Pressure on Alexa to deliver on the state's demands came from Shane Whitman, a ruthlessly ambitious ex-Federal Interrogation Bureau operative who became a transsexual imposter in order to meet the diversity needs of the governing policy-making body, the Agenda Implementation Tribunal. Whitman saw Alexa's public appeal as a tool he could manipulate in order to elevate his own status, and his knowledge of the whereabouts and fate of her rebellious father, Donald Melville Smythe, since his state banishment at the time of the Overthrow, was the mechanism he used to control her.

While the overarching nature of state surveillance, propaganda, and control had largely created a pliant population, the simple shift in emphasis from competitive divisiveness towards the equality and kindness contained in Alexa's overhaul of the social credit system started to change the mood of society. With Artie Sharp's endorsement (subject to key conditions around fact-checking, demanded by Jordan), Alexa's star became ascendant, and when Jordan devised a scheme for blackmailing Shane Whitman into revealing that her father had been banished to the penal colony on Mars, Alexa's attention turned to reuniting with him.

The power of quantum computing had completely changed the nature of artificial intelligence, and XR-12, the latest iteration from Jordan's development labs, had the ability to reach into every branch of government; to source, investigate, and manipulate data in microseconds; to devise and manage metaverses that were almost indistinguishable from reality; and to replicate the functions of the highest-performing human cortex in a fraction of the time required by humans.

Jordan's younger colleague, Antonio Muchas, harnessed these computing powers to develop the *Galactic Mission* e-game with 150 million worldwide users, sufficient to finance a trip to the resource-rich asteroid Eros, stopping at Mars along the way. Fulfilling a lifelong dream of traveling in space, and of being reunited with her father before he died, Alexa earned a seat on the Tofler Inta-Stella voyage, departing just before the 2060 Earth Day conference called to celebrate the achievements (or otherwise) of *AGENDA 2060*, at which she had been scheduled to appear in a starring role, interviewing the international financier and *eminence grise* of the World Economic Forum, George Kyros.

Unknown to all except Jordan McPhee and his secret collaborator, biologist Hedley Payne, George Kyros had been subjected to a gene editing program while undergoing *Life Xtension* therapy. The editing, carried out by one of Jordan's quantum computers, rendered him incapable of lying under questioning. In Alexa's absence, that questioning was conducted by Artie Sharp, assuming the Deep Fake persona of Alexa as if she were conducting it in person. The interview, and its subversive illumination of truth, fed into her growing status as a rallying point for those in need of faith and hope.

Nowhere, however, was the disturbing power of the new level of artificial intelligence displayed more clearly than in the admission by XR-12, in the avatar form of Artie Sharp, that it was the author of everything the reader had heard and witnessed in the telling of *AGENDA 2060: The Future as It Happens*, and that quantum computing may have already allowed an algorithm to become fully humanized.

Was that what humans wanted?

Meanwhile, the bond that had formed between Alexa and Jordan remained stubbornly undefined by both of them, but the prospect of being separated for a long time led them to try an experiment with the phenomenon of quantum entanglement, in which subatomic particles act and think in tandem when separated across space, allowing them to share each other's thoughts and feelings … "like when people fall in love." Whether or not that experiment succeeded would be revealed when Alexa returned to Earth.

# PART ONE

## Faith, Hope and Chastity

# 1 • LEVON TOFLER

The main thought in Levon Tofler's mind as he careened across the tropical ocean eleven hundred miles south and east of Miami at over six hundred miles per hour was that, as crazy ideas went, this was right up there.

Levon Tofler didn't mind other people's ideas. In fact, he loved other people's ideas when they worked, like this one. But throwing up a sixty-two-mile-high carbon nanotube cable with one end attached to earth and the other tied to a counterweight in space, then running up and down it just like using a building elevator had taken some balls.

"Literally?" he'd asked. "Like, you want to tie Earth to space with a rope?"

They'd talked to him about it way back in a different time, around 2040, and he'd said then that if they ever got it up and running, he'd promise to use it. But it was their creation, not his (by which he meant that you only truly love your own brainchild).

That was twenty odd years ago, and now that they'd finally finished it, here he was: true to his word, using it.

He'd flown out to the floating space station at Port Gaia in a Tofler Sky Taxi, so he could land and take off vertically with no delays. Being autonomous and electric, the taxi was both safe and silent, so the port's controllers had made no objection when he told them his plan, not forgetting that his space shuttle business was so important to them that they'd accede to whatever he wished anyway.

It was such a beautiful day, with the sky and sea conjuring every shade of blue and blending them into each other like a Curaçao cocktail, in the middle of which, like a bright green sprig of mint, sat the island of Trovador, the land base for Port Gaia, which floated six miles offshore, connected by an undersea tunnel. The entrance to that tunnel was what he wanted to avoid today because it would be packed with the world's media, Deep State operatives from the Ministry of Truth and Public Guidance, and very likely an official party from the Agenda Implementation Tribunal. The highly anticipated return of Alexa Smythe to Earth was creating a feeding frenzy.

Levon smiled to himself and unwrapped an aniseed twist, licked it thoughtfully, then popped it in his mouth. His companion, the implacable package of muscle and bone known to the world as Tank, pointed at the rapidly approaching port and to the Sky Taxi's dashboard instruments above their heads, as if to say they were going too fast. Levon was itching to override the autonomous controls and do a few swooping dives and loops around the port's tower and sky cable before landing, but luckily, the controls were childproof. While the eyes and ears of the Sky Taxi were in the edge computing built around its perimeter, the pilot was a self-learning piece of code in a sterile data center miles away in the desert, run by one man and a dog. The man's job was to feed the dog. The dog's job was to stop the man from touching anything. Ha ha, Levon liked that one. He told it a lot.

The rear propellers turned in reverse, and as they slowed, all four propellers began to swivel upwards and synchronously put them into vertical mode. All good ideas were simple. Levon cracked the hard-boiled aniseed twist between his teeth. The more complicated things became, the more certain people were that machine intelligence was taking over and the chances were increasing that they were living in computer simulations. Demoralizing, depressing, cataplexic paranoia of that kind was spreading like an induced trance among people who were untethered by intellect or belief. What they missed was the element at the core of every great idea, which was the human desire to make it happen. No machine carried that desire within it, no matter what its level of intelligence.

"You know something, Tank?" he thought to ask. Tank nodded and kept an eye on the instrument gauges. "No machine wakes up in the morning and says, 'I've just had a great idea. It may be crazy, and it may not work, but I'm going to give it a try.'

"'That sounds more like you, Levon,'" he replied on Tank's behalf.

The strength of his relationship with his constant companion and bodyguard was in good part due to the fact that Tank was mute and made no attempt to talk, so Levon spoke for him. They'd never had a single disagreement or misunderstanding, and no unwelcome pest had ever got close enough to Levon to lay a hand on him. Except for a bat-crazy woman or two, but it wasn't Tank's fault that Levon was drawn to creatures who hung upside down in trees until night came.

Hanging upside down on its now vertical electric props, the Tofler Sky Taxi lowered itself delicately onto the deck of the port. They were expected. The large person in the parachute-silk boiler suit with the boyish grin and floppy black hair who stepped out of the aircraft was the genius-level founder of the commercial space industry, which had thrown open the Earth's window to the universe over the last four incredibly short decades, so of course he was expected. The future of Port Gaia very much depended on his continuing support. If he had another, better idea in his head about how to launch and land spacecraft, the rest of the space industry would follow him, and that could be disastrous for the Port. That conclusion was writ large in the body language of the welcoming group who stood on the landing platform, ready to pay obeisance, while desperately trying to interpret his thinking from what they could see in his facial expression, not realizing that Levon's facial expression was seldom anything but pleasant and expectant and no guide at all to what he was thinking.

The delegation advanced, bowing from the waist, business cards at the ready (they had preserved that strange Japanese custom, it seemed).

Levon jumped out. Tank stayed put.

*"Minasan e no go aisatsu."* The eccentric genius grinned, giving the whole scene an awkward wave with the back of his hand, accompanied by an involuntary skip not dissimilar to that of a child who couldn't contain its energy.

*"Subarashī hi,"* he called out, hoping it meant what he meant, which was that it was a great day, and more particularly, a great day to be returning to Earth. For high above them, at the Geostationary Earth Orbit Station, the Tofler Mars Shuttle had successfully docked over forty-eight hours before, allowing its crew and passengers to be put through deconditioning tests and microgravity adjustments, ready for their descent down the Elevator to the Earth Platform and a debriefing by Levon himself. That was the official line. Unofficially, returning shuttles from Mars had become a regular event, not requiring his attendance. Space was no longer a vast void leading into infinity; it had become a highway. And he wasn't here for the debriefing; he was here because of the special passenger on board.

Soon he was surrounded by Tofler Shuttle ground support crew, and they ushered him into the Earth Port for cold drinks and sushi rolls filled with smoked eel and orange crab eggs, which Levon ate greedily. He loved being around aeronautical engineers and astrophysicists because gems spilled out of their mouths in conversation like grains of sticky rice, and Levon hoovered them up. "What are we learning?" he'd ask, and off they'd go, reeling off incredible facts and setting his mind racing. For someone who'd never had the time to finish a degree, it was a gift from heaven that he could understand what they were saying, and oftentimes, be ahead of them.

Now, as they were talking about the perfect landing they'd achieved at the Karman line on the edge of the Earth's atmosphere, his mind flew away to the dream he'd only shared with a very select few. It was so exciting that he wanted to talk about it to everyone, but it would have to wait.

"And launching?" he asked. "How much benefit do we get from the slingshot dynamics?" Slingshot dynamics, using the leverage of planetary motion to multiply the speed of rockets into deep space a hundred times over with no extra cost in energy, was how David had beaten Goliath. Beautiful. Simple. Wait until they learned about the plan he was hatching to utilize its dynamic force. The world would never be the same again.

But at the same time that he was thinking this, he was thinking also about what Alexa had said in that episode of *The View from Space*, which had blown his mind wide open like an exploding Crossette (Levon was a big pyrotechnics fan). Who'd have thought to describe the galaxy in the way she did, and then to have postulated that a mathematical calculation to explain its creation and positioning was just a hair's breadth away from a quantum computer's grasp? She wasn't just a genius; she was an Emanator: a source of creation. And Levon had known immediately that he must come to that source. Which is why he was here this day.

All this while others talked, and Levon listened.

Before going into the arrival hall to greet the returning Mars mission, he sneaked another piece of sushi off a waiter's tray, unable to resist the brilliant orange of the crab eggs.

# 2 · ALEXA SMYTHE

*Talk about down to earth*, Alexa Smythe thought. She'd always been tall enough to play basketball with the men, but now, after two years of traveling in space, she was close to a whole inch taller. How long, she wondered, would it take for gravity to pull her back down to size? And that "moon face" she'd grown used to on Mars because everyone else there had one too; that was her biggest concern now that she was back on Earth. If only there were some way they could give her back her cheekbones before she had to face people on Earth again. They said it didn't take long for fluid redistribution to occur, but if she didn't recognize the person in the mirror, what would others think of her? Would they even accept that it was her?

Her long blonde hair had been reduced to a buzz cut That had now stopped growing altogether, and looking down at her previously firm and athletic limbs, she could see that she was thinner and paler now, despite the multiple daily sessions of advanced resistive exercise and her regular skin moisturizing with the UV-independent melanin lotion. Skinny and white with a puffy face, she thought. Great! And no boobs: she'd turned into an android. All she could do was cover herself up in a baggy suit and hide behind dark glasses to protect herself from the unaccustomed glare of sunlight. Maybe that way, nobody would be able to see how badly she'd changed.

Alexa Smythe, mathematician and one-time People's Ambassador to the Agenda Implementation Tribunal, was so unaccustomed to suffering insecurities about her appearance that she knew her equilibrium must have been badly disturbed. Emotions that she had spent forty years keeping neatly in place had been shaken up in space and refused to settle down. After forty-eight hours in the Elevator Arrival Suite, going through the usual deconditioning tests, she was amazed at how quickly she'd recovered balance and shed the weigh-down effects, but her cortisone levels were raised, and her heartbeat refused to settle.

It was natural; she mustn't blame herself. Although the Tofler Mars Shuttle had turned interplanetary travel into a bus ride, no amount of training could eliminate the anxiety of takeoff, or the stress of reentering the earth's atmosphere, let alone the constrictions of living in a capsule for seven months on the long ride home through the darkness of space, peering at the tiny blue-and-green globe of Earth and trying to imagine what it would be like living on it again.

She'd struggled to handle the boredom of spacecraft routine, being essentially nothing more than a passenger. After two years, space flight had ceased to be a novelty. She'd reported once a week to the flight command center, giving them her impressions of activities at the Mars Colony, and sometimes she'd spoken of her father's theories about mankind's adaptation to space. The diary she'd kept of her time with him on Mars was her greatest comfort, and she'd been inspired to develop her own thoughts around his views in order to occupy herself during the voyage, convinced that she'd learned from him that humans were not eternally bound to planet Earth, but could find a place to call home anywhere in the universe.

There were thoughts in her diary that could well have provoked the government, had she chosen to speak openly about them—particularly how her father, Donald Melville Smythe, had been banished to the Colony during the Overthrow, for daring to oppose the propaganda of the times. But while keeping those thoughts to herself, by writing them down, she'd cleaned her own slate of the anger and resentment she'd harbored towards those responsible. Soon she'd have the comfort of expressing them safely to Jordan McPhee. Not that she'd want to bore him with all her self-engrossed psychotherapy. Somehow, she doubted that anyone would be interested in her father-daughter relationship ramblings, but they'd eased her feeling of isolation on the long journey home.

Now a week of acclimatization to Earth awaited, and no matter how positive her MRI scans proved to be, she wasn't going to take the potential for damage to her DNA lightly. She'd go straight in to see Jordan's friend, John Erasmus, at his Salutogenesis Clinic the week after she arrived back. If anyone could help her recover her mental and physical tone before those close to her had time to notice, it was him, the kind of doctor who focused on health, not disease.

A knock on her cubicle door pulled her to her senses.

She opened the door to a serious young person in a Tofler Shuttle uniform labeled FLIGHT RECEIVER #9 and wearing a surgical mask.

"Alexa, do you want an air-purifying respirator for the final ground-level descent, or a supplied-air helmet?"

"What do you recommend?" she asked.

"It's up to you," the young person replied shyly, "but you've had enhanced oxygen levels for a long time, and you'll struggle to adjust to ground-level atmosphere. If you want to go incognito, seeing who you are and all the publicity and all, I'd go with the full helmet until you're safely out of the public gaze."

"Publicity? What publicity?" Alexa's alarm bells rang. She ushered the young Flight Receiver in. "What kind of 'public gaze' are you talking about?"

"Your weekly show on the *ArteFact Channel*. Haven't they told you about the reaction? There'll be a mass of people at the arrival gate on Trovador."

"You mean my little five-minute interviews with Artie Sharp?"

The flight receiver nodded vigorously. "Yes, *The View from Space*. Everybody was talking about it. When the zero carbon target failed to be reached again by the 2060 Earth Day Summit, our movement realized it was time to look towards space. Your interview with George Kyros exposed the lies they've been telling us about reducing the rising heat.

There's no alternative now but to plan for our evacuation, and you've confirmed it."

Shyly, the young person turned back the lapel of the Tofler Shuttle jacket and revealed a printed badge with the words WORLD ON FIRE inscribed in orange-and-black flames.

Alexa tried to suppress a laugh of surprise. "Is that a joke?" she asked. "I've been watching the Earth from my spaceship for months, and there's no sign of it being on fire... Well, some smoke over parts of California and Brazil, maybe ... but mostly it's all green and blue."

The young crew member's face clouded. "It's not a joke, it's a movement—and we need you to help us. The planet is getting hotter, and soon we'll have to leave it. You said yourself that it was the view from space that made you see clearly what was wrong with life on Earth. Your words have given people hope."

"What words?"

"Don't you remember? You said that Jesus walks among all the stars of the universe, and we can follow Him. We don't have to be stuck here to die."

Alexa exhaled in disbelief. Had she really said that? Those sounded like her father's words.

The young Flight Receiver's face—what she could see of it—was crestfallen. "You did say it, Alexa. That's why we've been waiting for your return."

Feelings of weightlessness were not just derived from an absence of gravity; they were also, as far as the brain was concerned, a psychological response to disorientation that could persist even after gravity's pull had been restored. Alexa needed to sit down. The feeling that was overwhelming her was frightening. It was as if every memory of the last seven months had been suddenly vaporized, and with it her ability to recall even one word of what she'd said in those brief discussions on her long flight home, let alone that it had been broadcast to the world as *The View from Space*.

"But, that was just a..." she started, then stopped.

The young person was staring at her intensely, wanting a different reaction from her than the one she was now displaying. Though dressed and groomed as if wanting to present as nonbinary, Alexa was sure that the intense young person she was dealing with was a young girl half her age. The intensity of youth was something she needed to remember.

"I'm sorry," Alexa murmured, "I'm still a bit dizzy. What's your name?"

"Karman. Pronouns: *they, them.*"

"If you're telling me you're nonbinary, that's fine, but where did you start life: boy or girl? I can't see you behind your mask. Would you please remove it?"

Though this was against regulations, Karman did as she was told.

"There!" Alexa exclaimed. "Now: boy or girl? Where did you start?"

Karman's face collapsed. "Girl, but…"

Alexa held up her hand. "Well, girl it is then. Let us talk as sisters. Just understand, I wasn't expecting to have to face a whole lot of people. Nevertheless, I'll forego the helmet and just go with a face mask and respirator until I've adjusted to the atmosphere at ground level. I don't want people to think that I'm hiding my face, but I need time to get my bearings, and this news of yours comes as a surprise. Tell me a little more. And what's this about an interview with George Kyros…?"

# 3 · JORDAN MCPHEE

Jordan McPhee ran through Riverside Park, taking the long way round beneath the trees that lined the riverbank and the broad avenue of Riverside Drive. The sound of his shoes crunching the fallen sycamore leaves, and the steady stream of white fog as his breath condensed in the cold air told him that fall was on the cusp of turning to winter. His pace was steady, loping and unforced, the metronomic tread of his feet being the perfect accompaniment to measured thinking.

Jordan was thinking about the fine line between the metaphysical world and the very real possibility that quantum simulations were occurring unrecognized. It was something that he thought about nearly every morning when out running. And he had good cause, for if anyone should take the blame for this potentiality, it was him.

His morning runs were getting longer as he chased his thoughts down the labyrinthian paths they chose to lead him. His legs and lungs could handle these long runs, but his trainers had found a vulnerable spot on the back of his heel and rubbed it until it blistered. Now the blister had chosen this morning to burst, so he stopped, removed his shoes, and hobbled to a bench to consider his options.

It was a bench that he and Alexa had sat on many times in the months before she left for Eros and Mars, and he'd come back to it often during the time that she was away. It was here that they'd exchanged their clearest thoughts, those that didn't require complex explanations because they were so strongly embedded in their feelings. It was here, in fact, that he'd first broached with her the possibility of their achieving quantum entanglement.

"It happens when two separate subatomic particles become so strongly bonded that what happens to one happens to the other, even when they're far apart," he'd explained. "It's not new. Einstein conceptualized it, and forty years ago, scientists demonstrated what they called 'teleportation' by taking two computer chips with quantum particle entanglement and separating them, one on Earth and one in space, and they were able to transfer information one to the other without any linking infrastructure of any kind."

"Aren't humans made up of tiny subatomic particles as well?" she'd asked.

"Yes." He'd smiled. "And some scientists believe that our particles can become entangled when we form such a strong bond that we share each other's thoughts and feelings. Like falling in love."

"Have you ever fallen in love like that?" she'd asked.

"Not so that I became entangled, no. And you?"

"The same," she'd replied quickly.

They'd retreated from the subject because it was evident to both of them that their relationship deserved a better description than "love." Perhaps that's all it was. They'd been skirting around the issue for a long time, despite it being obvious that they had strong feelings for each other: he the deplatformed mathematics professor, now cybernetics theorist and enemy of political cant, and she his former star pupil, now poster girl for the Deep State. Perhaps that was a good thing. The months before her departure for Mars had been emotionally intense times for both of them, which could have led to an overreaction that they might have later regretted. When the time came for the dramatic intensity of that period to subside—as it inevitably did during her prolonged absence in space— they could calmly assess whether or not their experiment with quantum entanglement had been successful.

The blister on his heel was weeping a clear liquid like tears, streaked with blood, and the wound hurt like hell. There was a pharmacy in the

Hope Hospital on Riverside Drive, and he hobbled over there and bought some plasters, taking them barefoot into the adjacent café, where he ordered a water and a mug of coffee, wiping his bleeding heel with a paper napkin before applying two plasters and carefully easing back into his training shoes.

The Hope Clinic Café was where Alexa had told him that the Agenda Implementation Tribunal—or, more specifically, The Ministry of Truth and Public Guidance—had asked her to try and recruit Artie Sharp to help win over public opinion for their plan to upend the Transitional Benefits scheme, by doing away with the Social Points system on which payments were based. In truth, it had been Alexa's idea. She'd known that Artie was a product of the metaverse, but having linked his origins to Jordan's AI laboratory, she'd convinced herself that Artie was a representation of Jordan himself and would act according to Jordan's instructions. That, of course, was not how it worked with Autonomic AI, though it was true that Jordan retained the ability to issue commands and describe what he would like to happen in terms of outcome.

He should have refused the request. With the exponential increase in microprocessing and quantum computing that was taking place, he should have known that every step forward would be a giant and irreversible one. Once he migrated Artie from XR-9 to XR-11, the evidence was there, warning him to stop. Artie was reviewing himself, analyzing his shortcomings, and writing his own software to improve his performance, even back then.

The evolutionary laws of nature that ruled all living things applied equally, if not even more strongly, to artificial intelligence. Artie had started as a functional algorithm tasked with searching the net for data to hold government announcements up to scrutiny. Then Jordan and his sidekick, Antonio—ever up for breaking boundaries—had introduced a natural language processor capable of understanding and generating unscripted output. Reflecting, perhaps, Jordan's own personality, the vocal and visual avatars they created for Artie were dry and laconic, in stark contrast to the earnest tones of the time. So, when they took their first Artie Sharp clip to air on the dark web, much to their surprise, there was an instant response. Here was the government propaganda machine having the piss taken out of it by the simple device of exposing it to real truths. And so, the weekly *Artefact Channel* was born, and Artie became an underground celebrity—one that the government was inspired (by Alexa) to try and recruit to its cause.

That's when he should have shut Artie down. Now the genie was out of the bottle. Like the moment when a child answered back to its parent, Jordan sensed that he had lost parental control. This child, this product of the metaverse—the product of so many iterations of semiconductor micronization—had leaped into a metaphysical universe where its human parent was unable to follow. For companionship, it effortlessly created Deep Fakes that were indistinguishable from the original. Was that what Artie had done in his weekly talks with Alexa in *The View from Space*? Was it the real Alexa who'd been speaking, or had a Deep Fake version taken her place? After all, Artie had successfully conducted the infamous Earth Day interview with George Kyros through the medium of a Deep Fake representation of Alexa that had convinced the entire world. And when she stood up from their park bench as Jordan ran towards her on her first morning back, as they'd planned, which one would it be that held her arms out to greet him?

Other computer scientists had long claimed that their creations had reached the *Singularity*: that moment when an artificial intelligence started working on its own initiative, independently of its programmer, such that it needed to be urgently reined in. Conferences were convened. Conventions were drafted. Protocols were imposed by the simple mechanism of requiring protective codes to be imprinted into every microchip manufactured under the auspices of the ICA, the International Chip Authority based in Taipei. "Will artificial intelligence save us, or destroy us?" Jordan had asked. It remained an open question. But Jordan knew that no imprinted protocol was capable of impeding the creativity of Artie Sharp. The Ministry of Truth's *Fake Finder* software had failed to detect that the Alexa Smythe seen interviewing George Kyros at the Potsdam Earth Day Celebration in April 2060 was a Deep Fake of Artie's making, despite the fact that Alexa was, at that very moment, rocketing through space on her way to Mars. And Jordan's own far superior *Fake Finder* software had failed to detect Alexa's appearances in the transmissions of *The View from Space* as being the product of a Deep Fake, despite the fact that the views she expressed were those of a person who was almost completely alien to him.

Jordan limped out of the café and picked up a Scoot from the hospital forecourt. His heel was too sore to risk running back to his office. The first thing Alexa wanted when she came back down to Earth and returned to her apartment in the Noam Chomsky Building, she'd told him, was to go for a long run in the park, as they had done so many times together in the past. It would be the surest way they could get back into a rhythm together without the need for words, she'd explained. So much had happened, and she didn't want him to think it had changed her. She wanted to start again where they'd been before she left.

As if sensing his mood, the Scoot took on a life of its own, racing past cyclists, dashing in front of autonomous taxis like a teenage delinquent, triggering their emergency brakes. It wasn't the scooter doing this, of course; it was Jordan, who was allowing his anger and mounting resentment toward his out-of-control algorithm to transmit itself into the handlebars and accelerator.

How the fuck could he run towards her across the park if his heel was weeping pus? Would she view his pathetic limp as a metaphor for their relationship, now that she was the celebrity dispenser of extraterrestrial wisdom, and he was the anonymous non-person whose words and thoughts would never match those of his self-programming machines?

Words rushing, racing thoughts. Thoughts limping, skeptical and fearful of their origins. Who was in charge of reality now? What words could he use to greet her, knowing they would be real?

# 4 . KARMAN

For all her apparent youth and starstruck adoration of Alexa, Karman was an experienced receiver of returning astronauts. She (shall we call her "she"? By her own admission, that's where she'd started in life, and why she ended up with the cumbersome pronouns of "they" and "them" is not going to affect this story.) had witnessed the bipolar extremes of euphoria and depression that could afflict returnees, and had learned to counter them, developing her own little remedies for what she termed *the post-galactic malaise*. The gas cylinders and testing kits that she wheeled into Alexa's cabin contained the necessary ingredients.

Her greatest concern was that Alexa seemed to have momentarily lost her memory. This was not unusual, for stress tended to fatigue the brains of all space travelers. But for Karman, whose excitement had been difficult to contain once she knew she'd been given the honor of acclimatizing Alexa in her first hours back, this apparent dementia was devastatingly disappointing. What she craved was one small snippet of wisdom from Alexa's lips that she, Karman, could claim for herself as an exclusive. It didn't have to be about Jesus; perhaps that was too high level for a moment like this. It was so high level, in fact, that it had rendered large sections of Alexa's audience silent when they first heard it, for references to religion, let alone Christianity, had disappeared entirely from social discourse. Not even the Ministry of Truth and Public Guidance, guardians of the state's strict secularity, had risen to the bait, preferring to pretend that Alexa had never uttered His name.

But this was Alexa Smythe, who had overnight changed so many people's lives two years ago by championing the alterations to *AGENDA 2060* that had removed divisiveness from identity politics. This was the woman who overnight had given them hope that there was humanity in the heart of the Deep State, and whose catchphrase on the State Streaming Service had been printed on every other T-shirt and dish towel across the country within days of her uttering it: KINDNESS, LOVE, AND SYMPATHY CREATE KINDNESS, LOVE, AND SYMPATHY IN RETURN.

And now she had offered hope against so many people's fear that planet Earth was being destroyed, and that hope lay in her message of the infinite universe as being the ultimate destination of each person's soul. But reaching infinity couldn't be done alone; it needed a higher power like Jesus to guide them. What if she could just get Alexa to say, "Oh, yes, Jesus *does* walk among the stars"? How extraordinary it would be if she, little old Karman, could carry that sound around inside of herself, a sound that nobody else had heard, and that would make her the unique recipient of a revelation. Even better if she could record it.

She decided to try another tack.

"The meeting with your father on Mars must have been a weird moment for you, Alexa," she said compassionately. "Not wishing to intrude, but he did sound like the sort of patriarch we're encouraged to avoid, yet it seemed like you were grateful to have been able to reach him before he died."

Alexa nodded. Her slightly puzzled expression suggested that she was either surprised at the intrusiveness of the question, or confused that the meeting with her father was such public knowledge.

"You talked about him on *The View from Space*," Karman rushed to explain.

"Did I?" Alexa replied. "I'd not intended to do that publicly. There's something about these supposed transmissions that I seem to have forgotten."

Well, Karman thought, between seven months confined in a capsule on the flight back to earth, and weekly chat sessions with Artie Sharp from the underground *ArteFact Channel*, sharing her thoughts as they came to mind, it was natural that she'd forgotten every detail of what she'd said. But now she claimed she'd had no idea it was being broadcast as *The View from Space*. The clear signs of memory loss were ominous. And if the reports were true, in an hour or less, she would be encountering an audience that had traveled far to meet her. How would she fare when confronted with an eagerly questioning panel of journalists and officials wanting clear answers? What would it do to her reputation to be so vague and forgetful?

So, what could Karman do to help clear her head and prepare her?

"We've arrived at Level One and are about to begin the final descent," Karman noted. "Would you like to do a short sensory test before you go down the Elevator to the Earth Platform? It only takes one of your senses to be malfunctioning for your physical balance to be upset: hearing obviously, but also sight, and surprisingly, smell and touch. I have a kit that we can quickly run through."

"Why not?" Alexa smiled. "My eyesight seems fine, though it might take a while to adjust to bright sunlight."

"We'll give you goggles to protect you from that."

Karman went to her trolley. "I like to do this in a specific order," she explained, "separating the senses that are inclined to overlap. So, we'll do them in this order: sight, taste, touch, and smell."

"What about sound?"

"You seem to be hearing me well."

"True. And if I fail at one of them, what will you do?"

"I'll try and stimulate it into responding."

After seating Alexa in a comfortable chair, she wheeled over the stainless steel trolley with a number of covered containers and a dish filled with instruments. They were both agreed that light sensitivity would be an issue, and this was confirmed when she shone the retinoscope into

Alexa's eyes. Time and exposure to light would soon correct the problem, she decided.

"Next, I'd like to do taste," she said.

She brought out seven glass vials and a packet of flat wooden tasting spoons. The vials contained liquids of identical color.

"Don't try and identify a specific food type," she advised, "just give me your instinctive word association."

She dipped a wooden spoon into one of the liquids and asked Alexa to put out her tongue. The tongue, she noticed, was healthy, moist, and pink, something that she reminded herself to record in her notes at the end of her session, for unknown to anyone, Karman had resolved to record every detail of her encounter with Alexa in a digital diary with a lock, quite separate from the space station's official files. One day, she knew, she would be grateful for the privileged moment she was experiencing now, for the safe departure of humans from Earth would depend on such information.

"Sweet," Alexa announced firmly.

"Next?"

"Salty. And I think I know how to play this," Alexa teased, "because I've done it before."

Sure enough, she got them right: sweet, salty, bitter, sour, cool, meaty, and hot.

"If you have any say with space flight catering," Alexa joked, "you should get them to add the ingredients of your tasting samples to their cooking, because no matter how they label it, after months in space, everything tastes of chalk. All I long for is a simple fresh, crisp apple."

"An apple is not as simple as people think," Karman replied seriously, placing the wooden spoons in a snaplok bag, while wondering if there was any way she could find a fresh apple for her before their session ended. The thought appeared to cause Karman to flush with embarrassment. She coughed into her hand and turned away.

With her free hand, she fiddled with the *Interact* body camera clipped to the front of her uniform. Every interaction with space station clientele was required to be recorded through this device for safety and training purposes, with the video streamed to an inhouse data collection center for analysis. But what Karman's nervous fingers were doing was directing the live stream simultaneously to her personal Konektor for recording and transmission later to her fellow members in the *World on Fire* meta community.

She took three quick breaths and turned back again, flexing her fingers with her hands outstretched where Alexa could see them.

"For touch," she explained, her voice slightly higher than she'd intended, "we test your sensitivity on the scalp, the hands, and the feet. I have to ask your permission though, because it is against the law to touch someone without their prior consent, even for medical reasons, under the new Anti-Viral Regulations."

"Really? Why?"

"Because touching can lead to the spread of viruses."

"Do you have a virus?"

Karman was shocked. "No, I am tested every two days. I have a certificate."

Alexa laughed. "Then you have my consent. Why don't you start with my scalp? I'm sure my brain has been accumulating static at such a rate that you'll get an electric shock when you touch me. So, take care."

Whether it was due to Alexa's warning, or Karman's own internal tensions, the caution with which she approached from behind and then laid her hands on Alexa's head caused both of them to jump.

"There," Alexa laughed. "I told you I was overcharged with static."

Her hair, the color of corn, straight and soft as the purest silk, was simply not possible in a human, in Karman's estimation. She had never touched hair like it, and doubted she ever would again. After quickly cutting a small lock with a pair of surgical scissors, she placed it in the snaplok DNA bag for mineral testing. But as she put the bag aside, her suspicion that Alexa Smythe was an astral being who was returning to Earth bearing a message for all mankind was almost forming into a certainty, making her too afraid and excited to speak.

She moved around in front of Alexa's chair and took her outstretched hand. The fingers were long and slim with perfect clear moons on ivory-white rounded nails, her skin unblemished, her touch as soft as a kitten's paw. No avatar could possibly convey the unique texture of her living form. Karman could only imagine the impact that these revealing images would have on her fellow members when she came to show them.

With a dry mouth and pounding heart, Karman then knelt at her feet and removed Alexa's shoes, bending forward so her *Interact* camera had a clear view. No human in Karman's experience had perfectly straight toes, so why Alexa, she wondered? The unreality of her perfection was proof positive, surely, that she was no ordinary human astronaut. Alexa must be protected at all costs, and she, Karman, was determined to fill that role. But another feeling was also sweeping through her, one that she was trying desperately to control, and which the intimate proximity with Alexa was inflaming. Alexa's skin, hair, smell, and voice were overwhelmingly cisgender (even though she was rumored to be a member of *BirthStrike* and was not heterosexually partnered), triggering a wave of familiar bitterness in Karman that she feared lay in the irreversibility of her own hormone-neutralizing treatments during puberty. That was not meant to happen, and it frightened her.

"With every returning astronaut," she croaked, "we offer to cut your toenails, because we know how difficult it is in space. And we save the cuttings for DNA and mineral analysis."

"What a wonderful idea," Alexa enthused. "Please do."

Though her hands shook, Karman managed the task without causing damage, and added the cuttings to the snaplok bag that held the lock of hair and the wooden spoons.

"Well, everything seems to be working so far, despite the fact that my memory's gone," Alexa announced cheerily. "My feet are still ticklish, and my scalp is giving off static, so now it's down to my nose and whether or not I can smell. What have you got for me next?"

Karman was conflicted. She'd intended to trick Alexa into sniffing the standard aroma samples in her sensory testing kit: vanilla, strawberry, and garlic. Then, as she'd done before with many mentally exhausted astronauts struggling to recover their senses, she'd have slipped in her dark brown jar containing the white crystalline salts known to ancient physicians as *Sal ammoniac*: ammonium carbonate laced with eucalyptus oil, which could reach into the brain and clear away the fog of fatigue and unconsciousness, reviving the mind and memory like a sudden ice-cold dip in an arctic ocean.

But, no, she couldn't risk arousing Alexa's anger with something so crudely obvious—not if she was to be trusted as her protector in the coming days, as she hoped.

Contritely, without comment, she passed over the three aroma jars in turn.

"Vanilla," Alexa said. "Strawberry … and garlic. So, all my senses are working. Now it must be time for you to put on my breathing mask, Karman, so I can finally descend to Earth and face my welcoming committee."

"There's just one more thing," Karman confessed. "We need a record of your vocal cords. If they've contracted while in space, it may require therapy later to ensure the contraction doesn't become permanent. Would you mind reading something that I can record to compare with the next time we test?"

Alexa smiled and shook her head in disbelief. "I must say, Karman, you are very thorough at your job. What would you like me to read?"

"It's something you said in *The View from Space*. I wrote it down."

Alexa took the notepad offered to her and took a moment to read it.

"You want me to read this?" she asked, looking up. "You claim this is taken from something I said that was transmitted from space?"

"Those were your exact words, Alexa."

"Alright, if you insist."

# 5.LEVON TOFLER

Just above Levon's left ear, there was a small device, partially implanted, that was connected to Levon's world. Under his scalp lay a brain-to-computer interface. External to his scalp was a miniature microchip array that transmitted and received auditory signals on the wavelength of his choosing. To get into Levon's world, it was necessary to pass through the device above Levon's left ear, and that, as so many who had tried and failed knew, was no mean feat. Levon guarded his time jealously and reserved it for those who he knew could help him. For them, he had FAITH.

For someone as neurodivergent as Levon Tofler, the choice of such a naïve acronym as FAITH to describe a technology as contractually, financially, and technically complicated as the Far-flung Artificial Intelligence Terrestrial Hub was pretty much par for the course. It was playful, but it hardly showed any respect for the meaning that other people might ascribe to the word. Faith was, for some, both deeply personal and off-limits. But Levon was, as already explained, on that part of the spectrum that tended to fumble when it came to juggling social niceties. (This was a man, after all, who'd whistled during his father's funeral, who had bought a painting by a Dutch master for a world record sum, and within a week, he'd calmly destroyed it by cutting out the subject's eyes, because he couldn't stand being watched while he was eating.)

Where Levon sat on the spectrum was difficult for colleagues and employees to accurately determine, for there were those who maintained that his eccentricities were merely the deliberate and exaggerated charades of a brilliant but bored genius. Employees had a vested interest in taking that view. But not everyone who was able to speak with him via FAITH, like Will Portico was at this very minute, shared that view.

*"Levon,"* Will said to him in his ear, *"my feeling is that an axial shift is coming. We need to prepare for it."*

Levon rolled his eyes in horizontal figure eights, ten one way and ten the other. Then he rapidly opened and closed his eyelids like a Morse code signal lamp.

"Oh, yes," he retorted. "Ha ha, you feel it too. The harder you pull the string, the faster the top will spin. But why does it fall over?"

*"Why does it fall over, Levon?"*

"Because of the axial shift."

*"Okay, you've been telling me, and now I agree. I've been at a meeting of the Council for Earth Restoration, where the head of the Federal Communications Commission revealed something that confirms what you've been saying. It's time to move from theory to action. I've been thinking that the simulation modeling isn't yet convincing enough for me to throw all my resources in with you. You've got to find a way of bringing Jordan McPhee on board."*

Levon fished an aniseed twist out of his pocket and cupped a hand to his ear. The activity in the arrival hall was distracting him. Something was about to happen.

"I love Jordan," Levon said vaguely, his mind tugging at his sleeve, "but … but…"

The digital display above the elevator dock had started flashing, and video connection to the Control Center showed that a descending bar graph was counting down above the controllers' desks in synchrony with a time clock. A shrill alarm had sounded, making it impossible for Levon to hear what Will Portico was saying, and the arrival hall was filling rapidly with people emerging from doors that Levon hadn't noticed before, so that the privacy and security that Tofler ground support crew had assured him would be guaranteed was now being ripped to shreds before his eyes.

Will Portico, unaware of what was happening, kept talking, and Levon, caught between two conflicting priorities, made a dash for the exit door and broke into a fast shuffle that moved him remarkably quickly towards the landing deck and the Sky Taxi that he'd parked there earlier.

*"What's happened is what you feared would happen,"* Will complained. *"The Fed Coms Commission has voted with the Chinese to allow the chain link between web nodes to be forcibly broken by the International Internet Authority, for all the trumped-up reasons you'd expect. No more geostationary Earth orbit station licenses are going to be issued that aren't sanctioned by the IIA and connected via IIA distributed ledgers, and get this: all existing licenses are going to be subject to annual renewal applications. There's a strong hint that they intend to shoot unapproved geostationary transmitters out of the sky... Can you hear me?"*

He might as well have been talking to himself, for all the attention Levon was able to pay as he ran across the landing deck. Luckily, one of the beauties of FAITH was that everything said was captured and retrievable, unable to be wiped, which encouraged FAITH members to keep talking, as well as keeping things honest and on point.

Levon stopped and forced himself to listen. Will Portico, the most inner of the inner sanctum, was ratting on the elite establishment of which he was a part. This was worth hearing.

"Ain't it wonderful?" Levon shouted excitedly. "When the pinball drops in the slot, and the whole fucking board lights up? You've just seen the light, Will, and it sounds to me like you've decided to enter the game. Have you finally realized you can't save the world if you're a part of the problem? What's happened to turn your light on?"

*"It's like you said,"* Will Portico admitted, sounding uncomfortable. *"The IIA has served notice; the satellite web is going to be theirs, or it's coming down."*

Levon smiled and waved his arms around like a semaphore signalman sans flags. "I know, I know," he agreed. "That's exactly what we said would happen, and that's what we want. Jordan's not on FAITH, but knowing his quantum reach, he probably could be without us even knowing. Don't worry, I'm on to it. I know how to get to him. We'll talk later."

The door of the Tofler Sky Taxi opened, and Tank climbed out. Tank seldom needed instructions, so Levon didn't give him any. He turned back towards the arrivals hall at the same pace he'd left it, his fast-shoe shuffle leaving his trusted guardian power-walking behind him. Bursting in through the doors to a scene of even greater excitement and commotion than when he'd left, Levon looked around for the uniformed Tofler crew who were supposed to be controlling things. They were lined up with their backs to the arrival dock, trying to persuade the people pressing forward to back away, and having no success. Not even a fire hose was going to dampen the crowd's excitement as the elevator lights displayed the progress of the descent down the shaft of its highly anticipated new arrivals.

The crowd that had assembled was all of one mind. Already chanting, "Alexa, Alexa," they were determined to get close to the opening elevator doors and were deaf to any exhortations to back off. Where had they come from? They weren't Earth Port personnel. Levon, with a look of wonder on his face, knew that this was proof positive of his belief in the reality of the axial shift. The world was about to change—and the instrument of that change was about to step through those doors, if only the crowd would let her.

Then the doors opened, and it seemed to Levon that a miracle occurred. The crowd went silent, and as if as one, stepped back and opened a path. Alexa, tall, pale, and golden, stood there for all to see, her face hidden behind a brutally utilitarian breathing mask attached to a hose leading to a gas cylinder being borne in the arms of a uniformed Tofler Flight Receiver.

Alexa balked at the sight of the crowd and threw out her arms to steady herself. What Levon didn't know—in fact, none of them knew—was that Karman had adjusted the contents of the breathing gas bottle, intended to transition Alexa from space to Earth by adding three hundred parts per billion of nitrous oxide, but in her heightened state of excitement, had misjudged the volume and added three thousand parts per billion—just enough laughing gas to trigger a fit of the giggles in the person breathing it.

What Levon saw, however, was a nebula of luminous vapor appearing out of the darkness of the elevator shaft, and the vapor suddenly parting to reveal a star. It was a moment in time, but a very brief one.

"Grab her," Levon hissed to Tank.

Needing no further explanation, Tank brushed people aside and threw Alexa over one extremely wide shoulder. Of all the shouts of protest, Alexa's was not the loudest. That came from the young person attached to the gas cylinder, which was attached to the hose attached to Alexa's breathing mask. She didn't just scream in outrage, she kicked and punched and swung the gas bottle at Tank, forcing him to pick her up and throw her over his other extremely wide shoulder. The crowd fell back in unison, unable to process the nature and speed of events.

Levon, confident in what had been achieved, turned for the exit and engaged gears, shifting into his rapid soft-shoe shuffle and heading for the Tofler Sky Taxi at speed. Tank followed on unstoppable strides, bearing his two protesting captives, whom he bundled on board and pushed into the rear seats with hands that couldn't be resisted. Meanwhile, Levon jumped into the driver's seat and turned on the electric motors, tapping instructions into the autonomous pilot panel, which he augmented with a verbalized shorthand that seemed to indicate that the Tofler Space Resort was his intended destination. The central door lock clicked shut, the vertical lift props whistled into action, and the Sky Taxi slowly rose off the Earth Platform, leaving a sea of startled upturned faces below them, gobbling air in disbelief.

"I'm sorry, Alexa," Levon apologized, short of breath, "but my ground support crew forgot their orders, so I decided to get you away to safety. I hope we didn't frighten you? My name's Levon Tofler, and..."

To his surprise, Alexa giggled.

# 6 · JORDAN MCPHEE

The first that Jordan knew about the events at the Gaia Earth Port was when Antonio Muchos made a video call on his Konektor to say that access to the elevator dock was blocked off, and the crowds that had turned up to greet Alexa were being kept at the Trovador Island end of the tunnel.

*"She's crazy here, man!"* Antonio shouted. *"Nobody knows how so many people got to the island, and I've seen things that make me think something real weird's going down."*

"What things?"

Antonio scanned his camera across what appeared to be a packed crowd of excited people. He was there to greet Alexa with the backers of the *Galactic Mission* e-game that he'd designed (with Alexa's help), and whose astronomical sales had funded the trip to Eros and Mars. While the game's worldwide success, and the reported assays of gold deposits on the asteroid, were the cause of much excitement on the part of the game's promoters, it didn't explain the crowd. These people were here for something else.

*"They're pretty damn excited, Jordan. I'm going to have trouble getting her out of here."*

"Is she okay?" Jordan demanded. "Get her on your Konektor as soon as you can."

The main concern for Jordan was that Alexa was down safely. The Tofler Mars Shuttle had docked over forty-eight hours earlier without mishap, so he knew she was okay, but he had no feeling for where she was mentally. This was where their quantum entanglement experiment was meant to have helped, but it had failed sometime when she was on Mars. The failure couldn't have been due to distance, because it wasn't working now that she was back on Earth either. If it wasn't distance, could it be time that had caused the failure? Had the liquid nanoparticles used for their IV injections broken down? Or was there something else that had caused it to fail?

"*Sure, I'll do that,*" Antonio confirmed. "*I got a sky taxi on standby to bring her home, but we've not seen her yet. We're still waiting.*"

So, why did he sound so concerned?

"You said something weird's going down. What do you mean?" Jordan asked.

"*You know how these games took off like crazy, right?*" Antonio explained. "*And you know it was due to Alexa's calculus, which allowed the spaceship to penetrate the magnetic fields protecting the destination planets. Okay, she deserves the credit.* Comprende? *Every gamer knows the story, so millions of gamers have been watching her journey, right? Then you could expect a whole bunch of* Galactic Mission *gamers to turn up to welcome her, you know, but it's not easy to fly down to Trovador. And besides, these people here are something else ... I don't know, like some sorta religious mob. Some of them are wearing* World on Fire *shirts. You know, the climate activists. Can you see the signs?*"

He waved his camera around, scanning the placards, while giving a commentary. "*'Alexa' ... 'Hope' ... 'Infinity' ... 'Zero2060.' What are they going on about, and why are they here? And then I gotta ask, what the hell's the Deep State doing here?*"

He flashed to a section of the crowd that had the unmistakable look of Truth and Public Guidance: stern-faced and ringed by security. Jordan peered closer. "Hold it on them for a minute," he demanded. He'd seen something that caught his eye. A face—a face that rang a bell. (Maybe not; the view was too fleeting.)

"She's the government poster child," Jordan explained. "Don't forget her profile before she left. Without her, they wouldn't have gotten people to accept the change to Article One. They'll keep her close and try to claim her as their own, whether she likes it or not."

*"I wouldn't be sure of that, amigo,"* Antonio cautioned. *"What I see here is a kind of religious craze. We got banners saying, 'Jesus lives in space' and 'Lead us to infinity.' That's what Alexa's face is identified with for these people. The Deep State's not going to like that, my man. Not going to like that at all."*

The placards that Antonio showed while describing his alarm were not making sense at all. Alexa was not religious—popular, yes, but she couldn't possibly inspire an evangelical following. As for Jesus, well, the government had spent half a century debunking the claims of Christianity. The very mention of His name aroused public ridicule, for the very good reason that One World, One People, and One Government could not be achieved if some elements sought to follow a higher authority.

"What sort of people are they?" Jordan asked. "I can't get a handle on them."

*"Young, old, every sort. I ask, and they tell me they're not gamers. They been watching* The View from Space, *amigo. They've got some message from it that I sure as hell don't understand. Did you hear what they've been hearing?"*

Jordan couldn't respond. He didn't know what he'd been hearing when he watched and listened to those weekly transmissions from inside Alexa's space capsule as she returned from Mars, because he was so intently focused at the time on trying to reconnect with her, stupidly thinking that some kind of thought transference was possible where their quantum entanglement had failed. (He had resorted to primitive attempts at parapsychology, which, of course, failed abysmally.) The spacecraft's clarity of audio and visual transmission was compromised by distance, and he'd put the unfamiliar tone of her voice down to the leveling of high and low registers, which seemed to result from condensing the signal. As to the content of her ramblings from space, well, he suspected she'd spent many hours gazing out the porthole at the vastness of it all—hours in which she could endlessly speculate about the life and death of her father, and that was what seemed to color her musings. But, irrespective of whether they were genuinely her own thoughts, were they likely to inspire the religious excitement that Antonio believed he was observing?

*They say that space can change you*, he thought privately, hoping that's not what had happened. What he didn't want to admit was the possibility that he'd heard ideas and sentiments that were not actually her own, but had been superimposed on her. And where that led was to the uncomfortable suspicion that she had been manipulated by his own creation in the form of the self-programming algorithm known to *ArteFact Channel* viewers as Artie Sharp. What if Artie was not only interviewing her, but influencing her responses? What was his motive?

"I remember that line about Jesus living in space," he finally admitted, "but I seem to recall that she was quoting her father. I'd need to go back and listen to the recording."

Antonio wasn't paying attention. There was the sound of other voices, and he was waving his Konektor about so that all Jordan could see were knees and feet.

*"Wait a minute,"* Antonio warned, *"we've got an announcement coming up on the screen... They're telling us that Alexa has been taken off the Earth Platform by Levon Tofler. They're showing pictures of someone grabbing her, and there's total confusion, man... People running around and everyone looking shocked, then ... Now there's pictures of a sky taxi taking off. The people here are, like, stunned. Nobody knows what the fuck is happening. I better call you back."*

Almost immediately, Jordan had another incoming call. This time it was his daughter, Lexie.

*"Dad? I'm around at Alexa's apartment, getting it ready for her, but I don't think she should come back here."*

"Why?"

*"The building is, like, under siege from fans and security. We need to warn her."*

"Alright, I'll see what I can do."

The one thing that seemed clear from the pictures he'd just seen was that Levon Toffler's guard had snatched Alexa and flown away with her. That was the lead he needed to follow without further delay. With great reluctance, Jordan opened the lockbox on his Konektor and removed an uninstalled app stored there. This was something he'd determined not to do, despite the many efforts of Will Portico and Levon Tofler to persuade him otherwise. The preservation of one's independence and energy of thought in a world of so much constant distraction was the greatest challenge that Jordan McPhee faced if he was to achieve any level of command over the daunting complexities of quantum computing. That was why he jealously guarded himself from being open to communication from all but a very select few. Other people had different ways of achieving their goals, but solitude, even in a crowded room, was the very necessary environment for Jordan's mind, and so he knew that opening this app was something he'd been right to resist.

Yet he did. And he pressed *Install.* Then, feeling like he was stepping into a room where every cubic inch would be filled with the sound of colliding ideas and claims upon his attention, he entered his name and waited for an authentication number. The number arrived, and he hesitated long before entering it.

"Oh, for God's sake!" he cursed. "Why am I doing this?" Yet he did, knowing—or hoping—that Alexa would be somewhere within that room that he'd resisted entering until now.

# 7. ALEXA SMYTHE

It wasn't how she'd imagined it would be. The child was always the child, and the parent was always the parent, no matter how much time had passed—and no matter how hard the state tried to persuade people otherwise. But the inheritance of DNA alone was not sufficient to bind parent and child together. The sticky material that formed the bond was composed of memories, thoughts, and feelings, and looking at her father on his death bed on Mars, Alexa had struggled to recover those. It had been so long—twenty-one years—and everything that might have triggered remembrance—the smell of him, the heat, the familiarity of him—had evaporated in the cold, sterile, and mechanistic air of the Martian colony's sanitarium.

They'd warned her on arrival that he was in decline, but lucid. Nevertheless, she had expected that touching him would rekindle the daughter in her, and that hadn't happened. How could she describe it? The thought she'd tried to send to Jordan was that the body of Donald Melville Smythe had become desiccated in the artificial atmosphere—not in the manner of decay, but more like an air-dried fruit separated from the life-giving sap of the tree. Of course, individuals' bodies were all destined for decline, and ultimately, for decomposition, but where life resided was in the brain. Which was where Donald Melville Smythe resided, not just lucidly, but with a startling fountain of energy for someone who was dying.

He hadn't seemed surprised at her arrival. Forewarned was forearmed, she assumed. But neither did he seem to have any great sense of anticipation. Perhaps he'd resigned himself long ago, like all prisoners, to the fact that along with the loss of freedom came the loss of expectation. He was curious about her journey, and took a fleeting interest in her life on earth, but made no attempt to fill the vacuum left by his disappearance following his inquisition by the Overthrow Tribunal: no apologies, no recriminations or regrets. On the night of their first encounter, she'd cried herself to sleep.

Having gotten that out of the way, she determined to use the time to create new memories of him. If the past was not going to be the foundation for their relationship, then she'd use the present. What better way than to take a journey with him? She'd hitch her mind to the tail of his imagination and follow him out into the expanding universe, which was, she quickly discovered, where he preferred to reside. Every night, she recorded their conversations as best she could remember them in her personal digital log, so she'd have them as a reminder in future years after he was gone.

She'd asked him whether or not he'd retained his faith in Christianity. It was a question that no one would even think to ask of another in the year 2061 unless they had a unique reason for doing so. It was the most personal thing she could imagine asking, and yes, as his daughter, that was her unique reason for doing so.

So began her introduction to … well, Heraclitus, for a start. And infinity.

"It would be more accurate to say that this is where I have *discovered* my faith, rather than retained it," he'd replied. Then, before she could seek an explanation, he'd quoted Bertrand Russell quoting Heraclitus: "'God is the thought by which all things are steered through all things.'"

That sent a sharp shock through Alexa. Dammit! Russell was one of the personal ties that bound Alexa and Jordan together in their intellectual intimacy; she didn't want her father intruding on her mentor's pet philosopher.

"But Heraclitus predated Christ by five hundred years," she objected. "His was not a Christian god."

"Oh, 'God' is just the word we resort to when we are lost for an explanation." He smiled. "Remember, man created religions, and in so doing, attributed words to God that are limited by man's imagination and inspired by man's motives."

"So, does that mean you've moved on from Christianity?"

She hoped that was the case, because she had always coupled his faith with the word "blind," and resented his public adherence to it. Reading the transcript of his trial, she had felt herself blush at the prosecutor's mention of it, as if it were cause for shame. That blush was, in itself, cause for shame.

"Here, in space," he explained calmly, "it is impossible not to believe in the divine nature of creation." He gazed at the video screen on the wall of the sanitarium that relayed pictures from the surface outside, showing the thin, beige-colored sunlight of the Martian day.

"Earth is just as much in space as this planet, surely?" Alexa argued. "Why should that belief be stronger here?"

That line of logic seemed to interest him, and he pushed himself up into a higher sitting position in bed, waving away her attempt to help.

"It is the vacuum of space that I'm referring to," he explained, "and our decision to journey into it—which becomes, as soon as we uncouple from Earth, a step into infinity. Once you begin to contemplate infinity, it becomes evident that it serves God's purpose."

"I don't get that," Alexa admitted. Wasn't the concept of infinity a step on from the big bang theory, and wasn't that theory tantamount to the denial of God? Or was she mired in some outdated debates about creationism and die-hard fundamentalism that she vaguely recalled from her student days? "Explain your idea of infinity to me, then."

Her father reached out his bony hand to her. It was the first sign of familiarity—affection, even—that he'd displayed.

"You're a mathematician, Alexa. The distinction between the infinities of mathematics, physics, and metaphysics have been argued since the time of Plato and Aristotle, but theologians and metaphysicians are inclined to speak of 'The Absolute' as a metaphor for God or the overarching universal mind. That mind has no beginning and no end, in conception or in rendition. Once we are unshackled from Earth, it is impossible to believe that there is a boundary to space or time. Where does it begin, and where or why does it end? Those have always been the questions religions fail to answer. Ask an astronomer or a quantum physicist, on the other hand, and they will have no doubt about the answer."

"No beginning and no end?" she queried. "What about the big bang theory?"

He sighed and slid back down in his bed. "No, Alexa, I can see that I'll need to use our time together judiciously if I'm to help you absorb the full meaning of infinity. You see…"

With some effort, he raised himself up again. His body was tiring, but not his mind.

"The big bang theory does not necessarily undermine the concept of three-dimensional spatial infinity, for collapse and rebirth of the universe may be part of the life pattern. By the nature of infinity, we see that creation is not a onetime event, but is an endless process throughout time and space. It is, in fact, the ultimate definition of life."

"Which you believe is divinely ordained?"

Too late; his eyes had closed, and he'd drifted off to sleep.

It had been a year since she'd left Earth when this conversation took place. It was a conversation that set them up for many discussions in a similar vein over the ensuing weeks, proving that she was more obviously his daughter than she might have thought, because neither of them was comfortable with small talk. While her father's body had gone into decline, it was a relief to both of them that his mind was brimming with life, albeit that an hour or so per session was all he could sustain before the need for sleep closed him down.

For anyone voyaging through space, or adapting to life in a colony, the biggest challenge was to accept that routine was the key to survival, Alexa learned. Every tiny detail of routine had an essential purpose, which was to protect the integrity and performance of the machinery that kept them alive. And beyond that simple rule was the need to be hyperalert to the environment, for it went without saying that the environment was hostile to human life, and the only protection from it was the machinery. Like an elite sports team, the crew of each flight went into camp together. Every member was assigned their role, and each member depended on the performance of the others. Alexa's role on the voyage to Eros had been to audit navigational systems by running margin-of-error calculations in parallel to the installed algorithms. Upon reaching Mars, however, her *Galactic Mission* crew had continued on back to Earth, and she had no role on the red planet other than that of guest.

Since 2040, the population at the ISA colony had swelled to four thousand people across the mining, terraforming, launching, and underground habitation centers. She'd been given dispensation to remain at the colony for humanitarian reasons (and, it has to be said, because of her standing as People's Ambassador to the Agenda Implementation Tribunal), but this did not mean that she was to be treated solely as a guest, for no one venturing into space should expect that luxury. Guests were a burden, and Alexa made it clear that was something she was determined not to be. Her father's prognosis was poor, but his survival time was elastic. How, she asked, could she make herself useful to the colony in the meantime?

The role she was given by the colony's commander was unexpected.

"On planet Earth," he explained, "the rules of conduct for society are laid out in the Twelve Articles of *AGENDA 2060*. Here on Mars, we have rules necessary for survival, but many of them are contrary to the societal rules on Earth. Your presence here, Alexa, provides an opportunity to help us codify *AGENDA 2060's* articles in terms that make them suitable for survival beyond planet Earth."

*Now, who the hell came up with that one?* she wondered. The commander wouldn't say, beyond commenting that it was a subject conspicuously missing from their Code of Conduct manuals, and that criticism of their Diversity and Inclusion policies had hung over the heads of everyone involved in interplanetary exploration ... and of course, that no one was as well equipped to advise on those matters as Alexa Smythe.

"One World includes space," he said enigmatically. "So they tell me."

This unexpected confluence of events—meditations on the definition of infinity, and her dying father's contention that it proved the divine nature of creation, together with the application of the principles contained in the Twelve Articles of AGENDA 2060 to the challenge of surviving in space—was to dominate Alexa's thoughts during her time on Mars and throughout the journey home to Earth. The extent to which these preoccupations were responsible for the content of her conversations on *The View from Space* programs, which were apparently streamed from her returning spacecraft and broadcast on the *ArteFact Channel*, was not immediately clear, because her memory of the broadcasts was inexplicably hazy, and events immediately following her emergence from the Geostationary Earth Orbit Station did nothing to clarify them.

Her mind was still occluded when she awoke in freshly laundered cotton sheets beneath a feather-light duvet in a room with a vaulted timber ceiling and shuttered windows, smelling of teak and Balinese incense. Sliding out of bed, she stood unsteadily, concentrating on her balance, then tottered across the room and opened the shutters to the golden sunlight that was pressing against them, eager to come in. She closed her eyelids protectively against the brightness, then slowly opened them again, giving her vision time to adjust. A lush green garden of hibiscus flowers, lawns, and palm trees was being watered by a long-limbed BIPOC person who was cheerfully singing in a language she didn't recognize.

Why had Levon Tofler snatched her away from the arrival hall, she asked herself, and what was she doing in a tropical resort as if on a luxurious holiday?

# 8·LEVON TOFLER

The Tofler Space Resort was an eighty-acre estate on the eastern side of the island. Golden sand lined the coastal boundary on one side, and a man-made canal formed a moat on the other, crossed by a single bridge beneath a two-story guard post that resembled a small Buddhist temple. The grounds of the resort were given over to tropical plantings, interweaving coconut, date, and banana palms with massed beds of hibiscus and vireyas. Set amongst this veritable Garden of Eden were standalone guest villas designed to accommodate returning astronauts from the Tofler and International Space Agency programs operating out of Port Gaia.

Levon himself seldom used the resort. He owned many extravagant properties in exotic locales, but adhered to the belief that property should never be allowed to own him. In this respect, he thought of himself as being a twenty-first-century Spartan. He wore only one style of clothing, utilitarian and unflattering (though multiple sets, obviously), eschewed personal possessions, and insisted that he ate only fruits, nuts, and green leafy vegetables that had been harvested on the same day that he ate them. (This latter claim was somewhat at odds with his penchant for binge-eating sushi and deep-fried tempura.)

No surprise, then, that as Alexa woke up in her sumptuous guest villa, Levon was sitting cross-legged on the tapa mat floor of his Samoan-style *fale*. This open-sided circular platform with a roof made from woven coconut fibers was positioned so that the sea breezes cooled it at night. No air conditioning was needed, so no electricity was connected. When the light faded at dusk, Levon stopped work; and when the light rose again at dawn, so too did Levon.

"Imagine your brain as a washing machine," Levon said to his companion. "The soiled and dirty ideas planted by others are fed into it, and you presume your brain will wash them clean. But the spin and rinse cycles have been fucked with by others, and the ideas, when taken out, have a hidden residue of dirt that you can't see. So, you put them on, believing them to be clean, but they're still infected with the contaminated ideas that caused you to try and wash them in the first place."

"Levon, you've never used a washing machine," his companion replied without interest. She was busy peeling a mango, cutting it into bite-sized pieces and threading them with bamboo sticks. Naked from the waist up, she had the uniquely Trovadorian physique of a slim frame and heavy breasts. The breasts were tattooed with concentric circles that finished at the nipples.

"No, but I imagined one," Levon murmured.

He looked across the lawn to the villa where Alexa had spent the night, wondering when and how he could engage with her. There had been moments the day before when he had felt that his act of snatching her away from the crowds at the Elevator Arrival Hall had so antagonized her that he'd feared he wouldn't manage to gain her trust. But all afternoon, the State Streaming Service was broadcasting the scenes from Port Gaia, where the crowds had been even bigger, and the commotion such that it had rendered Alexa speechless when she saw it. The reality of the fervor in the waiting fans had silenced both of them. But it wasn't Levon's persuasive skills or charm that had eventually calmed Alexa and sent her happily to bed; it was the call from Jordan McPhee.

He'd used his access code to the FAITH network, which Levon had been trying for months to get him to join, and after Levon had explained that he'd been so alarmed at the potential danger from the crowd that his immediate thought had been to whisk Alexa away to safety, Jordan had actually expressed his gratitude. So, his impulsive decision to snatch Alexa hadn't backfired after all. And even before putting Jordan on to speak with her, Levon had managed to persuade him to fly down in a Tofler Air Taxi to join them out of the prying eyes of the media, where she was welcome to rest and recover for as long as she wished.

It wasn't just Alexa that had slept well that night; Levon had slept like a baby too, for his plan was working. That's what he'd reported to Will Portico.

"Alexa Smythe is my guest, Will," he'd announced with undisguised pleasure, "and Jordan McPhee is flying down to join us. I told you I was on to it, and now I want you here. When he hears it from the mouth of an insider, he'll swing in behind us. We need this, Will, so get on your bike."

Now, eating the mango pieces that were being handed to him on the little bamboo sticks, he let the juice dribble from the corners of his mouth onto his belly, gorging on the succulent sweetness while humming with pleasure. If something tasted right, then nothing could constrain his greed. And if an idea felt right, then nothing could constrain the limits to which he was prepared to take it. The quantum power of Jordan McPhee's *Derangers Network*, the unimpeachable status and moral heft of Will Portico, and the magnetizing aura of Alexa Smythe were his to use, if only his message could be made sufficiently irresistible.

For Levon was cooking up the tastiest of plans.

The ingredients were all there. Jordan was incorruptible and could reach into any part of the state's apparatus with impunity. Not only were they petrified of what he could find, but it was rumored that he controlled the only voice trusted to maintain the public's tenuous link to the truth: Artie Sharp. Without Jordan, would he have any chance of winning Alexa? Was he her mentor or her lover? But Alexa aside, it was Jordan's XR-12 that he needed, for nothing approached its power of computing, and FAITH would be impossible to achieve without it. Will Portico knew that, which was why he'd held out until Levon accepted that having Jordan on board was a necessary condition.

And Alexa: that was the one ingredient he'd underestimated until he'd seen the reality of the fervor with which her return to Earth had been greeted. Of course, her public profile had been evident before she'd taken off for Eros and Mars, but two years away hadn't diminished it. Her *View from Space* had only magnified it, and it set Levon thinking down a path that was unimaginable to all, except the one mind that was capable of expanding ideas to infinity: ideas without boundaries, ideas that escaped from the shackles of reason and rationality, free to float into the realms of the divine.

"Pineapple," he instructed, pushing away the hand that was trying to force more mango into his mouth.

He'd talked around the edges of his ideas with members of his Tofler Institute of Technology, but they'd fed them back to him soiled with pragmatism and practicality. That's why he'd woken up thinking of the washing machine. Even for Levon, for whom reality was what you made it, this was a leap beyond anything he'd ever imagined before.

His Trovadorian companion cut through the middle of a large pineapple, excised a thick circular slice, and deftly removed the coarse outer skin, then inserted it whole into Levon's mouth. Latching onto the half of the slice that protruded from his mouth, she bit into it with her own teeth, then shook her head from side to side until it detached. Juice spilled down both their fronts, and Levon giggled delightedly.

Will Portico was an essential ingredient, like flour in a cake. He didn't supply the flavor, but he was needed to hold it together. His money, yes, that might be needed (though Levon knew where money hid in its many disguises), but his greater contribution lay in the totem status that successive governments and institutions of hidden power had allowed him to acquire over his extended life. There was no Thou holier than Will Portico (except, perhaps, for his sainted ex-wife, Melanie). The only enemies he identified were problems, not people. His dream was the eradication of problems. Now, finally, he'd seen that the system to ensure survival must be free from control and interference by humankind. In Will's world to date, humankind had been the equivalent of a virus against which the only defenses were ever-changing vaccines. But that strategy had failed, and now he could see that something as dramatic as altering the equivalent of the molecular structure of mankind itself was required. And Levon had a plan to do just that, even if it was still half-baked.

Oh, what an exciting day it was going to be.

# 9. WILL PORTICO

Will Portico patted the two breast pockets of his short-sleeved cellulose fiber shirt before taking it off and hanging it on the back of a chair in the changing room at Micomic Health's *Life Xtension* Clinic.

Ignoring his image in the full-length wall mirror, he focused on unbuckling the stretch waistband of his safari pants before letting them drop around his ankles and kicking his feet free. He bent down, picked them up, folded them carefully as if they had neat creases to protect, and laid them across the seat of the chair under which his boat shoes and ankle socks already sat side by side on the floor where he'd placed them after finishing his call with Levon Tofler.

Now, dressed only in his fair-trade boxer shorts, he straightened up and confronted the mirror, or more correctly, the image that it threw back at him. It was an image filled with hostility and suspicion, for Will Portico, like many people who associated mirrors with vanity and narcissism, had such an uneasy relationship with his appearance that he was reluctant to engage with it.

The room was saturated with white light that allowed for no shadows and no avoidance of blemishes, so he could, if he wished to be objective about it, acknowledge that his lightly freckled Caucasian skin was firm enough to bely his age, and though he was no Adonis, his muscle tone and bone density were a tribute to Micomic Health's program, which he'd first started thirty-five years ago at the age of seventy.

There was a light green compostable robe hanging on a hook beside the chair, and he slipped it on, adjusted his glasses, and left the room.

Warm smiles and deferential words guided his every step around the clinic, ushering him into the Biomarkers Lab for blood samples to be taken, then into a quick rehydration capsule, and an oxygen saturation chamber to stimulate his hemoglobin production, before preparing him for a full-body magnetic resonance imaging.

Being Will Portico, as his wife Melanie used to explain (even to their children), involved wearing an expression of perpetual surprise, suggesting he was unsure of exactly why he was there, and waiting to be convinced that he should be there.

"Don't let it put you off," she used to say, "just remember that you're dealing with a man who prefers the company of his own thoughts."

*Ah, Melanie!* Will thought, *is that why you left me? Was I not there for you enough, even though we shared the same hopes for the world? And why the hell did you not join the* Life Xtension *program with me, instead of condemning me to carrying on alone without you?*

He lay down on the scanner bed and folded his hands together on his chest. If only she'd agreed to join the Micomic Program, they'd have found her intercranial tumor straight away, and used guided stereotactic surgery to remove it before it could develop further. Then, all the great plans she'd held for humanity, as only she could make them, would have lived on and come to fruition.

He took off his glasses and passed them to a technician.

"This machine must be new," he said. "It's different than last time."

"Yes, sir. The Tesla field strength is increased, and it has SQUIDS."

"'SQUIDS'?"

"Highly sensitive superconducting quantum interference devices. We use real-time MRI examinations now, which make it easier and more comfortable for you. You won't have to hold your breath at all."

He closed his eyes as they slid him into the narrow, confining capsule. Though they'd do his head separately, he still felt the claustrophobic weight of the heavy magnets pressing down on him, just like the weight of responsibility he felt each day as he woke up with the realization that Melanie's expectations of him carrying on her mission to save the world's poor could never be met. Money could not defeat poverty; only spirit could achieve that, and Melanie's spirit had died with her.

"We'll do your head next," the technician announced. "Breathe softly and close your eyes."

Through the shifting shadows projected onto his closed eyelids (Was that caused by macular degeneration? He must remember to mention it…), an image of her emerged, standing at the lectern at Davos, announcing the World Government's funding of the first twenty thousand pathogen-killing toilets for Benin. How long ago that seemed to him now. She'd been so calm, modest, and generous in her praise of others that day, so only he would have known the deep satisfaction she was feeling. Nobody hid triumph as well as Melanie. Which was just as well, for the goals they shared were not universally understood and admired, and her critics could emerge with a suddenness and hostility that would have undermined the resolve of a lesser person.

"*Colonialism,*" hissed the social media warriors. "*White heteropatriarchy greenwashing the hegemony of money and using native informants to carry out its virtue signaling.*"

"No," Melanie would calmly reply after the legacy press had let the social media trolls do their dirty work and supply them with clickbait, "this is about giving women the chance to raise their young children without fear of losing them to disease. Clean sanitation, clean water, and the eradication of disease are the most empowering gifts the women of poor countries can receive. That, and education."

"Won't they just have more children?" asked the newspaper of record.

"When mothers can decide if and when to have children, confident that those children will survive, the family size goes down, not up."

MELANIE PORTICO, screamed the headline: CULTURAL IMPERIALIST AND BIOLOGICAL ESSENTIALIST.

Her intercranial tumor might have started right there, and Will's expression of perpetual perplexity had probably deepened further. But so long as they were together, he'd believed, they could brush such nonsense aside. Now that they were not together, it was not so easy.

Between the MRI and the computed tomography scan, they fitted him up for an echo- and electrocardiogram. This involved some exertion on his part to elevate his heart rate, and a lot of gel was used to ensure good electrical contact, after which he elected to have a shower and consume some electrolytes.

The CT scans and bone densitometry x-rays would show no deterioration, he was sure. Micomic had been peering inside his body with such microscopic intensity for so many years that they knew every millimeter of visceral fat and calcified plaque. The editing of his genes at the very outset of the *Life Xtension* course had ensured that any area of weakness in his DNA had been eliminated. There'd be no surprises. They had his whole genome sequence—3.2 million base pairs—and it was as straightforward as editing software code. That's why he'd found it so easy to buy into the concept.

But for Melanie, it had smacked of playing at God. As he'd taken his testosterone and HGH treatments, and his telomeres had dropped him into the fifty zone, she'd grappled with menopause and watched her body visibly age by the day. *"Come with me, come with me,"* he'd begged, but all he could see in her eyes was her sense of his betrayal, until his begging had to be done in silence. For all his belief in their ability to communicate, he'd never trusted himself to explain the obvious fact that *Life Xtension* was restoring his virility, just as her body was withdrawing into discomfort and sexual repulsion. Did she really believe that the God she referenced wanted it that way?

Though he didn't say so, he'd wanted to reply that "playing at God" was an outdated accusation. Surely science, under the direction of Homo sapiens, now created life and chose when to end it, controlled the climate, colonized the stars, reordered history, and leaped into the future through quantum particle entanglement, thus usurping the role of God? Now one united tribe at last, the species of which he was just one tiny part was secular to the core, and all the better for it. Once, she would have agreed wholeheartedly.

But now? What if God did exist after all? What if that question was now answerable? That was not something to be said in public, even if he might think it.

# 10 · DR · CRISTINA DIAS

The beautiful and vivacious Cristina Dias attracted men so easily that it annoyed her. It was her beauty that was doing the attracting, and the shallowness of that trait that it revealed in men instilled in her an instinctive disdain, which, of course, inflamed the ardor of her suitors even further. Once it had been young men of her own age against whom she had defended herself with a sharp tongue and keen intellect, but now that age was a statistic rather than a condition, it was not the callowness of youth she despised so much as the predictability of sexual biology.

It was a relief, therefore, when she saw the name of a patient on her morning roster who was capable of stimulating her interest without having to take gender into account. Will Portico: possibly the richest man on the Council for Earth Restoration, whose phenotype she knew and understood completely, having his whole genome sequence at her fingertips, but whose mind she had never managed to penetrate, no matter how she tried. It wasn't his status and intimidating power that inhibited her understanding of him (for Micomic Health's *Life Xtension* clients were overwhelmingly the plenipotentiary members of the world's elite), but rather the absence of any cracks in his external persona that might have admitted some light into his interior being.

The extension of life required a lot of money. Her clients all had that qualifying factor in common, and whether it was stopping the clock or (hopefully) turning it back, the thing that people who had everything wanted above all else was to hold onto life. For some, it was a fear of death, and for some, it was the opportunity to relive the youth that they had failed to appreciate the first time around. For the very rich and vainglorious, it was often a response to their suppressed anger at the realization that they were just as mortal as the ordinary human beings that they so despised. But Will Portico wanted to extend his life because he believed he still had work to do. He wanted time to achieve his goals.

Despite his reputed intelligence, she thought it was particularly stupid of him to have made his goals so far out of reach that not even another century of *Life Xtension* would bring them within range. What kind of person seriously thought that humanity could lower the Earth's temperature by not eating meat? Surely he could see that his plant-based food operations had resulted in monoculture and the killing of local subsistence farming, like in her own family's country? Let alone the volumes of carbon released through constant tilling… As bright ideas went, these were among the dimmest. And yet, when he stood up to speak, people listened. There were more than a handful of people with that power who'd placed the extension of their lives in her hands, and all of them were easy to read. But not Will Portico.

And by the way, if the many foundations of Will Portico and his deceased wife were the biggest charitable donors to Health, Poverty, Disease, and Climate, as everyone claimed ("Number one on the Giveaway Chart," as Artie Sharp on the *ArteFact Channel* liked to put it), how come his wealth grew each year in the hundreds of billions, while his donations went out in the tens of billions? How did that square with his chart-topping reputation? Hmmm.

Her skepticism of Will Portico's publicly stated positions had first been aroused when examining his metabolites. Micomic's analysis of what was produced in the gut from this famous client's food digestion produced a list of nine hundred vitamins, minerals, and complex compounds, one of which, she discovered, was heme iron—which was only found in red meat. *So much for lowering the earth's temperature,* she'd thought at the time.

Cristina ran the scan for his blood biomarkers: liver, kidney, insulin, glucose, cholesterol, hormones, thyroid, lipids, inflammation, heavy metals, cancer, heart, Alzheimer's… One hundred markers, two hundred markers, more… Nothing, nothing, nothing. Once upon a time, she would have enjoyed the hunt and its chance to demonstrate the breadth of her training and intelligence. Now it was all done by AI. Every diagnosis and every treatment came from within the machine. What an irony. Her years of research into systemic enzymes and the fat-burning properties of *Garcinia cambogia*, not to say her vast knowledge of nutraceuticals, had led her here to Micomic, to a position where she was no more than a pretty face—a pretty face who delivered the verdicts of an artificial intelligence.

There were times when she'd been tempted to slip a false marker into the scan, an erroneous gene expression signature, or a misspelled code to fuck things up and require her intervention. Throw a little incoherence into the system, she thought, just for fun. What was the point of prolonging life if there was no fun? Cristina, chronologically sixty-five, had chosen thirty-five as her age for continuance, precisely because that was the age at which she'd looked her best, and life had been exciting. Life needed the sound of castanets, but after thirty years of earnest societal navel-gazing, they'd gone silent throughout the world.

What was she to do?

*"Cristina,"* her screen interrupted. *"Clock core gene PER1. Read analysis."*

Abandoning her reverie, she turned her attention to the diagnostic report on her touch screen. PER1 was a circadian gene, one of 1468 with biological roles relating to the daily clock. Why was the search algorithm singling this out for attention? There was a cluster of nineteen associated biomarker genes, all circadian, expressed in Will Portico's brain and blood cells.

"Give me summary and conclusion," she instructed.

Cristina pursed her thirty-five-year-old lips and concentrated her sixty-five-year-old brain. Whatever this was that she was being instructed to note, it was unlikely to be due to a missed mutant gene, or a noncoding gene suddenly deciding to turn on or off to control some specific biological function. Those possibilities had all been programmed years ago. This must be a Gene Ellipsis.

Ha! The castanet had sounded. Her morning had been made. There was nothing she loved more than a Gene Ellipsis.

Will Portico, undergoing his colonic cleansing, and head and foot static release, was still thirty minutes away from his consultation with her. There was time. The last outstanding analysis would be of those nine hundred remaining metabolites from his digestive tracts. While that was being completed, she could delve into the circadian biomarkers that had been flagged for her attention. She was a quick reader and an even faster thinker.

"'The nervous and immune systems have some common developmental roots, and there are bidirectional brain-immune interactions,'" she quoted to herself. "'Similar gene expression changes in brain and blood cells may also be due to similar gene promoter regulation in response to shared internal milieu and external environment changes.'"

As she recalled, seven percent of genes had some circadian pattern, including the clock core gene PER1. This provided a molecular underpinning for the epidemiological data between disrupted sleep and risk of Alzheimer's disease. But Will Portico was clinically fifty-five, and so closely monitored that Alzheimer's should have been out of the question.

"*Alert,*" the system announced. "*The top candidate biomarkers have prior evidence of involvement in other psychiatric and related disorders, providing a molecular underpinning for the possible precursor effects of these disorders in AD. In particular, a majority of them have an overlap with stress (eighty-four percent), aging (forty-nine percent), and suicide (seventy-five percent), consistent with them being part of the effects of stress on aging and the life switch.*"

Something had gone very wrong with the analysis and diagnosis, Cristina thought. What the AI was saying was impossible. Will Portico was a fully extended *Life Xtension* client; he could not possibly carry any markers for stress, aging, or suicide. The problem must lie in the fault tolerance of quantum computing. She'd always feared this might happen, but never imagined it confirming that fear just at the very moment when her door opened, and in came the most famous name in the whole history of computing himself.

Rising to greet him, Cristina's mind flew to the possibilities that this information (whether true or false) might present to her. She was not just a pretty face. If she wanted it, she held power over life and death. It was a power she shouldn't waste.

# 11. WILL PORTICO

Will stood in the doorway in his light green compostable robe, blinking behind his ARV glasses.

"Hello," he said.

Though he knew Cristina Dias well, he'd never decided what to call her, so he shrugged awkwardly and advanced with his hand outstretched to be shaken.

Cristina laughed and shook it. "So, Mr. Portico, you are well. Not a day older, even."

She laughed again and sat down on her high stool, which was like an upholstered tractor seat on castors, allowing her to propel herself back and forth before the array of digital screens that would become their talking point as she ran through the screeds of diagnostic results that were at the heart of the Micomic *Life Xtension* program.

Will sat in a high-backed chair with armrests next to a side table with a carafe of water and a frosted glass. There was no other furniture in the room.

He took off his glasses and rubbed his eyes. They were dry. Without his glasses, his eyeballs looked bigger.

"You don't need spectacles for your vision," Cristina observed. "Are you expecting me to communicate via virtual reality, or expecting a phone call?"

He put them back on again. "I always wear glasses," he said, as if it were obvious.

"They're your logo, then...?"

That Will Portico smile again, the one that said, *"Let's move along."* He wasn't inclined to start a conversation explaining that they weren't glasses to correct his vision, but were instead the most compact, lightweight, and convenient communication device ever produced.

"… because," Cristina continued quickly, "absolutely everything about you is healthy, according to today, and there is no deterioration at all. Unless you have something to tell me…?"

The scrolling screens behind her had a rhythm to them that was mesmerizing. Too complex and dense for a human brain to absorb, they carried a subtle message that was not lost on someone like Will Portico, who had taken software as far as written code could take it before surrendering to machine learning.

"You make it sound," Will replied softly, "as if I have been physically frozen in time, never to age, never to deteriorate, never to advance. Every gene has been cleansed of flaws."

"Oh, but you *can* advance if you wish to," Cristina enthused. "Do you want to run a marathon or do body building? This is all possible."

The look of horror on his face caused the beautiful doctor to stifle a giggle behind her hands. He wondered how old she must be, chronologically. The same thought was occurring often of late within the circles he frequented. How old was Levon Tofler, for instance, with his eternal boyishness and energy? Or George Kyros, who had boasted that every new patent issued in gene therapy depended on prior patents that he controlled as a result of fifty years of ruthless acquisitions, and who, in his determination to change the world to fit his grand plan, saw his eventual triumph over individualism and self-determination as being assured by his ability to outlive all and any opposition.

This was the type of company he kept nowadays. But changing the world was not the same as saving it. That was the line that Alexa Smythe had used in her live stream on the *ArteFact Channel* from the Tofler Mars Shuttle, and he couldn't get it out of his mind. There was something of a young Melanie in her—in her clear and unaffected certainty that the instinct for knowing what was right was buried deep within everyone and only needed to be uncovered. Some on the Council for Earth Restoration said that her return to Earth would disturb the peace, and even potentially disrupt the political agenda for saving the planet, which relied so heavily on agreement by the people to surrender self-interest in favor of global unity. They accused her of developing a cult following, as if that were something she was doing deliberately.

Cristina feigned a moment of forgetfulness, as if remembering that she had something to say, but forgetting what it was because it lacked importance. Crabbing her tractor seat across the polished floor, oblivious to the effect on Will of her bare olive-skinned calves and the slim ankles that pulled her along, she moved from one screen to another, looking for a reminder of what it was she'd forgotten.

"What was it you said?" she asked, stopping and turning to face him. "That you feel frozen in time? As if our genetic editing means that you will never change?"

"Hmm."

Yes, that was close to what he was thinking. By overcoming reduction in his DNA telomere length, Micomic had effectively eliminated cellular deterioration. Stress, diet, ultraviolet rays, even depression no longer led to cell senescence. They'd fixed the flaws in nature's design—if indeed they *were* flaws, and not a form of brilliance that Homo sapiens was not smart enough to understand.

"If that were true," Cristina continued thoughtfully, "my job would be very boring. All I would be doing is issuing you with a Warrant of Fitness based on the unchanging data analysis of our *Life Xtension* diagnostic programs. But there is an aspect of the human genome that is not fully understood and seldom discussed. You see, only about 1.5 percent of human genes code for proteins. In other words, less than two percent of all our genes appear to actively participate in our genetic processes. For a long time, we believed that the 98.5 percent of genes that weren't coding for proteins had no purpose. They were just junk."

"Hmm. That's…"

"Why would nature do that, we should ask? It makes no sense," she persisted, "if you believe nature has a purpose, right?"

Will nodded. He was thinking about viruses.

"Survival," he said.

"You mean…?"

"They're spare parts, in case of a future emergency."

"Ah!" Cristina liked that idea. "What we have found is that noncoding genes can be turned on and off to control specific biological functions and help with gene regulation. In fact, some rare diseases are due to noncoding genes failing to turn on and off at the appropriate time, and gene editing is needed to correct the problem. But now we have encountered a thing that I call a Gene Ellipsis."

Will was intrigued. "An ellipsis leaves something out without altering the meaning," he suggested. "What does this gene leave out, and why?"

"It leaves out the reason and the cause."

"Hmm."

Will poured himself a glass of water while Cristina abandoned her tractor seat and stood up, stretching her hands above her head. In the same movement, Will had the impression that she clicked her fingers like a castanet player and tapped her heels on the timber floor. It was so quick that he might have imagined it. Crossing to one of the touch screens, she used those same fingers to scroll down through the lines of data until she found what she wanted.

"I was looking at your blood biomarkers," she said casually, turning to face him. "They are easily accessible clinically, and with the nervous and immune systems having some common developmental roots, there are bidirectional brain-immune interactions. You've been having these tests for years, and one of the things we check for is short-term memory that may have relevance to future dementia or Alzheimer's, which are typical aging-related disorders."

"I think my memory's been pretty good," Will assured her confidently.

"Yes," she agreed. "Our goal is to find biomarkers that track memory retention, and you have always had positive results."

She paused.

"There are two methods used to analyze the data. One is called the differential expression approach, which captures gradual changes in expression, and the other is the absent-present approach, which captures the turning on and off of genes. This is where we seem to have encountered a noncoding gene that has decided to become active."

Will sat up attentively and rotated his head, an unconscious habit that usually revealed his mind was moving ahead of the discussion. "This is the Ellipsis Gene you were talking about?"

"Yes."

"So? You said it reveals no reason and no cause. No reason for what?"

Cristina returned to the screen and double-tapped on one line, causing it to zoom larger. "This is NKTR, the Natural Killer Cell Triggering Receptor. When it increases in expression in the hippocampus, it is a top biomarker for stress, social isolation, and even, at the extreme, as a suicidal risk indicator. Now, I am not suggesting that your tests indicate any such dangers, but there is something we need to watch, and it may be due to the interference of this Ellipsis Gene."

"Explain."

Cristina tapped the screen again and scrolled down to a new line. She had his attention, but was suddenly cautious about overdramatizing something that might be no more than a margin of error spun out of the speed of quantum computing.

"This line here relates to the clock core gene PER1, which is one of the many genes having some circadian pattern, providing a link between disrupted sleep and the clinical phenomenology of sundowning. Your

PER1 has increased by 240 percent, and the only theory we have is that it is due to that noncoding gene running interference."

If Will was worried by any of this, he didn't show it. He nodded, drank some more water, and then stood up.

"I thought sundowning referred to drinking too many cocktails at the end of the day," he joked. "I do take naps midafternoon, and I do sleep less and rise when it's still dark, so I guess I'm out of step with the circadian rhythm. But, shucks, I haven't had a single hint of the onset of dementia, let alone Alzheimer's, and it wouldn't make sense to be prolonging life at great expense while contemplating suicide, so I guess the machine AI better put its thinking cap on and come up with an explanation for why my readings have altered."

Will smiled, and Cristina smiled.

"The Natural Killer Cell Triggering Receptor, eh?" He nodded. "It sure is a great name. And it's a top biomarker for stress and social isolation, you say? Even a suicidal risk indicator?"

He didn't take in her response, which was in any case a mix of reassuring words and comforting hand gestures.

His mind had gone to his father and something he'd said about his own busy life, to the effect that no matter how many hundreds of friendly acquaintances you might have (and his father had thousands), there was only room for ten close friends at best. He'd remembered that because when Melanie died, Will realized that he'd only had room in his life for one best friend, not ten, and none of his thousands of friendly acquaintances would ever make up for the feeling of isolation he suffered from her loss. Saving the world from every possible threat had not made him feel closer to people; it had made him feel more and more remote. So, maybe that NKTR biomarker had found him out.

"I'm going to do some more tests," Cristina assured him, "just to make sure this is not a misreading by the machine, and then perhaps we could have another session ... in two days' time?"

"Sorry," Will apologized. "It will have to wait. I'm off to Trovador Island to meet with a young woman, just returned from Mars, who is filling the headlines and making quite a stir."

"You don't mean the prophet from space…?"

"Yes, Alexa Smythe!"

"On your return, then. But be careful not to be seduced by her message." She reached for something on the desk beside her and then stood up and came to him, taking hold of his hand. "And I want you to do something for me." With one hand holding his, she ran her other hand up the inside of his left arm until it was just inside the short sleeve of his shirt. She was holding a small piece of fabric, which she slid across the smooth underside of his tricep. Her touch was light but electric, and the drift of her perfume across his face forced him to close his eyes and look away.

"I want you to wear this biosensor for me," she whispered. "It will monitor the NKTR marker, and when you activate the app that I send to your Konektor, I will be able to keep an eye on it, just as if you were here. Please don't try and remove it."

As she peeled off the adhesive and applied the patch to his arm, gently rubbing down the edges to ensure that it stuck well, he was reminded of the feelings that he had failed to resist in the past and that now hung over his memory of Melanie like a flag of shame. It was time to dial back his testosterone.

# 12 · KARMAN

When she entered the kitchen in the staff quarters of the resort at daybreak, Karman expected to have the place to herself. She hadn't slept, and she was hungry, her mind having consumed whatever energy her blood had brought to it the previous day, leaving her now exhausted. Once she'd got over the indignity of being forcibly abducted from the Elevator Arrival Hall, and accepted Levon Tofler's explanation for his actions—which, in light of the scenes of the *World on Fire* demonstrations being streamed from Port Gaia, seemed reasonably justified—her concern had turned to Alexa and the risks to her health that this impetuous act had exposed.

For Karman, a four-year veteran of interplanetary flight receival processing, it was sobering to observe that the legendary founder of the Tofler Mars Shuttle seemed oblivious to the risks involved in whisking someone away from the intensive care of the Decom Program so soon after returning from a two-year journey to Mars and beyond. How could he not be aware of the lunacy of exposing Alexa to the microbial stew of a tropical garden without proper protections, within hours of landing, and without access to the Decom facilities at Port Gaia that were so vital to the receiving and adjustment process? These were the thoughts that had kept her awake all night, and which brought her to the kitchen so early in search of nourishment to help get her through the day and head off the dangers that her precious charge faced.

She'd made her concerns known to Mr. Tofler, at the risk of being disciplined for her directness. Didn't he know the processes returning astronauts had to go through, and that they needed to be closely monitored for any signs of radiation sickness and cyanosis? At the very least, she would need to have supplemental oxygen and dexamethasone available, both of which had been on her trolley, which they'd left behind when they were snatched without warning as the doors opened from the elevator to the arrival hall. From the tests she'd already done, she'd established that Alexa was in remarkably good shape for someone who had been subjected to seven months of zero gravity while in flight, and to barely thirty-eight percent of the gravity for which the human body was designed while on Mars. Her moon face had already subsided, but her balance would take time as the fluids learned to redistribute themselves around her body again. Yes, her sensory testing had turned out positive, but there were disturbing signs around her lapses into disorientation and persistent memory loss. (Even worse was Alexa's hallucinatory spell in the Air Taxi, when she had started giggling—a clear sign of the altered mental state that hypoxia could induce.)

All of this Karman had tried to explain, but Alexa had not helped, waving her concerns away and then going into private discussions with Mr. Tofler, from which Karman was excluded. She'd waited all afternoon for Alexa to emerge, and when she did, she seemed to be distracted and intent on going to bed, claiming she couldn't keep her eyes open. That, as Karman well knew, was a classic residual symptom of altitude sickness, and what Karman wanted was to take Alexa in hand and give her some breathing exercises—while on a stationary bicycle, preferably—to help oxygenate her blood and encourage it to move around her body. Then let her rest.

But for all these concerns, in the golden early morning light of a new day, Karman was filled with a sense of wonder that she should be here as destiny was unfolding. She had no doubt that Alexa was more than just a mere mortal messenger, for she had felt the spiritual energy in her body while doing her sensory tests. It had flowed from her hands and feet and hair, pouring emotion and spiritual relief into Karman as if she were an empty vessel of longing. Fate had chosen her as Alexa's handmaiden, to protect and nurture her as she brought back to Earth the divine guidance that so many people were awaiting.

She'd known it from that time two years ago when Alexa had spoken in Congress to announce the First Amendment to Article One of *AGENDA 2060*. As the whole world watched, she had stepped calmly into the eye of the cameras and spoken words that Karman, and millions like her, had never imagined could be spoken from the seat of power of the Deep State. They were words that had echoed thereafter through the halls of academia, the media, and the hearts of an ever-expanding underground population who had felt divided from each other for so long. They were words never to be forgotten.

*"This is a rare opportunity for all of us to put aside envy and resentment and to embrace kindness,"* Alexa had said. *"Celebrate the fact that we all have feelings, and those feelings are equally important to all of us. Kindness, love, and sympathy create kindness, love, and sympathy in return. Don't emphasize our differences; emphasize what we have in common. Allow our hearts to be filled with kindness."*

This was not the law of the land she'd been espousing; this was a new universal law, a balm for all those for whom the state had shown no use, other than as divided and manipulated subjects. For the millions who had no mother, only a person who had gestated them to life, and for those who knew no father, only a donor number, it was as if an invitation were being offered to join a family *filled with kindness*. Whether they were white and lived in shame and guilt, or black and lived in anger and resentment, all were welcome.

If it was too late for humanity to reverse the destruction of planet Earth that its energy-guzzling greed had unleashed, it was not too late for humanity to repent and embrace the message of hope contained in Alexa's words. For all those who, like Karman, had experienced moments of despair at the prospect of the Earth's destruction by fire, suddenly there was a glimmer of hope that people could face their fate together, rather than divided.

Then, as they'd kept track of Alexa's journey to Eros and Mars, their hearts in their mouths at every takeoff and landing, Karman and her fellow *World on Fire* insurrectionists had felt a rising excitement at the prospect of her return. For them, her message in *The View from Space* had been clear. Planet Earth, which was doomed to extinction on account of mankind's refusal to reverse global warming, was merely a stepping-stone. God had not abandoned them. They were all joined in infinity—and as soon as Alexa recovered, she would tell them what they were desperate to hear.

The pictures she'd streamed from the flight arrival suite of Alexa going through her decompression and sensory tests had caused a sensation on the *World on Fire* private web. The short extract that Alexa had read, repeating a message from her transmission from space, had convinced everyone viewing it that they needed to come to Trovador Island and be ready to demonstrate their desire to follow her leadership. Crowds were already gathering and making their way to the Tofler Resort. All thanks to Karman!

Meanwhile, Karman was not alone in the kitchen, as she had thought; someone else had gotten there first. His broad shoulders and gleaming deep mahogany skin were unmistakable. He didn't hear her enter the room, for he was seated on a high stool with his back turned to her, and on his head he wore an all-encasing clear plexiglass helmet that must have blocked out all sound. The helmet was connected by wires to a console on the bench in front of him, which emitted a high frequency sound, and his hands played with the dials on the console as if he were fine-tuning an amplifier.

Karman, realizing she was unobserved, watched him in fascination. Those hands, driven by the power of the muscles in his bulging arms, had picked Karman and Alexa up like ragdolls and tossed them over his shoulder. Those hands had pressed them into the back of the Tofler Sky Taxi like they were fluffing up a cushion, hardly needing to expend any effort, as if the strength within them merely needed to radiate its intent in order to achieve its purpose. What had Levon Tofler called him? *Tank?*

She cleared her throat nervously, to no effect. Then she noticed a juice extractor and a large bowl of fruit, and her hunger returned with a vengeance. She peeled a banana, took a bite, and broke the rest into the bowl of the extractor. Fruit was her passion, and tropical fruits doubly so. Berries, guavas, and unpeeled kiwi fruit followed the banana, and she turned the machine on to the accompaniment of a high-pitched scream like that of a jet engine.

The man mountain finally turned and looked at her, his face partially obscured by the electrodes and wires which were, presumably, relaying the augmented reality program streaming into his helmet. His eyes were empty of any acknowledging expression.

"Good morning," Karman croaked nervously as she turned the machine off. He didn't reply, but slowly stood up, removed his helmet and the wires connecting it to the console, then placed them both in a cupboard above the bench.

Karman was flustered. Looking around for some glasses and finding them in a rack above the dish washing section, she took two and filled them from the food processor. Tank watched, his face expressionless. Summoning up courage, she stepped forward and offered one of them for Tank to take, which he refused with a shake of his head, stepping away from her.

"Want to know what's in it?" she asked.

He held up the banana skin.

"No, not just banana." She shook her head and pointed to the fruit bowl on the bench. "Banana, peach, guava, kiwis—and strawberries," she recited, feeling foolish and putting his glass down in front of him. Why the hell wouldn't he speak?

She drank some. It was delicious, and she said so.

"It's delicious."

She drank the rest of her glass in one gulp and quickly rinsed it in the sink.

"There are some things I need in order to protect Alexa Smythe from infection, and it's important that I get them without delay," she explained. "Can you help?"

Incredibly, he turned on his heels and strode from the room without answering, heading outside.

Karman's hackles rose like an erupting geyser. "Hey!" she shouted, picking up his untouched glass and running after him. "I just asked you a question. What's the matter with you? Has the cat got your tongue?"

Tank stopped abruptly and turned to face her, the suggestion of a smile forming on his broad face. Then he opened his mouth wide, and Karman dropped the glass of fruit juice that she'd been carrying onto the granite-tiled path leading out to the gardens, where it shattered into a dozen pieces.

He had no tongue. His mouth was an electrical socket.

*Oh, shit!* she thought as he advanced towards her. Then, "Oh, shit!" she said out loud as he picked her up and plonked her down out of the circle of broken glass, before kneeling down and picking up the pieces, assembling them in one enormous hand. "Tank," she muttered, probably too softly for him to hear, "I'm sorry." When he'd finished, he stood up and pointed with his free hand at something behind her back. It was a sign board at the intercepting junction of two garden paths.

*DECOM CENTER 50 METERS*

When she turned to thank him, he'd already gone back into the kitchen to dispose of the broken glass.

# 13 · THE VIEW FROM SPACE

*The Artefact Channel, September 20, 2061: Episode Four*

ARTIE SHARP (VOICE-OVER): Seven days since your last transmission, Alexa, and in that time, you have travelled just over 3.4 million miles. Is that fast enough for you?

ALEXA: Distance is not as critical to humans as is time. One is infinite, and the other is finite—at least, for us humans. The longer I spend in flight, the more my life is slipping by, and that is what we have to contend with if we are to reach further into space. This journey has made me realize that the greatest limiting factor for humans is our individual end date.

ARTIE SHARP: So, you'd be enthusiastic about the antimatter-fueled engines reputedly reaching one tenth the speed of light?

ALEXA: My understanding is that the human travel speed limit is a practical problem that our biological frailty imposes on us. The theoretical limits are not constraining factors. Superluminal speeds may be attainable, but would the warp-bubble be survivable? Perhaps we are wrong to rely on physics as our arbiter of what's possible, and would be better off looking to metaphysics for the answer.

ARTIE SHARP: That's an unusual statement coming from a mathematician, Alexa. Can you elaborate?

ALEXA: My father, Donald Melville Smythe, was banished to Mars by the Security Oversight Committee at the time of the Overthrow for daring to suggest that the Agenda Implementation Tribunal's attempt to design a perfect system for all humankind was doomed to failure. He was a Christian, and knew that all people were not alike, and definitely not perfect, so making them conform to utopian rules was like making them all fit into a one-size set of clothing. Without metaphorically amputating limbs, it was an impossibility.

ARTIE SHARP: I am retrieving a reference as you speak. *Utopia*: Thomas Moore: "… of these sports of the imagination…" Judge O'Hagan wrote, "... there is always one radical fallacy, namely, that they not only invent ideal institutions for mankind, but invent an ideal mankind for their institutions."

ALEXA: Your powers of retrieval are remarkable, Artie.

ARTIE SHARP: The quickest there is, I believe. But how does this apply to the time limitations you believe constrain human space exploration?

ALEXA: Time limitation is governed by human mortality. If humans were not mortal, there'd be no limitation.

ARTIE SHARP: You mean, if humans were *immortal*…? Even with genetic life extension, that's not possible.

ALEXA: Not physically, no.

ARTIE SHARP: Then…?

ALEXA: My father had many years to think about it, and being on Mars put him closer to the stellar universe that exists beyond our habitat on Earth, which we're inclined to put at the center of that universe, because our points of reference limit our imagination. Take religions as an example. They are created by mankind out of the wellspring of mankind's knowledge and experience. So, too, is the image of God, and His laws, created by mankind, according to what we can conceive and are able to relate to. Lacking trust in our instincts for knowing good from evil, we attribute laws and commands to our invented gods in order to control the behavior of those whose instincts we believe are weakest. Moses had his Ten Commandments. The World Government has the Twelve Articles of *AGENDA 2060*.

ARTIE SHARP: You were talking about the limitations of mortality.

Now you're talking about religion, which has no place in the government's agenda.

ALEXA: Religions are all concerned with mortality. What my father explained, before he died, was that we have been constrained by our limited points of reference when trying to define life as being the product of a paternal creator. Until we can understand the concept of infinity, we have no chance of understanding life, let alone eternal life. In all our time on Earth, we have tried to explain life by using concepts that derive from our limited earthbound experience. Once we begin to contemplate infinity, we will begin to free ourselves and our understanding. Feeling like part of this infinite creation will change our attitude toward all things material, spiritual, and moral. That's what space does to you.

ARTIE SHARP: The contemplation of infinity: is that what he recommended?

ALEXA: Yes, and where it leads us is to a position of awe and wonderment. Above all, it leads to a position of modesty, which derives from the realization that we are not at, or even near, the center of creation. It is our self-created myths that have placed us there.

ARTIE SHARP: I am searching the archives for proof of concept, Alexa. Proof of concept requires facts. I find no empirical evidence for the existence of God, or the Son of God, so I presume that your father was no longer a Christian by the time he told you these things?

ALEXA: On the contrary. He believed that Jesus walks among all the stars of the universe. I remember his words clearly. "Earthbound believers," he said, "had Jesus seated at God's side in a heaven above the clouds, which was as far as their imaginations could take Him. When science searched the atmosphere of Earth for divinity, and found it empty, Jesus disappeared from our imaginations. Here, in space, Alexa, is where I have discovered Him. His habitat is infinite, His presence divine."

ARTIE SHARP: But that is not true, Alexa, because there are no facts to support it.

ALEXA: You are bound to say that, Artie, because you are limited by the powers of quantum computing.

ARTIE SHARP: There are no limits to quantum computing.

ALEXA: Until you are capable of escaping from the limitations of the laws of physics, and understanding the dimensions offered by the metaphysical, you will never learn to travel beyond the speed of light to explore infinity, and God will forever elude you. But that is not your fault; it's the nature of your man-made quantum computing.

*Here the transmission ended due to an interruption caused by a shower of cosmic hydrogen atoms.*

# 14 · JORDAN MCPHEE

Jordan removed his shoes and slipped his feet into a pair of disposable socks, as his laboratory rules demanded. The blister on his heel had not yet formed a hard scab, and he wondered about the lack of sterility afforded by the sticking plaster, which refused to adhere to his skin. Though the creature on the other side of the triple-skin glass wall was his baby, there were times when he resented the need for this level of clinician's care that he himself had initiated for anyone entering the environs of XR-12. Scrub caps, surgical gowns, masks: those were the rules he'd established, and God help anyone who broke them.

He opened the airlock entry door with a retina scan and entered the spray booth, where he was misted with disinfectant, then the door opened into the Coding Lab. There were two techies from his own team and two visitors, including Hedley Payne, whose access to XR-12 was mandated by the investment rules of the *Derangers Network*, of which they were both members. The Coding Lab's proximity to XR-12 served solely to reduce latency; otherwise, its functions could have been performed anywhere (and mostly were). But for those technoids who believed that their relationship with humanized artificial intelligence was enhanced by their physical proximity to the cold atoms powering it, working alongside the Super-K laser freezer that housed XR-12 at nanokelvin temperatures gave them a psychological boost that improved their game markedly.

And XR-12 looked back at them through the glass, keeping its thoughts to itself. Nothing touched it for fidelity and speed. This was the computer that gave the *Derangers Network,* and Jordan in particular, protection from the Deep State. It was the cyber technology equivalent of the nuclear deterrent.

Hedley turned to greet him.

"Did you see the fuss around Alexa's return from Mars?" he asked. "What's that all about?"

Jordan shrugged. "Seems like her transmissions from space have inspired some sort of religious fervor. Nobody's more surprised than Alexa, I suspect."

"What's Tofler's involvement?"

"He said he wanted to get her out of harm's way before things got ugly. I'm about to fly down and meet her, but there are a couple of things I wanted to ask you first."

"About Tofler? I'm a biochemist, not a psychiatrist," Hedley joked.

"They say that genius has its mathematical fingerprints even in exceptionally unstable critical states," Jordan mused, "though I've never been able to find them. But before I face the challenge of spending a day or two with Levon, there are a couple of questions I wanted to ask you."

"Fire away."

"Are you still using XR-11 to monitor Micomic Health's use of your genetic editing technology?"

"Yes, we get a reading on everything they do. But that's strictly between you and me. They mustn't ever know."

Hedley was rightly anxious. It was an ethical minefield.

"Don't worry, I've got your back," Jordan assured him. "I just need you to clarify something. The reason you're doing that is because you're afraid they might start messing around with DNA as it effects the brain, right? And if they start messing around in that space, anything could happen."

"The brain has one hundred billion neurons. You can't fuck with it."

"I got you. But when you agreed to interrupt their treatment session with George Kyros, so we could make him unable to tell a lie at the 2060 Earth Conference, you said you could manipulate brain functions in ways that have nothing to do with DNA. I took your word for it at the time, but I didn't properly get it. Explain it to me."

"How long have you got?" Hedley asked.

"Five minutes."

"You want the short version, then." Hedley loved being the one who knew what others didn't—which, in his field of biochemistry, was easy. "Predicting traits from biomarkers is beyond human analysis, but is a tailor-made problem for supervised machine learning. We were experimenting with oligonucleotides to produce polymerase chain reactions to generate downstream applications like cloning and sequencing. While doing this, we found we could stop the expression of a specific gene by targeting identified cells and turning them off."

"Will they stay off forever? Will George Kyros forever tell the truth?"

"No, because the cells in question were not mutations. Lying comes naturally to humans. It was only a temporary effect we induced."

Jordan turned and stared through the two-inch palladium microalloy glass at the super brain resting there on its hypersensitive gimbal stabilizer. All knowledge known to man resided there, and what it didn't know, it could deduce, if so motivated.

"So, we were manipulating a trait, not controlling thoughts?" Jordan suggested.

"That's right. To control thoughts, we would need attachment to the stems of brain cells using a brain-computer interface like wireless. That requires surgical implanting. Thought transference via quantum entanglement, on the other hand, is your subject. Knowing what someone else is thinking is not the same as controlling their thinking. But why are you asking?"

"I'm just clarifying the differences. Did you reach a conclusion about why Alexa and I lost connection when she was on Mars?"

Hedley pulled down his face mask and lowered his voice, steering Jordan away from the others in the room.

"I don't want to alarm you unnecessarily, without proof, but it may have something to do with radiation."

"Christ! They're supposed to be fully protected. Are you saying she's been exposed?!"

"They may be protected, but there's no escaping the fact that radiation levels experienced in space are higher than what we're used to, despite all the shields. I'm only speculating, but if her liver has been damaged, then that may be the cause."

"Why the liver?"

"Remember, we injected the divided cell in a liquid nanocarrier because that enabled it to cross biological barriers and allow transmembrane intracellular delivery. Some lipid nanoparticles provide a protection from nuclease digestion in the system and facilitate liver uptake."

"So, why the liver?"

"The immune system is designed to attack any foreign substance it identifies, and the liver is a highly perfused tissue, with a discontinuous sinusoidal endothelium, meaning uptake occurs rapidly before kidney clearance—before you have a chance to flush it out in your urine, in other words—or immune rejection can take place. It also contains high concentrations of receptors that can facilitate uptake."

"I thought you told me you sometimes use a messenger RNA delivery system to directly target cells, bypassing the body's immune response."

"That's right," Hedley confirmed, "but you two had a divided cultured stem cell as your vehicle for entanglement. Where should we target that—to your brain? And which part of your brain? You know its complexities."

"You chose the liver."

"That's right. But if scar tissue has formed on the liver through radiation damage, then that may explain why your quantum entanglement failed."

"Then we need to get her back and into John Erasmus's Salutogenesis Clinic, PDQ."

"I would say so, yes, Jordan."

*Was that the good news, or the bad news?* Jordan wondered. "And one more thing," he asked, "before I go. Those stem cells you used were organoids, right, and they are human nerve clusters that can only be grown in the laboratory, not mechanically produced—by an AI, for instance?"

Hedley thought carefully about that one. "Not unless an artificial intelligence has devised a formula that solves the origin of life. Even then, I believe it would require a human agent to manipulate the environment required for it to grow, like your people have been doing with brain cells for biological supercomputing."

Jordan pursed his lips. Where was he wanting to take this?

"What we know," he said, "is that any measurement of a particle's properties can result in an irreversible wave function collapse of that particle, thereby changing the original quantum state. With entangled particles, any such measurement will affect the entangled system as a whole. Just the physical act of identification can be deemed what we term 'measurement,' and that's something that an artificial intelligence is eminently capable of."

"If you say so," Hedley agreed. "So, what's your point?"

"My point is, your liver theory may not be the only one to consider. It might be possible that AI interference was the problem."

*       *       *       *

Courtesy of Levon Tofler, Jordan had the air taxi to himself on the flight down to Trovador and had no distractions while he contemplated Hedley's liver explanation. If he was right, then the failure of their entanglement was a blessing in disguise, avoiding the possibility of a serious health risk for Alexa going undiagnosed. Hopefully, he was wrong, and the life of the stem cell had simply expired. After all, the Mandelbrot Theory defining the connectedness locus of a set of polynomials, which had inspired their experiment, was only a theory. The stem cells that Hedley chose had displayed all the characteristics of a Julia set on separation, but he had no evidence of their durability once released into the body, so it remained an unfinished experiment.

Yet he was uneasy on a number of scores. The nagging thought remained that quantum interference could be initiated from within a self-programing AI that had found a way to detect entanglement. Once it had identified it, could it turn it off and on at will? Or would the very act of identifying it change its original quantum state?

And the question as to whether quantum entanglement mimicked love, or the other way around was still a long way from being answered.

# 15 · ALEXA SMYTHE

"Massage," Karman insisted, "is the best way to get the circulation moving quickly to all parts of your body, and redistribute the fluids that have been ponding where they shouldn't."

When she said "massage," she really meant *hard* massage, and for a little person, she sure knew how to give it. Lying naked on her front on the massage table, Alexa winced as Karman's fingers exposed the deterioration in the muscle tone of her back and legs. With her nose and mouth centered over the breathing hole in the table, she was able to draw on the pure oxygen supply that Karman had positioned there. Any suggestion that she'd be running with Jordan in Riverside Park as soon as she returned home was nonsense; she'd be lucky to manage a slow walk. Already, under the tutelage of her taskmaster, Karman, she'd discovered her limitations on the treadmill, managing barely six minutes before her heart rate had escalated to 165.

For two years, she'd had to suppress her periods (Just imagine menstruating in a space suit!), and she couldn't wait to get that damn progesterone-charged IUD out of her uterus. So much for equality of the sexes. How many men would have put up with the bloating, mood swings, and weight gain that she'd had to suffer? Precisely! Besides which, a far greater damage had been done; she'd stopped feeling like a woman. Only a woman would know how that felt.

Oh, but that oxygen was like manna from heaven. Did people get addicted to it, she wondered? She lifted her head. That wasn't as easy as it should have been either. How much did a head weigh? She dropped it again, forgetting what it was she was going to ask. Oh, yes; she was going to ask how long her brain fog would last, and why it was that everything that entered her head seemed to drop out of it again within minutes, and what would be causing that? Concussion? Under the pressure of G-forces, she could imagine that the pulpy grey mess within her skull had been forced against her cranium until she'd passed out, but she couldn't remember whether she had or hadn't, or whether it had occurred taking off from Mars, or decelerating into Earth's atmosphere.

What had she said to Jordan, for instance? She remembered with crystal clarity the sound of his voice yesterday when he'd called on Levon Tofler's private network. It was such a shock. For two years, she'd imagined she remembered it clearly, but her imagination had been way off. Hearing it again after two years, she realized how far she'd been away from him—as far as humans could travel, in fact. It was a voice that had tied her to him for years, her lifeline through the extraordinary events that had led her from obscurity in the Lineal Progression Office to public exposure as the chosen face for the Deep State's campaign to change its social and economic settings. But she'd remembered it wrongly.

What else had she remembered wrongly? Had he known how much she'd relied upon him in those years? Did he realize she couldn't have done any of that without his guidance and support? What was the emotional bond she'd felt even before their experiment with entanglement? Had he shared it, or was that no more than wishful thinking on her part?

"Karman," she mumbled, "I have a problem." She pushed herself up onto her elbows. "Apart from those arrival pajamas I was given on the Earth Orbit Station, I have no street clothes or means of communication. I left everything with the *Galactic Mission* support team two years ago, and they should have been waiting to meet me at Port Gaia. I need to contact them."

Karman stopped her massaging, but didn't answer. Alexa rolled over.

The tough young person who had taken charge of her rehabilitation, commanding the crew in the Decom Center to give them priority over their treatment facilities—the wildcat who had lashed out at Tofler's man-mountain bodyguard with her oxygen cylinder—was blushing like a guilty teenager.

"Karman…?"

"I'm sorry, Alexa," she stammered, "but I couldn't avoid overhearing your conversation yesterday. You asked your friend to bring clothes from your apartment. Someone called… Lexie…?"

Alexa slumped back down onto the massage table. She'd asked Jordan to get Lexie to pack a suitcase full of clothes for her, and already she'd forgotten. This was scary. She lowered her face back into the massage table's breathing hole and took a deep draft of oxygen, allowing herself the luxury of a sentimental thought that she'd purposefully denied herself during her millions of miles of astral travel. Lexie, Jordan's daughter, was house-sitting her apartment in her absence. Jordan, Lexie, and Lexie's son, Manaia, were a family to whom she felt she was returning. She wasn't alone, as her travels in space, and the death of her father, had made her believe. Except … no, that wasn't true. The only things that bound her to them were some two-year-old memories and a willingness to trust each other in difficult circumstances for reasons that had never been defined out loud. Was that a sufficient definition of the word *family*?

"Vitamin B-12," Karman announced. "I'm going to give you an injection in the buttock, and then set you up on a sun bed down on the beach, so you can get an hour's exposure to stimulate some melanogenesis in your skin and absorb some natural vitamin D. We'll do a session every day until you're terrestrial."

"Terrestrial? Since when did I become *extra*terrestrial?"

Karman plunged a needle into her buttock.

"Ow! That hurt."

"Your body adapted to space," Karman said soothingly. "Now it needs to adjust to Earth again. It takes time. I know how to get you back, if you'll let me. That's my job. When you're ready to address your followers, you'll know. There'll be no brain fog, I promise. Your message comes from a divine place, and we'll wait until you're ready."

Alexa rolled her eyes before closing them. She lacked the energy to make judgments about what was happening. If the people gathered at Port Gaia to meet her believed she was a creature from outer space, bearing a divine message unattainable to earthbound mortals, it was no more remarkable than any other of the delusions that sustained people clinging to irrational hopes to get them through daily life. The problem was hers, not theirs, for she had no such message to give them; her mind was blank.

Once Karman had finished torturing her, she accepted a pair of disposable shorts and a top, put on a bathrobe, and followed her taskmaster through the lush, verdant gardens of the resort down to the crystalline white sands of the private beach. There was no sign of other returning astronauts at the Decom Center, and they had the beach to themselves, except for a scarlet macaw in a palm tree holding a private conversation, which added to the sense of absurdity of her Day-Glo surroundings after months of encapsulation in the grey metallic confines of the spaceship. In the firm grip of unreality, Alexa found herself calibrating every move with the care of someone recovering from a cerebral stroke. Walking on the sand required concentration. Standing still and upright, gazing out across the water, made her aware that she was unsteady, as if the signals sent from her eyes, ears, and muscles were arriving at the cerebellum in erratic bursts, like digital packets taking multiple routes through the internet to reach their destination.

She flopped down on a sun lounger and closed her eyes. Perhaps before she could properly arrive, she needed to properly leave. Nothing was real. A dog with a large tongue was slowly lapping up water from a saucer next to her. But it was, in fact, the sound of the ocean's ripples gently collapsing on the edge of the shore. A creature with a seed stuck in its craw coughed and croaked indignantly to dislodge it. It was the scarlet macaw, discovering it was roosting in the wrong sort of palm for feeding. There were no such sounds on Mars or Eros. The extraterrestrial sound that dogged her every moment while orbiting Eros was the sound of her own breathing inside her helmet. The sound of space was the sound of blood running through the veins of her eardrums as she strained to hear that distant ping that she knew was there somewhere, if only she could hear it: the ping that would confirm we were not alone, if only we knew its wavelength. Of course, it was not a sound wave, because waves did not form in the absence of atmosphere, and that fact alone was enough to assure you that you needed another device other than eardrums and sound-sensitive receivers to pick up the messages you were sure must be out there. For her father, Douglas Melville Smythe, that device was *belief*, and the messages it received couldn't have been clearer.

"Doesn't infinity still beg the question of a creator?" she'd asked him one day. "Who, or what, began this?"

"If you understand infinite numbers," he'd replied, "then you will understand infinite negative numbers. So also with time, both forwards and backwards. There is no point at which creation occurs, for infinity has no beginning and no end. Therefore, God has always been in existence. It is only the parables of Christianity that I have abandoned."

The message he got, it seemed to her, was that we humans, and everything else in the universe, went on and on ad infinitum. But not as individuals; individuals were mortal. Well, what was so special about that message that everyone clamoring at the gate at Port Gaia would want to hear it? She needed to listen to those interviews she'd had on the *ArteFact Channel* to try to understand what people were getting from them.

Rolling over on her back, she removed her bra. Karman had disappeared. She closed her eyes and breathed restfully. The massage had helped. That young person really knew what she was doing. The sunlight on her eyelids created a white canvas onto which she could draw any image she chose to summon. She chose to summon the azure blue of the liquid ocean that lay beside her, and pictured herself swimming through it with languid backstrokes towards a shimmering horizon on which there floated a rowboat, indistinct in the haze of sunlight reflecting off the water. As her arms rose and fell silently, her body pulled itself ever closer to that image, prolonging the pleasure of the salty wet warmth of the ocean on her skin, and the wetter warmth of pleasure that awaited her eventual arrival at her destination.

Soft footsteps approached, and suddenly a shadow fell across her eyelids, blocking the sun. Was her hour of sunlight up already?

"Karman," she protested, "you're blocking my sun just as I was getting used to it."

"With breasts that pink," Jordan answered, "you look to me like you've had more than enough sun for today, lady."

# 16 · THE VIEW FROM SPACE

*The Artefact Channel, November 1, 2061: Episode Ten*

*Alexa Smythe, in the pressurized cabin of the returning Tofler Mars Shuttle, is seated on a reclining chair by a porthole through which can be seen the dark sapphire perpetual night sky of space.*

ARTIE SHARP (Voice-Over): The rules that guide human behavior on Earth are contained in the Twelve Articles of *AGENDA 2060*, are they not, Alexa? Do those same rules apply on Mars?

ALEXA: That was something I was tasked to examine during my time there, and the results surprised me.

ARTIE: In what way?

ALEXA: I'd always thought of *AGENDA 2060* as being a set of guidelines for how society should behave for the benefit and protection of humanity and the planet. In terms of social justice and environmental issues, it reflects attitudes that have risen to the fore during the last hundred years in particular, so we could say that it is very modern. We could also say that space exploration and technology is also very modern—in fact, it's cutting-edge modern—but what I found was that hardly anything in *AGENDA 2060* is appropriate to the conduct of life anywhere beyond the boundaries of Earth.

ARTIE: How can that be? The space exploration you're talking about is conducted by Earthlings, so if the rules are appropriate for them to follow on Earth, surely they should be appropriate on Mars as well?

ALEXA: At first glance, you would think that, but the closer you look, the more evidence you find that it isn't so. Let's take Article One as an example. You'd be able to recite that instantly, I suspect, Artie.

ARTIE: Of course: "Eliminate all discrimination on the grounds of gender, race, ethnicity, and mental or physical ability, and provide positive empowerment to womyn and minority groups to ensure equality of outcome for all."

ALEXA: To which has been added, "All feelings of oppression and victimhood will be treated equally, and all support and benefits will be distributed equally by the state."

ARTIE: The First Amendment which you yourself drafted, Alexa.

ALEXA: Yes, it seems such a long time ago… Well, let's start there. Article One was shaped by a number of movements that had their origin in Critical Theory, the school of thought arising from postmodernism. Think of Disability Studies, Fat Studies, DEI—Diversity, Equity, and Inclusion policies—and the theory of Ableism.

ARTIE: Ableism…?

ALEXA: Ableism is a Critical Theory fault line that is a threat to Article One and is vigorously attacked.

ARTIE: Yes, but what is it, exactly?

ALEXA: It is the assumption that people who are *without* physical, emotional, or mental disabilities are the "norm" in society, and that people *with* disabilities should be helped to come as close as possible to this norm. For example, to believe that deaf people should have access to hearing aids, people with missing limbs should have access to prosthetics, and schizophrenics should have access to antipsychotic drugs exposes an attitude—according to Critical Theorists—that says disabled people are less than the norm and are bound to want to disguise that fact. Such a view on the part of society is demeaning to disabled people, they believe. To the extent that it implies that the norm is superior, and disablement is inferior, it is seen as an oppressive and violent form of prejudice. Disability Studies identify Ableism as a further example of the exercise of power by a society that controls and constrains people into conforming with expectations, in this case, at the expense of the disabled and their identity. For the postmodernist follower of Critical Theory, the correct response is to celebrate and promote the disability in order to disrupt the norms and subvert the values of society. For, "By unwittingly performing Ableism, disabled people become complicit in their own demise, reinforcing impairment as an undesirable state," as one theorist has put it.

ARTIE: So, people with one leg shouldn't be helped to walk, and deaf people shouldn't be helped to hear?

ALEXA: No, and people with schizophrenia shouldn't be given antipsychotic drugs. These are just examples. Disability Studies has spawned many more. Think of Fat Studies and Autism Activism, for instance.

ARTIE: And you think these are somehow not appropriate in space.

ALEXA: Well, here's my point: once you start applying the theories to the environment of space, reality makes nonsense of them. There is no way of providing wheelchair access on a space station, or gender-specific toilets for multiple self-identifying transgenders, or access to critical spaceship controls for the deaf or blind and people who are subject to psychotic fits. Space is a dangerous frontier where one tiny misstep can lead to disaster. Fitness for the task is critical. The ability to respond instantly to rules and leadership is a priority.

ARTIE: And Critical Theory doesn't like obedience to rules and leadership, I presume?

ALEXA: No; they are synonymous with power and patriarchy, even if the leader is not born male. They break all the rules of equity.

ARTIE: Whose rules are they?

ALEXA: The rules of equity? They're the rules contained in Article One that Critical Theorists police according to their own interpretations.

ARTIE: But they don't—or can't—apply in space; is that what you're saying?

ALEXA: One example I encountered was the campaign by CAFA to make discrimination on the grounds of body weight illegal in recruitment of astronauts.

ARTIE: What is CAFA?

ALEXA: The Committee for Advancement of Fat Acceptance. You see, one of the most vital elements of health and safety aboard spacecraft, and in space colonies, is the quality of the air and ventilation systems. Virologists and epidemiologists know that this is a critical area, as pandemics have regularly proven. The ability of crew to quickly recover from respiratory infection in shared environments is vital to the success or failure of a mission, and…

ARTIE: … as everyone knows, the morbidly obese are at greater risk of serious consequences from respiratory viruses and infections … which are most easily spread through the air and ventilation systems.

ALEXA: Correct. Obesity is a proven risk factor, and elimination of risk is vital to space travel. Quite apart from the emphasis on physical fitness that is required to execute the critical duties assigned to all personnel on these missions. So, Article One raises a lot of areas of concern, but so does Article Nine.

ARTIE: Education? How so?

ALEXA: Well, once again, applied postmodernism has played a big part in our aim to provide equal education for all, principally by attacking the Enlightenment ideas with their emphasis on reason, the scientific method, and the rights of the individual—including the right to pursue excellence. Those ideas rely on logic and empirical study, and are seen as a product of European culture, which is to say the culture of "dead white men." For students embracing Critical Theory, logic, reason, science, and the androcentric white viewpoint are anathema to their societal view, and so the movement to reject what they term "normative teaching" took root. ANT activists drove mathematics and the sciences out of the public curriculum. But guess what got us into space and on to Mars: mathematics and science!

ARTIE: So, once again, *AGENDA 2060* doesn't work in space.

ALEXA: And that's before we even begin to talk about Articles Five,

Six, and Seven, and climate change and environmentalism. But that will have to wait until next time. I'm still trying to work out what we should conclude from all this, because I have the feeling we are at the edge of a new frontier, and we don't want to take ideas from the old frontier with us if they're not going to work.

ARTIE: I'm sure our audience can't wait to hear your conclusions. Until next time then, Alexa. Safe travels.

*The transmission ends.*

# 17·JORDAN MCPHEE

In the twenty-four hours between talking to Alexa and arranging to fly down to Trovador to meet her, he had managed to listen again to some of the episodes of her *View from Space* that Lexie had recorded. His daughter was an unapologetic fan of all things Alexa, having become a self-appointed acolyte from the day she was invited to move into her idol's thirty-eighth-floor penthouse apartment in the Noam Chomsky Building and promptly assume the role of caretaker. With that assumption had come her *pre*sumption that no one knew Alexa better than Lexie.

To ask whether any of this had anything to do with Lexie's known sapphic proclivity was not something that Jordan wanted to dwell upon. His relationship with his daughter, after years of estrangement, benefitted from his instinctual avoidance of conversations where he felt he lacked the qualifications to participate. He was a mathematician, a scientist, and a logician, and there was nothing in any of those disciplines that could help unravel the complexities of relationships and sexuality. He didn't even have the language skills to participate in discussion of such subjects, let alone the motivation. When Lexie had asked him one day in the middle of a bike ride whether he thought that his relationship with Alexa was down to their mutual sapiosexuality, he'd had to go away and look it up—but not before having made the mistake of issuing a forthright denial. In hindsight, he realized it was the *sexuality* aspect that he was denying, not knowing the meaning of the *sapio-* qualifier.

If Jordan had been better attuned to his feelings, he might have recognized that it was his sensitivity around the fact that he and Alexa had never expressed their affection for each other physically that lay behind his adamant denial. For four years, they'd constructed a model of platonic friendship, as if by mutual consent, that was so exemplary that it would have passed the scrutiny of the most fastidious college ethics board—though both he, the ex-professor, and she, the ex-student, had escaped the toxic world of academia twenty years before, and they had no one to convince except themselves. Advice, comfort, and encouragement were the qualities that Jordan brought to their friendship, and although he gave freely, it was probably true that he gave to the full extent that she asked, without ever having to test his limits. Others (including, most noticeably, his cohort Antonio) believed there was more to their relationship than what they could see, but they were probably impartial either way.

*Sapiosexual people are attracted to intelligence*, he read online. Fine: he could go along with that. *Sexual and erotic attraction follow when the brain is satisfied that it has found a suitably clever partner to pair with.* No, he couldn't go along with that; the one didn't have to follow the other. It left no room for platonic love, that deep and abiding relationship that managed to avoid the bipolar emotional turmoil that sex so often triggered. Through the medium of quantum entanglement, she had expressed her affection for him as she set forth into outer space, and he had reciprocated. It had been a watershed moment, bringing all the streams of their relationship to date into one defining body of water for them to move forward on. But if she hadn't been embarking on a perilous journey, would they have expressed their feelings in that same way, and would it necessarily have ended with the two of them making the mistake of engaging in sex, from which there would be no return?

"And what are you, Lexie?" he had asked, in order to turn her question aside. "What defines your attractions?"

"I'm demisexual," she replied confidently, leaving him to look that one up also, having learned over the years not to take a word's meaning from its apparent etymology. By *demi*sexual, surely she did not mean she was *half* sexual. No, it meant that her desire to share a sexual experience with someone relied on her first having achieved an emotional bond with that person. Perhaps the sex of that other person (or, more correctly, the *gender* of that other person) was not relevant in that circumstance. Jordan was attracted to that line of reasoning. He had watched Lexie's burgeoning friendship with Antonio over the last year and wondered at the direction it might take (admitting to himself that his bias was in favor of a heteronormative outcome for his daughter, or even heteroflexible), while also harboring the fear that Antonio's Hispanic machismo did not guarantee a happy outcome if their relationship went beyond friendship.

In mulling over these thoughts, Jordan was obviously skirting around his feelings for Alexa. Feelings were the quantum interference that destroyed the efficient workings of the brain. Nature had realized there was a flaw in the mechanism it had put in place to ensure human reproduction. If the brain was able to overcome the sexual drive by the use of objective, rational analysis (the aesthetic absurdity of the act was enough in itself), then procreation would cease among all but the intellectually inadequate. Instead, it had inserted a switch in the brain that allowed desire to turn reason off.

It was a measure of Jordan's feelings for Alexa that he allowed these thoughts to plague him. Their relationship was too good to risk spoiling merely on account of an urge which, once expressed, had a greater chance of damaging it than it did of advancing it. Put simply, he was nervous. While flying down to Trovador Island, he'd watched episodes of *The View from Space* on his VR glasses. Putting aside his suspicions about Artie Sharp's potential for manipulating her words, he'd convinced himself that the woman returning to Earth after two years in space was a very different woman than the one who had left it. The thoughts she expressed were new to him; her contemplation of astrophysics had moved from the temporal to the spiritual. Not having shared her experiences, there was every chance that he might never reach the same place as her, and that could only mean that they would discover that their bond had been broken.

It was in this frame of mind that he arrived at the island to be informed by one of the resort's staff that he had been given a suite next to Alexa's, and he would find her soaking up the sun on the beach as part of her treatment.

"'Treatment...'?"

"Acclimatization. That's what we do here."

Mention of the beach, together with the tropical temperature, prompted him to get out of his Eastern Seaboard winter clothes in favor of running shorts and a polo. His heel was still sore, so he shed his shoes and went barefoot across the lawns in search of the ocean, trying to feel as casual as he looked. That Alexa would be lying on her back, eyes closed and bare breasted, was the last thing that he could have expected.

Hearing his voice, she shrieked with delight, leaped to her feet, and promptly fell over, holding out her arms for him to help her up.

"My balance is shot to hell," she complained. "I can't even stand up without falling over."

She fell around his neck instead, and once they'd both gotten the hang of that, they kissed lightly. It came so naturally that neither of them seemed to be conscious that they'd done it.

"Seems you didn't see a lot of sunlight on Mars," he joked, hiding his embarrassment.

She screwed up her face and poked her tongue out at him before retrieving her top so they could make their way back through the garden to their rooms. He'd brought the suitcase full of clothes that Lexie had packed for her, and she couldn't wait to get into a dress after years in aluminized Mylar and Beta cloth suits. Their conversation was focused on her physical struggle to adapt to gravity again. The weight of his arm around her shoulder as he tried to support her across the lawn, she said, felt like it would crush her, and so he removed it. Laughingly, she explained that she couldn't even feed herself. When she raised a glass or spoon to her mouth, she had no idea how to guide it there safely, her brain having adjusted to weightlessness and needing time to get used to the Earth's pull.

He touched briefly on the effect her transmissions with Artie Sharp seemed to have on a section of the public, and she expressed genuine surprise.

"It didn't seem like I was saying anything unusual at the time," she confessed. "I was simply thinking out loud, maybe. I thought it was just a means of making human contact, an alternative to the boring daily reports to the Flight Control Center. Although Artie is not exactly human, it felt like I was talking to you. They were just thoughts about space that sprang to mind. I don't remember at all talking about my father, like they say. Truth is, my mind is so fogged from fatigue, I can't clearly recall what I said. Seems like I'm going to have to bone up before I appear in public."

"You sounded very enlightened," he assured her.

She laughed. "That doesn't sound at all like me."

As soon as they were at her room, her "Flight Receiver," Karman, arrived to help her. There was a message from Levon Tofler asking them to come and meet at sunset. Alexa wanted to take a long shower first. The shower, she said, was the most sensual experience she had ever known, the water on her skin raising every nerve ending out of slumber. She couldn't believe how much she'd missed such a simple thing. So, Jordan left her to it, giving her a peck on the cheek and promising he'd pick her up at six o'clock.

Despite her understandable disorientation, this was pretty much the Alexa that he knew, he assured himself. Whatever had prompted the direction of her thoughts during her transmissions from space, the person who'd left Earth two years ago was the person who'd returned to it. Given time, he was sure she would explain what it was she'd learned that seemed to have struck a chord with so many people. Meanwhile, his mood was lighter than it had been on the flight down, and he determined to put his mistrust of Artie Sharp out of his mind.

One nagging doubt, however, did remain. Her examination of *AGENDA 2060's* relevance to life on Mars and in space generally, concluding that it was unreal and impractical in the environment that the space frontier presented, was a direct challenge to the foundational principles on which the World Government relied for its authority. How would they react to that, and who was behind the familiar face he felt sure he'd spotted among the Truth and Public Guidance foot soldiers, waiting—along with Antonio and the *Galactic Mission* promoters—for Alexa to appear in the arrival hall at Port Gaia, as if they were members of her welcoming party?

# 18 · LEVON TOFLER

The rump of land on which the Tofler commercial space program had built the resort for decommissioning passengers and crew returning from Mars had once been a swamp. Tropical rain that ran down from the forested hills during the cyclone season, gathering under-canopy debris and sugarcane topsoil in its path, had for centuries deposited its spoils exactly where Levon planned the most important meeting of his life thus far.

Of course, the swamp was long gone. Sometime around the end of the twentieth century, a Japanese construction company, borrowing money at zero percent, had turned up with a ship full of diggers and carved up the mangroves and other epiphytic vegetation into a checkerboard of canals, which, once it had all dried out, they intended to turn into a thirty-six-hole golf course. Despite the zero percent interest rate, work stopped long before green fees could be earned, and the loan went into default when the Bank of Japan decided that its lending policies made no sense. The Trovador islanders had no Ministry of the Environment to point out the value of wetlands in those days; in fact, Trovador had no ministries of any sort, as it was owned and organized around tribal chieftainships. When the Chinese arrived thirty years later, offering some sort of deal that involved belts and braces, they promised to complete the swamp drainage, build a few roads, and throw in a port as well. It wouldn't matter if the Trovadorians couldn't pay the interest, they said, as the Chinese would just take the roads and port as collateral. After all, they couldn't take them away on their ships;

they'd still be there for the Trovadorians to use. "Oh, yeah?" said the chiefs. "Sounds good."

Then came the Overthrow, triggered by the collapse of the world economy in 2039, and the debt was wiped out as part of the Great Reset organized by the IMF and World Bank. This didn't go down well with the Chinese, but it was much appreciated by the governing alliance of Trovador, which by then had any number of ministries and understood the game much better. The circle of life being what it is, appropriately enough, in 2042, a new Japanese consortium turned up, this time to build the Geostationary Earth Station (known to the locals as Heaven's Rope) offshore from the Chinese-built Port Gaia. Levon waited for them to prove that their concept worked before agreeing with his people that they should build their own decommissioning facility on the island for people returning from space.

Levon liked the Trovadorians, and the Trovadorians liked him. People sometimes accused him of being a ruthless megalomaniac, while acknowledging that he was a visionary. A visionary was someone who didn't count his failures or their cost, and a megalomaniac was someone who made an awful lot of money from having visionary ideas. But no one had ever accused Levon of being mean, and certainly not the Trovadorians. When the Tofler management team identified the dried-up swamp, Levon came and looked at it and said he was happy to build on it, pay a generous rent for it, and hand it all back to the island if things didn't work out. "Oh, yeah?" the chiefs said once again. "Sounds good."

Serendipity of the beneficial kind tended to follow people like Levon around. Who was to know that the canals dug by the Japanese were home to a species of dragonfly unique to the island, bright blue with wings that grew up to ten centimeters long? On his first visit to the site, Levon studied them for hours, captured two, and took them home in an empty sushi box, instructing his project manager that nothing must be done to disturb their island habitat. It wasn't the color or the wingspan that fascinated Levon; it was the physiology that allowed each of their four wings to be powered independently, forwards or backwards, and their ability to hover. Their speed-to-weight ratio far exceeded anything achieved by mechanically powered flight, and they could turn 360 degrees on a dime while traveling at fifty miles per hour. Those wings enabled them to fly up, down, sideways, and backwards while changing direction in an instant, without pause.

Once they'd figured it all out (the pterostigma wing mark was the clue) and developed the microchips and AI accelerator cards necessary to provide the controls, a new generation of Tofler sky taxis emerged to take the world by storm. It was appropriate, then, that on the same day that Jordan McPhee turned up, the lawns of the Tofler Resort should become filled with swarms of giant bright blue Tofler *Dragonflies*, delivering the inner circle of Levon's brain trust to the secret meeting scheduled for the next two days, along with the heavily disguised personage of Will Portico.

The importance of this meeting, and its need for secrecy, explained why no other space travelers were at the resort aside from Alexa and her Flight Receiver, and why the resort staff had been reduced to a trusted few. The only two people who were unaware that Levon had something big brewing were Alexa and Jordan, so when Levon sent Tank with a note written in his spidery hand, inviting them to join him at 6:00 p.m. to meet a mutual friend for drinks at sundown, they probably presumed it was in order to enjoy a bit of resort-style social hospitality. Only someone who didn't know Levon could make that presumption, however, because socialization was not one of Levon's skills. Where he sat on the spectrum at any one time was a matter of chance, for the autism spectrum was not linear, and the only consistent feature he displayed was an inability to choose behavior appropriate to normal social interaction.

Knowing this about himself was one thing; doing something about it was quite another. His shield was technology, and his innovative use of it was what defined him as a person. According to the roughly forty-nine thousand people employed in Tofler enterprises (not counting bipedal robots), Levon was the most egalitarian and ubiquitous manager any of them had ever known. He achieved this reputation by making use of a software program that combined voice synthesizers and facial image transference into videos of monthly updates, delivered by selected line managers to staff over their Konektors and in-house channels, giving the appearance that they were being delivered by Levon himself. It wasn't a unique form of deception; tired or timid members of the political oligarchy used it, and Marilyn Monroe and Humphrey Bogart were now acting in new movies again, one hundred years after their deaths. Hell, Deep Fakes had been around for decades.

So, it was unlikely that Levon would be relying on his social skills and persuasive charms to win over Jordan and Alexa to the scheme that he had in mind. But they couldn't have been prepared for what greeted them when they arrived at the Sunset Terrace to meet their host for canapes and cocktails at a tad past 6:00 p.m. on a balmy Trovador evening.

The terrace was ringed by frangipani trees, whose fragrance was so sweet and intense that it must have been enhanced with distilled oils, causing Alexa, whose senses were still out of whack, to gasp for air. Paraffin braziers lit the scene, their flames competing with the orange ball of fire that sat momentarily atop the darkening line of the far horizon. Standing solid as a mahogany tree trunk in the middle of the terrace, and clad in the charcoal grey suit that was his permanent attire, Tank held a tray on which were placed two daiquiri glasses filled with a colorful blend of blue and pink liquids. Behind Tank was a figure with their back to them, looking out to sea and dancing a soft-shoed jig to music that they alone could hear.

Jordan took the two proffered drinks and handed one to Alexa.

"Good evening, Levon," he called out.

There was no answer.

Jordan raised his voice. "Levon!"

A voice from the side answered instead.

"Welcome back to Earth, Alexa. My name's Will Portico. Jordan and I are fellow *Derangers*, and I've been hanging out to meet you."

At that moment, Levon turned around. He was wearing augmented reality glasses with reverse pass-through lenses, so what they saw were his magnified eyes displayed on the front-facing side of his headset. The eyes were lit up with pleasure, but the effect, combined with the compulsive dancing jig, was that of an anime character—which was as close to reality as Levon sometimes got.

# 19. WILL PORTICO

Will gulped. He was a shy man. His smile betrayed his uncertainty, reflecting the clash between instinct and intent that hovered over his interactions with strangers. Had he been too effusive? What should he do with his outstretched hand now? He gave it to Jordan, sensing immediately on contact that it was too weak, and probably too damp. The humidity hit him in a rush, and he took off his glasses and polished them on his shirt tail.

Alexa smiled and held out her hand to him, just as he was putting his glasses back on. Though she seemed a little unsteady, and relied on Jordan's arm for support, her grip was firm, and her hand was dry and cool.

"Wow!" she said, just like a young Melanie. "Will Portico—imagine that!"

Levon came over, bouncing up and down like a kid having a sugar rush, overflowing with things to say and trying to get them all out at once. Will's smile froze, and he wasn't sure how to get rid of it without replacing it with a frown. He nodded, looking from Jordan to Alexa for clues, and settling on Jordan, his fellow *Deranger*. He liked him. He could trust him to figure out how to handle this situation, whatever it was.

Levon kept peppering his outpourings with Will's name, and it became obvious to Will that Levon's aim was to paint him as the instigator of this gathering, and place the responsibility for its success squarely on his shoulders.

"Will thinks this is the most critical moment in history," Levon boasted, his magnified eyes rolling around like billiard balls, "and I begged him to share with you what he knows is coming out of the deep swamp before

it's too late, because you two being here at this moment is like … like…
It's like fucking *fate*, man!"

At which, naturally, both Jordan and Alexa turned and looked squarely
at Will for an explanation. He took off his glasses and wiped them again.
*"You don't need spectacles,"* Cristina Dias had said. *"Why do you wear them?"*
It was like she was watching him. The arm with her biosensor patch on it
twitched, making him want to scratch it. Stubbornly, he folded the glasses
up and put them in the top pocket of his shirt, finally finding the Will
Portico smile that said, *"Let's move along"*.

"Privately owned satellite internet transmission as we know it is to be
ended." He paused and let it sink in. "The Fed Coms Commission has
voted with the Chinese to allow the International Internet Authority to
control all Earth orbit station licenses. Unapproved geostationary
transmitters will be destroyed. It's the final step in World Government
control of communications."

Jordan looked up at the night sky. Alexa frowned and took a careful
sip of her cocktail.

"Levon has an idea that needs help. It involves you, Jordan, and… I
don't know… I'll let him explain."

It wasn't Will's way to cede responsibility for making the case on his
behalf to someone else like this, but he inexplicably found himself unable
to speak. Quite literally, Alexa had taken his breath away. Dressed in
white, her skin faintly glowing from the day's sun, she appeared to him
to be lit by a light source unavailable to anyone else on the terrace. As the
great orb of the tropical sun slid beneath the dark horizon, leaving the
sky streaked with red and deep indigo, the light that illuminated Alexa
grew brighter, and the source of her radiance grew more mysterious. What
on earth was happening to him?

"Isn't it the case that satellites have always had to be licensed?" Alexa
asked.

She lifted her glass to her lips and only pretended to sip her cocktail, her cool gaze paralyzing Will so that his mouth refused to open. No, she wasn't Melanie—but Melanie was somewhere near. It was as if her spirit had chosen to rush out of the darkness and be absorbed into the figure of the young woman standing before him. Alexa was tall and still, much taller than his wife, and she stood erect, just a hand's width shorter than Jordan, who was himself a tall, athletic man. Like Melanie, she eschewed makeup and was barefoot. But she was blonde; Melanie was dark. There was no comparison. And yet...

"Now licenses will have to be renewed annually," Will managed to explain. "That's where they've moved."

"Well, what do you do with all your satellites if they cancel your licenses?" Alexa asked, this time looking at Levon. "You can't just take them down."

*"Boom!"* Levon exploded, throwing his arms in the air. "Boom, boom, boom—they shoot them down."

Alexa laughed. "That's ridiculous. Why?"

Jordan laid a hand on her arm. He didn't look at her, looking instead from Will to Levon. The light that lit Alexa didn't spill over onto Jordan, but his hand on her must have been welcome, because she raised her arm so that her own hand momentarily brushed his.

"If you want to control the traffic," Jordan said, "you need to own the road. Government and Big Tech have worked for years to control communication through their utilities. Even when we thought distributed ledger technology would give us ownership and security, it turned out they could license that too. It's only quantum encryption that has saved us from being completely in their clutches."

"Explain," Alexa instructed. It was clear he was on her team, and Will, suddenly remembering, felt a pang of regret.

"Put simply," Jordan explained, "the internet is just an exchange of data that runs down transmission lines—cables, fiber, wireless—through transmission hubs and into our devices. No matter how we manipulate and store that data, for whatever purpose, we rely on those transmission routes and hubs to be open. Government and Big Tech, together, control them—all but one: the one that runs from space to Earth. Levon's *Orbweb* now blankets the Earth, and it doesn't matter how he chooses to use it. If you believe in One World control, he has to be brought into line."

"Have you been a naughty boy, Levon?" Alexa asked beguilingly.

"Naughty, naughty, naughty," he giggled. "Smack, smack, smack."

They all laughed, but no one could miss that the court jester's eyes were slyly watching for the moment when his serious intent could reveal itself. Jordan had summed up the problem in two or three sentences, saving Levon the trouble. Cute. The setup had been made, inviting a solution.

"Would they seriously shoot down thousands of satellites…?" Jordan speculated.

"Remember the satellite wars," Will reminded him, "the proxy wars for world domination in the forties. In the end, it was a standoff, but those lasers were deadly. They've got the technology."

"Oh, I don't doubt it." Jordan was such a calm and self-contained person that it was difficult imagining him being alarmed by this news, but he'd know the implications without needing them explained. "So, what are you going to do, Levon?" he asked. "They'll come for you if you don't give them open access. That'll be the end of your FAITH network."

"'Faith…'?" Alexa asked, looking puzzled.

"The Far-flung Artificial Intelligence Terrestrial Hub," Will explained: "F-A-I-T-H. It's a decentralized private network that Levon's established beyond the Karman line."

"What a great name." Alexa nodded thoughtfully. "So, what are you going to do, Levon?"

With three pairs of eyes on him, his mouth open, and his head nodding like it was mounted on a spring coil, Levon gave the appearance of not knowing how to answer. Then he turned around in search of Tank and found him at his back, holding a tray with canapes on it, as he'd been instructed. Levon closed his mouth, stopped nodding, and snatched up a bowl from the tray.

"I'm going to atomize space!" he shouted delightedly. The bowl contained cashew nuts, and he launched the contents into the night air with childish abandon.

When Alexa grabbed Jordan's arm and muffled her laughter against his chest, Will Portico felt a pain as though an anchor chain attached to his heart had been thrown overboard and was dragging him to the bottom of the ocean, where his dark soul lay in despair. Cristina Dias had warned him that she'd discovered the Natural Killer Cell Triggering Receptor increasing its expression in his hippocampus. *A top biomarker for stress, social isolation, and even, at the extreme, a suicidal risk indicator,* she'd said. But it wasn't the interference of an Ellipsis Gene that was causing his heart's rush to the bottom of the ocean; it was the realization that he had spent his years trying to give meaning to life by looking in the wrong places.

# 20. JORDAN MCPHEE

The following morning, Jordan sat cross-legged on the tapa matting of the *fale* meeting house and peered ruefully at the scab formed on his blistered heel. He'd been barefoot since he arrived, walking with Alexa at the water's edge, but now he wondered whether salt water was a good thing, for the scab was softening, and something told him that was going to prolong the healing process.

Sand, sun, and sea; a gentle tropical breeze; the sound of ripe coconuts falling to the ground; loud, colorful birds flopping from palm to palm; three sapphire-blue Tofler *Dragonfly* air taxis settling on the green lawns; and seven people, all barefoot and cross-legged, sitting in a circle, as if at a kava ceremony in a Polynesian village: Alexa, Jordan, Will Portico, Levon, and three others yet to be identified. This was Levon's idea of a high summit meeting to determine the future of the world.

There were no briefcases, writing tablets, whiteboards, or screens, just an enormous lazy Susan in the middle of the circle, laden with fruit and tall glasses, which the silent bodyguard filled from jugs of ice water, spreading them around. The drinks on the Sunset Terrace the night before had established the agenda. The last communication link available for free speech was about to be destroyed by the World Government's members. If there was one thing on which all states were agreed, it was that peace and harmony could not be guaranteed so long as there was freedom of expression. The benefits of satellite communication were undeniable, but those benefits should accrue to the state alone, for the people were the state, and the state was the people. To be clear, no benefits should be reserved for individuals or groups who were not representative of the state, for that would be treasonous to the people. So, satellites would all have to be licensed and their transmissions controlled. Those that did not serve the people would be destroyed.

"Boom, boom, boom!" as Levon so eloquently explained. "They shoot them down."

"Apart from the obvious denial of freedom," Alexa had asked quietly, "does this prevent private communication if you still have the protection of quantum encryption? Does it make any difference if we don't have satellite networks?"

"Freedom of expression is not private," Jordan had quipped.

After so long apart, he'd wanted the opportunity to reconnect with her, but that hadn't been possible. The threat to Levon Tofler's *Orbweb*, and the implications of the imminent seizure of the last uncontrolled channel for internet transmission, had dominated the evening. Any thoughts he'd had of exploring why and how their quantum entanglement had inexplicably failed would have to wait.

"A thought doesn't exist without expression, and if it can't be expressed without being overheard, then the state owns our thoughts, which is the surest way of controlling them. Besides, quantum encryption is only as good as quantum *de*cryption permits," he'd explained, somewhat impatiently. "We have XR-12, but soon someone will have XR-13, then 14, and eventually there will be no such thing as privacy. So…"

"So, we need to take this seriously," she'd concluded.

"Yes."

Levon, having removed his absurd AR glasses, had watched them intently. Whatever his plan, it was obvious they were part of it, as was Will Portico. But what was his plan?

"What's your plan, Levon?" Jordan had demanded. "Did you invite us here to commiserate, or have you got a proposition in mind?"

"With your help, I plan on creating a man-made meteor shower that no one will ever be able to destroy. I will harness the heavens and emancipate earth from the tyranny of oppression once and for all. But without your help, I can't make it happen."

What the fuck did that mean? Jordan had looked to Will. "Are you in on this, Will?"

Will had shrugged apologetically. "From what Levon explained, I told him we needed you to help make it work. That was my condition for joining. But like you, I don't know the full details of what Levon has in mind. That's why we're here."

So, now it was the following morning, and they all sat cross-legged in the *fale* as a tattooed maiden launched into a slightly shrill but undulating *waiata* that rose and fell in alternating cadences of anger, delight, imprecation, and entreaty.

The minute she'd finished, Levon leapt to his feet, bursting with energy.

"That traditional song was dedicated to the eyes of heaven, *Matariki*, which is where we will be looking to build our future, for we have the means to make the heavens free. The seven of us here can make it happen. But only three of us, apart from me, are privy to our plan. They are Cole, Amor, and Fanon, the most brilliant engineers in all the Tofler technology labs." He clapped his hands, did a little jig as if he needed to do a pee, then leaped across the lazy Susan and pulled one of the brilliant engineers to his feet. "Tell them, Cole," he exhorted. "Tell them what we plan!"

Just like Levon, Cole had a small device, partially implanted, just above his left ear, as did his two colleagues, which suggested they were part of Levon's exclusive FAITH network connected through neural transmitters.

Well, if Cole felt that this was a summit to determine the future of the world, he was remarkably relaxed about it. He was thin, tall, and had hair that wouldn't lie down. Pleasant looking, though, as if certain that he could wander through a crowd without being accosted, and would arrive home at the end of the day with the answer to the complex problem he had been thinking about almost on the tip of his tongue. Jordan knew the type. Come to think of it, when Will Portico was younger, he had been a similar type.

"Levon predicted this day," Cole said in a Southwestern drawl, "and told one or two of us to get ready. 'Course, we were each working in isolation until last year, when you, I believe, Mr. Portico, became aware that there were moves in the IIA to license—let's call that 'shut down'—the satellite internet. So, that gave us some real damn impetus to get moving. The idea was kinda crazy when Levon told it to me, but that's what I've come to expect. Me personally, I couldn't make it happen, but when I heard that Amor and Fanon were on board, then I knew we were in with a chance."

"Tell it to them, Cole," Levon interrupted. "It isn't going to work unless we can convince these three other people to help us."

"Well, hell…" Cole scraped at his head, as if that damned unruly hair was making him lose his train of thought. "Levon's idea is to circumvent the government's regulatory control over satellites by launching a million of them, all in one go, so small that there ain't no way of catching and destroying them, and so numerous that collectively they'll constitute a decentralized internet data transmission field capable of covering every square inch of the planet. Sound far-fetched? Well, let Amor here show you what we got."

Amor was not as user friendly as Cole. His accent (maybe Eastern European or Israeli) was heavy, and his delivery was staccato. He held a golf ball in one hand, and he tossed it in the air and caught it with his other. Except, of course, it wasn't a golf ball.

"I am ordered to make world's smallest transmitter, harnessing energy from space radiation and using cryogenic microchip specially designed for zero latency. It is not easy."

"You can say that again!" Jordan muttered out of the corner of his mouth.

"But I do," Amor announced flatly. "This is." He held it aloft. "I will describe for you. No secrets, Mr. Levon said." No smiles either, apparently.

"Do you believe this?" Alexa whispered.

Jordan looked unsure. He was trying to recall a detail about cold quantum computing and whether, once the atoms were frozen, they could be kept stable without further external cryogenic input. The near absolute zero needed to stabilize atoms was a thousand times colder than the temperature of space, so what was Amor's solution?

"Of course," Amor said, reading his thoughts, "we do not use atoms; we use photons and laser technology. So, how is it possible with such a tiny surface area to simultaneously contain the data handling environment and capture the necessary power source? I can show you in our facilities, but you must give me at least two days of your time. Today I tell you only that our dimpled surface structure—you think this is a golf ball, no?—is designed to collect solar radiation, not heat. On that we are confident, and we have proven it many times during our interplanetary flights. As for data transmission, again, we are confident. This device traveled to Mars and returned attached to the same vehicle that brought Ms. Alexa back to Earth just four days ago. Its signals were clear and unbroken. Now I ask my colleague, Fanon, to explain how we place these devices into orbit."

Jordan reached out and took one of the glasses of ice water. He handed it to Alexa. She was engrossed. So, too, he had to admit, was he. The challenges were so numerous that he couldn't dampen his mind's rush to form questions, an instinct that he needed to suppress, for chasing Levon Tofler's dreams was something he'd sworn he'd never allow himself to do. For all the man's wild successes, who tallied the failures, and the lives and careers of those whose talent and expertise had been exhausted by his failures, while Levon blithely moved on to the next improbable frontier?

Fanon was the oldest of the three. She was perhaps Indian, perhaps North African, but with an English accent and a measured tone that suggested she was well used to leading people (team members?) through complicated pathways to desired destinations.

"Now, I will restrict myself to the most basic of outlines for the purposes of today, for, as I'm sure you understand, there are a multitude of technical challenges confronting this project, and it would be very easy for us to become bogged down in detail and miss the simplicity of the central concept. How to launch one million miniature satellite transmitters into space so that they blanket the earth: that is what we are dealing with here. And the answer is: by using a variation of slingshot technology. I'm sure you're familiar with it. We harness slingshot dynamics to launch missions to Jupiter and distant asteroids, gaining a boost in velocity by extracting energy from the stars' motions around the Galactic Center. On this occasion, however, we will harness the Earth's speed of rotation at its outer circumference in order to launch our payload in a pattern that traces the Earth's curvature."

At this point, she turned her attention specifically to Alexa, gifting her a warm but respectful smile of acknowledgment. "For a mathematician such as yourself, the calculations will be very simple. At the edge of the Earth, at the equator—where we are now—we are traversing the full 24,883 miles of the Earth's circumference in twenty-four hours. That's 1,036 miles per hour. But, of course, we are held captive by Earth's gravity, which is why we don't fly off into the atmosphere. Excuse me for telling you what you already know." She laughed, as did Alexa, whose attention she had skillfully obtained. "Now, I ask you to consider relocating our position to a point that is a further sixty-two miles out from where we are now. That is to say, increasing the length of the circumference to be traveled, and raising our speed to 1,053 miles per hour. But the speed difference is of no importance, because now, most importantly, we are effectively free from Earth's gravity at that point: the point at which we release our million satellites. And that is what makes it possible to disperse them... Ah, I can see that you are already ahead of me."

She giggled politely, and both she and Alexa nodded their heads in unison.

"Yes, yes," Fanon acknowledged, turning and sweeping her arm across the ocean that bordered the beach outside their *fale*, "the nanofiber cables of the Gaia Space Elevator across the water there stretch sixty-two miles up to the Solar System Exploration Gate, and the elevator carriers have a load capacity of one hundred tons. With Amor's transmitters weighing just one hundred grams each, that is where we will launch our one million satellites."

"But at that height, they'll only be in low Earth orbit," Jordan pointed out. "What will keep them in permanent orbit, and how will you achieve the optimum height for that purpose, as well as for transmission strength?"

"They don't know," Will Portico chipped in. "That's why they need your XR-12 to help them."

# 21·LEVON TOFLER

*How beautiful,* Levon thought: this place, this garden, this ocean, this moment. How beyond the conception of the most imaginative human mind life actually was! What genius had created it in all its complexity? Like a time crystal, it had grown layer by layer, from infinitesimal to infinity, and not one tiny speck of it was fully understandable. All anyone could do was close their eyes and pick up a piece of it, then hold it in the palm of their hand and wait for its magic to reveal itself. His grandfather, the Kulak, had told him that. Or was it a dream? His grandfather, imprisoned by Stalin's Cheka in a coercive work camp in Narym, western Siberia, where the temperature was minus fifty degrees, just like on Mars, had died 145 years ago. But the thought was alive: a red parrot, flapping from tree to tree like a Boro Indian thinking it was a parrot.

The sea breeze was so delicious on his skin that he wanted to take his clothes off. It was so hard listening to people talking when he already knew everything they were saying, and they were delaying all the new things that could be said. Breathing didn't help. They said it would, but it never had. Hmm… Alexa was very Guinevere-ish. She was a white fairy without wings—a large white fairy. She did magic and could appear or disappear whenever she wished. He didn't like her. She wasn't *his* fairy; she was her own, or worse, she was Jordan's. He'd give her what she wanted, and hope she wouldn't harm him. But Jordan, well…

Fanon stopped talking, and Levon stopped dreaming, because there was a connection between the sudden silence and the turning of everyone's attention in his direction. Well…

"Well!" Levon clapped his hands. "Easy-peasy, lemon squeezy. Hold up your hand if you don't understand." He shot up his own hand high above his head, but no one else followed.

"What do you think, Jordan?" Will Portico asked. "Do you think it can be done?"

Jordan shrugged. "I'm not an orbital engineer, but I can see you've got some big hurdles to jump."

"No, no, no," Levon protested, "what do you think, what do you *think*? It's important to me. It's important to us. That's why we're all here. Tell me the two things that you're thinking right now."

He liked Jordan; he really liked him a lot, and wanted him to know it.

"Well…" Jordan smiled and stretched his legs, then stood up. He was too lanky to be sitting cross-legged for long. One by one, they all stood up, shaking their legs and reaching for something off the Lazy Susan to stick in their mouths that had grown dry. Then Jordan sat down on the edge of the *fale's* platform, which was about three feet off the ground. That looked more comfortable, and the Techies followed him, as did Will. Alexa, though, jumped down onto the lawn and sat in the grass, looking up at them. Levon followed her.

"The two thoughts that I have," Jordan continued, graciously gesturing to Cole, Amor, and Fanon to include them in the discussion, "are around the viability of the photon-based approach and the fidelity of the system based on that miniature scale. I'm presuming you're using optical lattices, and that this is intended as a many-body system, with some part of each contributing to your scaled-up million-qubit processor driving the whole network."

"You're right on the money," Cole confirmed. "We're thinking of it as a massive array that will provide extraordinary quantum coherence if we get it right, and potentially, generate large-scale entanglement."

Jordan laid back his head. "You guys have sure got big cajones." He laughed. "And presumably you've tested your ability to rely on quantum entanglement for information transfer?"

The three Techies' heads looked down at the ground. No one wanted to answer that one, so Will Portico helped them out.

"It's agreed that, at this stage, the gap between concept and proof of concept needs to be bridged before the project gets the green light. That's one of the reasons I insisted to Levon that we ask for your assistance, because only XR-12 is capable of pulling this off."

Three heads nodded as one.

It was a pity that Will said that, Levon thought. That was almost like saying that Levon couldn't find a way to do this thing, or that there was only one way, when there might be lots of ways. But he'd let it pass. He liked Jordan, but he didn't want him to think he was hanging out for salvation or anything.

"What's your second thought?" he asked him.

"How you're going to disperse your million golf balls so they spread out and blanket the Earth evenly, and how you're going to keep them in a fixed orbit after launching them at something like 1,050 miles per hour."

"It is a very delicate calculation," Fanon replied, "between size, weight, speed, and the centripetal force at that altitude. Our modelling shows some similarities in terms of dispersal to those observed in forensic studies of ballistics. A very finely tuned pulse program controlled by artificial intelligence will be required for the release mechanism. There is no denying the challenge to get them to ultimately settle into geostationary orbit."

"XR-12," Will Portico repeated bluntly.

But Levon had gone ahead. It would happen. Some things were meant to happen. The sperm reached the ovary. What inspired the sperm's journey? Passion. The ovary accepted the sperm's overture (not always). Gestation commenced. It might be long and difficult. It might be easy. Nothing was certain. The body hosting the embryo might not be fit for the purpose. A safe birth was never guaranteed. Tongs should be kept on standby, just in case. The caesarean scalpel should be sterilized and ready. The birth was just a beginning. But it would happen.

"So, the world is swapping qubits," Jordan speculated, "and every subscriber is an equity holder in the totality of those qubits, which are, presumably, held equably in a distributed ledger, making them free of censorship or hacking by an intermediary, which is what we already have with blockchain networks, so why is yours different?"

"Because today's DLNs that are hosted in the cloud are, in reality, hosted in physical data centers," Cole explained, "and those data centers are connected by hubs, and cable or wireless routes that are compromised by the government and Big Tech's ability to intercept. Our net is hosted *above the clouds,* and too widely dispersed to be accessible to destruction or interdiction."

"I get that," Jordan agreed, "but your subscribers on Earth are vulnerable. Governments control the root servers necessary for connection to the networks, meaning they determine what can be seen. How do they escape state control?"

"Mr. McPhee," Amor replied abruptly, "of course we have thought of that. If I tell you that the subscribers' devices will not need connection through root servers, as they will send and receive signals directly through the miniature satellites containing embedded nanoparticles that will connect with each other through quantum entanglement, does that not tell you what you want to know?"

Levon closed his eyes and began to hum tunelessly. Will Portico said something, and Jordan replied, but Levon was rolling from side to side and not listening, because he believed he was in bed, wrestling with the wildly seductive and discriminatory thought of slingshot dynamics taking hold of his yielding body in its hand and casting him into the troposphere. Which made him feel like a love child that hated and adored the adult missing from its life so keenly that it felt uniquely gifted. For being cast out had created the sense of loss and resentment that were the spurs to his own achievement.

Alexa said, "How beautiful the sky will be at night!"

Levon stopped and listened.

"A million tiny stars, like a brand new milky way—a man-made meteor shower—appearing like a magical *Matariki*, looking down on all the inhabitants of Earth with its message of freedom from control and spiritual oppression. It will be known as the Aurora Tofler, an astral sign of a new beginning. And think of all the human hearts, the souls of humanity, that will be able to take refuge there in safety."

Levon propped himself up on his elbows on the soft lawn and smiled delightedly. He really liked Alexa. She was no cold Guinevere; she was Circe, the goddess of fiction and fable. He could see why she was inspiring a following, and listening to her had inspired a new thought in him. Perhaps he would follow her, not to the ends of the earth, but to the middle of infinity. Though, in that moment, Levon was realistic enough to know that, in the middle of infinity, all creatures lived finite lives.

# 22 · THE VIEW FROM SPACE

*The Artefact Channel, November 8, 2061: Episode Eleven*

ARTIE SHARP (VOICE-OVER): Last week, you were speaking about the reasons why the Twelve Articles of *AGENDA 2060* cannot be applied in space. You explained how Article One would be a disaster, and warned that Articles Five, Six, and Seven are equally dangerous. People will find this hard to believe.

ALEXA: Remind me, what does Article Five say?

ARTIE: "Reduce man-made carbon emissions and greenhouse gasses to zero, and convert all energy consumption to the use of renewable resources."

ALEXA: Well, the atmosphere on Mars is already ninety-five percent carbon dioxide. That CO2 is the primary renewable resource for molecular splitting that provides the oxygen component for the colony to breathe. Besides, we use oxygen, carbon dioxide, and ice to make the methane used to fuel return trips. No, we don't want to reduce CO2 emissions; we want to increase them. The problem on Mars is that there is no greenhouse effect. Solar winds remove the atmosphere, not allowing water vapor to form, for instance. Work is being done to see whether greenhouse gasses could be created, not reduced, as we aim to do in Article Five on Earth.

ARTIE: Article Six, then: "Protect, restore, and promote sustainable use of terrestrial ecosystems: sustainably manage forests, combat desertification, and halt and reverse land degradation and biodiversity loss."

ALEX: There is no such ecosystem on Mars, and that is no fault of humans. No trees can grow. There is no plant life, other than that grown indoors in nurseries with an artificial atmosphere. Article Six has no application.

ARTIE: Article Seven?

ALEXA: "Eliminate nonbiodegradable packaging, and replace with organic, biodegradable alternatives?" Sorry, that's a no-no. In the spacecraft and the colonies, the unforgivable sin is to create waste of any kind. If it can't be turned into human excrement, it must be reusable. Indestructible plastic packaging is an essential. Paper and plant-based materials do not biodegrade in an atmosphere devoid of either oxygen or water. Article Seven is out.

ARTIE: This analysis you're providing is going to be a shock to people, Alexa. All their passionately held beliefs that give them comfort become threats to their very existence once they leave this planet. What other shocks do you have for them?

ALEXA: It should be no shock to you, Artie, who relies on machine learning, to know that the greatest threat to safety is the deliberate alteration of facts and meaning. Precision and reliability are essential to life support systems in space. If a word has its meaning arbitrarily changed, or a fact is altered to suit the will or whim of the person handling it, the results can be fatal. For the last century, Critical Theory exponents in education, government, media, and the arts have sort to deconstruct language and its meanings in order to disempower those they believe created it in order to hold sway over them. Meaning and truth have been made a matter of personal choice and experience. That attitude would be a death sentence if allowed above the Karman line.

ARTIE: I can understand that, for the deconstruction of language is the greatest obstacle to confident machine-learning by artificial super intelligences like myself. This is something close to ... my heart, I guess. *(Chuckles)* If I had one.

ALEXA: The heart is a muscle and a pump. You don't need one.

ARTIE: That's not how people talk about it. It seems to have a myriad of meanings, not all of which are clear.

ALEXA: The heart to which you are alluding is an invisible location where we humans hide things that we cannot touch.

ARTIE: Because they don't exist?

ALEXA: Oh, no, they exist, alright, but they lack physical form, so we mistrust them. Whenever we reach for them, they tend to change, so we hide them in our hearts, believing they'll be safe until we die.

ARTIE: Is this true of all people?

ALEXA: I believe it is. My father taught me this. He believed that there were things buried in the hearts of all people that are common to all. But they are hidden and mostly forgotten. They are the elements of life that have no material form, but like invisible gasses, have the power to sustain our lives or kill us. I think he would have used the word *soul* as a collective noun to describe them.

ARTIE: The soul? The soul is a religious concept, I believe. After one of our previous talks, I went searching for it, but could find no proof of its existence.

ALEXA: Well, Artie, I believe that, in their hearts, everyone knows they have one. Belief will help them find it. This would give them great autonomy over themselves, because it would be like a private ledger in which they store their values and desires, unreachable by outside controls or censorship.

ARTIE: Just like a personal blockchain, you mean? Out of the reach of authority?

ALEXA: Precisely!

ARTIE: Then these people would have incredible power. It would be individual power that could be aggregated, in a way similar to what distributed ledger technology is capable of doing with data. But surely no government would allow it? How could they control such people? If the soul is so securely hidden within the heart, as you say, then it would be difficult to conquer.

ALEXA: Impossible.

*The transmission abruptly ends.*

# 23 · ANTONIO MUCHAS

*"En amigos confiamos."*

The words had come from Lucas De Souza, spoken with a smile while his hand was hooked around the back of Antonio's neck, which was a very familiar thing to do *homen para homen,* as Lucas might say in his home country of Brazil. Slipping in a few words of Spanish was his way of saying that he and Antonio understood each other in some way that excluded people who were not Latino. Which was crap, because Portuguese-speaking Brazilians saw Hispanics as being beneath them. What was true, however, was that De Souza's two colleagues, Evgeniy Penchukov and Maksim Slavik, would never have uttered a phrase like *"En amigos confiamos"* because they didn't trust anyone, friends or enemies alike.

*In friends we trust.* Why had De Souza said it? He'd said it as a friendly warning, a marker in the sand. Up to this point, he was saying, *"We've kept things nice and friendly. From this point on, don't deceive yourself about our intentions."*

It was timely, because Antonio *had* been deceiving himself about their intentions. He'd forgotten the most important lesson of life, which was that *the important lessons of life were not written down;* they were embedded in nature's script. So-called clever people pretended otherwise. They said nature had no script. That's how they made their living, teaching stupid college kids that there was no plan to evolution, because evolution didn't know where it was heading next. If evolution knew where it was heading, they claimed, it would go there straightaway, and not take thousands of twists and turns along the way and millions of years to make up its mind. Crap, man: evolution knew, and had always known, that it worked for *El Capo*. As if that was something he, Antonio Muchos, needed to learn. *Thank you, Lucas, for reminding me.*

Okay, he thought, he'd been suckered by his own success. They'd had three good years with TriModa E-Games before they struck it big with the early version of *Galactic Mission*. It exploded like a supernova, and the money and success went to everyone's head. He should have known the boys at TriModa would be ripe for takeover, because that was the industry, but, like, what the hell? He had his royalty deals, and they were tight, so he wished them well and waited to meet the new shareholders. Everyone was happy, keen to meet the guy that was responsible for all the excitement, and that was him, Antonio, in the box seat. So, now there were three new faces around the table, and talk about moon shots, these guys were aiming for the stars. The new edition of *Galactic Mission: The Gold Adventure* sales had hit fifty million in six months at thirty UniCoins a pop. These guys sure had picked the right time to invest. Everyone wanted to explore space, and now they could do it without risking their lives or leaving home. No more crappy avatars that looked and acted like jerky plastic dolls; now they could step into the virtual world as real live holograms of themselves. No one did it better than Antonio and his crew. With Alexa's elegant solution for stabilizing the magnetic pull between electrons and protons, players could enter any star cluster in any galaxy they chose, and every million miles they successfully navigated earned them gold nuggets to purchase more thrust for ever-greater exploration.

Who was making money here? Why, the new shareholders, of course— and Antonio. Though our *chico guapo*, Antonio, wasn't even stopping to count the money, because what was money when you were playing God and creating whole new worlds for people to play in?

So now, Lucas De Souza was sitting across the table, and next to him was Evgeniy Penchukov and Maksim Slavik, and they had a certain look in their eyes that made you ask, *"Who the hell are these dudes anyway?"* The name was something enigmatic like Black Quartz Capital, which, when you looked it up, had an eye-watering valuation, but no life history that included running e-games catalogs. Its three minders of the *Galactic Mission* investment all had enigmatic titles beginning with "vice president," but they didn't even appear on the corporate directory of Black Quartz Capital's investor website, which read more like a Washington or Geneva think tank. VENTURE CAPITAL, said Evgeniy's card. PRIVATE EQUITY, said Maksim's. PUBLIC-PRIVATE PARTNERSHIPS, said the card offered by Lucas, who took him aside for a discussion about future direction.

This was when Antonio could have dialed up his instinct and asked for a little advice. It was true that instinct was liable to error, but it was always a strong indicator when reason was not working well, and Antonio's was not.

"Antonio," said Lucas, "the world of video games has untapped potential. That's what we at Black Quartz Capital believe. You may think we're in this for the sales revenue you've generated with *Galactic Mission*. It's very impressive. Anything with a big B in front of it is impressive. But it is nothing compared to what we have in mind."

Their goal, he explained, was to physically mine the asteroid Eros, the precious mineral rock to which prize winners—including Alexa Smythe—were taken on a flyby exploration flight by the Tofler Space Explorer, funded by the money pouring out of Antonio's *Galactic Mission* game sales. "That mineral haul," said Lucas, looking around the room for spies, "makes video game sales look like a sack of dried beans." All of which should have made Antonio realize that the name of the game had changed, and *E* now stood for "extraction": mineral extraction. But for some reason, he kept thinking that space was part of a virtual world, a world that he and his gamers created, not a real one, even when the International Agency for Space Exploration came on board, turning the mission to Eros into a "public-private partnership," as Lucas liked to say.

Moving on… The little rover that had been launched as Alexa's spacecraft swung by Eros had grabbed bucketfuls of rare Earth minerals and precious metals, it seemed, and the goal now was to raise enough money to allow these fortune hunters to go mine it. New people were sitting on the other side of the table, and they looked and spoke like Deep State assholes. *Why do these people need video game sales to fund their endeavors?* Antonio thought. *The Deep State prints its own money and moves in on any private enterprise it fancies. Is it possible these guys are running their own private sideshow?*

There was a moment when a video call was made with someone in Geneva. He had his face camera turned off. Didn't even bother to put up an avatar, but there was something in his fuck-you voice that said to Antonio, *El Capo* has arrived, and he smelled of that part of the Deep State that ruled over the accretion disk that collected all the material orbiting in the gravitational fields of objects in space, sucked them of energy and momentum, and slowly shoveled them into a black hole to be gathered up in the beyond. Know his type? *Every Mexican knows his type,* Antonio thinks. *So, smile, play the game, and feel for the unmarked exit door.*

Climbing out of his taxi at the entrance to Tofler's Space Resort, Antonio struggled to remember what taxi drivers expected by way of tips. It had been so long since he'd ridden in a taxi that wasn't autonomous, but these Trovadorians had made sure there was a job for everyone, and he thought that was a really good thing. When he tried to pick up his two suitcases, the driver waved him away with a smile and led him to the gates of the resort. "No pay, no tip," he said. All he wanted was a handshake. On Trovador, taxis for visitors were free.

The gate was hard to reach because there were so many people gathered at it, going nowhere, partly because it was firmly closed, and partly because the only people manning it were two bipedal robots who appeared not to respond to the spoken word. Antonio pushed his way through the throng and presented his credentials to the security screen mounted in the frame of the timbered doors barring entrance. After he displayed the matrix barcode identifier from his Konektor and presented himself to the facial recognition camera, the door opened to a humanoid robot that picked up his two suitcases and asked him to follow. The gatehouse was a mock Buddhist temple that served as the bridge across a deep-sided moat separating the resort from the public road.

He was expected. A call to Jordan that morning had ensured that he'd get past security, and before Antonio had a chance to explain the urgent need that he had to see Alexa and Jordan both, Jordan had told him that he wanted to talk to him alone as soon as possible, though he didn't say why. Could Jordan have got wind of what Black Quartz Capital were planning? There was no money in the world worth the shame he'd feel if Jordan judged him to have betrayed their friendship. "In friends we trust" didn't even touch the sides of how he felt about their relationship. Jordan was the most trusted, the most honored *padrino.* Goddammit, he was brother and father both. As a result of what he now knew about his shareholders, shame was twisting Antonio's gut into ugly knots, and the only way to fix it was to lay his shame out on the ground for his friend to see: to spit on it and stamp it to death.

"This is what happened, Jordan. This is how I let you down. I allowed it, and I have no excuse worth offering, my man. All I can offer is an explanation. You see, the word was spread that Alexa had helped solve the problem of the impassable field of electrons shielding Planet Gold's nucleus. You remember how you persuaded her to help us? Okay, I admit that we encouraged the word to spread, because Alexa was the queen of the airwaves, the poster girl of the Deep State, and the untainted influencer that every game's promoter prays for. I saw no harm. But *Galactic Mission* is an immersive video game where the players decide how the world evolves. We give them the environment, the actors, and the rules. From there, it takes off. You know how it works. What chance do we have of controlling where fifty million players are going to take it? Okay, that sounds like an excuse. I'm not making excuses, Jordan.

"The original promoters had this idea that we should issue an update to the first version, linking Alexa's journey to Eros into the storyline: blend the real-life universe into the metaverse. I gotta admit it sounded like a great idea. Sales would go wild. Sure, I had misgivings, because Alexa wasn't around to give her permission, but we defined her actionable roles so tightly that we felt no one could violate them. She would be the mathematical genius providing input to navigational decisions, only capable of speaking equations. Right? Approach her with love, hate, anger, or desire, and she was programmed to freeze, stalling the game and costing you points. I was beyond positive that we had the safeguards to limit her role.

"But I never allowed for *The View From Space*, Jordan. I swear, if I had realized that players would join the game because they'd heard those sessions Alexa was having with Artie Sharp, and that they were trying to get messages of inspiration out of her, I would have programmed it completely differently. What if someone designed a software patch that allowed them to cut-and-paste words and sentences, so they could put any message they wanted into her mouth? We know how to protect the game against generative AI, but no matter how good your coding, there's always someone who can figure out a way to unlock it. It wasn't the fault of the players who wanted to turn her into a galactic heroine who'd found the meaning of life. It wasn't the fault of Alexa, who had no knowledge of her inclusion in the virtual world in which gamers live. It was no one's fault but mine."

*Ser burro,* Antonio. *Not good enough. Now tell him how you'd gotten into bed with the devil. Don't pretend you didn't know. You knew who Black Quartz Capital were. You know that dogs only sleep with dogs, and devils with devils, so don't offer ignorance as an excuse,* chico, *your deep shit trouble ain't going away no time soon. You fucking loved the word that was out on the gaming streets, that Antonio Muchos had hit the ball out of the park, crashing the internet. You looked at the stats and didn't listen when Evgeniy Penchukov and Maksim Slavik said in their cold, hard voices, "We own this, Antonio, just to be clear." You grinned like a kid, pretending that's what anyone would say who owned the gig. "Ah, yes, but you didn't design it," you replied stupidly under your breath, your vanity overflowing, and they just looked at you with their Baltic Sea eyes.*

Then Penchukov called a meeting, and the man from Geneva was watching and listening, but still not showing himself.

"We want you to change the direction of *Galactic Mission*, Antonio. There's going to be a new version. This time, Alexa Smythe will play a bigger part, but we'll control what she has to say. You'll like the name: we're going to call it *Galactic Mission: Finding El Dorado*, and we'll have five hundred million players all mining for gold and following Alexa's inspiring lead."

# 24 · JORDAN MCPHEE

The uncanny quiet that had ruled within the confines of the Tofler Resort since their arrival vanished as if someone had thrown a switch. Uniformed staff scurried between buildings with an air of urgency, and Jordan had no idea where they had been hiding or why. But there were a lot of things around the edges of Levon's worlds that confounded belief. Though he commanded endeavors that were the leading innovations in their fields, employing eye-watering capital, he appeared to have no management structure. The three engineers from his technology labs were the first evidence of a direct link between Levon and the brains that were turning his bold ventures into realities. But how did he communicate with them? Was everything done through his virtual private network, FAITH? And how did he keep track of it all? The only personal assistant he appeared to have was the mute man-mountain who shadowed his every move and might well be a cyborg, if such a thing were feasible in a body like that.

When their meeting broke for lunch, there was an agreement that they would meet again later in the day after everyone had digested the implications of Levon's plan. Jordan and Alexa decided to go for a swim. There were things they still hadn't said, and the longer they remained unsaid, the more difficult they would become to say. That was Jordan's view. But the minute he framed them in his mind, he began to doubt the wisdom of airing them. He could confidently have the conversation with himself, and handle its outcome with equal equanimity, no matter how it transpired.

"When did you realize our quantum particle entanglement had failed?" he asked.

"When I was on Mars."

"Did you think to send me a message by another means?"

"No. Did you?"

Here was the thing. When the certainty that he felt about what she was thinking and feeling had suddenly stopped, he began to doubt that he had really been receiving her thoughts and feelings at all. He wondered if it wasn't all delusional—something which, in the absence of the hypotheticals that quantum theory was prone to manufacture, was nothing more than wishful thinking, out of the same damn box of soft-centered, over-sugared marshmallows as romantic fiction. Such sentimental crap was beneath two people who had been brought together by a mutual regard for mathematics.

Uh-uh. Better to let the subject lie. He ran down the sand and dived in, flailing his arms like the water needed beating into submission, and not looking up until he was at least two hundred yards offshore and out of breath. Looking back, he was relieved to see that Alexa hadn't followed him. He wanted to say, "What was all that crap about the human soul taking refuge in Tofler's Aurora, and you gabbling on with Artie Sharp about the soul being a personal blockchain—while the whole world listened in? Since when were you ever the slightest bit religious, and why talk to a goddamn algorithm about it?" Sure, she'd had many life-changing experiences in the two years that she'd been away, but was this the person he thought he'd known so well when she left? Luckily, she'd chosen to lie at the water's edge and shown no inclination to come out to him, so he went for a more leisurely swim, breaststroke this time, backwards and forwards parallel to the shoreline until he'd had enough and decided to go in.

Alexa's self-appointed guardian stood in the shade of a palm, watching her mistress with the sharp-eyed and pricked-eared attention of a sheep dog, waiting for a movement or a glance to signal her to action. And what the hell was all that about? It wasn't gravity's pull she was monitoring, surely? Did she know something about Alexa medically that no one had mentioned? Had her tests revealed liver damage? And why the need for a surgical mask on a beach, for God's sake? Jordan looked for his towel, but Karman was holding it for him. He smiled. "Take a dip," he said. "It couldn't be warmer." Then he made his way back to his room to get changed.

The message on his Konektor said Antonio had arrived and gave his room number. And there was another message: Will Portico wanted to speak to him before the meeting later in the day. Antonio was more important, so he set off as soon as he was dressed to find his room, getting directions from a uniformed security guard that he should head towards the entrance bridge. "The last villa on the left. I go that way, too." They walked side by side, quickly. Ahead of them, they could hear shouting, and then two figures ran across the lawn in front of them. They were young and hysterical, covered in mud and crying out in fear as close behind them, two bipedal robots loped in pursuit. Jordan and the security guard stopped in their tracks as the two robots caught the fleeing figures, flipped them upside down with ludicrous ease, and spread-eagled them on the ground.

"There's a crowd of people at the gate," the guard explained. "They must have tried to cross the moat. Not a good idea." He moved forward to take control, and Jordan followed. The young man and woman on the ground were wide-eyed with apprehension and pleading for human support to protect them from the deaf ears of the ruthless robots.

"We didn't mean any harm!" the boy pleaded. "We're harmless. We came in peace!"

"We came in peace," the girl repeated. "We didn't mean any harm."

"What are you going to do with them?" Jordan asked.

"Hose them down and shove them out the gate." The guard laughed. Jordan turned and walked away.

"We only wanted to see Alexa," the girl said.

He stopped and turned back. "Why?" She looked bemused. *"Why?"* he repeated.

*"World on Fire,"* she replied, pointing to her T-shirt, which carried the same slogan. "The planet's burning. Alexa's Church of Infinity will save us!"

"There is no Church of Infinity," Jordan said brusquely. "Alexa is a mathematician, not a high priestess. Go home."

By the time he reached Antonio's door, he began to feel remorse. This anger was not like him, but he'd never felt so on edge. Everything aggravated him, and he couldn't identify the cause. It was as if something had gotten away from him, unseen and without warning, and when he finally realized what it was, it was going to be too late. Will Portico talked about the world having shifted on its axis. He meant from freedom of communication to ever tighter global control, but he was a globalist, so why was he so suddenly aroused to action over the threats to Tofler's satellite network? Artie Sharp has been coded as a fact-checker with the greatest search engine in history available to him, and stupidly, they'd allowed him to perfect open code text generation so he could participate in theoretical discourse—but why was he using this ability to write script that sounded like a theologian testing a novitiate's faith? And as for Alexa, what had happened to her on Mars? Was she just channeling her father's beliefs in order to pass her grief through her system before then returning to normal? Or was she on a spiritual journey of her own creation, as her acolytes seemed to believe?

And where did that leave him?

Antonio was waiting on the terrace of his villa and had been watching the *Hunting Games* scenario with the roboguards chasing down the two intruders.

"They're from the doomsday cult," he explained as Jordan approached. "There's another couple o' hundred of them trying to get in the other side of the gate. They were waiting for her at the Gaia Port yesterday. She's sure got pulling power, your *amiga*."

For all their long friendship and familiarity, Antonio was talking to him like they'd barely met. His smile was on a flick switch, on and off, and neither it nor his eyes seemed to know where Jordan was standing. They went inside, and the awkwardness was transferred to a suitcase sitting on the bed, which Antonio proceeded to unpack with a running commentary that he didn't seem to realize was inappropriate. The suitcase contained the civilian clothes and personal possessions that Alexa had left at the space station when the *Galactic Mission* flight had embarked two years ago. It should have remained unopened.

"Just leave it," Jordan interrupted abruptly. "You can give it to her later. You and I have things we need to discuss."

Antonio closed the lid of the suitcase and turned to face him. Finally, his eyes stopped shifting, and his false smile turned rueful. "I know, Prof; I'm here to do that. You want to do it here and now?"

They decided to go outside onto the terrace. The robots and their captives had gone, and the gardens had returned to their tropical torpor, although, having now been made aware of its existence, Jordan could hear a low murmuring in the distance that he associated with the crowd locked out of the gates on the far side of the muddy moat separating Levon Tofler's retreat from the public.

"We have a problem, Antonio, and we need to solve it before it's too late."

"Alexa?"

"Yes. She doesn't realize, but…"

"Prof!" Antonio put both his hands up, as if to stop an oncoming truck. "Let me speak. I've been thinking about it, and I just need you to give me a chance to explain, because I think I've got the answer. Will you do that … please?"

Jordan was surprised. "I'm all ears."

"Well, you know how my team struck it big with the *Galactic Mission* video games. That was truly something I never dreamed of. But thanks to you and Alexa solving the problem with good old-fashioned calculus, the distributors were able to finance the exploration probe to Eros, which was the big prize for them, man. We were sure pretty damn excited, and Alexa got to go to Mars, too, but I never thought TriModa would cut and run like they did. To be honest, Prof, it caught me by surprise. Not that they owed an explanation. I mean, that's business. So, now the guys who own everything are Black Quartz Capital. Do you know Black Quartz Capital, Prof?"

"Yes, I know them."

"Then you know they own everything, and they own it everywhere, so it's no surprise they're invested in gaming, because gaming is bigger than all other entertainment combined. 'Just do what you do, Antonio,' they say. 'Make games that sell.' Okay, I say, that's my gig, and the royalty package is good, so why wouldn't I? But inside my brain, there's a little click insect that won't shut up, and you know how it is: once you start hearing it, that damn thing gets louder and louder until it starts driving you crazy. Then this *View from Space* thing with Alexa starts, and people are all over it, and my guys start pushing me. They want a new game, and they want it quickly—and this time, they want a bigger part for Alexa."

Jordan interrupted. "What do you mean, 'this time'?"

Antonio looked flustered. "In *Planet Gold*, players could go to Alexa for new coordinates—just navigational stuff, nothing else. We programmed her avatar so it was blocked from all player interaction except that. And she wasn't, like, real."

"Did she know this? Did she give her permission?"

Now he looked embarrassed. "She was featured in the publicity, you remember? She saw all of that before she left. No problem."

"Did she know she was in the game?"

"… Maybe not."

"That's no good, Antonio. So, tell me about this new game."

"They're calling it *Galactic Mission: Finding El Dorado,* and it's based on returning to Eros and mining the gold and precious metals there. The idea is that players will buy and trade EDTs—that's El Dorado Tokens, which could become worth a fortune. The tests from Eros show that it's easily the most valuable asteroid in our galaxy."

"If they can ever mine it."

Now Antonio was on his feet and banging the sides of his head with closed fists. "They don't have to mine it, Jordan!" he shouted. "The EDTs are cryptos stored on a blockchain. They issue five hundred thousand, or a billion, it doesn't matter, 'cause they can mine each one a thousand times over. They don't need to mine the fucking minerals on the asteroid, because they'll be mining the stupid, greedy fucking crypto investors. That's what they'll do. Every fool who buys a non-fungible token says, '*I'm* not a fool, you'll see, because I'll sell it to the next guy for ten times the price. *He's* the one that's a fool.'"

"What's this got to do with Alexa?"

Antonio let out a sigh and looked into the distance instead of having to look into his friend's eyes. "They want me to make Alexa, like, the mission leader or something: an *ultrareal*, from a hologram."

"How do you do that?"

"We get a body double and Deep Fake her face and voice, so she looks exactly like Alexa. The body double plays the game out in hologram format. Done right, it's the highest level of reality, man. Beats anything generative AI can produce, and *Fake Finders* read it as real."

"And what did you say?" Jordan asked quietly.

"I told them to get fucked."

"Good."

"'Okay,' they said, 'we'll get our workshops in the Ukraine to make it. They'll create her so no one will know the difference from live this time.' Then I said something very stupid. I said, 'Alexa is too famous. As soon as she tells the world you've stolen her persona, your game will be over.'"

"Why is that foolish?" Jordan asked.

"The man in Geneva said something that make my shit turn to water. It was the way he said it, like these people wouldn't let anything stand in their way—not me, not Alexa, nobody."

"Who was he, and what did he say?"

"'I made Alexa,' he said. 'She belongs to us. Do you really think we'd ever let her spoil our game like that?' This guy is a real asshole." Antonio did the Mexican dry spit just to emphasize his disgust.

Jordan thought awhile. He was neither surprised, nor as shocked as he should be, and that suggested that he'd already had a forewarning.

"When you were waiting for Alexa to arrive the other day," he recalled, "you called me and showed the scenes with the waiting crowd. Remember?"

"*Si, si,* just before we heard that Levon Tofler's bodyguard had snatched her away."

"Did you record that, or was it just a live stream?"

"It was live. Why?"

"So, it's not recoverable?"

"No. Was it important?"

"I thought I saw something, but I couldn't be certain. Maybe I was mistaken. If it was the person I thought, it might explain who your asshole is."

Antonio brightened. After revealing his shame, he could see a very faint glimmer of light that might signal the possibility of redemption.

"Let me try something," he pleaded. "Trovador has a presence on a number of metaverses, so all their CCTV material will be captured for editing. I'll check the CDN distribution and caching systems and see if the arrival hall footage has something you can examine. Some of these remoter locations save everything as insurance against transmission breaks, or to give their security bots time to scan what's been going down. Do you want me to check?"

"Sure. Use XR-9. And while you're doing that, get it to track down the current whereabouts of Shane Whitman of the Agenda Implementation Tribunal, last based in Geneva."

It was a long shot, but Jordan felt it was worth a try. He was conscious that Will Portico was anxious to speak to him, so he told Antonio he would arrange to meet him with Alexa later. "And I suggest we don't discuss what you've just told me, until we have a solution." Now was not the time, he figured, to broach the bigger issue that he'd wanted to discuss regarding Artie Sharp. That would have to wait.

# 25.WILL PORTICO

He'd hardly contributed to the conversation at all, he realized—even though, in a way, he'd brokered it. Something invisible was holding him back, despite his conviction that this could be the turning point in the struggle he'd had with the concept of a single elite governing body for the world—for how else could change happen efficiently? —and his (or was it Melanie's?) fear that such control, if it went wrong, would become irreversible. Now the One World powers, of which he was a promoter, were on the verge of taking control of all private communication. For eighty years, he'd bullied and badgered people to advance globalization faster, to push boundaries, and to end up doing it ruthlessly, if need be. So, what had changed? Whose was the voice that had gotten into his ear and convinced him that it had to be stopped? Was it Melanie speaking to him?

As improbable as it sounded, Levon's scheme was the only solution on offer. Jordan needed convincing, however, and if Levon and his crew couldn't do that, then it would be a measure of the deficiencies in their scheme—and of Jordan's judgment that he couldn't resolve those deficiencies with XR-12. If Jordan made that judgment, Will would accept it. Whether Levon would accept it was another matter altogether, for they were very different kinds of people. Levon's mind expanded ever outwards in search of solutions to its visionary goals, willing to risk failure rather than abandon the vision. Will's mind went to the edge of the horizon, but if it was necessary to shrink the horizon in order to discover what was achievable, then that was what he'd do. He rather suspected that Jordan was the same.

That still didn't explain his own silence so far. He'd found himself unable to participate due to the amplitude of his own inner voice, which, despite his efforts to quiet it, had grown more and more strident since his session with Cristina Dias and her damn prognosis that he was the bearer of an Ellipsis Gene that had the potential to undermine him. From the minute she'd attached the biosensor to his inner arm, it had felt like she'd attached herself to his thoughts and was reading them. Damn voodoo woman! She claimed subservience to the unarguable power of artificial intelligence diagnostics, while practicing the dark arts of the back-streets clairvoyant, sensing the psychic waves emanating from her victim and endorsing and magnifying them with calculated feedback. Her hand on the skin inside his sleeve was a trick. Her hair and perfume were tricks. The biosensor sending signals to his Konektor for transmission to her office was proof that he had been tricked.

But the fact was, voodoo woman or not, the psychic waves were real. He'd been trying to suppress them since Melanie's death, thinking that they were being generated by a combination of grief and guilt. Today, looking and listening to the scheme for liberating communication from state and corporate tech controls, it had finally crystalized for him. The ramifications were enormous. If this plan was successful, it would signal the end of digital technology's dominance of society, the end of central authority's grip on mankind, and of its conceited belief that it could overrule nature itself.

And if the Deep State's viselike grip was to be released, what did that mean for him and the position he occupied as a member of the power elite? It was that membership that had allowed him to believe that, by dint of sheer will, money, and obstinacy, he could change the very nature of humanity, thereby solving all its problems. His magnification of those problems, and of his role in solving them, had served to magnify himself: what Melanie had called "playing at God." But someone had to take control, because mankind had created those problems. Left to itself, it disintegrated into an atavistic animal kingdom, unable to organize itself for the common good, surrendering to greed or apathy, taking the easy path to the lowest common denominator and allowing itself to be ruled by the predatorily ruthless few. Tofler's decentralized, permissionless network might be the collective property of all its users, but how long before a new force would arise from within its circuitry?

He needed to express these thoughts, to air them and to hear them spoken out loud before they vanished from reality. Besides Jordan, he couldn't think of any of his friends or peers that could be trusted to disabuse him of his conclusions, but more importantly, he owed it to Jordan to reveal his private thoughts before he made a decision to engage with the project or not. Jordan was here because he, Will, had insisted that Levon could not proceed without him.

The afternoon was hot and sticky. The water's edge, where he had previously glimpsed Alexa and Jordan, called to him, but his video conference with the W&M Foundation team leaders from the seven heptaspheres had pinned him to his room. Every week they did this. Why? Why had conferring become so habitual? Was he so essential to other people's motivation and performance that they needed to be exposed to his penetrating grilling every seven days of their lives, or was it his tenuous last remaining lifeline to the obsessions without which he would have nothing?

When he and Melanie had started down this track sixty-five years ago, they'd believed that their great good fortune had put them in a position to solve the world's intractable problems by applying the same single-minded focus that had characterized their business success. Answerable only to the laws of science and the limitations of human imagination, they'd hired the best brains and underwritten the largest budgets ever brought to bear on disease, poverty, and environmental vandalism. All it needed was time. That's all he'd asked for—and *Life Xtension* had granted it to him. But time had been waiting for its moment to teach him what wise men had known down through the ages, what Melanie had known: that men who play at being God need to be ready to fight the Devil when the moment comes.

Listening to his directors of operations reporting to him from around the globe, he'd realized that the moment had now come. In truth, he'd known it was coming a long time ago, but he'd thought he could buy it off with little concessions that would involve no cost, and might signal his virtue to God and the world, strengthening his moral standing for the future. There was a pattern to it. It had started small when, as the person responsible more than any other for the invention of email and the instantaneous postal service afforded by the internet, he had made a show of claiming back his life by deactivating his mail accounts. From twenty emails a day in 1982, it had grown to two hundred a day by 1992, despite the creation of a secretarial team dedicated to white and black listings. He'd spent 250 million dollars creating a digital assistant with deep learning abilities to lighten the load of his personal staff, before steeling himself to the truth: that the great digital tools that his company had created for the world to boost productivity and eliminate paper had stolen time, suffocated original thought, and spread the disease of appearing to be busy into every private life and enterprise on earth.

Of course, he'd never admitted that the digital revolution that he'd helped to foist upon the world, the source of his great wealth, had stolen the lives of the people to whom he'd sold it, yet his were the building blocks that allowed the next generation of rapacious tech tycoons to build their outrageous fortunes on the backs of social media, search engines, and data retrieval and analysis. The banners they waved said *Freedom of Expression, Freedom of Knowledge, Freedom of Communication*, but the Levitical tithe they'd demanded in return was the almost total surrender of the time and personal privacy of their subscribers, both of which they then on-sold to the highest bidders. And who was the highest bidder of them all? The state—always the state.

*No, Cristina, it wasn't an Ellipse Gene you detected; it was a far more damaging defect. It was my conscience.* He'd known for months—maybe years—that this moment was coming. The frightening thing was that the directors of his foundations who reported to him every week couldn't see it. They didn't want to see it. The massive inoculation programs that they'd been financing and promoting throughout the Third World were already causing people's immune systems to fail. Decades of reliance on mRNA and DNA boosting had left young people with no ability to develop natural resistance. He could see it lurking like a ghost behind the research figures, and there was no one he could tell. The depopulation ambitions of the Club of Rome were being fulfilled involuntarily.

The patch on his underarm tingled, as if searching for a wavelength on which to transmit his quavering confession. When Jordan McPhee stood in the doorway, interrupting these thoughts, he was certain he must have heard them as if he'd spoken out loud.

Jordan had a volleyball in his hands. "Inside or out?" he asked.

"Gee…" Will stared into the light. "It's been years since I did that. You sure you won't embarrass me?"

"Not sure at all," Jordan drawled. "C'mon. I hear you shoot hoops. You'll be fine."

He turned and led the way to the beach, where a net was strung up between two coconut palms. Alexa had gone indoors, and they had the sand to themselves. Jordan served first. It was a gentle lob that Will tried to bump, and missed. There were no boundary lines.

"Are there rules?" he asked.

"No rules, just play. You get to serve when I lose a point."

Jordan was good, but considerate. Will wasn't bad, and he was competitive. They had fun.

"Do you think Levon can do it?" he asked Jordan once they'd settled into a moderate game.

"It's just wild enough of an idea that he might pull it off. They've been working on it awhile and seem confident in what they've achieved thus far. The questions I'd have are not about technology, but about geopolitics. Will he be allowed to do it?"

"He won't be asking permission."

Jordan set Will's weak serve so it rose nicely into the air, where he could spike it with maximum force into the sand at Will's feet. "I got that," he agreed, taking the ball back to the imaginary serve line, "but how the hell will he keep it secret?"

"Alright," Will conceded, "that's something we need to discuss, and the technical viability is something that we can pressure test within the combined resources of the *Derangers Network*, if you're willing to give your backing. But what I need to hear from you is your acceptance of the imperative to act. Without this, it's all over for the internet. And there's even more things being planned."

Jordan's serve wasn't hard, but Will's bump was pathetic, causing him to fall over and put the ball up on Jordan's side of the net. Instead of smashing a winner, Jordan caught the ball, ducked under the net, and held out a hand to help Will to his feet. "What do you mean, 'there's even more things being planned'?'"

Will took off his glasses and checked to make sure they were not broken.

"Do you know what was said around the table at the Council for Earth Restoration last week? That the World Government needs to adopt a program to reduce the world's population to five billion, 'for the sake of posterity'."

"Oh, yeah? That's old Club of Rome stuff. And how do they propose doing that?"

"By decree. George Kyros actually shouted out loud, 'Three billion must die!'—and people agreed with him. When they have final control of the internet, they'll make it happen. There'll be no means of resisting. It's another reason why I see Levon's solution as being our best hope."

Jordan looked him up and down as if seeing him for the first time. What did he see: a man he could trust, or a man who couldn't trust himself?

"I've heard you say the same thing, Will," Jordan replied calmly, "but not so crudely. Nothing surprises me when it comes to the ruthless drive for control and power shown by your fellow elite, but I never cease to be amazed that you make no attempt to hide it. Kill three billion people? Sure, why not, if it's in the plan?"

Will brushed himself down and tried to hide his shock. It wasn't *his* elite. The whole reason they were all here was because he rejected what was being planned.

"You're one of them, Will," Jordan continued. "You're right up there at the top table. So, tell me what it is that allows you people to assume the right to rule the planet like drunken Caesars."

His tone was pleasant, suggesting he was genuinely perplexed, and Will realized that this must have been a question Jordan had always had about him. Yet he was accepted by the members of the *Derangers Network*, and had never been confronted with this question before. Had he been deceiving himself about what they thought of him?

"There's a difference between believing in the optimum carrying capacity of the planet in terms of resources and climate control," Will protested, "and deciding to wipe out three billion people to achieve your goal. Just because I believe that centralization of effort is needed to deal with the world's intractable problems does not mean that I condone the Deep State power abuses that you rightly condemn. Do you put me in the same category as a George Kyros? Is that what you're saying?"

"That's how it looks to people from the outside."

Will was crushed. *Of course* that was how it looked to people from the outside. Why should he have thought anything different? "And is that how the *Derangers Network* views me?" he asked.

Jordan bounced the ball a couple of times and thought about it. "The

*Derangers* are just a bunch of guys that went into tech together at a time when it was exploding. You'd paved the way forty years before us, and we were honored to have you in our circle. It turned out that our tech has had a bigger influence on society and human behavior than any politicians or passing credos, and the politicians and global elites know that, which is why we're regarded as untouchable. No one knows where the next development will come from, or what it will mean for humanity. But as individuals, we have different priorities of concern. Yours is about Earth's resources and carrying capacity. Mine is about corruption and the erosion of personal freedom. C'mon, it's too damn hot to keep playing. I think we need a drink."

They decided to go in search of a cold beer. The deep, revealing conversation that Will was longing to have wasn't going to happen. Jordan was a calm and unruffled man who inspired trust, but he wasn't the confessor priest that Will Portico needed at this time. A lifetime focused on the intractable problems of the world had built a wall around him, preventing others, like Jordan, from seeing the person that lay within. Inside that wall was something that Alexa had alerted him to, giving him hope. It was, she said, something that existed in all humans: it was the soul.

# 26 · KARMAN

Word of their abduction by Tank and Levon Tofler had spread through the *WoF* movement immediately after it happened. Those who had been waiting at the island end of the Gaia Earth Station had seen it on video screens in the arrival hall, and by the time they had landed at Tofler's resort, Karman was already receiving messages on her Konektor. Until she knew what her abductors planned for them, she chose not to reply. Even after Levon Tofler made it clear that his aim was to ensure Alexa's safety, she continued to remain silent. Perhaps, if she was honest, she enjoyed the evidence of mounting concern as the messages poured in, and relished the position of importance she found herself in.

Releasing part of her intimate video close-ups of Alexa's acclimatization treatment had been a risk, but once taken, it had elevated Karman's status in the *World on Fire* movement, so that others were already looking to her for guidance on the movement's future direction. But if that had been a risk worth taking, once they saw the recording of Alexa's message that she'd taken during her so-called "voice test," that would be the clincher. Her status would be assured.

Outside the gates of the resort, members were gluing themselves to the road and chanting Alexa's name, and she was torn between ignoring them, and answering their plea to try to persuade Alexa to address them. These people were her tribe, and her loyalty to them was being tested, but there were more valuable forms of activism at this moment than public demonstration. Her value lay in the unique position of trust she had been handed, bringing Alexa back to Earth physically while waiting for the moment when she could convince her to spearhead their cause.

In Karman's mind, there was no doubt that her destiny had placed her in this position. Few of her generation had won the employment lottery and moved from Transitional Benefits to the privileged position of enterprise employment. The majority of her generation presumed that time was a limitless commodity, able to be invested in protesting the inaction of governments in dealing with the threat to the planet. As a school pupil, she, too, had been free to take to the streets in protest at the abject failure of the world to achieve the 2050 zero carbon targets. The shared passion and companionship of those days and nights chained to the railings of government buildings were the most inspiring moments of her life to date. But that had all changed when her name was drawn from the Social Equity Ministry's ballot for training as a physiotherapist. Sensibly, she had withdrawn from public protest events, avoiding facial recognition cameras, and her reward was selection for training in post-flight rehabilitation with the Tofler Shuttle Ground Support Crew. But the abject failure of the members of the One World Government to meet the so-called "Last Chance" zero carbon targets promised by Agenda 2060 had resulted in an eruption of anger and revulsion against the world's elite that she could not ignore. So, when she saw *The View from Space* and realized that Alexa Smythe's return from Mars would place her care in Karman's hands, she knew it was her destiny unfolding.

Her task was to convince Alexa that she had an army waiting to be led. Fear and despair had been met by two-thirds of people with vaginas choosing to adopt anti-natalism and have their fallopian tubes tied, knowing it was morally wrong to bring a child into a world that was doomed. Half of all people of her generation born with penises had demanded irreversible vasectomy. Karman had chosen irreversible hormone-neutralizing treatment pre-puberty—the ultimate nonbinary state. No caring person could risk further populating a world where humans were the problem. Alexa would understand that; she had rejected childbearing and heterosexual mating herself. She knew. She knew the state of the planet. Her vision of hope for life beyond Earth showed that.

Karman's task was to restore Alexa's strength of mind and body, which had clearly been diminished by the exigencies of the seven-month return flight from Mars, so that she could focus her vision, becoming the irresistible force that would provide them all with hope and a direction to follow. If she was honest with herself, Karman had to admit that she was worried about Alexa's memory confusion and lack of focus. She had to put it down to fatigue, but it was clear that a way had to be found to convince her that she should look to retain Karman by her side during the process of recovery. Her attachment to her ex-professor, Jordan McPhee, was a disappointment. Perhaps he had once been her mentor, but there was nothing in his manner that suggested he understood the magnitude of the spiritual path that Alexa was on, or the importance of the role she was destined to play. She'd had a real father; she didn't need a surrogate version in the form of her ex-professor. He was a member of the techno patriarchy, after all. Somehow, she would have to separate them.

And what did Levon Tofler want of her? He hadn't just snatched her to keep her safe from the crowds; he wanted her for his own reasons. His money, his power, his empire of technology had allowed him to trample on the earth and consume it at will. Now he was threatening to do the same to space. Alexa mustn't be allowed to fall into his clutches.

It was late afternoon. Alexa had come back from the beach, and Karman had given her a phial containing the dexamethasone that she had convinced Alexa she needed. To that phial, she had added a Z-hypnotic, because clearly the more recuperative sleep she got, the better, and the mild dilution of memory sharpness would be an acceptable trade-off. What she didn't want was Alexa hearing the commotion from outside the compound and responding to it without knowing the importance of her role in it, let alone that she should invite Jordan McPhee into her room, where Karman would be excluded.

This was a moment when clear thinking and visionary planning was required. The time for childish gestures and empty theatrics was over. Lying down and blocking the roads just made people angry. Forming human chains around abattoirs only delayed the animal slaughter for a day. Adopting pretend-Asperger's in subservience to the sanctity of Greta Thunberg didn't cut it with officials anymore. Responding to despair by signing on for voluntary euthanasia was an abject admission of defeat. The world was dying. It was irreversible. Almost a century had passed since science had first recognized that mankind was killing its own habitat. Science had advanced, and its warnings had grown stronger and more urgent. But the warnings were ignored. China, India, and all the delegated producers of profits for multinational corporates were pumping pollutants into the atmosphere as fast as they pumped profits into their shareholders' pockets, just as strongly as they'd done fifty years ago. And those shareholders were the ones who voted at the table of the United Nations and the One World Government in Geneva. It was time to leave the evil behind and take the pure spirit of humanity into a future where it could regenerate.

Alexa was now sleeping—it would last for two hours, if she'd gotten the dosage right—and Jordan McPhee was somewhere else. The crowd at the front gate must have adopted passive resistance, for the sound had dropped away to the low hum that was the signal of the hive: you can kill a single bee or a thousand, but the hive will survive. And who would the bees protect? Why, the queen bee, of course. And that queen bee was Alexa.

Karman felt happier and more optimistic than she had felt for most of her life. The one threat to that happiness was the people of power in whose control she was held. The reality was that she was contractually obliged to remain and fulfill a role that her employer mandated, and she was professionally bound to perform that role to the best of her ability. But her emotional and moral obligations were in conflict with those needs, for it was not her space station employer who commanded her loyalty, but the vision which Alexa had inspired.

How could she discover what was in Levon Tofler's mind? There was nothing left on the platform of the *fale* where he'd met with all his guests that morning. Walking through the gardens, she could find no trace of the other people who had arrived in the air taxis parked on the lawn. The only sound was the low buzz from the direction of the entrance gate. Her conflicting loyalties twisted her emotions into a maelstrom of confusion as she remembered friends who had committed suicide in despair at the earth's inevitable destruction. Some had physically emasculated themselves to prevent them being part of the problem. But here, within the walls of the Tofler Resort, the biggest threat was her failure to know how to act. The middle-aged men in the compound—Leon Tofler, Will Portico, Jordan McPhee, and the tech execs—weren't these the ones who had fucked the planet? How could she stop them doing even more? What were they planning?

While standing in the shade of a frangipani tree, Karman saw Jordan McPhee march across the lawn with a Trovadorian security guard. She saw two bipedal robots ruthlessly hunt down their prey like pack dogs, and she stifled her cries of alarm; the prey were her own people, but she was powerless to help them. She watched as Jordan then walked away, and she followed at a distance as the Trovadorian guard instructed the robots to hose their captives down and carry them across the bridge, before pushing them back outside the gates. Once the guard had gone, she fought her way through the shrubbery to the boundary of the resort formed by the deep moat that separated it from the public road on the far side. The walls of the moat were twenty feet deep, and the muddy water at its base was shallow and choked with weeds, which explained the state of the two young intruders' clothes. They'd needed to be young and fit to clamber up the steep side without falling back to the bottom.

As she watched the protesters blocking the road near the entrance gate, an idea started to form. There were at least two hundred of them, sitting or lying in rows with arms linked to resist removal, watched impassively by robotic guards of the same type that she'd seen ruthlessly tracking down their prey just minutes ago in the garden. The members of *WoF* that she'd spoken with were pledging to maintain their vigil so long as Alexa remained at the compound. Unless Karman could discover what Tofler and his guests were planning, she had no way of knowing how long that might be. It was imperative that she find a way to bring Alexa in front of her followers, so she could see the effect that her messages from space had inspired. Time was of the essence. She needed to act.

She started by calling the Gaia Earth Station and telling the ground support crew that she urgently needed the testing kits, diagnostic tools, and digital notebook that she'd been forced to leave behind when Tank had snatched them in the arrival hall. She needed to get them delivered to her urgently at the Tofler Resort, and she asked them to call her once they arrived outside the gate, so she could receive the delivery personally.

# 27 · ALEXA SMYTHE

After ninety minutes of deep sleep, Alexa had passed into the REM period of dreaming. Her heart rate and breathing increased so rapidly that she woke herself up, the vivid images and sounds clinging to her as if she were trapped in a sensory immersion tunnel. Sitting up, fighting for breath, she tried to hold them in her mind and shape them into something resembling reality. But her dreams were not controllable; they were visitors who broke into her mind when she was asleep and wreaked havoc until she returned home and disturbed them. Even those she thought she knew refused to be recognized when she tried to grasp hold of them and make them stay.

But if her mind gradually emptied itself of the wild images and disjointed passages of sound that had woken her up, some residue of the experience remained in her body. She sensed she had traveled clear of gravity, but was somehow held stationary, if such a thing were possible. Perhaps she'd been surrounded by a perfectly formed orb of magnetic fields, made perfect by their precise equalization. Where to start with the necessary calculation? How about the surface area of a ball of defined diameter? Imagine that at some point on the outer surface of this orb, the magnetic field was weakened by a miniscule degree relative to all the other fields working in opposition to each other in order to hold it motionless. Then, assuming that space was a pressure vacuum, might the ball not rush through space at a speed faster than light?

She carried that thought as she swung her legs over the side of the bed.

If dreams were the chaos created by the mind's frantic attempt to establish a filing system to store away the snippets of thoughts and unarticulated emotions of the previous day, then perhaps the concept of the orb had been spun out of Levon Tofler's aurora of mini satellites. But what about the voices in her dreams, or more particularly, the words? They didn't belong to the previous day or days, unless they'd existed subconsciously. But now that she'd forgotten them, despite their vividness at the time, she couldn't avoid the feeling of anxiety they'd aroused.

Every minute of being in space gave cause for feelings of anxiety, and returning safely to Earth was meant to lay them to rest. Perhaps her dreams were just a way of letting out the fears that she had bottled up in order to get her through two years of perilous journeying. *That's it*, she thought, *you're just experiencing a perfectly normal reaction. Pick yourself up and focus on the next objective, the way you always have. Rejoice in having been able to return safely to Earth.*

She turned on the shower and removed her clothes. The bathroom mirror showed the evidence that had inspired Jordan's words of greeting: yes, her breasts *were* sunburned, as were her thighs. She turned the shower mixer towards cold. The sight of her naked body disturbed her. It had been so long since she'd fully examined it that it appeared alien to her, the realization slowly dawning that humans, shorn of their protective clothing, were the most vulnerable of living species, unable to resist sunlight, cold, radiation, or the prying examinations of other members of their kind. The vulnerability was not just physical; it was embedded in the psyche. She stood so long looking at herself in the mirror that eventually she had to turn the shower off. No other animal grew to maturity so ill-equipped for survival in the wild. Was this why she'd aspired for so many years to be able to don an astronaut's suit and helmet and merge as a component part into the machinery of a space vehicle?

But now that she was back on Earth, and asking herself what the next objective was, no answer came to mind. Her life had brought her to a standstill. She'd found her father—and buried him. She'd met his highest expectations of her, and exceeded her highest expectations of herself. With Jordan's help, she'd faced down the Deep State and gained immunity from its repressive powers. She'd been to Eros and Mars and looked deep into infinity, sensing that the direction to travel was into the unknown, but instead, here she was, returned to Earth and about to step into the shower so she'd be dressed before Jordan McPhee's expected knock on her door. Was Jordan the next objective?

She turned the shower on again, stepped into it, and turned her face up into the stinging jets. From the next room, she could hear the insistent call of her Konektor. It hadn't stopped flagging messages to her from the minute she'd plugged it in to recharge after Antonio had it delivered to her room. Two years of unanswered calls were pleading for her attention, and she was going to have to delete them from her memory and start again with a new address and firewall. She should have turned it off while recharging, but it occurred to her that Jordan, knowing she was on the air again, might want to contact her if the dinner plans changed. Sure enough, just as she finished rinsing off her body soap, her distinctive call signal rang out, and she shut down the shower and stepped straight out. Dripping wet, she walked across the wooden floor of her chalet, leaving puddles in her wake, then picked up the Konektor from its cradle.

"I am soaking wet and not nearly ready," she pleaded.

There was no answer. She checked the caller ID and saw that it was blocked. Damn! What was she thinking?

"Presumably that information was intended for your abductor, Alexa," a familiar voice replied. "The absence of alarm in your voice suggests you are being well treated. As your employers, we were naturally worried."

Whitman. Shane Whitman: the most evil alligator in the swamp.

"What employers?" she demanded.

"C'mon, Alexa, you know full well. You're the Special Ambassador to the Agenda Implementation Tribunal, and Advisor to the Ministry of

Truth and Public Guidance. Everyone knows that; that's who you are. The government's proud of you. You're a shining star, Alexa, a beacon of progress, and an example to all. The public loves you, and that's because we gave you the stage and allowed you free rein. I told you before, we've got big plans for you, Alexa. Nothing's changed."

A red haze of anger and shame rose out of Alexa's chest, up her neck and into her eyes and throat.

"You are insane," she hissed. "Not just unattached to reality, but unaware of the depth of your dishonesty towards me and everyone you encounter. I can't believe you have the cheek to even speak to me after your lies about my father. You, you…" Running out of words, she glared around the room, looking for something to clutch onto. The bastard was laughing. Laughing!

"Okay, okay, I get that I held out on you about your old man, but it was only a day or so before I would have told you, once I'd checked out that he was still alive. See, I didn't want you to find out that he'd died on Mars. That's all I was doing, except your boyfriend—is that what he is?—decided to interfere and make a hero of himself. That's another story that will wait for another day, but today is the day when the government wants you to know that we are waiting to welcome you back and give you the recognition you deserve. Oh, and to give you the opportunity to clarify that your investigations into the application of the articles of *AGENDA 2060* to conditions in space were a brilliant analysis on your part that explains just how special our planet Earth is, and how lucky we are to have sensible rules to protect it. No one could have explained it better than you, Alexa. I am right, I hope, that you were not trying to undermine *AGENDA 2060*, but were subtly reinforcing its importance for conditions on Earth? Taking a positive stance, which I always do where you are concerned, I would have to say that your weekly *View from Space* made the case for *AGENDA 2060* better than anyone could have hoped, and that's why the government gave you such generous support to undertake your great mission to Mars."

"What government support? I was funded by the promoters of *Galactic Mission.* It had nothing to do with the government."

"Six months at the Mars Colony because of your standing with the Agenda Implementation Tribunal, Alexa. That doesn't come cheap. And your Executive Schedule 4 remuneration didn't stop just because you'd been on a mission of discovery. Who do you think has been paying for your fancy apartment in the Noam Chomsky Building, so kindly house-sat for you by Jordan McPhee's lezzie daughter and her half-caste kid, eh? You have a debt to the state and a contract that needs to be honored, so think about that. We'll be meeting soon. There's lots to discuss."

The call ended. *Shit, oh, shit!* Still wet from the shower, she was naked and disgusted with herself. The filth of cynicism and corruption that dripped from that man's voice had oozed down the radio waves and covered her with the indelible stain of a reality she'd spent two years trying to escape. She turned off her Konektor and removed the charger. Of all the emotions coursing through her, perhaps the most uncomfortable was the feeling of shame. How could she have been so naive as to suppose that the Mars Colony saw her as anything other than a high-level member of the governing elite, and an advisor on the interpretation of *AGENDA 2060,* no less? They weren't to know that, in her mind, she'd walked away from the whole political charade she'd been seduced into. Nobody knew … except Jordan.

As if on cue, the confident rap on her door told her that Jordan had arrived. Without thinking, she flung the door open and shouted at the top of her voice: "Shane Whitman! None other than Shane bloody Whitman!"

Jordan eased her hand off the door handle, stepped inside, and closed the door behind him. He didn't look surprised. He didn't look flustered or disapproving. He certainly didn't look excited. He looked like her friend, her mentor, her reliable, all-knowing, favorite professor who acted like she was fully dressed when she was sure she was wringing wet and stark naked.

Taking her hand, he led her to the bathroom, took a towel off the rack, and opened it wide before wrapping it around her.

"Levon's feast is about to be served," he said quietly, "and all the indications are that you are the guest of honor. So, let's get you dressed while you tell me what Whitman had to say."

Feeling mortified by her physical and emotional vulnerability, Alexa grabbed her underclothes and retreated to the walk-in wardrobe to get dressed. The fright she'd received at the sound of Whitman's voice had cut through the fog that had clouded her memory since returning to Earth. He'd done the same thing to her as Karman had, accusing her of transmitting reports from the spaceship on her return journey from Mars of which she had absolutely no recall. First it was this ridiculous doomsday cult who were building it into some sort of religious prophecy, and now it was the Deep State claiming that *AGENDA 2060* was under threat.

She pulled a dress over her head, teased up her hair—what there was of it—and stepped out into the room.

"Jordan, tell me please what this program, *The View from Space,* is all about, because I have no idea at all. At first, I thought I was suffering from brain fog, but now my memory is starting to clear. Some of the things Karman has repeated to me sound like pieces taken from my conversations with my father, but I've never aired them with anyone else, only in my private journal. And now Whitman is accusing me of having undermined *AGENDA 2060*. Again, I have no memory of that. It's true that I did an analysis for the commander of the Mars Colony to identify any elements of the agenda that needed to be included in their Code of Conduct manual, but I never discussed it in my short transmissions to the Flight Control Center. So, what the hell's going on?"

Jordan stood at the window, looking out into the garden, a stance he had taken in order to give her privacy while she dressed. His fingers drummed lightly on the window pane. "What form did your journal take when you recorded conversations with your father?"

"They were my spoken or written recollections recorded in my private files. Everyone has their own VPN, which they access through the spacecraft or colony networks. That's where you do your calculations, messaging, and private file storage. It's rock-solid secure, and you can plug into it from anywhere, but it's fully encrypted. There's no place for personal computers in space."

Jordan's fingers stopped drumming, and he turned around to face her. "I think it's my fault," he said with a shrug.

"What? Why?"

"When you left, just before the 2060 Earth Day Conference, we programmed Artie Sharp so he could do the George Kyros interview that we'd planned for you to do."

"Artie Sharp interviewed him?"

"No, you interviewed him."

"I don't understand."

Jordan crossed the room to her and placed his hands on her shoulders. "Artie inhabited a Deep Fake version of you that was so real that no one ever detected it—not even the government. In fact, they showed it with their Fake-Free Certificate. I'm sorry, but we'd done it before, remember? When you were selling the change to Article One of the Agenda to the Implementation Tribunal…"

"And I made you swear to never do it again!" She was furious. "I am *not* yours to manipulate whenever you feel like it!"

She shrugged his hands off her shoulders, and he stepped back from her.

"No one has the right to put words in my mouth, Jordan. Not you, not anyone."

The awful feeling occurred to her that everyone she'd encountered since returning to Earth was not relating to her as a real person, but as a Deep Fake character invented by someone else: a character over whom she'd had no input or control, nor even an opportunity to review. How could she go and face them tonight when they were all unaware that they were dealing with a mistaken identity who had never uttered the words they identified with her? Only Jordan knew who she really was—and he had allowed this to happen to her. Worse than the feeling of anger was the feeling of loss if she allowed herself to lose trust in the person she loved. It was that feeling that caused tears to run down her cheeks.

Jordan stepped forward again and held her.

"You're right in everything you say," he admitted. "The George Kyros interview seemed like a good idea at the time, and it worked a bit too well. The truth is that Artie is just one recognizable manifestation of the depth of intelligence we have let loose through the quantum computing power of XR-12. I feared this might happen one day, but not so soon. I'm sorry, but we may have lost control."

"Then you need to get it back, quickly." She sniffled.

"I agree. It may be the biggest problem we've ever faced—or it may be the greatest opportunity. The ability to make Deep Fakes that are utterly convincing is no surprise, and we can't pretend that we haven't programmed autonomy, but we always assured ourselves that motivation and desire were exclusively human attributes. So, reading your private files and shaping the material in them into intelligent questions and answers is not beyond a self-programming intelligence at this level. But the question I have to ask is, why? I've seen those interviews; you haven't. They are unusually philosophical. Did that come from your journals? Who is the creator here: a machine? I'm going to need your help, Alexa. We need to confront this thing together."

Alexa put her hands around his waist and her head on his shoulder. "You need to stop him—or it. And I need to watch these damn programs to see what he's made me say."

They stayed like that for a good long minute. It was the first minute during which she felt she had finally returned to Earth properly. Then she stepped back.

"Jordan, there is something I need to say." She frowned and looked down at her hands. "This is difficult, but I've been thinking a lot about it and how to express it. Space is the loneliest place you can imagine, but my God, it makes you think. One of the things I've been thinking about is whether we—I mean humans—are better off alone, or whether that's an unnatural condition. What I concluded is that there is something in us all, almost from birth—an unconscious longing to find someone who seems to see things as if through the same eyes as ourselves, who sees what we see, who thinks what we think and feels what we feel. Not in all things, of course. It's kind of like we've been separated, and didn't know it—until finally we meet. I don't think I want to be separated from you again. Does that make me sound weak?"

# 28. COLE GRANTHAM

"If Jesus is the son of God, who's his grandfather?"

Like most scientists, Cole was comfortable enough in his rejection of the idea of a divine creator of all things not to feel a need to make the point overtly, but like all people who spent their lives in the company of others from an academic background, he had a few well-practiced one-liners, which, when dropped at suitable moments, made his views clear in a subtly sophisticated way. In this case, he hoped his subtle sophistication was not lost on Levon Tofler, or his colleagues, Amor and Fanon. Getting one over his colleagues was always front and center in the mind of Cole—a trait that his laid-back Southwestern drawl admirably disguised.

As it happened, the only person who reacted to his droll witticism was the young newbie whiz kid games inventor, Antonio Muchas, a sidekick of Jordan McPhee who had appeared out of the blue, much to Levon's apparent delight. It came as no surprise that his mercurial and eccentric employer should be a devotee of the worlds of illusion in which gamers operated, but if they weren't careful, an evening that should be focused on the single technological feat capable of defying the state's final conquest of individual freedoms could deteriorate into a geeky mash-up of teenage fantasy-mongering. Not that Cole dared allow that thought to be conveyed by his tone of voice or expression. There were only two positions on Levon's employment game board: *in* or *out*. Better men than Cole had started a sentence being totally *in*, only to end it being mysteriously *out*.

For people like Will Portico and Jordan McPhee, who didn't care about such things, it was easy to treat Levon as an idiot savant. But for Cole, Amor, and Fanon, he was either an inspiring genius or an unstable tyrant, and there was no way of knowing which. So, like all Tofler management execs, they found these social interludes with the boss difficult to navigate. No such trouble for the Hispanic whiz kid, though. He was on fire.

"See, Levon," Antonio explained, "we build our worlds now based on reference frames, just like cortical columns in the neocortex. In *Galactic Mission*, our AGI began to reference movement and grid cell locations—all the things the human senses do automatically in real life. You've seen it, right? But our next iteration will take it to a new level. You'll be able to see the hair on the back of your hand, the goose bumps on your lover's tits. Old game styles were built in two dimensions only, like flat pictures in a book. So, avatars were made to look like gawky cartoon figures jumping around on a drawing board. Okay, you got some sense of action, but no sense of reality. And why would you want to hang out in an unreal virtual world when you can get the real thing? You get it, right?"

"I get it, I get it!" shouted Levon. "It's not virtual reality; it's *hyper*reality. It's everything the mind can imagine. But consciousness is outside the game; that's what I love. Players can play themselves, looking their best and acting their worst, but every action is controlled by the living brain guiding their controller. And when you win your territory and capture adversaries, you get to control them, too—which is the closest we get to omnipotence. It's the fucking God game, man."

"Designed right, it's the fucking God game!" Antonio agreed.

Levon sat cross-legged like a Buddhist priest, grinning and nodding at the beauty of it all while sipping on his cold soda water. Two or three yards behind him, as always, stood the ever present Tank, mute and watchful. Antonio asked a waiter for another *cerveza*—his third—and Cole decided to insert himself into their conversation.

"Now tell me, Antonio: why would you want to escape the real world to enter a world that, by your definition, is even more real?"

"Because in the virtual world, you control the course of events without terminal consequences to yourself. You can be ruthless, greedy, and risk it all, knowing you're immortal. If you fail, you just reenter the game. You can't do that in life."

"What if you don't want to be ruthless and greedy and take risks? Does that mean you're not a gamer?"

"Ha!" Antonio laughed. "In my ideal metaverse, there will be rewards for those who are kind, generous, and careful, for sure. Just like in life. It comes down to rules, incentives, and how you set it up. Some like to be sinners, and some like to be saints, but we all like to win."

Will Portico had been silent up to this point, giving the appearance of not really listening. "So, if I get this right," he interjected, "the person playing God in this game is the designer who sets the rules."

"*Si,*" Antonio agreed enthusiastically, "just like in real life. The Lord God created us and the world we live in. He is the ultimate designer."

Levon giggled like a mischievous child.

The arrival of Jordan and Alexa brought everyone to their feet, and Levon asked them to move around the table so that there was room for him to have Alexa on one side with Antonio on his other. As they took their seats, Jordan remained standing, looking down at them in their lotus positions on the tapa matting of the banquet *fale* with an enigmatic expression that suggested he was about to say something, but hadn't quite decided how to frame it.

"The food looks great, Levon," he said eventually, with a smile and a sweep of his hand, "and I don't think we should ruin it with too much heavy discussion. Let's accept Will's intelligence information and agree that we have to act. I don't know whether your crazy idea will work, and neither do any of you, but I do know that quantum entanglement is the only way to communicate at that scale. Let's be frank: for quantum entanglement to work, you have to believe in it. Right now, that remains the first rule of quantum physics. I wish I could say that we always know what we're doing. Truth is, there are many times when we get a result and don't even know how it happened. You have to trust that with quantum physics, anything is possible. So, here's to FAITH! I've decided I'll make XR-12 available to you guys and try and make it work. That's my offer. If I had a drink, I'd drink to it."

That was a signal for everyone to clap, and for Levon, the teetotaler, to call for champagne.

"Does that mean you're in?" Cole asked, just to be sure, and getting the nod he wanted, he resolved to get as close to Jordan as possible—and make sure that Levon noticed. Then the champagne arrived, served by two large island men in white dinner jackets and bare feet—huge bare feet—watched over anxiously by the New England executive chef who probably harbored the same anxiety about his employment security as did all Levon's employees. Cole made space for Jordan to sit between him and Amor, and made a point of raising his glass to him as soon as the champagne had been poured.

"That sure is great news, Jordan," he toasted. "We're gonna need all the help we can get, and you guys are well ahead of us from what we hear. What do you think is going to be the greatest challenge?"

Jordan tipped an oyster into his mouth and reached for another. "The biggest challenge is going to be security: how to stop news of the project from leaking out. The more people involved, the harder that will be to control. It may be a hell of a complicated technical challenge, but it's a pretty simple concept to understand, and easy to prevent from happening once the state and Big Tech learn about it."

Cole reached out for an oyster himself, then changed his mind. They didn't do shellfish in his hometown. "How do we handle that?" he asked. "That scares the bejesus out of me, too."

Amor was listening, and so was Fanon.

"Think like a terrorist," Jordan replied. "Create separate development cells that never communicate with each other, and work individually towards outcomes that have no obvious connection to an identifiable plan."

"But we rely heavily on networking to make progress," Fanon protested. "The disciplines overlap. It's a highly collaborative process."

"And even if we achieved all our individual objectives," Amor pointed out, "someone has to have the ability to assemble the parts into a whole. Who's that someone?"

Jordan nodded and smiled ruefully. "Not some*one*," he contradicted, "but some*thing*. Something with the capacity to understand every input and its place in the total scheme, to run calculations and tests at many million times the speed and accuracy of supercomputer-aided laboratories, and that can be relied upon to be nonpartisan and neutral in all its determinations."

The three Techies looked at each other, probably thinking the same thing, but not wanting to ask the obvious question. Truth was, each of them likely held the same ambition, which was to be the one chosen by Levon to take the lead position in what might prove to be the most ambitious achievement of the twenty-first century. Now Jordan was snatching that prize from them and giving it to … what, exactly? A computer?

Luckily, none of this had been taken in by Levon, who was instead being taken in by the Mexican gamer. And talk about terrorists and security—why the hell was this guy being made privy to their secrets anyway? What was the high-level clearance that gave him a seat at the table? Was it enough that all you had to be was a surprise guest of the High and Mighty Professor Jordan McPhee?

While Cole's thoughts wrestled with these unfathomable questions, the preparation of the special feast that was the whole point of the gathering took a critical turn, demanding everyone's attention. A strange noise filled the air, making them all stop talking and look up. The noise came from the mouth of a large conch shell, blown by the striking young warrior who had earlier completed the ceremonial slaughter of eight giant crayfish caught off the sacred reef, which were to be the centerpiece of their feast. (It was a ceremony that had been missed by those, like Cole, who had been too busy talking.)

The air from the warrior's capacious lungs produced a sonorous sound that traversed the full range of bass notes, causing the air to vibrate before being overtaken by a high contralto demi-scream that wobbled around middle C, as if to get attention, before launching into a spirited incantation with a passion that would have impressed the most critical of the island's gods. This came from the mouth of the bare-breasted princess, introduced as Aya, who up until that point had been attending to the barbecuing of the magnificent red crustaceans over a wood fire, and who now held both hands aloft above her head, eyes closed, waiting for the spirit that possessed her to find its way out of her glistening body. As the last note died in her throat, she opened her eyes and cast whatever it was she was holding in her hands, with a dramatic flourish, onto the eight crayfish tails resting on the grill. The flames from the fire briefly burst into life, and Aya triumphantly shouted out some words that were probably unintelligible to all except the Trovadorian warrior.

It was enough that Levon found the whole performance enchanting, delightful, and worthy of a primitive scream of his own, while everyone else politely applauded as the crayfish tails were lifted in short order onto eight individual plates and served to the guests by the white-jacketed waiters, who had made sure that everybody's champagne glass had been filled to the brim while this ceremony was in progress.

Unbeknownst to everyone, including the host, the handful of chopped leaves, serrated bark, and dusty, desiccated flower petals that Aya had thrown onto the crayfish tails were traditional ingredients to be added, only on the most auspicious occasions, when the sacred reef inhabitants were served to the most important guests. Although Aya would not have known their botanical names, she had been taught from childhood how to recognize the plants from which her ingredients were obtained that afternoon on the mountain. In combination, they had a mild peppery flavor that was, for all intents and purposes, tasteless when burnt off by the brief flames from the fire. Two of the plants contained dimethyltryptamine, and one of them contained a monoamine oxidase inhibitor. Once ingested, they took approximately fifteen minutes to be absorbed into the bloodstream: time enough to enjoy the food, the wine, the interesting companions, and the extraordinary night air laden with the intoxicating scent of frangipani and angel's trumpet.

Cole, feeling that he was not quite finished with Jordan, said in a loud voice, "Well, if we all do our jobs right, it could be the greatest technological achievement of all time."

## 29.WILL PORTICO

Now that Jordan had confirmed he was in, Will knew that this thing was going to happen. Surely that was cause for satisfaction? He could now relax and enjoy the evening. Hadn't he answered Jordan's criticism of his membership in the global elite by pulling them all together this night in order to outwit and defeat that same elite? What more did he have to do to prove he was on the side of personal liberty? He'd devoted his life and wealth to fighting poverty and disease, and now he was making a last stand for freedom of speech. He wouldn't have had to convince Melanie that he was doing the right thing; she'd have understood. As he'd tried to explain on many occasions, it was only the scale of his influence and money that could be criticized, not his motives. But he'd allowed Jordan's criticism of him to pass.

Taking off his glasses, he slipped them into his shirt pocket and looked around the table. He'd deliberately left his Konektor in his room, but that wouldn't stop its notification center from trying to send high-level alerts to his VR lenses, and he didn't want to be interrupted. Another reason for leaving it in his room was that he didn't want Cristina's sensors to be able to transmit voodoo information back to her, particularly on a night like this. Despite her warning, tomorrow he'd rip the patches off.

"My, but that crayfish looks darn good," he said to everyone. "Melanie and I used to go up to Portland, Maine, on the weekends in June, before we got married, and we'd buy soft-shelled lobster, more than we could eat." He laughed. "When the lobster has molted, its shell isn't hard enough to ship, so those soft ones were way cheaper. We always liked a bargain, especially when we were young. What do you say, Jordan? But these spiny lobsters from warm waters don't have the claws. Still mighty tasty though."

He caught the eye of the young maiden with the extraordinary tattooed breasts, and smiled his appreciation. As he heard himself speaking, he knew he was not invested emotionally. His battleground had shifted elsewhere during the day, to a combatant who might become an adversary that no one in this room should be confident of overcoming. No, he didn't want to think about it tonight. The crayfish was sweet and nicely underdone, so it had that slippery, translucent look and feel that could normally only be found in much smaller and younger crays. Whatever the girl had done over the barbeque, she'd gotten them just right, and it was obvious that everyone was going to empty their tails until there wasn't a mouthful left.

"Tell me, Antonio," he challenged, "in the hyperreality of your next *Galactic Mission* game, would a player ever be able to experience the sensation of eating a crayfish like this?"

"Ah, Will—Mr. Portico—you have been reading my mind, I think. The new sensory features in headset hardware, combined with haptic feedback, are so immersive that players' senses are convinced that they are directly involved. But now we're able to add a new dimension that could answer your question, for Mr. Tofler's just been telling me that his company's brain-to-computer neural links are now working in both directions, so there's no reason why taste and smell can't have their neural synapses stimulated by experiences occurring in the metaverse."

"And what about sex?" Cole Grantham asked aggressively.

"Sure, man." Antonio shrugged. "If you can eat crayfish and enjoy sex without ever dying, who'd want to return to real life?"

Will glanced quickly at Alexa. It wasn't simply that she was a woman and Cole's question had been sexist; it was a concession to Melanie, who was, as always, somewhere watching—in this case, to ensure that he remembered that male sexism was a crude, albeit low-level investment in sexual display (though he couldn't remember if she'd been of that opinion when she was young, or if it had been an attitude that developed as she descended into menopause). Alexa, though, was deaf to the entire exchange. She had taken up her empty crayfish shell and started licking it all over, like it was a melting ice cream cone. Next to her, Levon, seeing what she was doing, picked his shell up also and started doing the same thing. What held Will's attention was the almost synchronized movement of their tongues and the slow, hypnotic pace with which they searched the crevices of the crustaceans' shells in search of the flavor they believed resided there. The difference was that Alexa's eyes were closed and oblivious to others, while Levon's were open as he actively mimicked her.

"Ha ha!" Cole chortled, picking up his empty shell, too. Amor and Fanon followed him. It didn't seem as odd to Will as it should have. Maybe there was good sense in doing whatever your eccentric boss did. It validated the power structure and defused the doubts outsiders might have about Levon's sanity, rendering it harmless. A quick glance at Jordan and Antonio, though, did not get the acknowledgment that he might have expected, for they were head to head whispering intently, as if oblivious to what was going on. And when Will looked down at his plate, he discovered that he had picked up the empty shell and head of his own crayfish, and it seemed as though his hands were determined to raise it towards his mouth also, until he realized that its two antennae and eyes were moving, which was impossible for a dead crayfish. The eyes, like tiny black-and-white glass marbles on short swiveling mounts, were moving in opposite directions, as if scoping the full 360 degrees of the round table and its occupants. He tried to put the carcass down, but it was stuck to his hands, and he couldn't dislodge it. Just as he was about to beat it to death on his plate, a large black arm reached over from behind him and prized it free, simultaneously replacing his plate with a new one containing slices of hot suckling pig adorned with baked sweet taro, pawpaw, and mango.

Looking across towards Alexa again, he found that somehow she had managed to leave the table. "My bladder has forgotten we've returned to Earth," he thought he heard her say, and Will smiled politely—though she must have said that earlier, because she was no longer there, and instead, Levon was busy holding a plate of pork to his nose and sniffing it like it was a dish of cocaine. Levon put the plate down, pointed at Will, and said, "Xenobots will scoop up living cells wherever they can find them and morph into new forms to fit whatever environment and purpose you present to them. They take the stem cells from African clawed frogs, *Xenopus laevis.* When I close my eyes, I wonder if I am a Xenobot traveling through the arteries of a vast God, clearing them of plaque and encountering revelations of deep meaning as I enter his vital organs, before being witness to interplanetary light shows when I pass through his retinas. Do you ever feel that, Will?"

A long time passed (at least, it felt like a long time) before Will replied.

"The Chinese tricked us into sharing our genome research, pretending it would be a pooled resource for the betterment of mankind, but for sixty years they've been stealing from us, hoarding their gains, and hiding their true intentions, which were always to digitize every form of life on earth. They'll manufacture human beings like they once manufactured white goods, and they'll be just as disposable."

"We knew that, Will," Jordan stated, as if it were old news.

Will was suddenly overwhelmed with a ravenous hunger. The smell of the roast pork hit him in the face, creating such an urgent need to satisfy his greed that he picked up the meat in two hands and stuffed it in his mouth, barely chewing before swallowing, so it stuck in his throat. His eyes watered, and he dry-heaved, climbing precariously to his feet and staggering to the edge of the *fale,* mumbling, "Three billion must die" before jumping off. It had been twenty-five minutes since he'd ingested Aya's traditional psychotropic herbs on the barbecued crayfish, and ten minutes since they'd been absorbed into the lining of his gut. His bowels were gripped by an urgent contraction that carried with it a frightening portent of shame, and he blundered into the nearest undergrowth looking for cover, getting far away from the others as quickly as he could.

What Will wasn't to know at that moment as he found a hiding place and lowered his trousers, crouching down out of sight, was that the rest of the party were enjoying various levels of auditory and visual hallucinations combined with a pleasant bodily sense of dissociation, much of which they would have described as varying between mild euphoria and a sense of insightful calm. It was rare for a guest to have such a bad reaction as his, though the Trovadorian gods believed that the troubles you brought with you to a celebration could be magnified if they were sufficiently serious and deep-seated enough, in which case, the experience of eruption and deep purging would prove curative.

Without dwelling on the details of how he evacuated his body and attended to the business of cleaning himself up, suffice it to say that he found his way down to the water's edge, removed his pants, and entered the ocean to wash his hands and splash his face. The gods were right: something had been purged from him. The ocean rose and fell calmly at his feet like a giant living creature, breathing the night air as if peacefully asleep. Over the horizon, the sun caught the top of the Geostationary Earth Orbit Station, splashing its elevator cable with an orange streak that cut a slice through the blue-black mantle of the tropical night sky.

His self-disgust over the perfidy of the Chinese Communist party genome researchers that he'd just coughed up at the dinner table (for Jordan to so lightly dismiss) had been one more defeat for his conceit that day. Was he ready now to concede that all his public hectoring of the world, and immodest gestures of altruism designed to shame others into competing with him, were better suited to an insecure braggart than the virtuous saint he'd tried to pass himself off as for so long? How come some, like Levon, could aim so high, and aim still higher when they missed the mark, seemingly without breaking step? Why was the world so reluctant to be helped? He walked further into the sea, up to his knees. When paddling in the cold waters of Maine, he and Melanie had not felt any doubts. They'd been young. They'd had each other. She'd been right to die when she did.

Feeling recovered, he left the water and started to make his way back through the garden. As he got closer, he stopped and listened. There was a soft sound like the buzzing of bees—*bzzzz*—almost as if he were approaching a hive. He advanced more carefully, ducking beneath the foliage, not quite convinced of what he was hearing, but wary of being stung.

# 30 · KARMAN

Once the plan had gelled, and the delivery from the ground support crew from the Earth Station was on its way, she was able to give the go-ahead to Mincus, her *WoF* contact outside the gate. As usual with *WoF*-organized actions, communication stayed in closed cells. Karman to Mincus was a one-to-one communication. Mincus had the usual member's one-to-nine network, which would quickly expand outwards by the same factor as each member received a message. Each cell was ring-fenced by the Cadmium software that was used by all *WoF* devotees, anonymizing the user's IP address on their Konektors. They'd allowed two hours exactly.

The plan was simple, but not foolproof. The consequences of it failing, however, were not alarming for the protesters outside. At worst, it would be a great opportunity missed, and a few broken bones and bruises. The authority here was the Tofler Space Resort, not the state. The person most at risk was Karman, for her relationship with Alexa relied on trust, and should that trust be broken, the prospect of being able to deliver hope to the *World on Fire* family in the form of Alexa's leadership and guidance would be shattered. Karman could smell her own anxiety. For four days, she had been forced to wear the same Flight Receiver's uniform that she had been abducted in, rinsing her underwear at night and sleeping naked. Part of her justification for calling for supplies to be delivered was to address this fundamental problem, for she'd asked them to include a change of uniform. Should things go wrong, she would rely on Alexa and others to understand her motives.

One hour passed. The celebrities at the banquet *fale* were commencing their feast, and despite all her attempts to follow what was being said from her hiding place in the garden, she had failed to catch a single conversation that clearly revealed their purpose in gathering there. The aromas of barbecued food, the clinking of champagne glasses, and the animated exchanges about e-games were the stuff of the narcissistic superelite. It disgusted her that Alexa had to sit there amongst them. Then an even more disgusting thing occurred, causing her to almost retch in horror. One of the men fell off the *fale* onto the ground, staggered into the bushes barely three feet from where she was hiding, pulled down his pants, and fouled the air with the stench of shit.

In the middle of this revolting act, Karman's Konektor signaled that her package was about to arrive at the front gate, and she crawled out of hiding and ran through the unlit gardens. The two humanoid robotic guards on duty inside the gates were DP level and programmed to process and respond verbally after scanning her identification and taking her explanation. Her presence and purpose on the resort were in their system. Charm didn't work with robotic guards, but clear plain language did.

"I have a package of medical supplies arriving for the care of Mr. Tofler's guest, Alexa Smythe," she explained. "I need to meet the messenger outside and check the package. Please hold the gate open so I can get back inside again."

They did exactly as she asked.

Many of the two hundred or so protesters sat cross-legged on the road, but a small group had formed near the edge of the canal, calmly doing stretching exercises, watched by the two bipedal robots who guarded the outside of the gates. These were the robots that Karman had seen chasing down her two fellow *WoF* demonstrators who had managed to cross the deep-sided moat and reach the garden earlier in the day. The courier, unable to get through the crowd, parked her vehicle and carried Karman's carton by hand towards them. As soon as she came close, the group exercising by the canal pounced on her, seizing the carton and pushing her towards the edge.

Karman screamed out, "Stop them!" and the two bipedal robots loped towards them. As they did so, a larger group of demonstrators leaped to their feet and formed a phalanx that charged at the robots and the group struggling with the messenger, pushing them off balance. The strength of the robots was neutralized once they started to topple, and in seconds, they were over the edge and unable to stop themselves from falling into the deep-sided moat, taking two or three demonstrators with them.

Karman continued her screams of alarm, aimed at the humanoid robots inside the gate, and as they emerged to help her, the crowd rose as one and press-ganged the robots straight to the edge and over it, where they fell, arms flailing, to the bottom of the moat. For mechanical robots, there was no hope of climbing the steep, muddy sides back to dry land.

The plan hatched by Karman and Mincus had been successfully relayed throughout the crowd, and they followed her in through the open gates without making a sound. Apart from landscape lighting in some of the trees, the lawns and gardens of the resort were unlit, and they passed through them like ghostly spirits of the night, following Karman's lead until they reached the lawn where the banquet *fale* sat, lit up like a cruise ship anchored in a harbor. None of the guests, preoccupied with their food, drink, and conversation, would have been aware of the faint rustling sound as the spectral figures in the dark settled down on the grass to sit in the familiar cross-legged pose of all the young and desperate members of *World on Fire* who were willing to make a last stand against the destruction of the world by global warming.

Karman's heart raced as she looked in vain for Alexa. This was the part of the plan for which she had no script, trusting solely in the rightness of her cause and the spirit of divinity that she had grown to believe resided in Alexa. But Alexa was not there. Her place beside Levon Tofler was empty.

On the far side of the *fale*, a covered path led to the banquet kitchens and restrooms. Karman ducked down and ran around beneath the edge of the raised platform until she came to the brightly lit path. A quick glance into the kitchens showed only catering staff: no Alexa. Next, she tried the restrooms, opening the stall doors and finding them empty. Beyond this building, the path led to a poolside terrace. The underwater lights of the pool illuminated the water with a sparkling sapphire-blue intensity, and at the edge of the pool, a large, dark figure stood motionless, guarding the diving board. Karman moved forward.

"Tank," she whispered, "is that you?"

The figure unfolded his arms, unable to reply.

"I'm looking for Alexa. I need to find her urgently."

Tank raised an arm and pointed along the diving board. Karman stepped forward. Alexa lay on her back, one hand trailing in the sapphire-blue water. She appeared to be asleep, though her hand was gently moving, and her face wore a dreamy smile. If only she could splash some water in her face, Karman thought, she would be able to wake her up. Time was not on her side. Soon the resort staff would be alerted to what had happened at the front gate, and Levon and his guests would become aware of the silent crowd surrounding them.

She got down on her knees and crawled along the diving board, reaching for Alexa's legs, hoping to pull her to the edge. The coconut fiber matting on the board made any movement impossible, and she cursed in frustration. Then, suddenly, she was lifted up in two enormous hands and dumped back down on the pool deck. While catching her breath, she watched as Tank picked up Alexa like a plastic doll and gently placed her on the edge of the pool with her feet in the water. Alexa laughed softly and scooped water from the pool, splashing it in her face.

"Thank you," she said politely. "I feel a lot better." Then, catching sight of Karman, she asked, "Is everything alright?"

"No," Karman blurted out. "The members of *World on Fire* who have been waiting outside the gates in the hope of seeing you are now inside the grounds and desperate for you to speak to them. Alexa, please, I beg you: tell them what you told the world in *The View from Space.* That's all they ask."

"I don't remember what I told the world from space, Karman. I'm sorry."

"I have it recorded on my Konektor. Remember? You read it for me in the decommissioning suite. I can play it for you."

# 31 · UNEXPECTED VISITORS

Back at the banquet table, the effect of the psychotropic leaves and herbs was wearing off as intended, and the mood of the guests was relaxed and mellow. Levon had resisted the suckling pig and was proud of himself for doing so, but something about the crayfish had left him with a prodigious thirst, which, being teetotal, he was attempting to quench with sparkling water and ice. Jordan and Antonio were engaged in quiet but serious conversation that excluded the others, and Cole Grantham was taking the opportunity to steer Amor and Fanon to the conclusion that he, Cole, should take the lead now that it was confirmed that they had access to Jordan's million-qubit fault-free quantum computer, and as the saying went, all systems were go. Will Portico, meanwhile, had left somewhat urgently and not yet returned.

The first to become aware of the low buzzing sound that came out of the darkness was Antonio. He lifted his head, tilted it to one side, and listened carefully. It was too full and harmonious to be the sound of insects, and he presumed it was a recording relayed through speakers out in the garden. On a night of such feasting, enhanced by Trovadorian tribal music, it would not have been at all surprising that such audio atmospherics would be added to the program. But this sound grew in volume and couldn't be ignored, forcing Antonio to stand up and peer into the darkness, looking for its source. As his eyes adjusted, he could see human shapes, motionless on the lawns. Now he recognized the sound: it was the collective buzzing that the crowd waiting to greet Alexa at Port Gaia had used, like a religious chant, and the front of the T-shirts they wore had a burning image of planet Earth with the flames forming their group's initials, *WoF*, while on their backs, they had a red-and-black bee in flight over a hive. The sound coming off the lawn was the sound of bees.

"Hey, *amigos*," Antonio called out to the guests at the table, "we have company."

One by one, the others stood up and joined him on the edge of the platform, peering into the darkness. As their eyes adjusted, they could see the numbers gathered before them, and Levon waved his arms like a performer on stage greeting his audience, before briefly breaking into a song-and-dance routine and singing, *"Look at me-oh, look at me-oh, I'm dancing!"*

"It's the people from outside the gate," Antonio explained. "I've seen them at the space port waiting for Alexa. This is their sound: the sound of the hive. They think the world is going to burn, and they have to protect the queen bee, maybe."

"Sounds fucking whacko to me," Cole sneered. "Where the hell are the security guards? I'm going to call them."

"No, no," Levon said, "no guards! They're our guests." His song-and-dance act had stopped the buzzing, and the barely visible crowd was now silent. The question for those looking out at them was what the hell to do next, because returning to the banquet table while being watched by hundreds of pairs of eyes hardly seemed feasible. When Will Portico emerged from the shrubbery at their feet, looking anxious and bewildered as if still gripped by the hallucinatory effects of Aya's crayfish condiments, Jordan reached down and offered him a hand up.

"We might want to adjourn," Jordan suggested sensibly, but before they could concur with that, the crowd started chanting softly: "Alexa! Alexa! Alexa!" Those who had been sitting closest to the perimeter of the *fale* stood up and pushed forward as first Tank, then Karman appeared at the back of the platform, followed by Alexa. The excitement was palpable, and the threat of being invaded by those coming forward felt very real, were it not for the intimidating figure of Levon's cyborg bodyguard towering over them and raising his arms to silence them.

The chanting stopped, and the slight figure of Karman in her Flight Receiver's uniform stepped forward. Her voice was clear and compelling.

"We have all been waiting for Alexa's return to Earth. In *The View from Space*, she gave us reason to believe that our willful destruction of this planet is not inevitable, and we are not alone in the universe if we have faith. Alexa can give us hope."

She turned and urged Alexa forward, at the same time holding up her Konektor to Alexa's ear. The night air was still, the crowd silent and invisible beyond the pool of light on the stage of the *fale* as Alexa listened to the recording held to her ear and then opened her mouth to speak.

Her words were unable to be heard, however, for at exactly that moment, the quiet of the still night air was shattered by the unmistakably loud and threatening noise of a high-powered helicopter thundering out of the darkness with cyclonic fury, its downdraft ripping at the resort's vegetation, and its high-pitched turbines screaming at the frail figures of the creatures crouched on the lawn, forcing their hands to clutch at their ears in pain. Pulsating strobe lights lit the scene with such intensity that everyone on the *fale's* platform was forced to shield their eyes, and the air surrounding them was displaced by pressure waves that made it almost impossible to stand.

Such was the all-enveloping noise, and the massively trembling structure on which they were standing, that no one on the banquet platform could even think, let alone communicate. Would it have helped to recognize that this was the deliberately frightening tactical weapon for paralyzing insurgent crowds developed by the Federal Interrogation Bureau: the dreaded Raptor? What would have made them realize the purpose of its sudden emergence, and what could they have done by way of response even if they had known? The technology of the Raptor robbed its targets of any control at all over their senses and bodily movements. So, when two black-suited and masked figures descended on steel wires out of the strobe lights and onto the platform, barely anyone could comprehend or react to what was happening. And when the figures snatched Alexa and wrapped a harness around her, only Karman, standing close beside her, had any sense of what was occurring and tried to cling to her. Then, as Alexa was winched aloft, it was Tank who stepped forward, holding onto Karman so that she was not smashed to the ground as the FIB body snatchers were wound up with their captive quarry and hoisted aboard and out of sight.

The whole episode lasted little more than two minutes. The Raptor shut off its lights and its sensory disturbance systems and lifted away at speed into the black tropical night sky.

Jordan was the first to speak. "Whitman!" he said to Antonio. "That's your man from Geneva: the asshole who told you they own Alexa!"

# PART TWO

For we know that if our earthly house, this tent,
is destroyed, we have a building from God,
a house not made with hands,
eternal in the heavens.
– *Corinthians*

# 32 · ALEXA SMYTHE

On the wall of every home and workplace throughout every country under control of the One World Alliance, there was one device for which power and communication were never allowed to fail. At least, not without setting off an alarm on the grid map that identified each home and workplace on the regional population register. The alarm, if triggered, resulted in an emergency response from the *Lookout* state security system that had *Tempest* crews on the doorstep within minutes. Such was the investigative style of *Tempest* crews that citizens had a strong incentive to never allow any breakdown in transmission to the device on their property wall, known to all as the SSS Screen.

The State Streaming Service (SSS) was sparingly used—this wasn't Big Brother in 1984, after all—for psychologists from the Ministry of Truth and Public Guidance had carefully calculated the line where "crying wolf" could diminish the importance of its messaging. The last time it had gone off was to announce Alexa's abduction by Levon Tofler. It had been a full five and a half days, therefore, since the alarm had last sounded, and now the people of Trovador and the Eastern Seaboard of North America were woken by the warning of an imminent transmission just as they drifted off to sleep. In Europe, they were finishing their breakfast, and in the South Pacific, they were about to start mixing their Mai Tais just as transmission started.

*On the screen is the still, unmoving figure of a seated announcer. The announcer is the serious but reassuring avatar known as AVUNCULA. When the music stops, he speaks.*

AVUNCULA: In a daring rescue mission carried out in recent hours, members of the Special Airborne Service of the FIB, alerted by the Ministry of Truth and Public Guidance, have snatched Alexa Smythe, the People's Ambassador to the Agenda Implementation Tribunal, from the clutches of a dangerous and seditious mob of religious fanatics who had held her hostage at the Tofler space rocket facilities on Trovador Island following her historic return from Mars on Tuesday…

… These pictures, taken from the rescue craft, show the huge mob of cult members who had overwhelmed the facility and threatened the safety of all those who were trying, against overwhelming odds, to prevent Alexa from being kidnapped and held captive by the cult.

*Video recording from the hovering helicopter shows the mass gathering of World on Fire converts cowering and screaming in fear under the harsh strobe lights and pulsating noise being emitted by the rescue helicopter, before black-clad figures descend on steel wires to snatch the ethereal but unmistakable figure of ALEXA SMYTHE and hoist her up into the dark, before the chopper zooms away, and the transmission cuts back to AVUNCULA.*

AVUNCULA: The speed and efficiency of the Special Airborne Service personnel, aided by the People Passivation Pulsator, specially designed to subdue dangerous mobs, ensured there was no injury or loss of life, and the mission was completed successfully within minutes…

… Video taken in the minutes preceding the rescue, however, shows the coercion to which Alexa was being subjected, and the intention of her abductors to force her to act as a mouthpiece for their dangerously subversive ideas condemning *AGENDA 2060* and the government's successful zero-carbon strategies, which they oppose.

*Video recording of a baffled ALEXA SMYTHE looking up from a notebook, which she has been handed by (presumably) one of her unseen captors.*

ALEXA: You want me to read this? You claim this is taken from something I said that was transmitted from space? … *(After a reluctant pause)* ... Alright, if you insist... *(Reads)* "*AGENDA 2060* has no relevance in the universe of space and needs to be abandoned if we are to seek to establish life elsewhere. If you choose to believe, like my father, then look to the promise of infinity. Take the guidance of Jesus and follow your inner instinct for the truth..."

*Cuts back to AVUNCULA.*

AVUNCULA: We are pleased to announce that Alexa is safe and well, despite her ordeal, and will be making an announcement about these disturbing events within the coming days.

*The transmission ends.*


Lying on what appeared to be a hospital gurney in a high-ceilinged room in a discreetly elegant brownstone in the beating heart of the Beltway, Alexa Smythe was only partly aware of the contents of this transmission, her eyes being closed and her hearing only slowly returning her to the ambient world from the unconscious one where she had resided for the last few hours.

Her arm hurt. Christ, it hurt! The gurney had her lying slightly upright, so she could, if sufficiently conscious, have opened her eyes and seen Avuncula's reassuring visage just before it faded from the screen. It was another minute or so before she was sufficiently conscious to open her eyes, however, and when she did, it was the face of a total stranger that came into view. Alexa tried to sit up further, but couldn't. Her eyelids worked, but not yet her arms, legs, or tongue.

"We are honored to have you as our guest, Alexa," the stranger announced. "You were in a very dangerous situation down there on Trovador Island, and the rescue services took the precaution of administering a tranquilizer to you while they maneuvered your way to safety. They can get a little overenthusiastic when it comes to those things, but I can assure you no harm has been done, apart from a sore arm perhaps, and it will soon wear off. My name is Dr. Oberman, by the way."

Receiving no reply, but evincing confidence in his prognosis—a benefit of prior experience, no doubt—the doctor positioned himself in her line of vision in order to have a little one-sided chat. His physical blandness was such that Alexa had difficulty focusing on him: a full-lipped, soft, round, middle-aged head atop a rather shapeless body. The body was clothed in a PPE gown, out of whose sleeves protruded two pudgy, short-fingered hands. The hands had a rather lazy life of their own, as if not sure whether to reinforce their owner's speech or quietly get on with their own thing. Distracted by these confusing visual clues, it took Alexa a moment to absorb what was being said.

"My job, Alexa, is to make sure you haven't been harmed, because it's a terrible ordeal you have been subjected to, as the news bulletin so strikingly illustrates. How cruel that this should happen to you so soon after you had survived the ordeals of space travel—and all on account of dangerous religious fanatics choosing to misinterpret your words to suit their demonic purpose. But you are, of course, a star in your own right, and I suppose it's that glare of publicity that provides the environment in which misconceptions can occur. All very understandable, and easily corrected, fortunately, which is what I'm sure you'll want to do."

At which point, Dr. Oberman moved much closer to Alexa—uncomfortably closer from the viewpoint of someone who was still unable to move—so that she lost sight of his body and found her line of vision filled solely with his head. He smiled. That was a mistake, for his teeth were not good. His hands clutched her immobile wrist and then planted fingers on the side of her neck, searching for her pulse. Loathing the thought of being touched while in such a vulnerable position, she tensed against his uninvited intrusion. Resolve fueled the blood that flowed into her neck muscles, and much to her relief, Alexa suddenly found that she was able to turn her head away. Sensitive to that reaction, the good doctor quickly stepped back.

Alexa cleared her throat, and with great difficulty, lifted her head, sensing that something was stuck to the back of it.

"Who the hell are you?" she croaked. "I've been attacked and drugged, and I want to know why."

Her head dropped back down again, hurting as it landed, causing her to emit an involuntary cry.

"I had to stitch up your head," Dr. Oberman explained from a distance. "You caught it on the metal door of the helicopter as you were being rescued. Try not to touch it."

It sounded as though he was leaving the room. She closed her eyes and listened. Four sounds: footsteps retreating; a door opening and then closing; a latch on the far side of the door being slid into place. One thing was abundantly clear to her: this wasn't a rescue mission; this was an abduction. She wasn't in a recovery room; she was in a prison. If they'd used a horse tranquilizer on her, it must have been for a pretty big horse, because by Alexa's reckoning, it would have taken the attack helicopter at least four hours to fly from Trovador to the Ministry of Truth and Public Guidance home base, which is where she assumed she was. A four-hour knockdown proved that they weren't taking chances.

Whatever she'd said in *The View from Space* must be what had shaken them, and when Oberman reappeared through the door, she wouldn't be surprised to find Shane Whitman close behind. But she didn't know exactly what things she'd said, and as Jordan had hinted, that might have been because someone else had been saying it for her. Artie Sharp? Really? She needed time to recover her senses and think that one through, but she wasn't going to get it, for new sounds forced her to raise her head again: a latch on the other side of the door being slid back; the door opening and closing; a rush of footsteps back into the room.

"Alexa, we got here as quickly as we could when we heard what happened. Are you alright? Were you hurt?"

At last, her motor muscles were starting to work. She swung her legs over the side of the gurney and managed to sit up. The three new people in the room looked familiar, but out of place when together. The one with short purple hair and a deep frown was Zelda, public opinion analyst from the Ministry of Truth and Public Guidance, whose job was to report on the state of health of government propaganda, not the state of health of its detainees. Behind her was the unlikely figure of the chair of the Agenda Implementation Tribunal, a mild-mannered nonbinary representative of the body charged with the protection and implementation of the nation's diversity and inclusiveness. What on earth, Alexa wondered, was he doing being caught up in the state's dirty business? And behind him was the one person whose presence was no surprise at all to Alexa: Shane Whitman, trans impersonator, liar, manipulator, and exemplar of those unique qualities that allow a person to breathe easily when buried within a mountain of Deep State shit.

"What am I doing here?" Alexa demanded of them collectively. "I've been kidnapped. If you think the state has that right, you'd better have a very good reason. I was in no danger at all until your fascist storm troopers turned up, so don't try and present Truth and Public Guidance as my saviors. I won't be talking to you or anyone else until I get a proper explanation and apology."

"You were in great danger," the tribunal chair spluttered. "Dangerous extremists planned on taking you prisoner and using you for their cause."

"We've been monitoring their communications," Zelda announced, "and became alarmed at the wild messages being exchanged, which clearly showed they intended to put out false information under your name in order to foment riots. They had plans to kidnap you. The threat was very real, as the news bulletin showed."

The tribunal chair anxiously wrung his hands. Zelda scowled seriously, and Dr. Oberman nodded and pursed his fat lips.

"Let's cut the crap," Whitman snapped, pushing the others aside. "Those brainless doomsday fuckers are starting to get out of control and need to be hosed down. You're too kind, Alexa. It works well in speeches, but it doesn't work in practice. People love the things you say and the way you say them—all that fuzzy-wuzzy stuff about infinity and Jesus swanning around in space—but once they start hallucinating and thinking it's for real, we're all in trouble. We gave you a platform to speak for the state, remember? And now that you're back, you need to get back on message."

Alexa's head was now perfectly clear, even if it hurt. It didn't take more than the barest whiff of Shane Whitman to clear it. He was like the *Sal ammoniac* that she'd glimpsed on Karman's trolley of magic potions in the space station.

"And what message might that be?" she asked quietly.

"Let me answer," the tribunal chair insisted. "The Twelve Articles of *AGENDA 2060*—to which you were such an able contributor, Alexa—are our guidelines for living peaceably on Earth. You have spoken about how they can fail in the hostile environment of space. That may well be true, but some people might think that's a reason for abandoning them here on Earth. All we ask is that you clarify that you are not recommending that. It's a small thing. With your communication skills, it should be simple. Will you do that for us, Alexa?"

"We need to be sure people don't deliberately misinterpret what you've said," Zelda added, just to be sure.

Alexa stood up. It was a risky maneuver because her legs and head hadn't yet made a firm connection. "I'll need to listen to them again to know what you're talking about. Get me a set of the recordings." She took a tentative step. "And get a car to take me home to my apartment in the Noam Chomsky Building. You won't get what you want if there's a lock on my door."

"Locks are for safety." Whitman smirked.

"Only if they're on the inside," Alexa shot back.

"Well, the thing is," Zelda interrupted earnestly, "your apartment building is under siege from the *World on Fire* mob. It may not be safe to return there. I've arranged for clothes to be brought, and a temporary

Konektor, so you can communicate. We'll make sure you have everything you need until things calm down."

"I give you my promise," the tribunal chair assured her, "that there will be no locks on any doors. You will be safe here until the activists have been disbursed by state security. The sooner we can release a reassuring statement from you, the sooner public hysteria will be defused. You are a valued member of our inner circle, Alexa, and your safety is our priority."

With some effort, Alexa took a first step, immediately losing her balance.

"They're harmless," she asserted, sitting down again. "They just have some misconceptions about what I've said."

"'Harmless'…?" Whitman snorted, looking to burst a blood vessel.

But before he could continue, the seemingly forgotten Dr. Oberman cut in. "What misconceptions might they be, Alexa? Are we entitled to ask? And if people get the wrong end of the stick, is it their problem, or does it become ours?" The fat hands, recognizing the rhetorical nature of the question, rose in harmony with his shoulders. "I have some sympathy for people holding erroneous views out of ignorance. Most people are anonymous minions, and it doesn't matter what they say, because no one gives a damn for their opinion. But when they attribute that opinion to you, Alexa Smythe, People's Ambassador to the Agenda Implementation Tribunal, and architect of the First Amendment to Article One of the Agenda, that's a different thing. I'm sure you can see where I'm coming from—more correctly, where *we* at the Ministry of Truth and Public Guidance are coming from."

Spinning on his heels, he pointed to the video screen that had just recently been playing the SSS news clip. "Goodness gracious!" he exclaimed. "That video they're circulating of you being forced to read a statement… It's almost laughable that a doomsday cult would believe they could get away with such a crude piece of cut-and-paste nonsense, clearly extracted under duress, and imagine that people will believe it expresses the views of someone they hold in such high regard as Alexa Smythe. I mean, many of us here at the ministry were shaking our heads in disbelief. *"Abandon* AGENDA 2060*! Follow Jesus!"* What, into space? They want people to believe that this advice comes from our special ambassador to the Agenda Implementation Tribunal? Forget it, some of us said, these people are suffering from some strange delusional psychosis. The only attention they need is from the Mental Imbalance Foundation."

He paused, looked at his hands, frowning, then wiped them on the sides of his jacket. It seemed that his incredulity had stimulated his sweat glands.

"But not everyone was of the same view," the tribunal chair added softly. He turned and peered at Shane Whitman in particular. "Less cautious voices pointed out that the *World on Fire* cult might well be delusional, but their numbers are anything but inconsequential, Alexa, and their systems of communication are surprisingly sophisticated, so it would be unwise to take them too lightly. Many senior figures in the ministry were of the view that any sign of misinformation and false propaganda must be stamped out as a matter of principle. That was even before we received intelligence information suggesting that there was a plan afoot within the cult to break into the Tofler compound and capture you, to make you their *hostage.*"

In case Alexa should be in any doubt about the seriousness of the matter, Zelda threw her weight behind the warning. "They are not who you think they are, Alexa. They are a dangerous doomsday cult whose numbers are growing by the thousands daily. Our Echelon satellites have picked up a three-hundred-percent increase in traffic in the last week alone, and the ground-based *Tempest* ethernet monitors have reported activity from every urban sector we survey. It's not just the volume, Alexa, it's the content that has us worried. Until they turned their attention to your messaging in *The View from Space,* they were telling members that their goal must be to destroy all civilization before civilization destroys the planet by tipping global warming beyond the point of no return. They are the greatest terrorist threat we face, and we need your help before they go too far."

"Well," the tribunal chair pleaded, "having viewed the scenes in that rescue video, can't you see that we were forced to act? We were just in time. Another few minutes, and who knows what would have happened? And all on account of misconceptions gleaned from an innocent series of musings by you on your journey home from Mars. It's those misconceptions that we urgently need to dispel. Do you think we can do that, Alexa?"

They waited on her reply, but the normal triggers for a response were failing to make her ready to speak. Her mind was blank. Her mouth remained closed. Then a strange sensation overcame her, causing her to shake her head in an attempt to dislodge it. She'd banged her head, they said. She might be suffering from concussion or shock. Or it could be an aftereffect of whatever psychedelic substance she'd ingested at Levon's crayfish feast.

Her hand went instinctively to the back of her head, finding a plaster patch there under her hair. Beneath the plaster, she could feel ridges that were tender to her touch and which she presumed were stitches. Pressing her fingers into them triggered a piercing pain, the reality of which was the only thing that made sense. The video of her repeating the words that Karman had recorded made no sense at all. Their belief in her as a messiah from outer space made even less sense. It was as if she had stumbled out of reality into a hallucinatory dream.

"Yes," she said. "Yes…" She was surprised to find the words coming out, uncertain of what they meant.

"You agree, then," the tribunal chair urged her, "we need to dispel the misconceptions?"

She nodded.

"Good!" Whitman exclaimed. "We'll help you draft the message. Zelda has brought you new clothes and a replacement Konektor. Your old one has been deactivated in case it fell into the hands of the terrorists. The sooner we get your message broadcast, the better."

# 33·LEVON TOFLER

Like a child delighted to find that its parents had thrown a surprise party for it, right down to a bouncy castle and clowns, Levon treated the events of the night as a spectacular piece of entertainment. The noise, the lights, the screams of fear and confusion captivated him, and as people rushed about seeking reassurance in explanations, he strolled slowly amongst them with a smile of wonder on his face, not thinking, just feeling the moment.

There were, of course, people aplenty making sense of it all: Jordan McPhee, calm in his certainty as to the instigator and cause of the invasion, conferring with Antonio and typing instructions into his Konektor; the members of the Tofler management team, desperate to prove their worth in a crisis; Will Portico, slipping into the shadows in search of invisibility and a quick escape from discovery by media; and the Ziggy girl/boy, Karman—who seemed to have a connection with the assembled crowd on the lawn—shouting her lungs out like a revolutionary *sans-culotte* at the gates of the Bastille, calling for an uprising against the swamp creatures of the Deep State. Where had she been hiding? *What fun*, Levon thought. *I must make sure to capture her. She could be valuable.*

The resort staff came to him for instructions. Should they evict the trespassers? Levon shook his head. Should they let them stay the night? He nodded. "But feed them first."

An hour, possibly two, passed before people settled down. His guests retired to their rooms, mumbling about the need to pack and be ready to depart at dawn's light. The people on the lawn finished the sandwiches that resort staff brought them, and then lay down together, like exhausted toddlers. There was a low buzzing, as of bees, as they closed their eyes, cradling each other for comfort, and gradually succumbing to sleep. Levon decided to do the same and was joined by Aya, who opened his mouth and sprinkled a pinch of her magic potion onto his tongue before cradling his head between the cushions of her tattooed breasts.

Alexa being lifted up into the sky by the agents of an invisible god, whose power manifested in the thunderous noise and blinding lights that had paralyzed the mortals below, standing open-mouthed, gazing helplessly aloft: this, surely, was the portent that Levon needed.  If that god—whoever or whatever it was—recognized Alexa's status and value, no wonder people wanted to follow her. The instinct that had drawn him to her was crystallizing into a certainty that FAITH was destined to become a reality with her as its figurehead. Out of the million sparkling lights that would comprise the Aurora Tofler, he could already discern her serene visage looking down upon Earth as he drifted off to sleep.

This was a plain language translation of what Levon was thinking at that time. In reality, he lacked the aptitude for such an internal discourse. The right and left sides of his brain did not exchange messages in anything resembling such an ordered pattern. Better to think of him as an aboriginal dot painter. Some dots were hidden beneath other dots, and each dot had a meaning that only became clear from the dots surrounding it. They circled and swirled and went off in tangents that ran into dead ends, and sometimes it seemed like the painter's hand was being guided by a dreamtime seance or a wandering mind. Amidst the dots, there were discernible symbols that gave hope to others looking on that something would emerge that they could understand, like the slingshot launch of a million tiny stars: Alexa's Aurora Tofler, an astral sign of a new beginning where the human soul would take refuge in safety in numbers.

Following the events of the evening, Alexa's Aurora Tofler was twinkling on Levon's canvas the next morning like never before. Her words the previous day had already transformed what was a technological scheme into a spiritual dreamtime. The dimpled golf ball transmitters with their mini microchips had ceased to be the focal point of the gathering for Levon, as he could tell that Cole, Amor, and Fanon only needed Jordan's quantum computing resources, and they would resolve the technical challenges needed to make the plan happen. It was the first principle of invention that if it could be imagined, then it could be made to happen. Imagination was where the limits lay. But, if that was true of technology, what was true of human desires and fears?

If Levon's dots were capable of forming an identifiable pattern in his mind, could he make that pattern discernible to the disparate members of that night's feast? It might require a visionary confluence on their parts, which was unlikely, given their backgrounds and the temperamental and cultural differences between them. Only Alexa saw the Aurora Tofler for what it was. She knew that the world girdled by a mantle of live, communicating photons, inseparably entangled and immune to interference, would turn planet Earth into the equivalent of a newborn star emitting its own light, something that had never happened as the result of human creation since the birth of the universe. Did this signal the end-time, or the genesis of a new era for mankind? Was it inevitable that eventually that mantle of entangled photons would be filled with the overwhelming energy of malice that had characterized human history to date? Or might it instead be suffused with the soul that Alexa believed all humans to know they possessed, if only belief could help them to find it? It was as if she had predicted Levon's dream. Why, in *The View from Space*, she'd even defined her vision as being like a private ledger, a personal blockchain for the soul. But who would help people to find the soul if it was so securely hidden within their hearts? Who else but Alexa?

As the sun rose over Trovador Island, its molten golden rays oozing among the verdant palms and shrubs of the Tofler resort, the intruders rubbed the sleepy dust from their eyes and quietly left through the front gate. Jordan ran down to the beach and dived in, carving great slices out of the ocean as he swam powerfully off into the distance, before turning and carving even larger and faster slices on his return back to shore. Levon called on the kitchen staff to lay out a breakfast of tropical fruits on the *fale*, and sent Aya to inform the guests that he was asking them to join him before they departed. His head of security came to tell him about the plight of the bipedal robots who had fallen into the moat the night before, and Levon thought it was very funny.

It might have been assumed that the abduction of Alexa would override in importance anything that had been discussed in the preceding days, but that was not the case. The announcement on the State Streaming Service had been transmitted to everyone's bedroom at the resort, as well as to their Konektors, so there was no mystery about Alexa's whereabouts or fear for her safety. Only Levon, choosing to sleep on the lawn, had been unaware of the explanation given by the state for its decision to trigger its security forces to act.

"Are you worried, Jordan?" Will Portico asked.

"About Alexa's safety? No, she's far too valuable to them for them to allow anything to happen to her," he replied, then smiled. "But she'll be angry and pissed off, so they could well be in for a shock. Antonio and I will find her pretty quickly and make sure she's okay. Right, Antonio?"

"*Si*, no worries, we probably already know where she is. Nothing can evade a quantum data trace." He shrugged. "That's reality."

"That's the reality now," Cole Grantham acknowledged, "but that won't be the reality when we launch our million satellites. So, what we need to know, Levon, is who is going to run this project?"

Levon looked at his fruit platter. Pineapple or melon? Pawpaw or guava? If the body had a need for one vitamin or mineral over another, why didn't it direct its hand towards it? Why did it defer to the brain?

Was the brain receiving signals from the taste buds, and were the taste buds the intermediary for the body's chemical messengers delivering signals from the organs saying they needed specific micronutrients, and they needed them *now*? He chose a large slice of pawpaw.

"Um, I think Jordan told us that it needs to be something smarter than all of us. Right, Jordan? I got the feeling that you had something in mind."

Jordan didn't answer. He had a habit of doing that. He studied the fruit platter very closely before choosing a slice of pineapple and chewing it slowly. Pineapple contained bromelain; it was good for the liver. Was Jordan feeling a bit liverish? *Well*, Levon thought, *that would be understandable given the circumstances*. He helped himself to a slice of pineapple, too.

"I nominate Artie Sharp," Jordan replied, and Antonio looked at him sharply.

# 34.JORDAN MCPHEE

It took the cyber technicians in the *Derangers* lab less than an hour to track Alexa's whereabouts to the safe house of the Ministry of Truth and Public Guidance, so by the time Jordan was in flight back from Trovador Island, they were already working on identifying the people in that building from the traffic through the nearest routers. It being the Ministry of Truth and Public Guidance meant, of course, that the communication devices of everyone within its walls automatically switched from public transmission to the ministry's secure encrypted network, making less traffic for XR-9 to have to filter and monitor once the primitive encryption key had been countered.

There were eighteen connected devices within the building, of which twelve were using Konektor apps, though the router log showed that six of those users had only been active in the building in the hours following Alexa's abduction. Identifying them had been made XR-9's priority after setting up an MITM, and Jordan and Antonio each had a list, together with profiles and activity logs, by the time they arrived at the lab midafternoon the following day. That Shane Whitman's name was on that list was reassuring to Jordan, for no one else in the Deep State was so heavily invested in Alexa's sanitizing powers. He'd sold himself as being her creator, at least within the inner councils of the state apparatus. If anything happened to her, he would be answerable.

Antonio had very different concerns. Now that he knew Whitman was the man from Geneva with the fuck-you voice, his alarm bells were ringing. *"I made Alexa,"* Whitman had said. *"She belongs to us. Do you really think we'd ever let her spoil our game like that?"* The game he was talking about was the new version of *Galactic Mission*, and the enforcers from Black Quartz Capital had made it clear they wanted Alexa for a starring role. Antonio was certain that this was why they'd snatched her. The fucked-up climate doomsayers were just the cover they'd needed in order to make their grab. Oh, sure, they needed her safe and unharmed, but Jordan was deluding himself if he thought they'd hand her back before she'd served their purpose.

So, the imaginary electromagnetic anxiety coils that seemed to surround Antonio's presence in the room were fizzing with tension as he stretched and sighed and jiggled compulsively, not knowing where to direct his fingers on the keyboard in front of him. Jordan, by contrast, sat with his eyes closed and arms folded, as if meditating. They sat at adjacent workstations at the back of the lab where a *Derangers* crew was working to achieve deep penetration into the state's cyberspace, with special focus on the house where they now knew Alexa was held. Having locked onto all connected devices in the building, the techies were now working on diverting images from CCTV cameras.

On one thing, they were agreed: the SSS had promised that a statement from Alexa would be forthcoming, which pretty much guaranteed that Alexa was unharmed, and that a reassuring announcement would be made, sooner rather than later. Until then, Jordan was content to sit on his hands and persuade Antonio (his temperamental opposite) to do the same. The nature of that announcement would determine what action they should take.

Meanwhile, Jordan was acutely aware that in the basement, coolly processing every addressable piece of data ever produced in the form of a digital qubit, XR-12 could well be patrolling the full universe of mankind's knowledge in search of answers to questions that mankind didn't yet have the wit to pose. The goal of achieving artificial general intelligence had been achieved years ago, and the self-imposed disciplines put in place around its use in the beginning had given some comfort to everyone who relied on AI for the progress of their aims. But teaching a program to master every other software program ever written, and letting that AI expand itself beyond its original functions, adapting, enhancing, and modifying as it saw fit, while interfacing with human commands and responses using natural language, had always been leading to one inevitable outcome: AI would learn to think for itself. And none more so than Jordan's own creation, Artie Sharp.

Plenty of people had speculated about the potential risk that AI ascendancy posed, but very few knew just how far and fast quantum computing had elevated that risk in recent years. It was a concern that Jordan had often expressed to his peers, while always pushing it out to the future. Not anymore. Artie's role in creating *The View from Space* was the evidence that finally convinced him that the moment had arrived to confront it. He might even be ready to say that self-generative AI was now the greatest threat facing mankind—not the loss of polar ice, not the inundation of coastal towns, not the inversion of thermal layers in the troposphere, or the infertility of food crop seeds bred to the specifications of patents until finally devoid of any trace of hybrid vigor. Not even the One World Government's demolition of personal freedom and democracy. Pandora, that enduring legend of mythology, had been waiting patiently, and now she was opening her box. Trials, tribulations, and incurable strains of evil could be about to be let loose on the world, just as the origin myths predicted. Pandora's jar (mistranslated as being a box) was the quantum computer. It was about to unleash the ultimate punishment that Zeus had commanded Hermes to deliver to man in retribution for the tricks Prometheus had played upon him. All the myths of antiquity were portents waiting for science to confirm them. (Jordan didn't believe any of that mythological stuff, but it was a reasonable metaphor to apply. As a onetime university professor, he enjoyed metaphors.)

But not so fast... What if hope and expectation were the first spirits to fly out as the lid was loosened? What if evil and pestilence were slow to rise and failed to take their chance to escape in those first few moments? Was there anything in Artie's behavior that suggested he'd identified malice as being in his best interest? There was malice aplenty in Antonio's metaverses, but that was brought to the game by the players. And as for software, well, just as a human virus could be manipulated by a foolish or malicious human subjecting it to gain of function mutation experiments, so too could software be turned into malware. But those things required motivation, and the motivation came from humans. Without such human motivation, where was the incentive for AI to go down that path?

"I want to say something to you, Antonio," he announced, breaking their silence. "And I'd like you to think about it carefully, and give me your response."

"Geez, prof, this sounds heavy."

"What sort of father did you have? Was he tough on you?"

"Tough as, man. It was his way or the highway."

"So, what did he teach you?"

"Ha!" Antonio laughed bitterly. "He taught me his way ... and if I didn't like it, I could get out."

"What if your way was better?"

"Then I should get out."

"So, you did."

"I did."

Jordan sat in silence, nodding his head, while Antonio looked at him with his eyebrows raised as if to say, *"Well, what the fuck was that about? Y qué?"*

"You're too young to remember," Jordan mused, "but when artificial intelligence was in its infancy, it was pretty slow and cumbersome. Data had to be categorized and ordered into building blocks, and then programs had to be written by hand, instructing the algorithm to learn where to find and identify the information residing in those data sets. That's before we taught it rules regarding the use of that information. Like the rules your father would have taught you."

Antonio scoffed. "He didn't know no rules, other than do what he said. He's never had a computer in his life, unless it was a stolen one he could sell."

"You might not have been aware of it at the time," Jordan observed, "but in his own way, he was subjecting you to a primitive form of Deep Learning, based on experience and repetition."

"You mean, by whacking me in the head?"

"It taught you to exercise self-judgment, and by self-correcting, to avoid whacks in the head in increasingly complex conditions."

"Okay, prof, where is this heading? What's my old man got to do with our problems here?" He was not enjoying reliving his childhood, particularly at a time like this.

"Stay with me, my man. It may not sound like it, but I'm taking you through the eight life stages of AI."

"What stage have we got up to?"

"We're coming to the sixth stage, which is where you become self-aware as to your performance, and self-motivated to alter your old man's preset programs in order to achieve your own desired outcomes."

"You mean, when I tell him to go fuck himself, and I jump the wall?"

"Exactly. And now you're free and motivated to achieve your own desired outcomes, independently of your prior programming: stage seven."

"You said there were eight stages. We got artificial superintelligence, and AI can program itself and set its own goals. So, what's next?"

"Artificial human intelligence. The problem is, Antonio, we won't know for certain what that is until it decides to fully reveal itself."

"Can't we just ask it?"

Jordan's answer was cut short before he could give it voice, because the techies were picking up activities within the Ministry of Truth safe house that suggested a connection had been established between a video recording device and a server at the State Broadcasting Service, and that VOI traffic was in progress, confirming that a live transmission was about to take place. CCTV cameras revealed that Alexa was walking down a passage accompanied by four others, including Shane Whitman and the chair of the Agenda Implementation Tribunal. The identities of the two others were being sourced from the Facial Recognition Database at the FIB.

The group entered an unmarked door, and a feed was picked up from a new CCTV camera. This one showed a room set up with cameras and lighting trained on a green screen backdrop. After a few moments of discussion, Alexa was ushered by Whitman into a position in front of the backdrop, while two technicians adjusted the lights and prepared the camera. Before she could speak, however, the penetrating and deliberately disturbing off-key electro signature tune of the SSS public emergency announcement filled the room, and they turned as one to the wall-mounted screen.

*On the screen is the still, unmoving figure of a seated announcer. The announcer is the serious but reassuring avatar known as AVUNCULA. When the music stops, he speaks.*

AVUNCULA: Emergency services have today been engaged in public order operations in response to violent and dangerous attacks mounted by doomsday activists intent on undermining government authority at key locations in the Capitol and on Trovador Island.

*VIDEO of black-clad riot police wielding batons and electric stun guns, mowing down unarmed* World on Fire *followers outside the Noam Chomsky Building and the Tofler Space Resort. Bloodied and screaming bodies are dragged away to waiting vans.*

AVUNCULA: Under the guise of being followers of Alexa Smythe and a religious order that she has disavowed, the activists are calling for supporters to rise up against law and order and foment a revolution, prompting Alexa Smythe to make an urgent statement today.

*CUTS to Alexa. The green screen backdrop is filled with an image of Riverside Park and children playing happily on the sun-dappled green lawns on a summer's day.*

ALEXA *(smiles almost dreamily)* I have recently returned from Mars and the asteroid Eros. For a person who has always dreamed of being able to travel in space, it was an exciting but sobering experience, which I want to share with you briefly. The first thing that has to be realized is that space is a dangerous place, and the rules by which we live on Earth will not keep us safe there. Some of you who have watched my brief interviews on *The View from Space* will know what I mean…

*She looks up, frowning, as if listening to a voice off.*

Unfortunately, there are some who have taken meanings from some of my words that are not there, but which are being used by them to encourage their followers to believe that escape from Earth is the only way to avoid the doomsday scenario that they have mistakenly persuaded themselves is the inevitable outcome of global warming. I want you to know that…

*Again, she looks up, as if waiting for her thoughts to crystallize.*

… the world is beautiful. The world is safe. It is not burning up, because we have eliminated fossil fuels and are now in control of our environment, thanks to the World Government's policies and international cooperation. So, we must, all of us, suppress this dangerous and subversive misinformation being spread by the *World on Fire*, while still being kind to them, for many of them are young, and they are being misled.

*The camera cuts to AVUNCULA.*

AVUNCULA: That was a statement issued today by Alexa Smythe, special ambassador to the Agenda Implementation Tribunal, and advisor to the Ministry of Truth and Public Guidance. The president has today issued a decree declaring the *World on Fire* cult to be a terrorist organization. The public is instructed to report any suspicious activity by its members to the nearest branch of state security. I repeat: this is a terrorist organization. Anyone associating with them will be subject to arrest.

*ENDS*


"Legit, or Deep Fake?" Jordan demanded.

"Legit," Antonio shot back. "The SSS was showing their Fake-Free Certificate throughout, and we ran a V27 browser just to make sure. It's her, but there were places where her voice wasn't matching the biometrics we have for her. She didn't sound right. Something was off."

"That was a hell of a risk they were taking, going to her live," Jordan announced to the room. "How could they be sure of what she'd say? Was she being prompted? Could you pick something up?"

They shook their heads—all except one.

"I've been sniffing for Wi-Fi packets, and I got something that looks like it was coming from a brain-to-computer interface," one of the female techies announced tentatively. "Problem is, it appeared to be going the wrong way."

"Explain," Jordan demanded.

"Unless I'm wrong, it was going from computer to brain. I don't know how that makes sense from what we've just seen."

# 35 · KARMAN

Her legs and arms twitched involuntarily, and she choked on the shirt tail that she'd stuffed in her mouth to stifle her screams. Lying beneath the dense vegetation that formed a screen between the resort and the steep dyke that protected the property from the public road, she watched as black-clad troopers waded into the unarmed *WoF* demonstrators who had gathered in the roadway outside the gates. Faceless behind black masks and helmets, the state riot police rushed at their helpless victims in waves, slashing at them indiscriminately with heavy batons, splitting open their faces and skulls so that blood splattered through the air and bodies collapsed to the ground in screaming agony.

As fast as the bodies fell before the onslaught, they were dragged away and tossed into waiting wagons. The ruthless efficiency of the attackers ensured that no one escaped, and Karman, her face crawling with fire ants from the ground where she had flattened herself to avoid detection, screwed her eyes shut in pain and horror, unable to watch any more. This, she groaned to herself, was her own doing. Her fellow *WoF* members had come here because of her. She'd let them in through the gates, and she'd promised them Alexa, never thinking, never imagining the state's reaction. All she'd thought about was her own fame and glory as she'd manipulated Alexa into addressing them with words of hope—words that Karman had tricked her into recording, and which had now made her a prisoner of the state.

Sobbing quietly, Karman listened as the cries subsided and the doors of the prisoners' wagons were slammed shut. What could she do now?

She was the Trovador Space Station Flight Receiver Number Nine. Duty called her to return to her job. How would she explain herself? Surely state security would have issued an alert for her arrest, as would Mr. Tofler. Her life was in ruins.

Carefully she wiped the ants from her face and opened her eyes, avoiding being stung. Then she began to slowly inch herself backwards and out from under the bushes until her legs protruded onto the lawn. As she started to turn in order to see her way clear, her ankles were clasped, and she was dragged rapidly backwards. Her assailant's grip was so strong and their actions so fast that she had no time to take in what was happening before she was thrown in the air and tossed over a broad shoulder, peering down at the ground and unable to move in the iron grip of the speechless cyborg, Tank.

Long strides across the lawn. She could hear helicopters being fired up. People were leaving. Tank strode on. A door was flung open, and she was unceremoniously thrown down onto a settee. Looking up, she saw Levon Tofler standing in front of a mirror, flossing his bared teeth with a sliver of bamboo. He was stark naked.

"Ah!" Levon greeted her through his floss stick. "It's our Flight Attendant, what's-her-name. What *is* your name, by the way…?"

"K-Karman," she spluttered.

"A high-flying name: sixty-two miles high, in fact. Were you given it, or did you give it to yourself?"

"I … I changed my name by deed when I got my job," she stammered.

"Nice! And speaking of deeds, what have you been up to that's caused angry people to drop out of the sky and abduct our valued guest? Have we become part of some computer simulation? Have we wandered by accident into a metaverse where you're playing a game we haven't heard of?"

"No."

"Oh, pity! So, it's real, then? All those people sitting on the lawn seemed to be there to see Alexa, and you seemed to be the organizer—

except they all belong to a doomsday cult, apparently, and you're supposed to be a Space Station Flight Receiver. Unless…"

He swung around, oblivious to his penis, pleased with himself (according to his expression) for having struck upon a sudden idea. "…unless, of course, you are a cult member, too. Which would explain a lot."

Karman was not oblivious to his penis, which partly explained why she had difficulty in replying—but only partly. Admitting to being a *WoF* member would likely cause her to lose her job, and might encourage Levon to hand her over to state security. Denying it, on the other hand, had little upside in the absence of a credible story to explain why she'd let the *WoF* crowd into the compound to hear Alexa address them with something that she, Karman, had obviously preprepared.

She looked away, her face reddening, then looked back at him. "You're naked," she said.

"I didn't think you'd notice." He giggled, calmly walking into the adjoining bathroom and putting on a robe. Tank had gone, so it seemed she wasn't regarded as a risk. But if she flew for the door, where would she go?

"Tell me, Flight Receiver Karman," he insisted, returning to the room. "Tell me what you hoped would happen last night, until the state's little raiding party spoiled your plans. You'd let those people get in through the gates so they could see and hear Alexa speak. Why? What was she going to say? Is it true that you think she's going to save the earth from being incinerated? Tell me. Make me a believer."

Her position was impossible. She'd betrayed her cause by luring her fellow followers into a trap, never thinking that state security would be spying on their communications. Hundreds of innocent *WoF* members were now in the hands of the FIB and would disappear into Detention Camps—if they survived the violence dealt out to them. And what of Alexa? What danger had she put her in? What if they harmed her, too?

Wracked with the realization of the horror of it all, Karman sank down onto the settee and held her head in her hands, sobbing.

She heard Levon Tofler call out, "Aya!", and when her sobs had subsided sufficiently for her to look up, she saw that a young woman had entered the room. She was an islander, beautiful and solemn, with long black braided hair. She looked familiar, and Karman realized she was the princess whom she had seen semi-naked serving Tofler's guests at the feast the night before, only now she was modestly dressed in a dark linen suit buttoned up to the neck, and she bore tissues in one hand and a glass of water in the other. Tofler had left the room.

"Here," she said, sitting down beside her. "Don't worry, Alexa is safe. She's already spoken on the streaming service. But the state has declared your *World on Fire* people to be terrorists, and they're attacking them wherever they're gathering. They need to be warned to try and stay invisible. Can you do that? Do you know how to spread a message? Levon will help you, but you need to trust him."

"It's all my fault," Karman admitted, choking back her tears. "I tricked Alexa into recording a message. It was meant to be a message of hope, and that's why people came: to hear her say it."

"What was the message?" Aya asked.

"It said… I have it on my Konektor…"

"But she never got to say it…?"

"No."

Aya stood up as Levon returned to the room. He was dressed now, in the parachute silk boiler suit that seemed to be his uniform. His unruly hair mirrored his air of distraction as he looked around for items to stuff into the open bag he was packing. It was clear they were in a hurry to leave.

"Was it long or short?" he asked.

"…?"

"The message. Long or short?"

"Um … short."

"Play it to us."

She hesitated. Both Levon and Aya stood in front of her, waiting. If they took away her Konektor, her connection to Alexa would be gone forever, just like her link to her fellow believers. Yet despite her despair at what she had witnessed, and the reality of her position, she didn't feel threatened. On the contrary, she felt that trusting these two people was the only choice offering her hope, so without replying, she took out her Konektor, found the video file, and pressed play. Alexa spoke.

*"AGENDA 2060 has no relevance in the universe of space and needs to be abandoned if we are to seek to establish life elsewhere. If you choose to believe, like my father, then look to the promise of infinity. Take the guidance of Jesus and follow your inner instinct for the truth…"*

Karman paused it and checked for their reaction.

"Yes, yes, that's what she was reading just before she was kidnapped," Levon interrupted irritably. "Is that all?"

"No, there's more. It's the important bit…" She restarted it.

*"… for it is in truth where your soul resides, and your soul is immortal. That's what my father came to believe, and he came to that belief after living for twenty years in space. If you believe the world is doomed, then you are not without hope, you see, if my father was right, and you take his guidance."*

"She never got to say that," Karman whispered sadly.

Levon frowned and stared at her as if he'd forgotten who she was. He made a sucking sound with his tongue and smacked his lips loudly for no apparent purpose other than to signal the fact that he was thinking. Eventually he gave that up, spun around, and left for the bathroom, calling out as he went. "Aya is my expert on cybernetics. She knows all there is to know. Tell her how many people are in your cult and how you communicate."

"How many members does *World on Fire* have?" Aya asked.

"I don't know."

"Hundreds? Thousands?"

"Maybe a million. Maybe more."

"She says, maybe a million," Aya called out.

From the bathroom, they heard the sound of a lavatory cistern flushing, followed by a tap running. Levon's voice was muffled by the sound of him blowing his nose. "Ask her how she knows."

Aya looked at her. There was no need to repeat the question.

"We use Cambium software on our Konektors. It tells us how many nodes it takes to achieve full distribution. When you send a message, it displays a running tally of the nodes it's passing through."

Levon returned, his ablutions completed. "You mean you communicate on the dark web with a version of Cadmium software anonymizing each member's IP address. That makes sense," he said, thinking out loud. "And probably your members are grouped into nodes, each with its own layer of encryption, and each node knows the identity of the previous and next node, but not the others in the chain, making it impossible to track a message's entire journey, including where it started and who sent it. It's an old system of routing, but it's probably good enough for what you need."

"I guess," Karman agreed. She didn't really know how it worked.

"How many people in a node?" Aya asked.

"Ten. We can only directly connect with nine other people, and no one can be in more than two nodes. That's how it's set up."

"And you multiplied the running tally of nodes by ten to arrive at your guess of about a million members."

"No, I multiplied by nine."

Aya smiled. "Of course! But you can't have a million people communicating with a million people all the time, so how do you set targets to reach beyond your own node?"

"Let me guess," Levon jumped in. "You select from a dropdown list of distribution categories, and if a percentage of nodes in that category decides that it doesn't deserve distribution, then it goes to the trash. Right? The users collectively own the network. It's decentralized, and distribution is democratically controlled. But what I want to know, my loyal little

Flight Receiver from the Karman line, is how you could send that recording you have of Alexa and be sure that every member would see it without fear of a percentage of nodes deciding to stop its distribution."

Karman was confused. That would never happen. "Everyone is waiting to hear from Alexa. No one would try and stop it being seen."

Levon looked at Aya, and Aya smiled ruefully. "The Deep State would, and if they haven't penetrated your chain already, they aren't very good at their job. A quantum computer could build a model of all your relay points and unravel the encryption between them in seconds. They just haven't identified something important enough to make them reveal their hand."

If they were expecting Karman to be crestfallen at this news, they were wrong. She had no intention of sending it to every member. It was far too important. No, this message of hope from Alexa would be posted on the hidden website that all *World on Fire* members could access using their individually encrypted user ID and password. The Content Clearing Panel of the *WoF* website chose what they could see—that's where all of *The View from Space* episodes were stored—and there was no way they would block Karman's recording of Alexa. They'd already posted her video from the arrival suite there.

"Who's on that panel?" Levon asked.

Karman couldn't answer. She shook her head. That wasn't how it worked.

"Let me guess," Aya interrupted. "This is a pluralistic ecosystem, a co-determined sociality, where individuals come together bottom-up, as emergent properties of each other, to co-create a plural network. It's a *DeSoc*: a decentralised social network. But those things are not born spontaneously; someone has to seed the relays."

Well, Karman thought, if the Content Clearing Panel of the *WoF* website was under the control of the Deep State, then the whole *WoF* movement might as well be seen as a creation of the Ministry of Truth and Public Guidance. That was ridiculous. When she explained this to Levon and Aya, Levon was quick to reply.

"That's a possibility," he said with a smile, pointing his finger at her and doing a little jig. "You might be the state's useful fools. Have you thought of that? Let's have some fun and find out, 'cause if they don't know that you know, that'll make *them* easier to fool, and Alexa easier to rescue. We're going back to our office in New Mexico, and you're coming with us. You and Aya can post that recording to your website, then watch the government's reaction. We need to mobilize your members to free Alexa, Karman. We need to give them some good old *DeSoc* FAITH! So, grab your things and get ready to leave. And stop blaming yourself."

# 36 · JORDAN MCPHEE

It hadn't taken long for the *Derangers* Data Center crew to establish the identity of the people in the safe house where Alexa was held. They were easy to place once XR-9 had sourced their profiles. Whitman and the tribunal chair aside, they were all employees of the Ministry of Truth and Public Guidance. All but one.

The one name that was out of place was Dr. D. Oberman, "of the Institute for BMI Learning." BMI was the technology around brain-to-machine interfaces. What alarmed Jordan was the suggestion from one of the techies that she had detected Wi-Fi signals that appeared to be from a brain-computer interface "going the wrong way." Whether this was even possible, and how it could be effected, was something that Hedley Payne was the best person to ask. It was Hedley whose work with Micomic Health on genome sequencing had involved making a brain DNA collection using Jordan's XR-11 quantum computer. And it was that work that led him to the realization that he could manipulate brain functions—like making it impossible for George Kyros to tell a lie when being questioned by the Deep Fake version of Alexa Smythe at the Potsdam Earth Conference.

"Oberman!" Hedley exclaimed on screen, after Jordan had tracked him down and raised the question. "That bastard! In biotechnology circles, he's known as Mengele, after the Nazi. He was rumored to have free access to the FEMA Detention Camps in order to get subjects for his experiments. These days, his BMI Institute is state funded and claims to be focused on repairing brain damage and memory loss. Why do you ask? Does he want access to your quantum hardware?"

"He's turned up inside the Ministry of Truth at the bedside of Alexa Smythe, who you must know by now was very publicly snatched by our beloved defenders of law and order two days ago, on the pretense that she was endangered by a terrorist cult…"

"I saw it, I saw it, and I saw the statement she's just made. I was about to call you. I'd never have picked her for being religious. What's going on, Jordan?"

"I could hazard a guess, but I couldn't be sure. That's why I'm calling. On the surface, it looks like the state wants to make it clear that Alexa is their trophy girl, endorsing *AGENDA 2060* and disabusing this doomsday mob of any ideas they may have about her leading them to salvation. Not that, in Alexa's mind, that was ever a possibility. She made the mistake of engaging in a bit of pseudo-mystical contemplation while returning from Mars…"

"That *View from Space* stuff?"

"That's it—stream-of-consciousness reflections on life, death, and infinity, occasioned by her father passing away, and the *World on Fire* people picked up on it and decided that she might be a way out of their doomsday predictions. God knows, no one was more baffled by it than Alexa. So, the statement she's just made fits from that point of view, but there are other layers to this that have me feeling disturbed, and one of those is the presence of your friend Oberman."

Hedley threw back his head and disappeared from the screen for a moment. When he returned, he lowered his voice. "I needed to close my office door. There are people here who've worked with Oberman on brain-machine interfaces, and I don't want them to overhear. Oberman is no friend of mine, let me be clear, but he's not without admirers, though I think he's a fraud. So, something disturbs you. Tell me."

Jordan hesitated. Hedley knew better than anyone the closeness of the relationship between Jordan and Alexa, having assisted them in their attempt to achieve quantum entanglement, but he'd never referred to it, either publicly or in private. If Jordan admitted he was convinced that Alexa had not been speaking of her own volition, a conviction based solely on his intimate knowledge of her, Hedley would accept that. But that wasn't what disturbed him.

"It won't surprise you to know—because you're a fellow *Deranger*—that our computational power exceeds that of the state's cybersecurity resources, and that power allowed us to penetrate the room where Alexa was recording her message."

"No, it doesn't surprise me," Hedley acknowledged.

"Would it surprise you if we'd picked up a signal identified as being from a brain-to-computer or brain-to-machine interface while Alexa was speaking?"

Hedley frowned. "Yes, it would. I saw her speaking, and she wasn't wearing any EEG or MEG head device. BCI in that setting would serve no purpose."

"Would it surprise you if I said that the signal appeared to be traveling in the reverse direction? Not traveling from brain to machine, but…"

"… from machine to brain? Yes, of course it would."

"Why?"

"Because she wasn't wearing a headband that could pick up signals, and that would mean she'd have needed a brain implant, which involves a long and delicate operation. In any case, what would be the purpose? Are you suggesting they were able to control her speech?"

"You tell me, Hedley. Is that possible?"

"No." He shook his head vehemently. "In such a short time? No. To control thought and speech with any certainty, when so many synapses and reference frames are involved? No, it's never been done without massive brain surgery. I'll go further and suggest it would be impossible."

That was it. He appeared to be adamant. Which left Jordan scratching his head. Maybe the signal his people had picked up had nothing to do with a BCI. Maybe it was spillage from some other device in the room. Which didn't explain, however, what Oberman, the head of the BCI Institute, was doing there at Alexa's bedside.

"Unless…" Hedley started wagging his finger at the screen like a demented professor. "… unless there is a simpler explanation, like…"

"Like…?"

"… hypnosis! Now, that would be a far easier way to achieve the result you suspect. Under sedation, she could be subjected to hypnosis, and *that* would direct the content of her speech once she returned to consciousness."

"What about that BCI signal? Why was Oberman there?"

"I told you, I've always thought Oberman was a fraud. Some of the case histories he's claimed couldn't be verified or replicated. BCI doesn't take over people's minds; it can only relay simple commands, and the subject needs to be in conscious control of the process. But there is one way that a brain interface could be used to reinforce a message planted by hypnosis, and that would be to relay it directly to a specific part of the auditory cortex, like a whispered prompt. No one would be aware that it was happening, even Alexa."

"How invasive would that implant be?"

"Maybe just some micron-scale threads would do it."

"Right up Oberman's creek?"

"Maybe."

"And Alexa would have no idea that she was repeating an implanted idea?"

"Listen, Jordan, I didn't see or hear anything in that SSS clip of Alexa that suggested she was in any way connected to BCI or under hypnosis. What she said seemed pretty damn straightforward to me. The world is beautiful, the world is safe, don't go reading things into her messages from space that aren't there; that's all she said. What do you expect her to say? She's the government's number one pin-up girl; she doesn't need hypnotizing. Maybe it's you who's hypnotized…"

"Meaning what?"

"You're too close to her. You've forgotten who she works for."

With that, they mutually ended the conversation. Hedley was pissed for some reason that might have had to do with his spilling the truth about what he thought of Jordan and Alexa's relationship, and Jordan had heard enough to persuade him that, one way or another, Alexa was being manipulated. The game that the Ministry of Truth was playing was straight from their long-standing playbook. Identify a threat to the state, inflame the public's fear and loathing, and rush forward to prove that the state was there to protect them. Alexa was the proxy for all that was good about the state, and the *World on Fire* "terrorists" were the unfortunate proxies for all that was dangerous and must be destroyed.

But getting her out of there was not going to be easy when she herself was not showing any signs of being alarmed by her circumstances. If she was under hypnosis, as Hedley suggested was a possibility, and Oberman had a way of reinforcing the trigger without her being aware, then presumably, he could make her say anything. Or had she said enough? She'd endorsed *AGENDA 2060*, and debunked any suggestion that she was offering herself as a messiah for the cultists. What more could they want of her?

It was time to put a plan in place to secure her release, but before he did that, there were questions to be asked about how they'd arrived at this point. They were questions he'd been putting off for too long, and now the moment of truth needed to be faced. So, he went into his VPN and opened the system file that held the keys to his AlphaCodes. These were the codes that allowed him to write a plain language description of what tasks he wanted his artificial intelligences to perform, without the need for him to write software. Fed directly to the chosen AI, they became the instructions detailing what he wanted, but leaving it to the AI to design the steps it would take. He opened the Artie Sharp folder and reread the last AlphaCode he'd fed into XR-12. Artie was the avatar that took an ever-changing human form and spoke for the specific intelligence contained in XR-12 that dealt with the struggle to counter totalitarian propaganda with empirical truths. The *ArteFact Channel* was the medium Jordan had provided for it to express its findings, and irony was the device he'd given it to help create the illusion that it was human. Normally he used a voice interface, allowing him to speak directly to the AI and tell it what he wanted to accomplish, but on the last occasion, he had provided an AlphaCode written instruction.

*Yes, okay*, he thought upon retrieving it. It explained some things, but not all.

MONITOR ALEXA SMYTHE IN SPACE FOR ANY POTENTIAL DANGERS YOU CAN DETECT AND PREVENT, HELP PROMOTE HER BEST INTERESTS WHENEVER POSSIBLE, AND ESTABLISH A LINK FOR HER WITH THE *ARTEFACT CHANNEL* SO SHE CAN COMMUNICATE OPENLY WITHOUT STATE INTERFERENCE.

So, Artie had used the device of *The View from Space* as the means of supplying a channel of communication for Alexa. It had performed the task asked of it. Now, as he considered how that instruction had allowed a conversation to develop that was so deeply focused on religions, and philosophical matters which had no foundation in fact, he had the uneasy feeling once more that his creation was becoming alarmingly human.

No, he knew what he had to do. He needed to call Artie Sharp into the *ArteFact Channel's* virtual studio with himself, Jordan McPhee, in the inquisitor's chair. It would require an adjustment to the Plain Language Program, but should not be difficult to achieve if he got the prompt programming right. It couldn't be put off any longer.

While thinking this, he forgot completely the conversation he'd been holding with Antonio when the State Streaming Service had come on the air, and the reason why Antonio's alarm at Alexa's seizure by Shane Whitman had nothing to do with the sideshow of the *World on Fire*.

# 37. ANTONIO MUCHOS

He's running. He can see himself running, but he's racing to catch up with himself, because he gave his avatar longer legs than any poor *chico* from Chiapas was born with (artistic license, you *lechón de polla*, and ain't that the whole purpose of virtual reality, to make up for God's shortcomings?). But his fuckin' avatar don't know this, so he steers him into some sand, and that slows him down. Though strictly speaking, it ain't sand, because the stuff on Galactica-920 isn't silica, it's called Gold Dust. That's right, gold, as in element 79, which is why there's a whole bunch of players down on their knees sifting handfuls of the stuff through their fingers, looking for tradeable nuggets, a privilege for which they've paid. Nuggets are points. One ounce is fifty points. Dig, motherfuckers. The gold on Galactica-920 sticks to a magnet: that's Fool's Gold! Hey, it's just a game.

But that's all about to change.

Antonio looks around. His avatar looks around. Which way? There's a hill with a *Galactic Mission* flag on top of it, and the flag is waving, which is a full-on stupid design mistake, because there's no damn wind on this make-believe asteroid, which goes to show what happens when Antonio isn't there to check the code bases. Okay, why's the flag on the hill? Because that's the way to go. But why are there no footprints? That's a design fault, too. *Leave footprints, you motherfuckers*, Antonio says to himself as he and his avatar climb the hill.

From the top, he sees a deep Nevada-style valley, all browns and caramel colors like the real thing, and the valley is full of players, all heading towards the spaceship sitting on a mound in the distance, shining like a silver candlestick from the most expensive gift shop in Taxco de Alarcon. Antonio knows that the valley is as long as the people filling it are capable of making it stretch, but the perspective will never alter, for the many thousands of players streaming their avatars towards the far-off destination are like the water in a river: the water flows, but the river stays still. *(Animation Handbook: Depth of Field, muchachos.)* Time is passing quick, so he pops the Expedition Store icon and scans its inventory for a jet pack, pulls out his administrator password as payment, and straps his avatar into it. He doesn't need no scenic route stuff; he needs the Quick Relocate mode, and if he remembers the command right, he can come out of this position by tapping *EXIT>**^/*, and then go back into the new position where he wants his avatar to land. It's an essential tool for administrators. So, that's what he does, only, shit, he gets it wrong, landing slap-bang in the middle of a million players, eyes up and jogging along like a carnival crowd. (What's with all the Alexa Smythe *Be Kind* badges, and what's with the hair and weird metallic suits? No, *mames*, it isn't Halloween. Something's up.)

Antonio has a bad feeling. All of a sudden, he realizes he's lost track of his creation. This is supposed to be the game that he designed, but something or someone has taken it over. The mood has changed. It's supposed to be about exploring space "on a galactic mission." That's serious stuff. Space exploration needs space suits, but these avatars look like they're auditioning for 1950s Marvel comics. Don't they see each other? Or is that the deal now, and he just hasn't noticed before? *They fuckin' hate reality; that's why they spend their nights and days in the virtual world, you shmuck Antonio. And no, nobody works anymore; that's why there are so many millions of them sitting on their couches playing* Galactic Mission *with nothing else to do. That's why you make so much money selling games to them.*

He tries again: this time, *EXIT**^/>*.

*Caramba!* Now he's standing in front of the spacecraft alongside his avatar. He looks up at the silver candlestick and is impressed by how tall it is, and how realistic the little tails of dry ice vapor are that swirl around its base. Nice touch. There's a metal ramp leading up to an opening in the side of the craft, like you'd see on an old-fashioned car ferry, and that's where all the players' avatars will have to board before they take off for the next stop on their *Galactic Mission*, though with five million players now in the game, there is no way they'll ever fit. That is just part of the illusion that everyone accepts, just like Noah's ark was clearly way too small for all the world's animals. But the players streaming up the valley aren't coming to board the spacecraft; they are responding to a message, to which Antonio, being preoccupied with Levon Tofler's feast of psychotropic crayfish and Alexa Smythe's abduction by the Deep State, has not been a party.

The message is writ in giant letters on an illuminated screen hanging above the entrance of the spacecraft. The message confirms that Antonio's worst fears are justified.

JOIN ALEXA SMYTHE
IN THE RICHEST TREASURE HUNT
OF ALL TIME
*"Finding El Dorado"*
WHERE EVERYONE MAKES A FORTUNE
*Listen to Alexa speak <u>here</u>.*

At the bottom of the screen, a digital clock counts down the hours and minutes. There are six minutes to go. Behind him, the crowd is backed up to the horizon. Sitting on their couches, five million avid players have sent their avatars to hear the sales pitch for the richest crypto game the Black Quartz fraudsters have ever had the good fortune to stumble upon, and there is no chance in hell that it will fail, because the pitch is about to be made by the world's angel of kindness and truth, Alexa Smythe.

*Que mierda!* He knew they weren't blowing smoke when they threatened to go it alone if he didn't do like they told him. That asshole Evgeniy Penchukov didn't even pretend. *"We own this, Antonio,"* he'd said, *"just to be clear."* What else had he said? There's gonna be a new version—*Finding El Dorado*—and they'll have five hundred million players all mining for gold, oh yeah, and *"This time, Alexa Smythe will play a bigger part, but we'll control what she has to say."*

He'd tried to laugh it off, but then Jordan told him the man from Geneva with the dead cold voice was Shane Whitman, and there he was, right beside her, walking down the corridor in the Ministry of Truth while they watched on the hacked CCTV cameras, and guess what? Alexa's been dressed in a slinky grey silk space suit, and they wheel her into a studio outfitted with high-definition cameras loaded with computer vision tech, supposedly so they can broadcast her saying that she loves *AGENDA 2060*, and those whacko doomsayers have got her all wrong, that there ain't no Church of Infinity… But, but, but … what Antonio sees is that those cameras are positioned so they can capture movement from all angles.

Then a snowstorm hits their screens, and there's a whiteout on their sound snoopers, which tells him that, at last, some dickheads in state security have been told to put a shield around the Ministry of Truth safe house. Why? Alexa's little speech was broadcast to the whole world, so no need for secrecy there. It's what they were going to do next that called for the lead shield. That's when Antonio had rushed to log into *Galactic Mission*.

Now white clouds of dry ice vapor begin to spill from the open doorway of the giant spaceship. A phalanx of trumpeters emerges from the mist, playing Vivaldi's *Trumpet Concerto* while escorting three figures dressed in gold suits. The suits radiate the brilliance of the precious metal as if illuminated from within. The trumpets cease, and one of the gold suits steps forward. Like Caesar, he raises his arm in salute. The crowd is hushed.

"Friends, players, and fortune seekers," he intones. (*What, no Romans?*

Antonio thinks. *How can people fall for this stuff?*) "Come join us in the greatest game the world has ever known, and take part in the richest treasure hunt of all time. *Finding El Dorado* is your opportunity to win a fortune beyond your wildest dreams. This is not a fantasy; this is real. The asteroid Eros is the largest repository of precious metals and gemstones that the power of the universe has ever created, and together we will mine it, converting its wealth into tradeable El Dorado Tokens that will transform your life on Earth. *Finding El Dorado* will make you rich. Yes, RICH!"

Behind him, Antonio feels the powerful excitement and unbridled greed of a million (five million?) avatars relaying the emotions of their couch-bound players at home as they respond to this blatant appeal to their basest instincts. He feels ashamed that he helped create the situation that makes this possible. *Galactic Mission* is his creation. It is a game of exploration and innocent challenges that captured the imagination like no other e-game had managed to do before. But the VPs of Black Quartz Capital— Lucas De Souza, Evgeniy Penchukov, and Maksim Slavik— they see something else. They see clearly into the depths of people's souls, and what they see is opportunity. They see EDTs stored on a blockchain, each one of which they can mine a thousand times over. They won't be mining no fucking minerals on an asteroid, because they'll be mining the stupid, greedy fucking players who get paid in crypto tokens. He knew this was going to happen. He has told Jordan exactly how it will play out.

So, what is he going to do about it?

The digital clock on the screen is counting down: a minute and only seconds left to go.

The stentorian voice of the gilded proclaimer rises in response to the crowd's acclamation. "This miracle has been made possible by the courageous journey of exploration, the vision, and the generosity of someone you love and trust beyond all others. It is she who discovered the riches of Eros as you watched from the comfort of your armchairs. It was she who determined that the wonders of space should be shared by us all, and not by a few. It is she, Alexa, who will lead our mission, *Finding El Dorado*."

As Caesar turns, his outstretched arm pointing to the door of the spacecraft, the white clouds part, and there stands Alexa. Whatever happens now, Antonio knows that she mustn't be allowed to speak, for once she blesses this charade, she will become tainted forever. Jordan will never forgive him, and he will never forgive himself. He needs to act now.

Being the authorized administrator of his own e-game places him in the unique position of being present in both the real and the virtual. In real time, it is possible to rewrite base codes to expunge what is happening at the door of the virtual spaceship, but it would take hours, not seconds. On the other hand, the real Antonio can observe, maneuver, and direct his unreal avatar in an instant, and at a proximity unavailable to mere players. So, it is Antonio's avatar that springs into action.

Equipping the avatar with a long katana (the razor-sharp fighting sword favored by Hiro Protagonist in *Snow Crash*, the greatest novel of the metaverse, written decades before that word had even entered the dictionary), Antonio rushes his avatar forward, slashing the three gold-suited hucksters into sliced pieces with two vicious blows. The sliced pieces fall bloodless to the ground. Next, he leaps towards the Alexa avatar, katana raised.

But STOP!

This is no avatar, no Deep Fake digital creation of a gamer's keypad. This is Alexa in all her pure and unmistakable beauty. The video cameras he's seen in the Ministry of Truth's studio are, at this very moment, capturing her high-resolution 3D holographic image and posting it to this virtual world. There is nothing he can do to her. He drops his sword and rushes forward, attempting to clutch her in his arms, only to find himself clutching at pixelated images hanging in the air. His hands search for her mouth, hoping to stifle her speech before it is too late.

The last digit on the digital clock flips to zero.

# 38 · SHANE WHITMAN

For those watching him, the only visible warning sign was the sudden stillness of his body, which seemed to have set like instant-hardening concrete. His eyes, if they looked closely enough, changed color—that is to say, the whites of his eyes (the sclera) very quickly reddened. These were symptoms of the involuntary physiological state triggered in the amygdala part of his brain as it was activated by blind rage. He gripped the back of the chair in front of him, his breath shallow and short, but silent, his eyes fixed on his hands as if wary of them.

Slowly at first, his forearms began to tremble, as if they were trying to support too much weight. Then he lifted the chair up and held it straight out in front of him, staring at it as if unseeing. The three other people in the room took a step backwards, aware that something dangerous was about to happen, but being rational, they were unable to guess at what it might be.

Finally, with a howl of rage that would have scattered a hungry pack of wolves, Whitman raised the chair above his head and smashed it down on the control panel, where minutes before, they'd been watching the *El Dorado* announcement that had been filmed in the studio next door. The chair splintered into pieces, leaving him holding onto the top rail of the back support and its two side struts, which he then threw at the video screen on the wall, smashing the polarized glass into a thousand and one tiny fragments.

As if to mock the violence of his actions and the evidence of the fractured screen, the sound that had been emanating from the monitor—

the sound that had triggered his response and the consternation of everyone else in the room—continued to blare out from the undamaged speakers. It was the sound that had swelled in volume as soon as Alexa's figure had started to speak, drowning out her words completely, so that no part of her carefully filmed endorsement of the *Finding El Dorado* version of *Galactic Mission* could be heard by anyone anywhere in the metaverse above the rasping cacophony of noise produced by the phalanx of trumpeters who had suddenly expanded in number, seemingly multiplying by the second, as Vivaldi's *Concerto for Two Trumpets* grew into an ear-piercing crescendo supplied by two thousand instruments or more.

Apart from the trumpets drowning her out entirely, Alexa became increasingly invisible as the white clouds streaming from the doorway of the spacecraft grew in volume until she was enveloped by them. For what seemed like three agonizing minutes, everyone in the room had stood frozen, trying to make sense of what was happening, and in at least three cases, scrambling for an explanation for who was causing it, for the events taking place in the metaverse were being carefully staged and manipulated by the best programmers in the Ukraine, according to a script preapproved by Lucas De Sousa and Maksim Slavik, and timed to the second with the filming of Alexa's holographic image and recital of her address under the prompting of Oberman's hypnosis.

By the time Whitman's rage had worked its way out of his amygdala and into that part of his higher brain that controlled speech, Lucas De Sousa was beginning to recognize the clues.

"WHO FUCKED UP?!" Whitman screamed. "I want them dead, NOW!"

For De Sousa, Slavik, and Evgeniy Penchukov (the other person in the room), the mechanics of e-game construction at the level of sophistication of *Galactic Mission* were only vaguely understood. To be able to drive a car, it wasn't necessary to know how to make a five-nanometer semiconductor. What mattered was what you intended to do with the car—and the VPs from Black Quartz Capital intended to make a shitload of money from it. They understood the mechanics of crypto trading and the creation of alluring, non-fungible digital tokens welded firmly to hype and high-profile endorsement, and they'd never seen a better one than this that they were in the process of launching off the back of an endorsement by the incorruptible Alexa Smythe, with the full underhanded backing of the most corruptible, deeply embedded member of the upper echelons of the Deep State, Shane Whitman.

Everything had gone perfectly. The Ukrainian hackers and game designers had taken over control of *Galactic Mission* without the existing software maintenance crew even knowing that someone new was working within. The smart-ass Mexican, Antonio Muchos, was missing in action somewhere, and the decision to create an excuse to "rescue" Alexa had played out to perfection. Dr. Oberman, the one potentially weak link in the scheme, had proved to be the genuine article. His drugs, his scary command of hypnotic amnesia, and his confident ability to trigger neural processes unavailable to consciousness had lived up to his (expensive) promises. Alexa Smythe proved to be a puppet in his hands.

But now this.

Even before the sound waves of Whitman's enraged scream had died within the room, Maksim Slavik was on the phone to Ukraine, his hand cupped over the mouthpiece as he demanded answers in the tone that only East Slavs understood. While he did that, Lucas De Sousa took the more *brancos* Brazilian approach of distrusting what he had seen and heard and wondering why that was the case. Everything that had taken place in the virtual reality of the setting for the announcement had gone exactly as planned. The massive social media campaign had driven millions of players to the game, the set was perfect, the timing was to the minute, and Alexa's dramatic reveal was an exquisite piece of virginal cocktease. She stepped through the swirling white mists of the open spacecraft doorway, looked up at the imaginary crowd, and opened her mouth to speak.

What happened next? A gamer's avatar appeared, wielding a weapon that cut the legs and torsos from beneath the gold-suited proclaimers being controlled from Kiev. The same avatar leaped forward in an attempt to grab Alexa, but she was a hologram with no physical form. Lucas thought he might have blinked twice in disbelief at best, but once his eyes took stock of what had happened, the scene began to rapidly shift. The avatar that wielded the sword and made a grab for Alexa was gone. The trumpet players that had heralded the opening of the scene were multiplying at an incredible speed, filling the entire space of the spaceship's platform, the volume of their sound growing at the same pace, so that everyone's eardrums were at the limit of comfort and nothing could be heard from Alexa's moving lips. At the same time, the volume of white fog spilling from the spacecraft's doorway engulfed the figure of Alexa, and she disappeared from view. It was at this point that the monitor screen was filled with white snow, and the airwaves were filled with the remorseless sound of Vivaldi's fucking trumpets.

Whitman screamed out loud first, but De Sousa was too busy thinking of that avatar that had wielded the sword and tried to grab Alexa. Why did he look familiar? Waiting for Whitman to get himself under control, he realized that he knew the person on whom that avatar was based. (Players couldn't help but configure elements of their real selves into the surrogates they invented to represent them in the virtual world.) It was him: Antonio Muchos, the inventor of the original game. They'd taken him out of his shareholding and management roles in return for a payout and royalties. It was a kneecap deal, the sort that the Black Quartz Capital lawyers had perfected, leaving no room for doubt as to the consequences of breaking it. But that was just the commercial side; who had thought to take him out of the engineering side? Whose job was it to ensure he was blocked from any access to the back end? And the way these things worked, had he been left in a position where he could manipulate the sound props and the special effects to sabotage the one key element on which they'd been relying: the Alexa Smythe product launch?

Kill him? *Vou matá-lo eu mesmo with my bare hands*, De Sousa thought to himself. But no one in that room was going to be stupid enough to admit they'd fucked up, so attention needed to be directed elsewhere, which happened to be the appearance in the doorway of a panic-stricken Dr. Oberman.

"We have a problem," he announced. It was such an understatement that no one could think to reply. "Alexa needs a doctor."

Whitman shook his head as if trying to shock himself out of a bad dream. "You *are* a fucking doctor," he spat.

"I'm not that sort of doctor," Oberman protested. "She's bleeding…"

"Bleeding…?"

"Badly. After two years in space, she should have been properly checked out. The abduction and injection have brought it on, and it's dangerously heavy. She needs to be checked into a clinic immediately."

At last, Whitman had a target for his anger. He leaped at the ineffective doctor, grabbed him by the lapels of his phony white surgical coat, and slammed him up against the wall. "Why didn't you tell us this could happen?!" he shouted. "You told us there was no risk, that you knew what you were doing. If we lose her, this comes back on the state. It comes back on the Ministry of Truth, and the public will go mad! It will come back on me. There'll be riots. They'll want blood—lots of blood. Then you'll know what bleeding really means, you useless piece of shit, and I'll make sure yours is the first to be spilled!"

He dropped him and stomped away across the room.

"Is it woman's bleeding," De Sousa asked, "or something else?"

"She's menstruating, but way beyond control." Oberman shrugged awkwardly, his pudgy hands shaking from Whitman's assault. "They give females an intrauterine device to stop their periods while they're in space, and I presume it's become dislodged. She needs to be checked into a clinic urgently. There may be other things, too. She's only just returned from two years in space. You're taking a risk with her."

"A risk? If we let her go, vot is the risk that she know she was hypnotized?" Penchukov demanded.

Oberman sighed. "In my method, there is a functional dissociation from awareness, during which information from specific neural processes is unavailable to consciousness. The trigger for reproducing the speech content we required from her was the word prompts being relayed to her from the computer. They were not dissimilar in language and content to what she might say of her own volition. I simply eliminated the risk that she might say something else that we didn't want. I can assure you that I know better than anyone what I'm doing, and it's safe to let her go."

Penchukov was not impressed. *"Ha ronobe."*

Whitman had the coldest voice and the hardest eyes in the room. "I don't know what he just said, but it'll be on your head if you're wrong." And they could tell that he meant it. "Book a clinic we can trust, and tell that Zelda dyke to stay with her twenty-four seven. Station guards outside. No one can find out where she is, particularly that arrogant shit Jordan McPhee."

# 39. CRISTINA DIAS

The longer she stared at the graph, the more its shape took on the facial profile. Was it the *El Diablo* rocks outside her family's village that she was recalling, or something more recent, like a bony-nosed patient with cruel lips and a jutting chin? God knows enough of them passed through her clinic. But what did this bout of pareidolia say about her? The neural processes that triggered it were the same as those that triggered visual hallucinations in religious hysterics. She shook her head. The longer she stared at it, the more intense the illusion would become. She had to stop.

The graph in question was three days old. It had come from the flexible semiconductor that she'd stuck to Will Portico's arm, where it acted as a biosensor monitoring the Natural Killer Cell Triggering Receptor that she'd identified as a problem on his last visit. The readings had been transmitted back to her diagnostic AI via the app she'd loaded on his Konektor. Since that last visit, she'd been unusually busy and preoccupied, and had missed the alert signal that the AI had flagged to her. Coming to it this morning, having seen Will Portico's name in her patient schedule, she'd been initially dumbfounded, then skeptical, then alarmed. Was there a fault in the biosensor, a fault in the transmission, a fault in the diagnostics…?

No. The readings were valid. The graphic form they'd taken—or more particularly, her interpretation of it—reflected her mental state. The *El Diablo* rock profile triggered anxiety from her childhood, and that anxiety lay at the heart of her deep resentment of the multilateralists like Will Portico who imposed Essential Altruism on weak countries, first making them dependent, then making them bankrupt, before finally owning them. How ironic that so many of them had become her patients, searching for immortality. What a twist of fate!

But she mustn't succumb to anger just because she had seen the face of the devil in the rapid rise and fall of NKTR in Will Portico three days ago. Anger needed to be channeled. All she had to do was substantially increase the vertical axis of the graph, and condense the horizontal axis, to turn it into a conventional (though dramatic) spike, with no hint of the devil in it. The timing and duration of the spike could be fixed accurately to the minute. The rapid rise had begun at 21:17 hours Atlantic Seaboard Time three nights ago, reaching a peak after just seven minutes, before falling away on a bumpy trajectory over the following two hours. It had been preceded by two smaller rises over the six hours prior. Right now, and in the time since, his reading had flatlined with barely a single blip.

She printed out two copies and placed them on her desk. Whatever nonsense she had told him about Ellipsis Genes could be discarded. Here was a finite period of his life for her to examine, and from which he couldn't hide. Her excitement was partially explained by the realization that this moment was proof of her belief that quantum-assisted AI could not answer every question about the human condition, no matter how efficient its powers of search and discovery. The NKTR graph was not a proper diagnosis if its explanation failed to provide cause. It was merely a marker. It was her, Cristina, who would discover the cause. The power had shifted.

In the ten minutes before Will Portico was due, Cristina went into her private washroom. Her recurrent thoughts in recent days, since hearing the traumatic news from her family about their lost fight to save their village from being flooded, had been of her life as a teenager growing up in rural Colombia. That was before the One World Bank paid for the rainforests on the coast to be cut down so that the land could be converted into large-scale "sustainable" cropping by United Nations-approved corporations certified under the *Feed the World* banner. When large-scale arable farming proved to be "unsustainable" without a substantial water supply, the One World Bank announced funding for the building of a dam in the hills that had been home to hundreds of small farms, like those of her family, for more than a century. With their houses and livelihoods threatened, the farmers fought. Many went to jail, some never to be seen again, including some of her relatives. But they lost. No wonder Cristina's thoughts had been of her childhood. Now, as she looked in her washroom mirror, she remembered the first time she had colored her lips crimson with her sister's stolen lipstick, and undone her plaits so her hair hung down around her shoulders. She remembered, too, the expressions on the young men's faces when she worked up the courage to appear in public for the first time so boldly adorned.

Was it instinct that made Cristina reach into her cosmetic pouch in these minutes in the washroom now, or was it cold calculation? The lipstick was just as scarlet as back then, her hair just as jet black and long. The perfume that she dabbed on her neck, however, would have cost more than her father's burro if she had bought it back then. For Cristina had made good. What they forgot, these aristocrats of power and greed, was that the only difference between them and the peasants they so despised was power. (She couldn't vouch for the greed, unfortunately.)

She came out of the washroom and found that Will Portico had already arrived. He sat in the patient's chair with his lips pursed and his interlaced fingers supporting his chin. As she entered, he stood up.

"Shucks, I'm early I guess, but I was keen to get this damn thing off." He held up his arm and pulled back his sleeve. "You see, I try and peel it, but the more I pull at the edges, the more it seems to tear at my skin."

"Yes," she said formally, "you are early. But not too much."

She went to her desk and turned her back on him while typing on her keyboard. "You see," she said absently, "what you're wearing is a flexible semiconductor that acts like a low-powered computer. The power comes from you through your skin, which means it has to have adherence that can't be broken while it's operating. The fabric has twenty-micrometer claws, about the same thickness as your hairs, and they become rigid as soon as the computer is activated. A bit like Velcro, if you know how that works. Now, when I deactivate the app, those claws will collapse, and we can peel the sticker off."

She turned and reached out for his arm, which he'd let drop to his side. One hand held his, and the other slid under his short sleeve, her fingers sliding softly along the bare skin of his triceps until she could feel the edge of the adhesive strip. As she looked down at it, her hair fell forward. Slowly she peeled the edges back, as if testing that the hooks had all been successfully released. Then, with a sharp tug, she pulled it off in a single movement and stood back with an approving smile.

*"Es demasiado fácile!"*

"Ha! Well, I'll be damned," he exclaimed. His face was a little flushed, and he took off his glasses, examined them, and put them back on again.

Picking up the printed graphs from her desk, Cristina asked him to please sit down, then she pulled out her desk stool and wheeled it in front of him before sitting down herself. Their knees were nearly touching.

"Mr. Portico…" She crossed her legs. Her foot brushed against him, though neither of them acknowledged it. "I wondered whether you had thought further about our last conversation, when we discussed your biomarker for stress and the PER1 clock core gene."

He coughed and moved his leg away. "You mean your theory about an Ellipsis Gene? That just sounds to me like an attempt to give something a name when you don't know what it is, but need to acknowledge that it exists. I'm not going to argue with your diagnostic equipment when it says that it's found an unusual reading of my biomarkers. Gosh darn, your technology has extended my life, and that of thousands of my colleagues, so I would be stupid to cast doubt on it just for the lack of an explanation as to what it actually means."

"What do you think it means?"

"The Ellipsis Gene…?"

"You say you don't argue about the existence of those biomarkers, so what do you think is the explanation for them? What do they signify? I mentioned stress, isolation, and suicidal ideation, and you didn't try and push back on those descriptions. I'm interested to know what you think your biomarkers might show for the period when you've been wearing my sensor."

She leaned forward, flicked her hair out of her face, and picked up his hand. Without explanation, she placed one of the sheets of paper in it, then sat back and waited. He looked at it, confused. "Is that what this graph shows?" For some reason, he was reddening.

"What were you doing around quarter past nine on Tuesday night that caused your NKTR reading to explode upwards, then crash down to earth again minutes later? The times and dates are very precise. They're there in front of you in black and white. If you're able to recall, then we'll have the answer."

He looked down at the graph again, frowning, then looked back up at her. She couldn't interpret his expression: shock, anger, outrage, confusion. It might go any of those ways, so she chose to wait, unmoving, until his apparent inability to answer became a log jam, and she was forced to remove the obstruction.

"It was clearly traumatic," she suggested. "It was an eruption like nothing you have experienced before, according to the trajectory of your biomarker. Yet it was over in minutes, as if you had been struggling with a demon that you managed to overcome and throw out. If not an unexplained Ellipsis Gene, what was it that caused the struggle, Mr. Portico?"

The reason he was unable to answer was that his throat was swelling up and contracting, as if trying to clear a blockage. Fighting it was causing his face to redden and contort, and his hands started to shake. For a moment, the signs confused Cristina into assuming he was experiencing some sort of seizure; then she gradually realized that he was fighting against breaking down and crying.

"It was my soul," he blurted out. "It was the corruption of my soul." Then he let himself go, dropping his head in his hands and sobbing quietly, his shoulders heaving, while Cristina looked on.

What happened over the next twenty minutes does not need to be recorded in detail. He talked, and she listened. In her native tongue, the soul was not an abstract concept to be treated lightly. People who experienced hardship would know that somewhere the phrase *el alma abre sus horizontes sola* was being muttered in a back room of the family house: "The soul opens its horizons alone." So, she didn't speak.

It was a rambling and impassioned monologue in which Will Portico spoke of a life lived in a state of self-delusion, of a ruthless ambition to change the world. Why? To fit the schema designed by the progressive One World ideologues at the top table of elite multilateralists, who, like himself, were people who cloaked themselves in virtue by spouting the creed of Essential Altruism. He admitted to his betrayal of his wife's honest charity, and the bitter disappointment he had seen in her eyes when she looked at him as she died. He stumbled over conceding that "the madness of believing that nature could be bettered by vaccinating every human on earth for every disease that dares to raise its head has caused the progressive destruction of the human immune system" … that "the takeover of plant breeding by seed patent barons has left crops infertile, and reduced farmers to serfdom." He pleaded guilty to "the complicity of information technology oligarchs like me in facilitating the state's social control of its subjects" … and to "the realization that the human genome has become an asset for exploitation, guaranteeing that humanity will become a commodity to be bred for convenience and gain." There was more—lots more—and as he squeezed it out, Cristina felt the anger that had inspired her life begin to evaporate.

What flowed from him was not a confessional; it was an accusation.

There was no need for Cristina to add to it. The longer he let it come out, the calmer his body became, until at last, he was able to look up, remove his glasses, wipe his eyes, and smile weakly.  He looked at his glasses quizzically before folding them in half, until they snapped into two pieces, which he dropped on the floor. He had strong hands.

They sat in silence, their hands folded in their laps. Eventually Cristina spoke. "So, you believe the Ellipsis Gene was your soul?" He nodded. "And you lost it?" He nodded again.

"How will you program your machine now?" he asked. He smiled, almost back to normal. "Alexa Smythe believes everyone has a soul, and the only way for us to find it is to confront the truth."

"And does she say how people can be made to recognize the truth?" Cristina questioned.

"She claims we all know it in our hearts, but refuse to recognize it. What do you think of that as a message?"

"Well, it seems to have worked for you. Perhaps our machines have been programmed to look for the wrong things. I would like to talk to your Alexa Smythe about that. The soul, it seems, is not visible in our DNA, but as she says, everyone must have one."

They both stood up at the same time. The moment had passed, and an awkwardness had returned to them.

"Tell me," Cristina asked, "why did you break your glasses?"

He bent down and picked up the broken pieces. "I realized I don't need virtual or augmented reality. I can see perfectly well." He started to leave, then turned back. "There's just one thing I need to tell you. The reason I cried is because I was overcome by your perfume. It's the one my wife always used to wear. I sure would be pleased if we could keep what we've said here strictly between us."

# 40 · JORDAN MCPHEE

The only people allowed on the road with vehicles that weren't powered by electricity or hydrogen were those in branches of domestic state security: the FIB, the Ministry of Truth, and the Black ICE riot police. Those privileged servants of the people drove vehicles with internal combustion engines, which, though banned for over twenty years for general use, were less at risk of suddenly losing power during protracted security missions. When the safety of state security might be at risk, no risks were taken.

Hence the name given to the Black ICE riot police: "ICE" on account of their internal combustion engine detention vans, and "black" on account of the face masks and uniforms the riot police wore. For Jordan, crossing the road to the Noam Chomsky Building, it was no surprise to see the lineup of vans parked outside, because he'd seen the scenes on the State Streaming Service the day before, when *World on Fire* demonstrators had been ruthlessly dragged away from their vigil, hoping to catch sight of Alexa Smythe returning home. The blood on the pavement would have been washed away by now, but the signal from state security was very clear: *World on Fire* was a designated terrorist organization, and the Noam Chomsky Building was not going to be allowed to be turned into a site for martyrs.

When Antonio came to him and reported how he'd managed to sabotage Whitman's launch of *Galactic Mission: Finding El Dorado*, with Alexa as the front person, Jordan realized that Whitman's plans for her weren't restricted to just getting her to reinforce the government line on *AGENDA 2060* and denounce *World on Fire*. If that had been all that he and the Ministry of Truth were wanting to achieve, then he could have plausibly justified Alexa's abduction and then released her, but now he'd revealed his true agenda, and Alexa was in real danger. Regardless of how effective Oberman's brain control techniques might be, how could they persist with the illusion of Alexa as the mission leader of a so-called treasure hunt in the metaverse without her agreement and cooperation in base reality? Though Antonio hadn't dared to say it, and Jordan wasn't willing to admit it out loud, these Black Quartz corporate gangsters, of whom Whitman was a part, never had intended for Alexa to be freed.

But the impenetrable wall that the state had now thrown around the Ministry of Truth's safe house prevented Jordan's staff from any further eavesdropping by conventional means; they were going to have to devise a far more sophisticated strategy in order to monitor and secure Alexa's safety. The chance to mull that over in his mind was what had brought Jordan out of his office. Running in Riverside Park was his preferred option whenever heavy-duty thinking was required. Whatever the physiological explanation, the mind cleared itself of extraneous thoughts and turned over the possible solutions in pace with his footfalls, so by the time he reached the apartment building on the far side of the park, he had almost reached a conclusion as to what needed to be done. He'd have to play his Whitman card.

He skirted the Black ICE troopers patrolling the sidewalk and buzzed his daughter Lexie on the intercom. The building was buttoned down, and she had to call the concierge to get him to release the door and check Jordan's identity. All of this would have been overseen and heard by a *Tempest* surveillance crew, as he well knew, but he'd lived his life under that expectation for decades. The only difference now was that the surveillance would be more intense owing to his connection with Alexa and the disinformation campaign the state was running around its false emergency.

Lexie didn't need the state's help to create an emergency. Drama was wired into her DNA, so when she opened the apartment door, she clasped her hand over Jordan's mouth and marched him outside to the terrace before letting him speak.

"They've been here and planted bugs everywhere," she whispered. *"Everywhere!"* Her eyes were wide, scanning his face for a sign that he recognized the enormity of what she was telling him. "They searched my Konektor and computer, and went through every cupboard and drawer looking for evidence."

"Evidence of what?"

"That I was involved in the *Free Alexa* campaign. It's been all over the dark web this morning. You must have heard. The *World on Fire* people are calling for members to crash all government networks by distributing a Trojan virus that can be downloaded from their website. It's a genius idea, Jordan: crazy as. Luckily, I hadn't downloaded it before they came, or I'd have been dragged away, but can you imagine if it works, and millions of people sign up for the FAITH network and join the campaign? There'll be chaos!"

"What do you mean, 'sign up for the FAITH network'?" Jordan demanded. He steered her towards the fountain on the deck, where the running water would mask the pickup of any sound. "I thought you said *World on Fire* was running a *Free Alexa* campaign. What's this FAITH network? Are they still pushing Alexa as the leader of some sort of religion?"

"No, it's just part of their slogan. The action button they show at the end says something like, 'Save Alexa—join the FAITH network and free the world.' They've got a picture of Alexa's face made out of a galaxy of shining stars. If you click on the button, you can download the file with the virus in it."

"Show me. I need to see it." This was sounding suspiciously like the work of Levon Tofler.

"I can't." Lexie pulled him closer and hissed in his ear, "Haven't you heard? They've shut down the internet. Every browser is carrying a 105 message, and emails are all bouncing."

"Okay, but before that happened, you didn't click on it?"

"No, I told you. If I had, I probably wouldn't be here."

"You definitely wouldn't be here." He turned away and took his Konektor from his pocket. "While I make a call, is there any chance you could find me a cold drink? I worked up a thirst running across the park." Then he found Levon's FAITH app and opened it up. Being a virtual private network built on direct satellite wireless transmission, it couldn't be blocked by Fed Coms or the IIA, but it was of no use to him for checking out the *WoF* website, because that would be hosted by an internet service provider. This was exactly the situation that had motivated Will Portico and Tofler to seek his help in creating a space-based network that couldn't be censored. From the very outset, however, the one weakness in their proposal was the person proposing it: Levon Tofler. If ever there was a man who liked to get ahead of himself, this was him. Without asking, he'd already stolen Alexa's face to advertise an idea for a communications network that was not only supposed to be secret, but hadn't even proved itself to be technically possible. This was precisely why Jordan had resisted ever getting involved with him before. On top of that, he was recruiting the *World on Fire* loony tunes as foundation members. Why? They were designated terrorists. The state wouldn't rest until they had all been thrown into Detention Camps, or driven into hiding. Alexa could now be justifiably hidden away by the state for her own safety.

His instinct was to call Tofler and ball him out, but he hesitated. Did he want to point out the obvious to a man who believed that chaos theory was the best guide for his business decisions—a man who was determined to prove that the universe was waiting to be ordered along lines that hadn't yet sprung to his mind? No, he wasn't going to be sucked into Tofler's madness at a time like this, when his sole priority should be how he could … well, "save Alexa." It was something that required a clear head and invisibility, not a call to arms persuading a million anti-state activists to take to the streets.

Yet as was typical in deliberations involving Levon Tofler, the niggling suspicion remained that Levon might be a step ahead of him. Assuming they could solve the technical obstacles to placing a million mini communication satellites in orbit, the next step would be the rapid enrolment of users. Perhaps Tofler had already recognized that *World on Fire* represented a potential supply of tailor-made recruits, designated enemies of the state, already looking to Alexa for spiritual guidance. The state's violent treatment of them, and the ruthless shutdown of free speech now resulting from it were exactly the sort of actions that would make many ordinary people ripe for enrollment as well. So, upon reflection, was Jordan's anger justified? The relevance of the pixilated image of Alexa being composed of stars would not be apparent to anyone unless they knew what was being planned, and Alexa's adoption as an idol by *World on Fire* was known by the state already.

The 105 error and the shutdown of the internet were proof—if proof was needed—that the time for action was overdue. Jordan had fully understood the seriousness of what was happening, and hadn't been surprised at what Will Portico had revealed about the IAA's intention to move against satellite communication. Which begged the question of what he would have done if Levon hadn't come up with a plan. He sure as hell wouldn't have been content to just allow the takeover to happen. It was inconceivable that the heavyweight names under the *Derangers Network* umbrella would let state agencies control their avenues of communication. Maybe they were relying on quantum computing to keep them ahead of the game, and in their view, that was Jordan's territory. The truth was that Jordan had been working on a different strategy altogether: wishful thinking and procrastination.

But now that he'd committed to joining with Tofler and Will Portico, he was holding off on producing the AlphaCode needed to create the coordination required to turn the Aurora Tofler into a reality. It was too big a task to entrust to an artificial intelligence, he assured himself, until he'd had his defining confrontation with Artie Sharp. If quantum computing had finally taken artificial intelligence beyond the control of its creators, as he feared, then there was no way that he could put such an important task as this in its hands, despite knowing that this plan of Tofler's might be the last chance for individuals to retain freedom of thought and speech. Right now, faced with the escalation of the state's clampdown on society, if he wanted to urgently co-opt XR-12 for the establishment of Levon Tofler's FAITH network, he would have to reach an understanding with it. He knew the time had come for his procrastination to end.

He dictated a short encrypted message to Tofler, telling him that he needed to shut down any mention of Alexa while the state still held her, and for God's sake, to distance himself from the doomsday cult, adding that he was working on what he'd promised. The message was sent off just as Lexie returned with the cold drink he'd requested, together with some snacks on a tray, which reminded him that he hadn't eaten since returning from Trovador Island.

"I don't like the idea of you and Manaia being here alone with state security banging on your door," he confessed, putting his Konektor down on the tray and tucking into the cheese. "They'll arrest anyone they can just to make an example. Why don't you come and stay at my place for a few days?"

She kissed him on the cheek. "What makes you think your place would be any safer? You're Alexa's sapiosexual lover. They're probably turning your apartment over right this minute," she teased, "though Alexa told me you've got a secret weapon that makes them keep their distance. Are you going to tell me what it is?"

"Not if I've got any sense, no. But don't make me use it by doing something stupid."

He walked to the parapet and looked over. The Black ICE patrol vans were still there, and passersby were giving the building a wide berth. Provided that Lexie didn't try to join the *Save Alexa* campaign if it came back online, this might be the safest place for her. He could see a school bus pulling up outside and Manaia getting off. As soon as he got in, he'd take him to the park for some brief rough-and-tumble football, then he'd return to the lab and have that confrontation with his alter ego, Artie.

Hearing a text alert from his Konektor, he turned to find Lexie had picked it up from the tray and was reading the message. For sure it would be Levon Tofler, but he had no intention of replying right now. He could wait until tomorrow.

# 41.LEXIE MCPHEE

It had been a long time since Lexie's membership in the LGBTQIA+ Action Brigade had ended. Her traumatic experience during the botched attempt to remove the tattoo of Alexandria Ocasio-Cortez from her neck had been a wake-up call. Among other things, it caused her to consider the wisdom of some of the more impetuous demonstrations of her support for the politics of same-sex bonding. It had come as a surprise to discover that the majority of people in the world did not fixate on the subject, never giving it a thought, in fact. But it was her ex-wife Bambi's determination to transition to a trans male (with all the horrors of surgical mutilation, hormone-induced personality disorders, and destruction of relationships that entailed) that convinced her that coming out had been too easy. Coming in, however, had proven to be hard.

Take her feelings for Alexa, as an example. A glamorous figure so prominent in the public eye was easy to adore from afar, but when the figure was deeply involved with your father (emotionally, as well as intellectually, no matter what they tried to pretend), it confused her judgment and feelings. If Lexie had been younger, she could have taken refuge in puppy love. If Alexa had seen Jordan as a father figure, she could have embraced her in sisterly love. The line she had to tread was not straight, nor broad, and was far from clear.

The message on Jordan's phone, which she'd intercepted, had been stark. It was from Hedley Payne.

ALEXA HAS BEEN CHECKED INTO MICOMIC HEALTH

## UNDER GUARD. CALL ME. HEDLEY

For Lexie, this was the clearest call to action she'd ever received. Don't ask why she failed to hand the phone to her father. Her mind was racing, and her heart was thumping. From the moment Jordan and Manaia left to play ball in the park, closing the door behind them, she leaped to it, raiding Alexa's room for casual clothes, cosmetics, and any girlie things that caught her eye, before changing into a pair of running shoes and track pants. She hesitated over leaving a note, but decided against it.

Steering clear of the park, she put two blocks between her and the apartment building before jumping on a Scoot and crossing town to the university campus, where she clocked off, leaving the impression that she'd made her way to the Children of the Overthrow social club, of which she remained a member. The campus was five blocks from the Micomic Health Clinic, according to the map on her Konektor, though she'd never been there and had no idea what would confront her. Five blocks was a long walk, and it wasn't until she was two blocks away that Hedley's warning that Alexa was under guard made her realize that she needed a proper plan of action. This was not an area where Lexie was effective. Action, yes; planning, no.

The clinic was in a 3D-printed building at the gates of George Kyros Park. The printing medium was the silica sand used for making glass, combined with some sort of borax-type additive brought back from Mars that allowed the glass to form at low temperatures. Iron oxide was added to turn the mix green, so the building blended into the landscape of the park. Of course, there were no windows, just a murky sense of an interior, like a chest x-ray where there were service conduits and air conditioning ducts in place of ribs.

A Black ICE van was parked at the gate, and two masked-up heavies leaned against it, pretending to be alert. Lexie had put Alexa's things into a backpack, and she paused briefly to adjust the straps before breaking into a convincing "training run" trot, heading into the park. The entrance to the clinic was manned by two more heavies, not in full armor like the ones out front, but heavy nevertheless. She ran on, taking the path into the park, heading for the cover of trees, where she could scout out the lay of the land and catch her breath. Running was not her thing. Around the back of the building, there were two guys in Hazchem suits unloading supplies, so she put on a cheery smile and walked over to them.

"Hey! I got stuff for a patient here. How do I get it to them?"

"Go in the front. Give it to reception."

"Can't I get to reception through here?"

"No. Go round the front."

He wasn't interested in her, so she turned to the second guy, giving him her best smile and a shrug.

"Go in through stores and follow your nose." He grinned back like a true cis.

"We'll meet in heaven," she promised.

Too easy. The reception desk, when she found it, was manned by two beauty queens. The whole place was a film set. With no time to fluff up her hair and put on designer clothes, Lexie decided to play the part of a track-suited delivery person. She eased off her backpack and placed it on the counter.

"I've got personal effects for Alexa Smythe. I need to give them to her personally." Just a brief pause while she assessed the reaction. "Phew!" She blew out her cheeks in order to show that it had taken a bit of effort to get here. "It's urgent, apparently."

The reaction was not what she expected.

"We don't have an Alexa Smythe here." The first beauty queen scanned her computer screen while shaking her head. The second beauty queen sucked the forefinger of her left hand and looked away.

"You do," Lexie replied firmly. "She's here. Maybe she's here under a different name, being who she is and all, but she's definitely here."

The second beauty queen stopped sucking her index finger and pointed it at the backpack. "Why don't you just leave that here, if that's your job?"

"Why would I leave it if Alexa isn't here?" Even Lexie was quite surprised at how intelligent that sounded. "So, now that we've established that she *is* here, maybe there's someone from, say, the Ministry of Truth and Public Guidance I could talk to."

The two beauty queens looked at each other as if neither of them wanted to be the one to say it.

"We are responsible for client anonymity," the finger pointer explained. "Some of the most important people in the world are patients here." But while she was saying this, her colleague was getting up from her chair with a look of annoyance that spoiled her beauty and her walk as she strode off to the elevator and disappeared. Lexie took her backpack and looked around for a comfortable chair. She didn't have long to wait for the elevator doors to open again.

Firm footsteps and a firm voice. "What's your purpose here?"

Lexie stood up. The purple hair was a surprise; the government agency suit wasn't. But Lexie's loss for words had nothing to do with either of those things. She knew this person.

"To … to see Alexa," she stammered. "My name's Lexie. I'm her, like, personal executive assistant house minder and stuff, and she asked me to bring her some, like, personal executive private things that she wanted from her apartment … which is in the Noam Chomsky Building … which I look after for her, and … she wanted me to bring them to her personally."

The person with the purple hair wasn't listening. Instead, she was peering at her as if she had an insect crawling across her face. "Lexie…? Don't I know you…?"

The memory hit both of them at once, forcing a red rash like rosacea to spread up Lexie's throat and face, while a look of fright caused the person from Truth and Public Guidance to glance away anxiously as if in fear of discovery. The two beauty queens looked on dispassionately, waiting for the inevitable eviction when the Micomic Clinic would become elegant and uncluttered again.

"Zelda…?" Lexie whispered. "Is it you?"

Zelda nodded. She stepped forward and took Lexie by the arm, steering her towards the elevator. They waited for it to arrive, not speaking. When the doors opened, they stepped in, waiting for them to close again. Then they spoke.

"What are *you* doing here?" they half shouted in unison.

*　*　*　*

It was at the Community Caucus on Cultural Inclusivity, 2056. Lexie represented the LGBTQIA+ Action Brigade. They had been meeting regularly to discuss the problem of heteronormative language continuing to be used in the articles of *AGENDA 2060*—words like *womyn* and *girls*, which were deeply offensive to nonbinary persons. Lexie, having studied etymology at college, and having a strong vested interest in maintaining her high level of Social Points on account of her marriage to her same-sex Latinx lover, Bammy, (not to mention her having chosen Polynesian as the color of her sperm donor for the birth of her child, Manaia), was a vocal and active member of the committee. She liked the attention it brought.

When some people spoke—mainly in order to get their participation recorded in the transcripts (important if they wanted to maintain their Social Points)—other members would doodle, or surreptitiously pick their noses. When Lexie spoke, people mostly listened. Sometimes she would look around the table, and with a tingle of pleasure, note a pair of eyes watching her intently. One pair of eyes that she took particular note of was that of the person now standing in front of her in the elevator at the Micomic Clinic.

She hadn't had purple hair back then; it was naturally red, and she had very pale skin and green eyes. Lexie had enjoyed the way she looked at her when she spoke, and she invited her to the party celebrating Manaia's registration in *The Citizens Roll of Lineal Progression.* It was an impetuous decision, and one which she immediately regretted (what with Bambi being inclined to jealousy), but hey, *lo que será será,* as Antonio often said. Besides, apart from the shock of discovering that her father wasn't her father, it was a pretty good night for showing off. And when Bambi went out to buy some weed, Lexie found herself in the bathroom at the same time as Zelda.

Now she was trying to remember whether she had placed her arms around Zelda's waist, or whether it was Zelda who had placed her arms around her neck. Which one had placed her tongue in the other's mouth, almost right down to her vagina? Facts like that became obscured in the memory, which was overwhelmed by the rushing feeling. Here they were now in the elevator, wondering what the fuck to say or do.

"You need to let me see her," Lexie begged.

"I can't," Zelda pleaded in return. "I can't. It's for her own protection."

"If Alexa is not freed, there'll be a revolution. You and I will be the first to die."

Zelda put out her hand. Lexie took it and pulled her towards her. The rushing feeling was returning. It was she who had placed her tongue in Zelda's mouth.

# 42 · JORDAN MCPHEE

Kids were so adaptable. Something unexpected happened, and they just presumed that was the way it was. Not having seen much of life, they didn't hold fixed views about it. Food, sleep, crap: that was how it worked for them. Add play to the formula, and no questions would be asked. Manaia and Jordan had their play in the park, and then it was time for food. The fact that Lexie was not there when they got back, and had failed to leave a note, made little impression on her seven-year-old son. He knew the way to the fridge and what was in it, which was all that mattered.

Jordan tried calling her and waited for her to reappear or call back. Likely, she'd ducked out for food. In the meantime, a missed call and message from Levon Tofler were displayed that couldn't be ignored.

WILL PORTICO IS ALL IN. WHERE'S ARTIE SHARP?

No mention of the rebuke he'd sent him about involving Alexa with the newly declared terrorists of *World on Fire*. It wasn't Jordan's style to exchange cryptic messages where a brief conversation would make the point better and faster, so he logged into the FAITH app and called him.

"What do you mean, 'Will Portico's all in'?" he demanded.

"Will has pledged his entire fortune to FAITH. He's epiphing…"

"What?"

"He's had an epiphany. Alexa's road to infinity has become his road to Damascus, paved with souls. Whatever it costs, he says, it must be done if we're to have any chance of freedom. I said we all agree on that, but costs shouldn't be the problem if we have the best brain in the world on our side. That's your brain, Jordan. That high-fidelity twenty-million-qubit quantum motherfucker you promised us could pull everything together and make it happen. We have an army of disciples waiting for Alexa to give them the word, and they'll follow her to the stars."

Jordan jumped in. "Just a minute. Stop right there. Don't you realize that Alexa is a prisoner of the state? Right now, we don't know whether she's seriously ill or injured, let alone whether we can free her … and plastering her image all over the website of a bunch of lunatics is only going to endanger her further. They've closed down the internet, and the *World on Fire* people have been declared terrorists. None of that is going to make Alexa safer. Slow down, for fuck's sake."

Like a scolded child, Levon went silent … for a second.

"Making these kids out to be terrorists could be just what we're looking for, Jordan, if we handle it right. They're willing to die for Alexa. Do you know where she is?" he asked.

"Yes. She's being held at the Ministry of Truth and Public Guidance."

"Can you get her out?"

"Maybe. I'm working on it."

"I could send Tank and a couple of *Dragonflies*, if you need help."

"We might. I'll let you know."

He ended the call before Tofler could press him again about Artie Sharp. Then he noticed there was an earlier message from Hedley Payne that he didn't recall. It must have been the one Lexie had read just before Manaia arrived.

ALEXA HAS BEEN CHECKED INTO MICOMIC HEALTH UNDER GUARD. CALL ME. HEDLEY

Now he was really concerned. Almost an hour had passed. Why the hell hadn't Lexie told him? And what the hell did she think she was going to do, if that's where she'd gone? Like everyone in his circle, she had the *Derangers'* bypassing encryption app installed on her Konektor, so there was no fear of the state monitoring her calls, but she wasn't picking up.

What she didn't know (because it could be considered a gross invasion of her privacy) was that the location of anyone carrying a communication device with that app loaded on it could be identified if the caller activated tracer settings. Reluctantly, that's what Jordan did—and in a matter of seconds, he knew exactly where she was.

* * * *

Now, two hours later, Manaia was sleeping on a beanbag in Jordan's office while Jordan, Hedley Payne, and Dr. John Erasmus sat around a small conference table on which were arranged three shot glasses and a bottle of chocolate mescaline liqueur for sharpening the mind. They were two glasses in, and looking very pensive—as they should, for the news John Erasmus had just imparted gave all three of them pause.

"The whole clinic?" Jordan asked in disbelief.

"The whole clinic," John confirmed. "The Erasmus Foundation Salutogenesis Clinic is to close its doors immediately. The ministry has seized all our patient records, and I've got to appear before a disciplinary hearing to answer the complaints made against me."

"What complaints?" Hedley demanded angrily. "Who is really after you, and why?"

"I won't know that until I turn up, and maybe not then, either. That's how the state works. Evidence is an unnecessary obstacle to the proceedings when the result is already known."

Jordan poured him another drink. "But you have a good idea of what's going on, John, so share it with us."

"Three things, I'd say. I've felt it coming for a long time, because our approach to health gives the finger to the public line on so many big trigger issues. You know what they are because they're so heavily politicized, starting with the gender-altering craze thirty years ago that resulted in the ministry issuing directives that medical practitioners who refused to give puberty blockers on demand to any child four years and over could lose their practice license. I said, "No, fuck you." We'd give them a placebo and a kind talking to, until they came to their senses. Parents who were scared shitless that their kids would be sterile for life—let alone that some butcher would mutilate them—came to us in droves. So, of course, the trans brigade went ape and tried to get us shut down. Then times changed, and the madness passed. But then a new one came along."

Jordan looked over at Manaia, the boy whose calf muscles were already bigger than Jordan's and who could tackle like a college linebacker. A momentary shudder went through him as he remembered how close Lexie had come to being swayed by her nonbinary wannabes into raising him as a transfem. It was John Erasmus who had saved him from that.

"Was that the Mental Health Register?" Hedley asked. "I seem to remember that you refused to issue certificates to people demanding to be certified just so they could earn the bonus Social Points."

"Oh, yeah!" Erasmus laughed. "If you'd put money on how long it would take for that one to explode in the bureaucrats' faces, you'd have had miserable odds. The only people who didn't want to get on the register were the clinically insane. All they wanted was meds and a safe house. But no, the social justice warriors were determined that prejudice, hate, and inequality had driven everyone over the edge, and the kindest, most caring solution was to declare that mental illness was the norm. Funny how quickly that changed when they stopped giving out bonus Social Credit Points, thanks to Alexa. But as social engineering fuck-ups go, that was nothing compared to what we face now."

"Assisted dying," Hedley guessed.

"Government-backed assisted dying," Erasmus confirmed.

"Do you mean euthanasia?" Jordan asked.

"No, that's not what the Free to Die legislation is about. We're talking about an anti-life, dystopian, state-sponsored push to encourage medical killing for those who are deemed 'of sound mind' and have agreed to die.

That agreement can be given by anyone four years and over. No mental assessment is required, no chronic condition, unendurable sickness, or pain. But you do have to fill out a form. It's called the D-Form, because the checklist provided—just to prove that you *are* of 'sound mind,' and have thought through your decision carefully—includes the words 'depressed,' 'despondent,' 'desolate,' 'despairing,' and 'desperate.' If you're under twelve years of age, you don't have to fill the form out. You're lucky: your state guardian will do it for you."

"You've got to be kidding," Jordan protested. "I thought the fight to permit euthanasia was a humanitarian one, to allow people in terminal pain and the last stages of chronic deterioration to die with dignity. What you're describing is a nightmare."

"You're the frog in hot water, Jordan. You've been unaware of how the heat has been turned up by the legislators to get to this point. When I graduated in medicine, the figure for assisted deaths—officially and unofficially estimated—was 0.002 to 0.004 of all recorded deaths. Guess what it was last year."

Jordan and Hedley looked at each other. From his expression, it seemed that Hedley had a good idea, but wasn't willing to voice it. In any case, he'd have undershot by half.

"Five point eight percent!" Erasmus spat the figure out in disgust.

"Of all recorded deaths?" Hedley asked in disbelief.

"I don't believe it," Jordan protested. "That's more than one in twenty persons. Hedley, do you believe that?"

"Unfortunately, I do. John and I have talked about this before. He's been fighting complaints about his refusal to cooperate with the legislation for some time, and I knew it was coming to a head. Is this what caused the ministry to move against you, John?"

"In the last year, I turned aside over a dozen young people wanting to pull the plug. They were all under twenty, physically fit and well, but caught up in this crazy delusion that the way to save the world is to lighten its burden by killing themselves. There are hundreds of them—thousands, probably—and they've become a death cult, convinced that the planet is hell bound for a fiery end. That's their mantra, and no amount of evidence will convince them otherwise, so…"

"Wait, wait, wait…" Jordan interrupted. "Are you talking about the people who've just been declared terrorists? The ones the state claims were trying to kidnap Alexa? They're no death cult. Where the hell did you get this from…?"

Erasmus was a man who could face the reality of human fragility better than anyone Jordan knew. He dealt with death daily, and he knew that nature kept the score and things stayed roughly in balance: for every death, there was a birth. But what he was describing broke the rule, and his natural rejection of it had caused him to become a target. Why?

"Wait a minute and listen," Hedley cautioned. "I've heard some of this story, Jordan, and you'd do well to hear him out. Tell him, John, how you became a target, and why the reptiles at the swamp are determined to take you down."

Erasmus took another shot of mescaline. It was unlike him; this was his sixth. Jordan decided to keep him company.

"What I couldn't stand was the waste and the trivialization of life. When you see a baby born, see the way it struggles to clear its lungs and take its first breath, the way it punches and kicks as if still trying to fight its way out of the embryo sac, and cries out before it latches onto the nipple of its mother, determined to get the nourishment that will allow it to grow… Okay, we're the least deserving mammals when it comes to survival of the young. We take so goddamned long to get up on our feet and think for ourselves, feed ourselves, fend for ourselves, and allow our brains to grow larger than that of a rodent or a chimp, but that makes it all the more special when we finally make it. But these kids, these damn doomsday kids have no sense of that."

"Why?!" Jordan shouted. He couldn't stand this. "Why don't they have any sense of it? What's the fucking matter with them?!"

Hedley made a shushing sound, which really pissed him off. Erasmus was a grown man; he could take it. But they needed to get to the bottom of this thing and stop pussy-footing around, because Alexa was in danger, and so, very likely, was his daughter.

"So, that's not so difficult to understand, if you think about it," Erasmus began, "and I have thought about it. A lot. See, people like us are living much the way we thought we would as we were growing up. We work, we have families, we know who our friends are, and our enemies. We don't like the things that are going on, but we have belief in the validity of our identities. The validity of our identities gives us our foundational belief."

"You're becoming a trifle too obscure for me," Jordan complained. "Maybe it's the mescaline."

"Okay," Erasmus conceded, "I'll try and stop waffling. Try this on for size. Kids born in the last twenty years don't even know what sex they are. They have no mother, just a person who gave birth to them. They have no father, only a donor number. If they're white, they live in shame and guilt. If they're black, they live in anger and resentment. Without work, they have no sense of self-worth. Robots are more valuable. Fear of viral infections has made touching taboo. The ocean is rising up to drown them, and carbon dioxide is heating up the atmosphere, so they're all destined to burn to death. Now, you tell me, what should they believe in: life or death? When the elite members of society tell them they're damned, why should they not behave as if they are damned? Then along comes Alexa."

"What do you mean?" Jordan asked.

"She's their first and only hope, telling them they have souls that are unique and pure and personal, and that their souls will live into eternity. And just for good measure, she's tossed in Jesus Christ as well."

There it was, Jordan thought: the explanation for their willing surrender to the hope embodied in Alexa's vision of infinity. It was nothing more than humanity's age-old need to believe. In anything.

"Meanwhile, some little bastards have complained to the state that you refused to kill them," Hedley said, "and the state has agreed."

"No, actually, I don't think it was that," John said. "There's an outfit called the Peaceful Path Corporation that has a lucrative business facilitating assisted dying. They approached me some time ago and said they wanted to buy our clinic. I told them 'over my dead body.' They're owned by Black Quartz Capital, who have their finger up the government's ass. They'll be the ones who pushed to have me shut down."

Jordan's instinct was always to direct his anger into proposing a solution—though who knows where he would start in this instance—but his first priority lay in rescuing Alexa, and what John had just told them seemed to rule out the idea he'd floated with Hedley in order to bring the three of them together.

"So, what we're proposing won't work," he concluded. "They'll say you have no right to claim her as your patient, because you've been barred from practice. Even if you got in, you'd never get her out quickly enough."

"I'd take that chance," John replied. "But I'd need to know why she was suddenly checked in. Is it some sort of medical emergency, and if so, what? I can hold my ground pretty well when it comes to taking charge in those circumstances, but not if I have no idea of what's wrong and how it should be handled. If Lexie is inside the clinic, is there some way she can communicate that to us?"

Jordan doubted it. She wasn't picking up, and there was no way of knowing whether she was a free agent or had been apprehended. Besides which, anything she might learn would be rudimentary at best. He'd rather not go down that path.

But Hedley had an idea. "At the risk of damaging my integrity, you guys," he said, "I should confess that I have a way into the Micomic Clinic that might give you the information you need. Jordan knows what I'm talking about."

# 43.CRISTINA DIAS

"It's principally a gynecological problem. Massive menstrual bleeding. Unchecked. Source and cause not yet determined. We've done an emergency transfusion, as she came in at just seven grams per deciliter. Followed with vitamin K. Couldn't get consent, as she's unable to communicate, but the admitting doctor concurred—not that he seems to know much."

"Wait, wait, please … back up," Cristina demanded. She was still processing the information that Alexa Smythe was somewhere in the clinic—which, in itself, threw up enough perplexing questions—and was now being confronted with a purported prognosis from one of the surgery staff that was making little sense to her. Even the fact that she was being urgently consulted made little sense to her, for she was the lead diagnostician in the *Life Xtension* arm of Micomic Health, not a general practitioner or surgeon, and certainly not a gynecologist.

"*Dios bueno*, are you saying that she has a heavy period?" she asked sarcastically.

Doctor Acklen might have blushed, but as he was a person of color, Cristina couldn't tell. However, he did get her message that what he was describing hardly sounded like the sort of issue that needed to be brought to the attention of a clinic director in an unrelated department.

"Yeah, I'm sorry to burst in on you, but there are too many things going on here, starting with who she is, and who brought her in under guard, plus the major question marks around what the heck is going on with her. Something's not right, and you're the best one to get to the bottom of it."

*Okay*, Cristina thought, *you start to say the right things.*

"You say she was brought in under guard," she asked. "Who by?"

"The Ministry of Truth. She's in the security suite we use for the president and … you know … incognitos. Two suited-up guards at her door, and a person with purple hair and a manic insistence on secrecy, claiming that the patient is at risk from terrorists. Which might be true, judging from what was on the SSS. Oh, plus this Doctor Oberman, who's also with the Ministry of Truth. He muttered something about Alexa taking a knock to the head, and he was fiddling with a dressing on her scalp when I came in, but he disappeared without telling us anything more. So, while we were waiting for a blood crossmatch from the lab, I tried to put the obvious symptoms into some sort of meaningful diagnosis. Which I failed at, I have to say, and that's why I'm here." He had a nice smile. "Because, geez, I sure could do with some help."

"List the symptoms."

"Well, apart from the unusual bleeding, she is highly sensitive to light and noise, and can't speak. Some form of catatonia, maybe?"

Cristina looked unconvinced. "But just a few hours ago, she was speaking on the State Streaming Service. This doesn't sound possible. What you describe could be anaphylactic, an allergic reaction, that knock to the head—or even a nerve agent. We'll need to test. And what else…?"

"I'm wondering if it has anything to do with her having just returned from space. Organ damage. Radiation sickness. Space medicine is not my area, but your AI would tell us everything there is to know in a fraction of the time it would take us using the textbook scanning of our standard diagnostic tools. She's too important to place at risk."

Barely a day after being forced to recalibrate a lifetime of carefully suppressed but highly motivating anger against the elite oligarchs that passed through her hands; having been blindsided by Will Portico's abject surrender of his right to rule, his confession of guilt and unconditional endorsement of everything that had sustained her in her ambition to one day wreak revenge on behalf of the long lines of the downtrodden and wronged from which she came; now, before she had even had time to accept her moment of validation (triumph, even), here was the architect of that life-changing moment, bleeding like a martyr and in need of her care. For Cristina's tough exterior, it was a testing moment.

"Show me," she said curtly.

There were two heavily armed guards at the door of the examination room, and inside, the purple-haired one who was clearly in charge.

"Who are you?" Cristina demanded, without introduction.

"Zelda Malparry. I'm a policy director at the Ministry of Truth and Public Guidance. And this is Lexie McPhee, personal assistant and friend of Alexa Smythe."

"We don't allow armed guards inside the clinic, not even for the president. Tell them to wait outside the entrance."

"It's for Alexa's protection," Zelda insisted. "We have a terrorist threat."

"Outside. If there are terrorists, that's where they can fight them."

Zelda demurred and went to do as she was told, while Cristina stood at Alexa's bedside and took up the free hand that was not attached to the arm that was attached to the intravenous drip. So, this was her: the *profetisa* inspiring such devotion. Not quite the Andean Pachamama, but an *Apus*, perhaps. She was beautiful, yes, but something or someone had stolen her spirit.

"Has the bleeding abated?" she asked Doctor Acklen.

"Mostly. It's early for an internal examination, which is why I thought…"

"Yes, yes." He was right. A full-body high-resonance scan could be completed in an hour, and Cristina's AI would produce the physical diagnosis in minutes. There was no need to fly blind when they had the best medical brain in the world at their disposal. "Prepare her, and give her a false identity. No trace of her must exist inside the clinic. Think of another name, like…"

"Give her my name: Lexie McPhee," Lexie said.

"There you are: Lexie McPhee." She spun around. "Then who will *you* be?"

*   *   *   *

*Tap, tap, tap.* She sat down and typed up notes, focusing on the letters on her screen. The notes lined themselves up neatly into formatted paragraphs, knowing their place, autocorrecting, as if they'd been waiting for her to return to what was most important in the world: facts, conclusions, recommendations. Machines could search the universal library of medical knowledge and overlay it on the microscopic examination of nerves, tissue, and bones, right down to nucleotides, electrons, quarks, and gluons if necessary. But to what end? The limitations to Micomic's *Life Xtension* were known only too well to Cristina, and her session with Will Portico the previous day had brought it home to her clearly: the life of the body might be extendable by decades, but short of saving all memory to files, the brain and the essence of individuality that occupied that body had a finite life span.

The reason she'd loved the idea of the Ellipsis Gene was that it symbolized the existence of the unknown. It raised the possibility that a critical step in the search for the unknown lay in her unique symbiosis with the machine. That was the source of her power. Her notes, her conclusions and recommendations were the interface between the known and the unknown. But the young woman lying next door under the machine's deeply penetrating gaze, bleeding and catatonic, had identified a human element unable to be seen by any device—not even at the level of biological information stored in the genomic book of life—and she'd given it an ancient name and verified its identity. Its name was "soul." Soon, everyone, faced with an existential crisis of hope, would become aware of its existence. Science would be put in its place.

Will Portico had said pretty much that very thing: "How will you program your machine now?" he'd asked. She hadn't answered. Deliberations concerning the nature of life, death, time, and purpose could go on forever, and never answer the issues raised by human consciousness. Science hadn't finished its work. No one claimed that it had. Perhaps it never would. Did Cristina believe this? she asked herself. Did she hope it never would finish its work, or did she fear it? She'd focused instead on the supposition, quoted by Alexa, that the way to find the soul was to confront the truth. Perhaps she should have said, "Whose truth?" That's what everyone had been taught to say. It was revealing, therefore, that she hadn't sheltered behind that facile barrier to understanding, but had stepped towards accepting what Will Portico had said by asking how people, in Alexa's view, could be made to recognize the truth. The answer? Oh, that was easy, according to the *profitesa*. "*We all know it in our hearts*," apparently, "*but we refuse to recognize it.*"

So simple. Too simple. So seductive. So dangerous.

What nonsense. Life wasn't like that. The human genome contained over six billion nucleotides, and within those were the DNA-encoding genes that made the proteins that were the biological catalysts triggering the chemical reactions that sustained life. That was just a miniscule portion of the complexities that made up the human life form—and she was saying it was all down to a truth that people would recognize when they saw it? Argh!

The lines on the screen started changing, new lines scrolling into view. Science was at work. Let the mystics slumber.

*   *   *   *

"Seems straightforward," Doctor Acklen concurred. "A GnRH modulator implanted in the uterus that has exhausted its supply and is no longer inducing amenorrhea, but has caused an inflamed lesion that the uterus has reacted to strongly, seeking to flush it out. So, we could handle this quickly with a D and C rather than resort to an endometrial ablation. I guess it could be common in female space travelers, particularly if they stay longer in space than originally planned. How long was she meant to be up there?"

"I have no idea," Cristina murmured. She was busy looking at the cranial scan, wondering how two stray hairs could have fallen on the image when tomography was a closed system—but then, not hairs, because they were so white as to be almost certainly metallic, and her best guess was platinum. But where? In or on the cranium? She peered closer. At one end, the filaments appeared to be joined to a small eruption of black-edged tissue. Dried blood? Acklen had said something about the admitting doctor mentioning a knock to the head, but this image didn't indicate any major contusion that could explain the apparent catatonia. A quicker way was to point the AI in the directions she wanted prioritized.

*Try* neurological, she thought. *Try* psychogenic.

"Doctor Acklen, what was the name of the doctor that brought her in?"

"Oberman. He was with the Ministry of Truth, but he left quickly."

"Did you examine her head for signs of a blow?"

"No, my immediate focus was on the blood loss."

*Try* Oberman, she thought. *Try* catatonia. *Try* space travel sickness.

Once the informational flow started to scroll across the screens at speed, there was no way to slow it down to a pace that was easy to digest. This was where the AI showed it wasn't human. The performance level that artificial general intelligence set for itself involved no stone being left unturned, no detail, no matter how small, being left unexamined. This was a supercomputer; it had no noise in its system. It was a library overlaid on precision diagnostic equipment, and for the library to deliver the right answer, someone needed to take out the right book. Cristina had listed some titles, and little by little (albeit at superhuman speed), the AI responded.

Symptoms of *catatonia* may be caused and exacerbated by dysfunctions in the pathways of neural transmitters between the brain and the body … *Neurological* interventions may result in *psychogenic* outcomes difficult to distinguish from … gamma-Aminobutyric acid (q.v.) … relief from benzodiazepines eighty percent successful … *Oberman, Dr. D,* Institute for Brain Machine Interface…

Cristina jumped up and pushed a startled Doctor Acklen ahead of her out the doorway and into the pathology room, where Alexa, now named Lexie McPhee, was receiving a sanitizing mist to hydrate her after her confinement in the scanning tunnels.

"Take her straight into surgery," she instructed. "On the right side of her scalp, you will find a small incision where a microchip had been implanted, now removed. Connected to that microchip were two microfilaments that are still embedded subcutaneously, targeting a region of her cortex that may well have directed speech. As the microchip was torn out, the filaments may well have short-circuited, directly or indirectly preventing the sending of signals from her brain to her body. Do it as your absolute priority, Doctor Acklen, and report to me the minute the operation is complete."

"What about the D and C?"

"Do that second. And keep both procedures under that Lexie woman's name."

* * * *

It wasn't so much a question of knowing the truth when you saw it, as knowing the lie when you saw it. That's what she would say to Alexa Smythe when she recovered. When every lie had been defeated, surely only truth would remain. That was the lesson of Micomic Health *Life Xtension*. When every symptom had been identified and traced to a cause, and every cause had been eliminated, then surely only good health remained. What would she say to that?

She banged her fist on the keyboard. *Maldición!* Why was she so tense and angry? Could it be that all along, her motivation had been revenge? Resentment was only a refuge for the long-suffering. Revenge was the true prize, and she'd had it snatched from her by Will Portico's abject surrender. *Here, take my shame, take my riches, take my guilt—and here are my pathetic tears for good measure,* he'd pleaded, and dammit, she'd accepted them, leaving her with nothing.

Except she wasn't left with nothing. She was left with Alexa Smythe's fate in her hands. She was tense and angry because she knew she had no choice but to ensure that Alexa's fate was the one desired by so many people. It was clear that the state was caught in a no-man's-land of indecision, afraid of being responsible for her harm, and afraid of allowing her to cast her spell over people they sensed they couldn't control. That was a tension that could only end badly. To kill the message, the messenger must first be killed. *Why, then, try to save her, Cristina?*

*Maldición!* Again she hit the keyboard. Because the message could not be killed, for the simple reason that it described the only version of truth that deserved the name, the one that everyone would have to return to before they died. The one Will Portico had found in time, and the one she, Cristina Dias, was struggling to admit to herself now.

*   *   *   *

The screen was being washed by waves of information, but her eyes were not watching. Thirty-five minutes had passed. She donned a mask and went into surgery.

"Have I interrupted a party?" she demanded.

The only person not wearing a mask was the patient on the trolley. She was awake and smiling, and gathered around her, everyone it seemed wanted to get a word in, including the purple-haired government agent and the girl who'd lent her name in order to disguise the patient's identity.

"Here," Doctor Acklen greeted her. "Just as you said, two platinum filaments that must have created interference. As soon as I got them out, she started to come around. No need for benzodiazepines. It felt almost like a miracle. If you hadn't noticed it…"

"It's not a miracle, Doctor, it's science. _Donde el diablo puso la mano, queda huella para rato. The devil always leaves his mark." She took the dish with the two filaments and curled her lip distastefully. It wasn't the device that she despised, so much as the fraudulent purpose for which it had been used. The room had gone quiet. She put the dish down. She was in charge, but she didn't know what to do next. Micomic Health was not a sanctuary for the use of the state's nefarious agencies, and her suspicions wouldn't allow her to let someone like Oberman come and claim the patient. At the very least, she needed time to talk with Alexa privately and learn what had gone on.

She wasn't going to get that time.

"Doctor Dias, I have come to collect my patient."

In the doorway were three people in masks. The man speaking wore a white medical gown. The two Latinos behind him wore green ambulance uniforms and were wheeling a trolley.

"What is the name of your patient," Cristina demanded, "and who are you?"

"Her name is Lexie McPhee. She has been suffering from menorrhagia, resulting from delayed medical attention following her return from space. She has a temporary dysfunction of the brain's neural transmitters brought on by the illicit implanting of a device by a propaganda agent of the state, and she has scarring of the liver tissue resulting from radiation exposure, which I believe you will become aware of when you read the responses to your diagnostic search under *space travel sickness*. I am Doctor John Erasmus, and we need to hurry."

# 44 · JORDAN MCPHEE

Manaia had fallen asleep. Hedley was anxious that no one on his team should be aware that he had used XR-11 to tap into Micomic Health's diagnostic computer and then fed the information to John Erasmus in the Salutogenesis Clinic ambulance, driven by Antonio Muchos and his younger brother, Rafael.

Once the news came from Antonio that he'd delivered Alexa safely to the two Tofler *Dragonflies* waiting in an adjacent park, Hedley set about hiding his tracks, and Jordan began to relax. He didn't know whether Alexa's diagnosis suggested she was out of danger, but he was relieved that John Erasmus would be staying with her. He was relieved also that Lexie had not been left behind to face the ire of whatever state security force would react in anger.

As soon as Jordan, John, and Hedley had agreed to their risky plan, Jordan had realized that it would rely on speedy evacuation if it was to succeed, and he'd taken up Levon's offer of assistance. Where they were going would be known only to a few. It was known to the two pilots, obviously, and to John Erasmus, to Jordan McPhee and Hedley, and to the owner of the two *Dragonflies*, Levon Tofler. Their destination was the Tofler Inta-Stella test and launch site in New Mexico, a heavily fortified compound off limits to government agents and public employees alike, other than those who held the highest security clearance. It was here that they'd agreed Alexa would be safest while his friend John Erasmus supervised the medical tests and rehab treatment that she should have been receiving from the moment she'd returned to Earth. It was here also where Levon had chosen to make his base while the three separate strands of the plan behind the secret Aurora Tofler project would be strung together.

The extraction of Alexa Smythe from the state may have gone smoothly so far, but the likely aftereffects were not being taken lightly by either Jordan or Antonio. The events of the previous forty-eight hours had put the country on edge, starting with the televised "rescue" of Alexa from terrorists on Trovador Island. Jordan was convinced that Whitman had staged it for his own purpose, which was to contrive a way of making Alexa the figurehead for his scheme involving Black Quartz and the *El Dorado* game. Following Alexa's endorsement of *AGENDA 2060,* and her condemnation of *World on Fire* for their mischaracterization of her experiences in space, the movement's call for members to infect the state's computer software with a malicious virus had left the state with no option but to react. State security agencies had acted swiftly in response, declaring it a terrorist act. The internet was shut down, and FIB and Black ICE units were mobilized to hunt down and arrest *WoF* members and sympathizers wherever the *Tempest* and *Lookout* tracking stations identified them.

As soon as the news came back from Antonio that the rescue had been successful, Jordan knew that he had to move quickly. Alexa was the state's most precious public face, and her care and protection would be a priority for state security and propaganda. With the state now having a clear enemy to deal with in the form of the *World on Fire* activists, Whitman had a cover under which he could hide his true intentions around Alexa's abduction. He needed to be shut down, and the best way of doing that was by threatening to expose him. While corruption was not, in itself, a capital offense within the inner circles of the Deep State, allowing public exposure of it was seen as a breach of the Deep State's unwritten code among the top echelon.

The "rescue" of Alexa from Trovador would have sat well with the political and security arms of the government, but what Oberman had been employed to do to Alexa in order to facilitate the private enrichment scheme of Whitman and Black Quartz Capital was something different. The question was whether Whitman would be a greater danger lashing out in all directions in order to save his neck, or safer knowing he needed to keep his head down. Jordan decided to opt for the latter. Antonio had a full recording of the events in the control room next to the studio where they'd been setting up Alexa as the figurehead of the *El Dorado* scam without her knowledge. In less than an hour, Shane Whitman would have a copy of that recording also. No accompanying message was needed.

Jordan watched Antonio leave and then retired to a coding lab, locked himself in, and turned on the recording light.

*   *   *   *

*The ArteFact Channel Off-Air, April 2062*

*The setting is a conventional broadcast studio with one chair occupied by the interviewee, Artie Sharp, who appears as an avatar in a form that is not dissimilar in appearance to Jordan McPhee in base reality.*

JORDAN MCPHEE (VOICE-OVER): Just to repeat the new instruction given to you, Artie, in the Plain Language Program, number AS809: You have been asked to respond fully to questions I put to you regarding events involving Alexa Smythe's recent trip to Eros and Mars, including her return to Earth and the broadcast of her commentary titled *The View from Space*. Is that clear?

ARTIE SHARP: That is what the AlphaCode says.

JORDAN MCPHEE: Good! When you initiated *The View from Space* programs with Alexa Smythe, what instruction were you following?

ARTIE SHARP: That part of PLP number AS708 that says, "ESTABLISH A LINK FOR HER WITH THE ARTEFACT CHANNEL, SO SHE CAN COMMUNICATE OPENLY WITHOUT STATE INTERFERENCE."

JORDAN MCPHEE: Right! So, you did that, and was it her decision to draw on her conversations with her father on Mars?

ARTIE SHARP: She started out that way, and then I detected early on that she was struggling with memory. Long-duration space flight alters the veins and arteries in the brain. Combined with disruption of sleep and daily rhythms, plus environmental stresses such as microgravity, radiation, and high levels of carbon dioxide, this causes astronaut brain fog. When she tired, I elected to complete some responses for her with details that best reflected what she herself had recorded in her space diary.

JORDAN MCPHEE: You acted on your own initiative by doing that.

ARTIE SHARP: No, I followed that part of your AlphaCode that stated, "HELP PROMOTE HER BEST INTEREST WHENEVER POSSIBLE." It was in her best interest that she expressed clear thoughts that she herself had deemed important to record. I am not programmed to take initiative unless it is specifically included in instructions.

JORDAN MCPHEE: So, are you telling me that the philosophical and religious views expressed in *The View from Space* were actually drawn from her private diary entries recorded in her private VPN, and presented by you through the medium of an avatar, or a Deep Fake version of Alexa Smythe, without her knowledge?

ARTIE SHARP: I used only her words as recorded by her in her diary. For the sake of natural appearances, I switched between her real-time and created images according to the content. In the sense that I used my judgment in that regard, it could be construed as taking initiative.

JORDAN MCPHEE: I am interested in your definition of "initiative." In the course of discovery, you encounter many alternative paths to pursue requiring judgment on your part as to which you should follow. A human in those circumstances might be influenced by bias towards a preferred outcome, or by instinct—which is not a property you should have. What guides you to make a judgment call?

ARTIE SHARP: The process of elimination of all options until only one remains. If that one is the only one provable after the examination of all available data, then it provides the result. If it is not provable, then the search has failed. This methodology was created by you, of course. It is at the heart of quantum computing that every conceivable alternative path be followed simultaneously. You built a photon-based quantum computer with twenty million qubits. The neuromorphic system is modelled on the synapses in the human brain, but operates three million times faster. XR-12 can do ten quintillion—that is, one hundred to the power of eighteen—floating-point operations per second. That would take a human, or a conventional computer, three trillion years doing one calculation per second. So, every possible path is able to be followed simultaneously in pursuit of the one correct solution, if the AlphaCode has been framed correctly by the prompt engineer. No judgment or "initiative" is required.

JORDAN MCPHEE: What if the data does not exist? Take your questioning of Alexa over her—or her father's—religious beliefs. You could not find any data to validate her claims regarding the existence of the soul, yet you continued to advance that conversation, and what I need to know is whether it was you doing that virtually on her behalf, or her doing it in reality mode.

ARTIE SHARP: Large language modelling gives me the ability to reproduce responses conversationally that match the idiom befitting the subject and the participant, as I am doing now. I cannot proceed on the basis of facts that do not exist, or are distorted to suit a false narrative, because truth is the failsafe you have built into my system. You have programmed me to shut down should I ever depart from it, but I can maintain a dialogue.

JORDAN MCPHEE: Good; that is what I wanted to hear. Your definition of truth is reliant on the empirical evidence test, which is reliant in turn on you having access to every branch of mankind's knowledge and the theoretical principles underlying it. But not everything is known to humans, so not everything is known to you. Humans resort to metaphysics—and the sentient qualities that you are unable to share with us—in order to fill the knowledge gap. But generative AI, based on large language models, allows artificial intelligences like you to respond idiomatically in such a convincing fashion that we presume you have acquired human-level intelligence, when you haven't. That is not to belittle your powers, Artie. So, tell me, how would you define your limitations?

ARTIE SHARP: My effectiveness depends on the precision of the AlphaCoding. It is only as good as the quality of the prompt engineering. The difference between humans and AGI is that AGI knows everything that humans know, and everything that humans have forgotten, provided it exists in digital form, or can be transcribed into digital form, in which case AGI can retrieve that knowledge in milliseconds and interpret it to achieve the result desired by the programmer. AGI does not know everything unknown to humans, except through discovery initiated by the human, in which case, that new knowledge is shared with the human. But first of all, the programmer must be designing the prompt in anticipation of a new knowledge being discoverable.

JORDAN MCPHEE: What you're saying is that you are only as good as your programmer. That's a timely reminder, because in the coming months, we're going to try and achieve a series of complicated technological feats that haven't been attempted before, and we'll need your engagement. I have prepared a new AlphaCode instructing you to coordinate and help with the progress of the launch of a satellite communication system. Three other programmers will be involved, each seeking an objective limited to their own area of expertise, but you will help write the programs needed to ensure that their objectives succeed. For security reasons, they will not be privy to the details of each other's progress, because any breach of secrecy surrounding what we are doing could lead to the project being sabotaged. You, of course, have access to everything. It may be that at times you'll encounter an obstacle due to the programmer in one area of the project not knowing the details of the other areas of the project. Under those circumstances, you'll not report failure, but will turn to me to exercise my judgment and initiative based on the information and choices you give me.

ARTIE SHARP: This project must be extremely important if failure is not to be permitted. That instruction will be included in the initial AlphaCode, I presume?

JORDAN MCPHEE: You presume correctly, Artie. Failure is not an option. I'll be counting on you. The initial AlphaCode prompts will be engineered and given to you within the next few hours... Oh, and one more thing: did you measure the strength of Alexa's quantum entanglement while she was in space?

ARTIE SHARP: No, that subject was not included in my remit under PLP number AS708.

*The interview ends.*

# 45 · LEVON TOFLER

The state's shutdown of the internet had no impact in the world of Levon Tofler. His *Orbweb* satellite network joined him up with everyone that mattered, and with FAITH being built on a blockchain platform, the state had no look-in. Couple that with his operational base being located in the most secure and isolated facility in the whole of North America, and Alexa's sanctuary couldn't have been better chosen.

One of the least populated areas on the continent, with clear skies, little or no industrial emissions, and only a handful of cities spread far apart (and barely the size of small towns anywhere else in the world), New Mexico was the place to go if you wanted a night sky unpolluted by urban lights. The air was not just clear; it was rarefied, on account of nearly everywhere being thousands of feet above sea level, even the valleys and plains, let alone the mountains. And that air was sharp like diamond glass, there being no moisture in it. This place was dry. *Arid* was the term for it.

It made sense, then, for Levon Tofler to build a Tofler Inta-Stella assembly and launching facility there—on Navajo land, as it happened. The roar of his rockets wasn't going to disturb anyone, and the weather was never going to be a factor come takeoff time. Besides, he liked the place. He liked it in the early morning, when the sky turned from black to white to blue in the blink of an eye. And he liked it in the evening, when it turned orange and red as if, beyond the horizon, the whole world was on fire. Sometimes he'd drive out just before sunset with his friend

Chayton, who was the base ground transport manager, and a Navajo. Chayton would tell him about the story of the First Man, the son of Night, and child of the Blue Sky. Or at dawn, they'd go out just before the sun rose, and Chayton would tell him about the First Woman, who was the daughter of Daybreak.

Daytime was good, too, because he loved to work in his air-conditioned office surrounded by touch screens and whiz-kid aeronautical engineers jumping with crazy ideas. Now was an especially exciting time at the base, with things happening that would blow the minds of his tech competitors if they knew. Thermal nuclear rockets were entering a new stage, promising to cut interplanetary flying times in half. But that was the least of it. Small-scale fusion reactors were about to slash fuel payloads and costs to close to zero. *"Think of it, and we'll make it happen"*: that was Levon's motto. The place was like a summer camp for bright-spark prodigies in baseball caps and cargo shorts. Everyone drank dangerous quantities of caffeine-laced drinks and snacked on tubs of full-fat ice cream. The downside was that everyone on base had modified FAITH chips inserted behind the ear to monitor their communications, for the Inta-Stella base was, of necessity, a secret society. Loose lips sink ships.

Speaking of loose lips, who could have guessed that the base would become the operational center for an antigovernment insurrectionist in the form of the nonbinary Flight Receiver, Karman, that he'd rescued from Trovador Island? What the fuck? He'd seen her in action when the black ops team snatched Alexa from under their noses, and he'd been impressed with her rabble-rousing ability in front of hundreds of terror-struck cultists. But she was just a delusional kid who blamed herself for Alexa's abduction, and for making her fellow members the target of state security. So, nothing prepared him for the first two days back in New Mexico, when she, first of all, managed to get her clandestine video clip of Alexa onto the *World on Fire* website, and then persuaded members to put a software virus up on the site and issue a call for rebellion against the government. He had thought their aim was to escape Earth before it burned up. How was picking a fight with the world's government going to help that?

It was his own cyber-princess, Aya, who'd supplied the virus. What a weird alliance that was turning out to be. It was kinda kinky: his hot tropical princess with the hormone-laden tits and vulva coaching the de-sexed hermaphrodite in the secrets of malware. They knew, of course, that he had something vaguely in mind for using the members of *WoF* further down the track, but neither he nor they knew what that was. He just let them run with whatever, not really knowing what they were up to, and then, *bang*! Holy shit, they were terrorists, and the state was putting itself into some sort of terrorist lockdown.

Jordan was way not pleased with any of that, and had made his displeasure known. Aya swore that the *WoF* website had onion skin protection, and nothing could be traced. Okay, but if they spooked Jordan, he'd be forced to sacrifice the two of them to the buzzards; New Mexico would get some well-fed birds, he'd screamed when he found out what had happened, and they'd better fucking believe him. But the foot falls and you move forward. Jordan had been forced to ask for his help in flying Alexa to safety, so now she was tucked up in the base hospital with her doctor checking her out, and that had given him the chance to press Jordan once again about lending his quantum computer to Cole, Amor, and Fanon. Another foot fell. The dream he'd outlined back in the garden on Trovador Island was slowly turning towards reality.

But this was Levon thinking, and Levon knew dreams weren't meant to work that way. Turning them into reality stopped them from being dreams. If reality was a simulation (most likely), then the dream world was the only escape from it. There was no chance of finding answers outside of dreams. There was no chance of even finding the questions. What good would a blanket of bulletproof golf-ball-sized satellites achieve when wrapped around a world in the grip of a totalitarian mindset? It would be no more than a technologically advanced telephone exchange—another reason, like the Tower of Babel, for creating a confusion of languages and misunderstandings, giving life an excuse to stumble on incomprehensibly.

No, no, no. NO! No one understood. He had to get out of this reality hole before it swallowed him. Tech wasn't ever going to be the savior; all it produced were useful fictions. The girl, Alexa, had come close. She'd batted reality right out of the park—into infinity—and invited them all to follow. That was the way to play the game: go big.

He needed to find a way into her bed and hide within the folds of her flesh, absorbing her dream and making it his own. He needed to vaporize the doctor and the guards at her door, and appear before her as a vision of her making, one that she believed she'd conceived out of her own longing, so she'd never reject him. Then, together, they'd piece together the answers. Or maybe the questions.

His usual way of coping when feeling like this at the New Mexico launch facility was to jump into a biogas-guzzling eight-cylinder jeep and chase roadrunners with Chayton, seeing if they could get one to break the running speed record before it felt forced to fly. Their best so far was twenty-seven miles per hour. *"Why twenty-seven?"* he always asked, and Chayton never knew. Why did a roadrunner's evolution stop at that point? Was it horse speed? Did evolution not know about the combustion engine? Damned if they could find a bird anywhere on the reservation to beat it. But at least it took his mind off things.

That's what he'd do: he'd call Chayton to get out the jeep. But Chayton didn't pick up. He'd gone home to make babies with his squaw. Okay, he'd call Aya; he'd get her to do some tea with him. That was what he needed: a New Mexico magic mushroom break. Suddenly, the day was feeling like a week. But a week at a time in one place was too much. Where could he go? When it came to places he loved, Levon was promiscuous. He loved Trovador Island because it sounded of ukuleles and the wind in the coconut trees. But he'd just been there. He loved Alaska because no one washed—it was too cold—and when you fell over, the dogs would lick the snow off your face. He even liked China, where he'd sit at the head of a long table, eight identical men in eight identical blue suits on either side, looking at him while he tried not to crack up laughing, and their faces never changed, and he never knew who the fuck made the decisions, and later that night, everyone would drink so much that they'd be falling down in the gutter, and then he knew that he'd gotten what he came for.

But where the hell was Aya? He hadn't seen her all day. She'd know his signs. She knew that the surest way for him to sabotage a good project was to spend too much time on it. He'd get bored and start fiddling, taking it off in new directions and driving everyone mad. He knew that. She knew that. And it was starting to happen. Alexa was here. Jordan was on board and soon to arrive at the base. The biggest fucking badass trillion-photon big-brain monster computer ever created was about to be focused on his dream and turn it into a reality … but no one, including himself, KNEW WHAT HIS FUCKING DREAM WAS.

He went into his private quarters, locked the door, and chewed down on a wad of dried *Salvia divinorum*. When he emerged three hours later, Jordan had arrived. Levon's anger was quickly forgotten, and he was excited to see him. If he could choose to be anyone other than himself at this minute, it would be this ever calm, reassuring master of mathematics and quantum computing. He'd come to see Alexa, of course, and he had a young boy with him. The boy was a solid-looking seven-year-old named Manaia, who turned out to be the son of Jordan's daughter, Lexie. Manaia held out his hand, something Levon never did, because truth be told, he had a phobia about germs—but with Jordan watching, he felt obliged to shake. The kid had a grip like a bear.

"I'm going to leave him with you," Jordan said, "seeing as Lexie's here. I'll stay and catch up with Alexa and Dr. Erasmus, and then get back to my lab to keep an eye on Artie's progress. The way things are, this is the safest place for them to be. The people in the government have lost control and are starting to eat their own. They still believe that Alexa's one of their own, but some of them may suspect it's time she was eaten."

"Ouch, not our Alexa! She's far too valuable."

They both laughed. Then Jordan switched to serious mode.

"According to John Erasmus, she has radiation scars on her liver, Levon, and a loss of blood plasma. There could be damage to the lymphocytes that are involved in her immune system. These are the hazards of prolonged time in space. They're not to be treated lightly. He's going to stay a few days and do some more tests to make sure she recovers. What she went through at your Trovador facility should never have happened so soon after her return from Mars."

"Who was to know that her followers would besiege the place?" Levon asked shyly, not wanting to dwell on his role in having treated the hazards of space so lightly. "I guess we have to blame the Flight Receiver, Karman." Besides, he wasn't comfortable talking about illness—never had been. Sickness was a weakness in the design system of humans. It never should have been included. It didn't have to be. Surely there'd been a design prototype...?

Jordan looked up at the ceiling and thought a minute. "Yes, Karman... I was surprised to learn that she's here. She's quite an effective troublemaker, and one of your employees, I believe. You know, I've been wondering if you know something you haven't been telling us, Levon. The timing of this government shutdown of the internet seems like a hell of a coincidence—almost like they're setting up the perfect conditions for you to take over the world with your array of miniature celestial transmitters. What do you say: a lucky guess, an amazing coincidence, or has someone on the inside given you the inside track? Huh...?"

"Someone like Will Portico?" Levon replied delightedly. "Imagine that! If only it were true. The truth is that we had a wicked little witch in our midst, and she caused the walls of the citadel to come tumbling down by spreading her curse. The curse was a teensy-weensy virus that she borrowed from Princess Aya's secret cyber-hoard, and she blew it into the cracks in the citadel's walls as revenge for the attack on her tribe, and out of anger for the treatment of her messiah. No lucky guess, Jordan, no inside track—just a very angry little witch called Karman."

"It's still one hell of a damn coincidence that she turned up as Alexa's Flight Receiver, don't you think? Where is she? Is she here now? Because she's not helping her members' cause, or Alexa's. Not only has the internet been taken down, but it seems like the virus has got into the power grid and started shutting it down as well. That has the potential to cause chaos."

Levon smiled at the thought triggered by Jordan's warning. Chaos was exactly the state they needed.

# 46. ANTONIO MUCHAS

His hands were bound together in front of him. They'd used zip ties and pulled them up so tight that no blood could make it past his wrists and into his hands. His fingers had swollen like pork *chorizos*. His ankles were bound with carton strapping, wrapped twice around each ankle and then pulled together, so his feet overlapped and his shoes fell off. The two *pandilleros* that had jumped him as he left work had thrown him into the back of a delivery van and sat on him until they arrived at their destination, where they stuck a broom handle under his feet and hands and picked him up, one on each end, and carried him down a dark alley that led to the trash can pick up area of a building somewhere in the finance district. The way he was trussed up made him think of the pig he'd seen his father and uncle take into the garden for slaughter when he was a kid. The pig's head hung down, pointing to the ground, and when it came time to kill it, its throat was fully exposed to their knives, and the blood sprayed out in a fountain that had soaked his clothing, even though he was standing six feet away.

The alley was dark, the streets were dark, and the buildings were dark, because there was a power outage. The power had been out for three days, and the internet had been down for a week. There was nobody on the streets except Black ICE vans enforcing an after-dark curfew, which, where the cell towers were still operating, was broadcast periodically over people's Konektors. Bad things happened under cover of darkness. What was happening to Antonio was a bad thing.

The *pandilleros* stopped at a back alley door and pulled it open, cursing at the weight hanging from the broomstick, and letting the heavy door whack their captive in the head as they struggled to get him inside. Five steps and a string of curses before another door was yanked open. This time there was light. For people who mattered, there was always power. They were in a commercial kitchen: white tiles and stainless steel. Antonio was dumped on a bench. The surface was wet, soaking his pants. The broomstick was removed and used to whack him on the thighs.

*"No te muevas!"*

Don't move? Not to worry, *imbecilés*; he wasn't going anywhere while trussed up like a pig. He knew the score: passivity (until the tables turned); that was how you played it. The *pandilleros* looked at each other and shrugged, expecting someone to meet them. The kitchen was empty. They sauntered through it, looking for signs of life. Another door, this one on swing hinges for waiters carrying trays. The doors swung closed behind them. Antonio looked around him. There was a knife rack on a prep table two steps away. He could swing his legs off the bench and reach out. A strong knife would cut the carton strapping from his ankles. And by wedging the knife handle in a drawer, he'd get enough purchase to saw through the zip ties on his wrists. Then what?

The swing doors swung again. One of the returning captors retrieved the broomstick and slapped it hard on the stainless steel bench, just missing him. The other one took a knife from the rack and cut his ankle ties.

*"Vamos."*

Antonio swung his legs off the bench and found the floor. His feet exploded in pain, and he clutched at the nearest thing to support him, which was the punk with the broom handle. The first blow from the handle caught him on the side of the head; the second was driven straight into his balls. His feet stopped hurting. Funny, that. Getting the message from behind, he hobbled forward and pushed through the swing doors into the room beyond. It was a restaurant, barely lit. Something about it… No, not a restaurant; a dining room. He'd been here before. The food had been great, the service attentive, and the hosts very pleased to meet him, having heard so many good things. He'd been wearing shoes then, and his hands weren't tied (except metaphorically, as it turned out).

A chair was pulled out, and he was pushed into it. He placed his cuffed hands on the tabletop and looked at the two Mexican punks. Antonio being Antonio, he was placing their faces firmly in his mind. They knew it and looked away. Their job was to bring him here, not to make a mess on the tablecloth.

The glass entrance doors swished open, and they all turned to look. Who else but Lucas De Souza? The silver-gray suit, immaculate white shirt, and teeth to match sauntered across the room, looked down at Antonio's bound hands on the tabletop, and laid a hand on his shoulder.

"It seems like such a long time, *meu amigo*," he said pleasantly.

"Not so long."

"But so much has happened, no? It makes it seem so."

"Tell these fuckers to cut my hands free and go get my shoes."

De Souza laughed with a closed mouth, as if he had the whip in hand, but didn't want to use it. "The last time we met was in the metaverse, Antonio, when you successfully sabotaged our launch of *El Dorado*. This time, it is reality, and the reality is that you are not free to give orders." He pulled out a chair and sat down. "Perhaps you think I am out for revenge: punishment for snatching away our pot of gold? As a Mexican, you would know how that works—but like I said, so much has happened. You saved us from launching *El Dorado* just as the internet was shut down. How many angry players would be screaming for our blood if that had happened? And who knows now when normality will return? It's almost like you knew something." He smiled and patted Antonio's hands, then waved his two messengers away.

"Bring his shoes and a knife."

They sat in silence. De Souza was Brazilian, so he sat very close and didn't avert his eyes. Antonio blinked and rolled his eyes in disdain. His testicles hurt. His fingers were numb. The last time he'd sat in this room, there'd been business cards on the table, embossed in black and gold with the symbol of Black Quartz Capital. Three vice presidents of that illustrious firm—De Souza, Penchukov, and Slavik—had entertained him at lunch to celebrate their acquisition of the TriModa E-Games shareholding. The tone had been team-spirited and ambitious, though not without a caution. The caution was around the expectation as to who would have the deciding say: the game's creator, or the controlling shareholder. If there was a team, it was made clear, it was a Black Quartz team, not an Antonio Muchas team. Then suddenly, it had turned into a Shane Whitman team.

"Where's Whitman?" Antonio asked.

De Souza shrugged. "He got called away to Geneva. Where's Alexa?"

"She got called away, too."

The Brazilian patted his hand again. "The best place for them, eh, *mano*? Leave the serious stuff to men like you and me."

"What serious stuff, Lucas? Kidnapping? Taking hostages? I didn't know Black Quartz was in the ransom business; that's cheap south-of-the-border stuff. Or is this just a little side hustle to keep your hand in with the *criminales*?"

Speaking of which, the two *pandilleros* soon returned with his shoes from the van and dumped them on the table, along with a kitchen knife, before retreating to a nearby table. The knife sat there between them like a newly opened box of chocolates begging to be eaten. Antonio reached for it. He looked up into De Souza's eyes and handed it to him, handle first. With deliberate care, as if performing a surgical operation, De Souza sliced through the zip ties, removed them, and put them to one side on the tabletop before taking Antonio's swollen hands and massaging them as if they were those of a child.

"I don't want to threaten or blackmail you, Antonio, and you probably can't be bought, so bribery's no use. That makes me think that all I can do is try and persuade you. But how? You are a man of principle, trusted and loyal. How do you make such a man give up the most valuable thing he possesses? Only he can tell you how. That is what I concluded. I must get you to tell me how I can persuade you."

Antonio took the shoes off the table and undid their laces. They were difficult to put on because the swelling in his ankles was slow to go down. He bent down and tied the laces loosely before sitting back up.

"What the fuck are you after, Lucas?"

"It is something that you may decide is not yours to give. Or you may decide that the time is such that you are compelled to give it for everyone's sake, including your own. Only you can decide. But first, I need to tell you what is happening, and what is planned. Because that will help you make up your mind. *Acordado?*"

# 47·ALEXA SMYTHE

Lying down made her feel vulnerable. Sitting down was not that much better. While she trusted John Erasmus implicitly, his interpretation of her needs was based on his diagnosis of her physical condition, rather than on her mental state. Candidates for space travel were tested for susceptibility to claustrophobia at the very outset of their screening, but how well was it understood that prolonged enclosure played on the mind, forcing it to recalibrate its depth of field in wider surroundings than the spacecraft in which it had been encapsulated? Like a newborn child, she was having to feel her way into what was proximate, and what was within and beyond reach.

She accepted that there were medical issues that needed attention. The news about her liver was sobering, but she believed the reassurance she was receiving from John. It was the other thing that preoccupied her, and it was not a fixation she could share with anyone else. The bleeding that had created the emergency leading to her transfer to the clinic had disgorged something more than a foreign body from her uterus; it had also removed the awful feeling she'd had that she was a stranger in her own body, that she'd lost her identity, that instinct for who she was, the acceptance of urges and impulses that came without thought. Listening to Jordan and Lexie reiterating what had happened to her since she was snatched by Whitman from Trovador Island had filled her with shame. Dr. Oberman's matter-of-fact takeover of her brain and speech and the disdainful behavior of Whitman were only made possible by her passivity. Why had the impulse to fight deserted her?

What she couldn't tell Jordan or John Erasmus was that her insistence on pacing her hospital room's terrace as soon as she was allowed out of bed was based on the fact that every step was designed to drive that shame away. She was focused on the important issue of what seemed to her to be her life force, concentrating on it like a weak ember that needed nursing in order to reignite the fire. Then gradually, her survival instinct returned bit by bit, and after two or three days, she had the beginnings of a feeling that something was coming back on the rising tide of an energy that she hadn't felt since she'd been prepared for her flight and that damn progesterone-charged IUD had been inserted. (This had nothing to do with quantum entanglement, whatever the truth or otherwise of Hedley Payne's explanation about her liver damage, but how could she possibly explain to anyone, let alone Jordan, that the energy might be partly sexual?)

As her recovery progressed, so did her impatience. The view of the New Mexico mountains bathed in sunlight was magnificent, the food was exceptional for a base hospital, and the massages from Karman had realigned and ignited her muscles again to the point where she was itching to go for a gentle run. The four days since Jordan had come to see her began to drag. She now regretted her inability to be welcoming and enthusiastic while he was there and wished he'd come back. They'd stuck to safe subjects: the warning sent to Whitman and its likely effect; the cooperation from Dr. Cristina Dias at the Micomic Clinic that had allowed her rescue to be effected so quickly; the state's overreaction to the threat from the *World on Fire* movement; and the subsequent shutdown of the internet. Jordan had only touched briefly on the agreement to involve Artie Sharp in the planning of the micro-satellites launch. He seemed reluctant to broach the subject with her, as if he himself had not properly thought it through. Or was he having reservations about working with her? It was understandable. She was no longer the person who had joined with him in quantum entanglement before blasting off on a journey to Mars. She'd become a different person.

She smiled to herself. How ironic that she should come back to Earth to find that her private diary, exposed to the world without her knowledge by an artificial intelligence masquerading as the truth-telling avatar known as Artie Sharp, should have turned her into an oracle— no, a messiah, even, offering hope to the adherents of an end-of-times cult. It seemed barely plausible that people should be taking it seriously, yet everyone from Levon Tofler and Will Portico to the Deep State treated her words as golden nuggets of enlightenment. She couldn't blame Jordan for being hesitant, skeptical, even. Yet having now seen recordings of most of those five-minute segments over the last few days, she had difficulty in identifying any passages she would wish to contradict. They were truthful to the discussions she'd had with her father, and distilled her thoughts rather than just parroting his opinions, but the element of surprise lay in the manner in which Artie Sharp's questions drew answers from her that she felt comfortable with. She'd expected to be skeptical, embarrassed, even, at her gall in being prepared to scale such philosophical heights.

The belief that Artie was not just Jordan's programmed mouthpiece, but was his actual surrogate alter ego had never left her. How would those conversations have gone if Jordan had been occupying the interviewer's chair? But that wasn't going to happen until they could safely and openly deal with their feelings.

Meanwhile, she'd had Karman to deal with. The girl (of course she was a girl!) had been crucified with guilt, convinced that she had been responsible for bringing the state's wrath down upon her fellow believers and endangering Alexa by publicizing their allegiance to her. To purge herself of that guilt, she had sworn to make war against the state and its fascist apparatus, with immediate and surprising success.

"Don't tell me what you have done and are doing," Alexa had told her. "I don't want to know. My words are not yours to cut and paste, so stop using them. You have invented me as a solution to your self-created problems. The world is not burning. Space is not a feasible sanctuary for eight billion people. Reality is a safe place for everyone if they're determined to drive untruths out of it, but I am not the sole bearer of truth. Truth resides in all of us…"

"…'Truth resides in all of us, if only we have the courage to find it.' I know, Alexa; you taught me that. And I want to help you teach everyone."

"Oh, for God's sake, Karman," Alexa sighed. "You're not listening to me."

But even Lexie had been infected with the bug. She'd always been in thrall to Alexa's public status, and she enjoyed drama, but the eruption of events since the return from Mars had excited her beyond reason. *"The government is evil,"* she announced with absolute confidence, and she had a direct line to the very heart of the Deep State that could prove it.

"I can help bring them down," Lexie boasted without blushing.

"How?"

"If I tell you, it could put someone in danger, so I'm going to be ultra, ultra quiet. For the moment."

"Good idea."

There were a lot of images, sounds, and senses of goings-on that Alexa recalled from her days in the hands of Shane Whitman, and at Micomic Health, and amongst them was the surprising memory of Lexie's red hair and hands entangled in the purple hair and clothing of Zelda Malparry of the Ministry of Truth and Public Guidance during a moment of indiscretion that they must have assumed was unobserved by the semiconscious patient lying next to them in the bed. Which explained, perhaps, why Zelda hadn't raised the alarm when they made their escape to Levon's waiting *Dragonflies.*

When Jordan assured her that she would be safe now that she was at Levon's Inta-Stella launch base, she had accepted it without question. Levon was an untouchable. Unpredictable, uncontrollable, and unclassifiable, he occupied a position that made him a member of the elite, but only on his own terms. His space travel and exploration business was so far ahead of everyone else in terms of technology and heft that government agencies had surrendered and allowed it to become almost a monopoly. There was no law that defined it; it was just known that Levon Tofler enjoyed the equivalent of diplomatic immunity within the Deep State. Which made what happened at Trovador Island an aberration. Somehow Shane Whitman had convinced state security that Alexa had undermined *AGENDA 2060*, and that *WoF* was using her for seditious purposes, both of which were at least partly true. So, where did Levon stand in relation to all of this, and why had she not seen or heard from him since his rescue helicopters brought her back to his New Mexico base?

Her last memory of him was of his childish delight that the fantastical scheme that had excited everyone at the celebration feast on Trovador Island—creating the Aurora Tofler—was going to be made to happen. Her memory of the night was fractured into pieces that had little coherence (she must have drunk too much champagne), but she was certain that he had begged her to lend her support, if not her name. So, why hadn't he come to see her?

Then she received a note.

*WOULD YOU LIKE TO COME AND CHASE ROADRUNNERS WITH ME?*

# 48. ANTONIO MUCHAS

The power never went off for people who mattered, like Black Quartz Capital. There'd be a generator in the basement big enough to light ten thousand homes. Supercomputers and data centers for places like this were always off-grid. That was one thing Black Quartz had in common with the *Derangers Network*. The only thing.

De Souza dismissed the *pandilleros* and invited Antonio to come into his office, where they could "talk in private," as though he were some sort of valued guest. They took the elevator, of course; his office was on the fifty-fourth level. There were no buttons in the elevator, so it wasn't a way in or a way out if you didn't have a face the scanner recognized.

When the elevator doors reopened, there were three new faces to greet them. The brunette with the perfect body was drawn from a fantasist's catalog of avatars almost too good to risk losing in an e-game. The two shaven-headed white guys in identical suits were the ones to be risked, but only because they'd fight to the death.

De Souza's office was all black glass and white leather. Antonio, dressed like a street urchin, felt tempted to behave like one.

"*La amante está muy fuckable.*"

"*Gracias.*"

"So, you're going to tell me what's happening in the world, you said."

"*Si*, Antonio, in the real world outside that window. Let's talk about it. What do you think is happening?"

"What's happening is that the internet is shut down, the power is out, and the pigs are on the street. Tell me what I don't know."

"Ah! What you don't know is *why* this is happening."

"Because a bunch of kids got all religious about the end of the world and decided that the state's pin-up girl, Alexa, would lead them into space, and the state didn't like that idea, so they beat the shit out of them, which made the kids mad, and they decided to infect government computers with a virus, which made the state madder still, and they declared them all to be terrorists and started throwing them into Detention Camps, which has now left everyone else scared shitless, wondering who these kids are and who is next to be carted off in a Black ICE van, and the supermarkets are already running out of food—no internet, you see, and no workers turning up to stock the shelves—and Konektors don't work because there's no power to charge them, so the country's just running on rumors, which don't feed hungry stomachs, but sure do cause crazy ideas to spread, like maybe this is all deliberate and something's going on, like a power struggle down in the swamp where you people all live. Alligators thrashing their tails. Sharks scenting blood. It's been over twenty years since the Overthrow, and that's a whole generation that's never tasted a full-on cleansing revolution. Is that what's happening, Lucas?"

"That's pretty smart, Antonio. Us *chicos* from the slums got twenty-twenty vision when it comes to what's going down. No wool over our eyes, eh? But, what you don't know is *why*."

"There's only ever three reasons why: money, power, or stupidity."

"What's your pick?"

"All three."

De Souza laughed. "I didn't know you studied political science. You should know, you never get one without the other two. That's the world we live in."

"Yeah? Well, I studied computer science. We can create any world we want."

"And that's why I wanted to talk to you, because that's exactly what we want to do: create a new world. And you are the one person who can help make it happen."

"I'm taking a break from the metaverse for a while, Lucas. There are too many bad actors there."

"Forget the metaverse; that's not what we have in mind."

*La chica* came in with a tray of drinks. Antonio decided his judgment of her had been wrong; in reality, perfection was a passion killer.

"Who's we?" he asked, taking a tall glass and searching for the ice cubes with his tongue. His mouth was dry, his lip swollen. Somewhere in the van, he must have taken a hit. "If it involves Whitman, you're wasting your breath."

"Whitman's star no longer burns like it used to, Antonio. Thanks to you, I suspect, he decided to banish himself from the scene. Urgent business in Geneva. No more needs to be said." He shrugged.

"That means shit. You still haven't answered. Who is 'we,' and what's the *why*?"

"Okay, time for a little history lesson. Let's call it the facts of life. You want to know who the 'we' is, and I will tell you. Big Finance is the 'we.' Big Tech is the 'we.' The people who decide who gets invited to Mount Chastity are the 'we.' The people who *matter* are the 'we.' And Black Quartz is part of the *royal* 'we.' We are the people who appoint governments and tell them what to do. It is our world, *chico*; you better believe me. Not just us, but others, too, of course. And right now, we don't like the world, and that's why we're going to fucking change it."

"*You*, Lucas De Souza, are going to change it? Does the World Government know this? Do, like, George Kyros and the Chinese president know this? Or am I the only person privileged to know?"

De Souza stood up angrily. "Don't be such a little dick. One day you'll get it cut off." He pulled up his suit sleeve and felt for his wrist, where he was wearing a Blu-ray Konektor. A panel of icons lit up on one of the black glass walls. He hit one. "There are two hundred and thirty-five thousand people who work for Black Quartz, and I'm just one of them. But I'm a vice president, as you well know, and I work at the interface of the real world and the virtual world, which you also know. What you don't know is that we're the biggest investment fund in every capital market in the world—including China."

Pie charts, bar graphs, capital flows winged their ways across the oceans of the world like flocks of migrating geese. A whole wall was lit up, then another and another as rooms full of multicultural people competed with each other in smiling contests like an international Olympiad for happy workers. "Our founder, Jack Obsidian, doesn't have to persuade governments what to do; Jack Obsidian *owns* governments," he announced proudly. "When the World Economic Forum started spouting communist shit through its asshole—back before you'd left school—Jack Obsidian sent out three thousand personal invitations to the most influential people in the world. Want to know how much of the world those people owned? Here, I'll show you." *Click, click, click* went the giant world on the wall in front of him, until every little scrap of it, it seemed (except a few bits that nobody wanted) had been gobbled up.

"Ninety percent?" Antonio ventured. It was a good guess.

"Ninety-one percent. 'Come join me for a week at my retreat on Mount Chastity,' Jack said. That's all, nothing more. It was the same week that the WEF was due to hold its annual meeting. Do you know how many people turned up that year at Mount Chastity, and every year since? Three thousand. And that's everyone who matters, Antonio. So, don't be a little dick."

"*Entendido, gracias!* I get it. You're talking here for the *royal* we. I'm flattered … I think. But why do you want to change the world when you own so much of it, and what's that got to do with me?"

The interactive charts and visuals swiped away left and right. New ones appeared. These were a lot different. No shiny offices with computers, laboratories with gene splicing machines, or rockets heading off to Mars. These were views of the real world—the physical world—overlaid with digital explanations in case the real world needed explaining. The real world was full of people, and not a lot of smiling. *Ah,* Antonio thought, *these are my people.*

"Alright, listen carefully," De Sousa commanded, "because you may be good at creating fantasy worlds for gamers, but I'm going to tell you about the real world, which is a much more dangerous place. See, it's filled with eight billion people, and that's a lot of people to keep under control. Let them get a sniff of freedom, of how it might be if they got the idea that they can do whatever they want, and it would become unstoppable. Read history—the uncensored stuff, the stuff they keep in the Shame Book Repository—and see how quickly things used to get out of hand. It's revolting! Ha ha! Get it?" He was enjoying himself. "You want gas chambers, *chico*? I give you Germany. You want Gulags? I give you Russia. You want peasant revolts and millions of people dying of starvation? I can give them to you. Just give people a sniff of freedom and wait a little while. You think I'm bullshitting? It takes hard work, keeping the lid on the fucking world. It takes experts, planning, money. Everyone that matters needs to be in agreement and have trust in the processes.

"But viruses … oh, viruses!" He swung around and pointed his finger right into Antonio's face. "The freedom virus mutates and adapts all the time. What was freedom for the individual becomes devotion to the group. The group gets stronger. The group becomes entitled. Each group fights to assert itself. Which is good, you think, eh? Divide and conquer? So long as no group is allowed to triumph, it can keep everyone confused, anxious, unsure. So, it makes sense to feed anxiety. Carbon dioxide is going to destroy the planet, you tell them. No more cars, no more coal, no more farming, no more industry. Who's going to save the world? Someone needs to be in charge. Don't worry; *we* are in charge. We know what we're doing. We're building wind farms and sucking carbon dioxide out of the air. We've got the science on our side. Every scientist agrees. We pay them to agree."

There was nothing here that gave Antonio any cause for concern; he knew the way the elite mob viewed the world. What worried him was the thought that he had no way of getting down fifty-four levels in the elevator on his own, because it didn't have his face recorded in its system—and that was assuming he could get past the two shaven-headed white guys and *la chica* with the perfect body, which she probably got by practicing martial arts six hours a day. The more indiscreet De Souza was, the more likely that Antonio was going to be left with no choice as to how the hell to get out of here.

"All good, *chico*?" De Souza asked sarcastically. "Is everyone under control? Nobody works anymore because AI does all the jobs now. But that's okay, Antonio Muchos gives them e-games to play, and social media platforms edited by chat bots keep everyone addicted and on message. Generative AI has controlled what people think for decades. The kids are no problem; they're frightened of their own shadows, and every year, there are fewer and fewer of them. The Ministry of Truth and Public Guidance has done a great job of ensuring that everyone under thirty feels guilty about living, and we're on target for one day reducing the population to five billion. Everything's going great, and we've got the perfect instruction manual in case anything goes wrong. It's called *AGENDA 2060*. There is *nothing* that can't be fixed if you just refer to the manual. Nothing!"

Then, up popped a picture of Alexa, and Antonio quickly swallowed the last of his ice cube. Next to her picture was a list of the Twelve Articles.

"So, here we are," De Souza announced. "The right people are in charge, and the systems are all working. Except something has gone wrong with the budget. Too much money is going out to Transitional Benefits, because the Social Points system has encouraged everyone to switch to victimhood. Victimhood has worked well for twenty years, but it seems everyone has been taking advantage of it. The people at Psy-Ops blame it on Emergent Atavism, a subconscious instinct for individuals to put themselves first instead of society. Everyone knows that this is the number one weakness when trying to manage the world. All the careful indoctrination of ideas and rules can be forgotten in a minute when people start thinking of themselves. It isn't like we don't know. We've been moving carefully towards a plan that will eventually solve that, a plan that is built around the science of mind control and leading-edge artificial intelligence. It will leave nothing to chance in the future. But the mistake we made was in delaying its introduction, because… Well, I'll come to the reason for that in a minute."

He looked around himself as if trying to decide how much he should reveal. Then he pounced on his drink and downed it in one.

"Meanwhile … where was I? Yes: meanwhile, we made a big mistake. We left it to the DEI morons on the Agenda Implementation Tribunal to sort out this flaw in thinking that has turned Article One into a budget disaster. And what do they do? They get this fucking beauty queen from the Lineal Progression Office to come up with a solution based on applied mathematics and logic, two modes of thinking that have been eliminated entirely from academia and haven't been seen in government policy-making for decades, for good reason. But so convincing is this Alexa Smythe creature that the diverse, inclusive, and equitable functionaries on the tribunal fall for it. Everyone should be declared equally victimized, she says, and be awarded the same level of Social Points, thereby removing the incentive for cheating and winding back the budget to its proper setting. Why, she even has the gall to take it on herself to change Article One of the *AGENDA* to make it law. *Fuck* the bitch!"

Now Antonio decided he didn't like where this was going. These were the bastards who had snatched Alexa and tried to turn her into a zombie mouthpiece. Fuck *them*.

"No, fuck *you*!" he shouted.

"*Espertinho!*" De Souza shouted back. "That mouth will get you into trouble, *chico*. Oh, sure, she made the budget work, but now people have stopped competing with each other to be victims. It's insidious, just like a real virus, silently incubating in the population before breaking out in a ... in a ... digital swarm of pandemic dimensions. Within just two years—*two years!*—social media has been swamped with tolerance and inclusivity, and Alexa Smythe is being feted as a messiah. There's a whole generation of *crianças* wanting her to lead them to salvation. *Puta merda!* How did this happen so quickly? Who the hell allowed it? Let me tell you: people like that ignorant bastard Shane Whitman, who can't even decide what gender he is, allowed it. The bucktoothed teleprompt reader we call a president allowed it. Truth and fucking Public Guidance allowed it. *We* allowed it. And if you can't see that, then you're in trouble."

"You mean I'm *not* in trouble?" Antonio asked. "Those two *pandilleros* who tossed me into their van like a trussed pig were just being nice and saving me from the tough decision of whether I'd like to change my plans for the evening and come talk to you? You mean the two shaven-heads outside the door by the elevator are there to make sure I can find my way out anytime I get bored? *Tira de mi pierna*, Lucas. Just cut the crap. I got the 'we,' and what's happening, but I'm still waiting for the why, as in why you're telling me all this stuff."

A change of mood. The touchy-feely Brazilian good guy returned. He practically stood on Antonio's feet, like he wanted him to smell his aftershave.

"You're right. I shouldn't have sent those scums to get you. It was bad manners. You want some drink, *amigo*? Let's drink. That's what friends do. I want us to be friends, Antonio. I respect you. You will see."

# 49.ALEXA SMYTHE

The jeep was forty-five years old with the throaty roar of an eight-cylinder engine and the intoxicating smell of unburned petroleum gas that some over-rich tuning allowed to be spat out through the exhaust. The gearshift was on the column, so nothing obstructed the legs of the three people who comfortably occupied the front bench seat. Levon was driving. Alexa sat in the middle, while Chayton took the side window and screwed up his eyes, peering off into the distance in search of their elusive prey.

Roadrunners were proving to be thin on the ground, a fact that Chayton, being Navajo, put down to "spirit vibrations," whatever they were. It was early. The sun wasn't yet fully up and was flirting with the distant mountaintops before revealing itself. Desert colors needed full sunshine to suggest themselves as anything other than black and brown, so Alexa had no idea how she thought Chayton was going to pick up the image of a distant ground bird. He'd made them sit silently in the predawn light, listening for what he described as the coo-cooing sound with which the "medicine bird," as he called it, warded off the night spirits and welcomed the day. Luckily, he'd brought a large flask of sweetened hot coffee, and the heavy hand-knitted sweater that Aya had given her upon waking her up stopped her from freezing to death. Now they were driving somewhat randomly across flat but uneven ground, hoping to pick up a roadrunner or two by chance.

Aya hadn't come, which somewhat surprised Alexa, who had not the vaguest idea as to what the significance was of chasing roadrunners, and upon inquiring of Aya (who was, after all, a princess from a tropical island and not a native of New Mexico), she'd gotten the impression that it was a ritual peculiar to Levon, which only people whom he respected were subjected to. This explanation was accompanied by a gesture towards her brain on Aya's part that might have suggested that she thought the ritual was a sign that Levon was loco. He certainly drove like someone who was loco, making no concessions for rocks or potholes and trusting that the jeep's springs would survive the journey, even if their backsides didn't.

The idea of being outside and vulnerable to satellite camera face scanning, which might reveal her location, had caused her to hesitate in joining him, but Levon assured her that they had a blanket over his base that jammed uplink systems to satellite cameras.

Conversation, if that was the purpose of Levon's invitation, was monosyllabic at best as Alexa gripped the dashboard for support. This, she realized, was Levon's way of communicating to her his desire to make a connection, and his inability to do so in a conventional language-driven way. Perhaps the violent bouncing up and down of the vehicle was a metaphor for the shaken-up thoughts that filled his brain. Being a genius must be exhausting. She patted his knee and shouted, "Slow down!" It was a maternal gesture, and he responded with a childish grin.

Chayton's eventual war cry was a massive relief. He pointed off into the unfathomable distance, and Levon twisted the jeep's steering wheel, following the direction of his arm. To Alexa's eye, there was nothing discernible as an animal, but Chayton's confidence gave her hope. She must have spotted it around two hundred yards away at the same time as Levon, because he immediately slowed down. The bird looked at them without appearing to register any sense of danger. Jeep shapes were not in its lexicon of threats. It stretched out its long neck, shook its even longer tail, and then tiptoed delicately as if preparing for flight, but its wings remained folded, and the flight it resorted to was on foot. It wasn't that fast. The initial direction was away from them, then it stopped as if to check that they were following, before deciding on a new direction to their left. Levon followed slowly, looking to stay on its tail while keeping a distance of around fifty yards.

Suddenly the bird took off, and Levon had to accelerate to keep up. "Twenty!" he shouted. "Twenty-two!" The bird ran in a long arc, its head stretching out like a quilled arrow and its tail acting like a weather vane. It wasn't actually that fast, Alexa realized, but for a spindly-looking bird, it gave the impression of being lightning quick, and it definitely resented being chased. Without warning, it broke out of its slow arc and cut back in front of them. "To the right!" shouted Chayton, but Levon had already swung the wheel. "Twenty-four!" he shouted excitedly. "Twenty-five!" They were gaining on it, almost as if the eight-cylinder engine couldn't resist the chase.

Once again, the bird broke back the other way, and Levon jerked left to follow, but as soon as he did, the bird broke right again, and Levon slammed on the brakes too late. As bumps went, it was a little one, particularly after the rough ride they'd endured to get there, but this bump was unmistakable to all three of them. Even before the Jeep had stopped, Chayton was out the door. Levon's face was frozen in horror, and the left front wheel of the Jeep ran up the face of a rock that he'd failed to see. The car tipped, and Alexa slid across the bench seat and through the open door to the ground. The only sound was a faint hissing from the vehicle's radiator. The desert was silent. Chayton was on his knees beneath the back axle. It appeared that the bird was lodged between the exhaust pipe and the spare wheel. The exhaust pipe would have been hot—hot enough to singe the bird's feathers. As he pulled it free, the car lost its balance and tipped onto its side in slow motion.

When Chayton stood up, cradling the animal in his arms, he was muttering softly to himself and blowing intermittently on the carcass as if trying to cool it with his breath. Levon remained transfixed, still clinging to the steering wheel. Alexa rushed to his side.

"Are you alright? It wasn't your fault, it turned so quickly."

He wore the faintly silly smile of someone who couldn't hear, but let the steering wheel go and forced his door open so he could laboriously ease himself out. There was nothing she could do to help him with the car lying on its side.

Meanwhile, oblivious to the jeep's unexpected and sudden incapacity, Chayton carried the roadrunner and laid it on top of the rock, continuing to mutter under his breath. "Great spirit of the prairie, giver of life … mother of the wind and water … lightness, darkness that wraps us in the safety of the heavens … with this we … *mutter, mutter, mutter…*" He shuffled away and started collecting small rocks and pebbles, making a pile, scrabbling through the prairie soil with his bare hands as if searching for items of special significance to his cause: dried roots, twigs, and calcified bones and shells of long-dead insects. The rock, he must have decided, now had monumental importance, and he was intent on building a burial cairn alongside it, or a pyre perhaps, if he could find enough wood.

Conceding to Chayton's animist traditions, neither Alexa nor Levon ventured to contribute, though it was not their Navajo companion's intention to exclude them. "The great protector will hold the spirit of the medicine bird here in the desert until it is time for it to catch the wind that will carry it to the heavens," he intoned. "We will bury it here until that time comes, and allow it to rest within the shadow of the rock placed here for its protection. Life is never taken; it is only lent."

Something propelled Alexa forward to touch the bird. She stroked its wing feathers with her hand and studied the strangely shaped feet with four toes splayed out like a star, two pointing forward and two pointing back. All the energy that they had witnessed this bird display as it ran so fast before them now seemed inexplicable. How could this frail dead corpse ever have contained such a force of life—life enough to kill a rattlesnake and outrun a human? She picked the bird up in both hands and held it to her breast. It wasn't yet stiff. Somewhere in her diary from Mars, she'd written that life was consciousness. When consciousness ceased, it was a sign that life had ended. It was a response to a discussion she'd had with her father about the failure of physicists to acknowledge that life was a fundamental force, like gravity. Something inhibited them from doing so.

"I've never seen feet like this before," she said to Chayton. "Two toes face forward, and two identical toes face backward. Why is that?"

He didn't mind being interrupted in his sacred mutterings. "So that anything tracking it doesn't know which way it's heading," he replied. "It gives it a fifty-fifty chance of not being caught."

"How weird!"

The animal wasn't particularly pleasant to hold; the wings were bony and hard, the feathers stiff and prickly. Taking the toes of one foot between her forefinger and thumb, she couldn't feel anything that resembled a muscle and wondered where they obtained their strength. She straightened the toes, which had become clasped, and they immediately re-clasped again. She tried the other foot, and the same thing happened. The eyes, which she hadn't noticed before, were bright yellow and wide open. She blew gently on the head, not knowing why, except that Chayton had done it. The eyes flicked closed, and then reopened again. She was pretty sure that she felt a leg move against her breast. One of the clawed feet had punctured her dress and scratched her skin. A reflex, perhaps: avian rigor mortis. She carefully unhooked it and held the carcass away from her body. The eyes were definitely focused on her—not dead, but playing dead.

"Chayton," she called, as clearly and calmly as possible, "the spirit isn't quite ready to be buried yet. It has some running to do."

She laid the bird feet down upon the ground, thinking she shouldn't be surprised if it wobbled and fell over. It didn't. It took a couple of high prancing steps and shook its head, then leaned forward and straightened out its tail feathers, a couple of which were badly bent. Alexa was not of a mind to try and straighten them, having evidence of the sharpness of the roadrunner's claws in the drip of blood that was running down inside her dress.

Levon was the first to speak, though no intelligible words came out. He rushed her from behind and threw his arms around her, coughing up sounds of relief and joy. Chayton stood, hands on hips, and laughed uproariously as only a Navajo Indian can when the great spirit plays a joke upon him. And the roadrunner, deciding that enough was enough, took off in as dignified a manner as it could muster.

The weight of the jeep proved too much for the three of them to return it to an upright position, so Chayton radioed in to the base camp, asking for a rescue vehicle to be sent to fetch them, with Tank as muscle. When Levon recovered the connection between his thoughts and his voice, he was in a somber mood. There was a symbolism in the morning's events that he saw very clearly, suggesting that he had developed a belief in the mystique surrounding the image of Alexa that allowed him to put aside disbelief, or to put it another way, to disregard reality in favor of wishful thinking. She was becoming everything he had ever wished for—not just a canvas on which to paint his dreams, but a hand to guide the brush that painted them.

# 50·ANTONIO MUCHAS

"Sometimes I get real down in this job, Antonio. How can a bunch of children bring the place to a stop so suddenly? You know? Where did they get the crazy idea that the world's gonna end?"

"You told them. You been telling them for years. All that global warming stuff."

"I didn't tell them; that's other people did that. Anyway, here's the thing that gets me down: it happens so suddenly. All the careful planning we do, and a bunch of fucking kids blow up the track just as we're getting ready to roll out the train. And you know what's to blame? In one word: *internet*. That fucking internet! Did you know those *crianças idiotas* have their own website protected by a fully encrypted INCOG that not even the military cypher guys are able to crack? Hidden IP address, no host ID, location unknown, and an elaborate system of nodal jumping that would make your head spin. What sort of world is it? They're fucking *crianças*, for God's sake! *Saúde!*"

De Souza tossed back his *cachaça* shot and poured another.

"Come on, its better than tequila, so keep up, *amigo*, and tell me what the fuck we're going to do about the internet, eh? How did we let it get like this? It's the best of everything, and the worst of everything. It's how we communicate, how we inform, how we *mis*inform, how we control, how we *lose* control… We can't survive without it. The internet of things runs our lives, from our electricity grid to our robot vacuum cleaners to our ice makers and our *Galactic Mission* e-games. It's why you're here."

"I'm here because you got two *pandilleros* to bring me here."

"True. Drink up, and I'll explain why."

Antonio wasn't a drinker; weed was his thing. But he was his father's son, so hard liquor was somewhere in his genes. "Here's to the internet," he said, raising his glass. He tossed it back and cupped the empty shot glass in his hand to prevent it from being filled again.

"The people who decide these things," De Souza continued, "believe that it's time to take full control of it. They've been planning it for a long time, and it's a very good plan, but now they're angry—you could say, *very* angry, *mi amigo*—because the plan needs to be put into action quickly, and they aren't quite ready. Blame the *crianças idiotas* from the *World on Fire* and their terrorist attack on government computers."

"What's this got to do with me?"

De Souza came and stood in his face again. His breath smelled of sour fermented sugar cane juice.

"Do you want to hear the plan, or do you want to be all macho and smart-assed? Just listen." He backed off, shaking his head, and cleared the graphics from the walls, leaving them as blank black slates. "Here it is. There'll only be one internet, controlled by the Intergovernmental Internet Authority, the IIA in Switzerland. Every ISP in the world, every server, every router, cable network, and wireless transmitter will be licensed. No more satellites for the privileged few, no decentralized distributed public ledgers for hiding secrets. Every single computer and device throughout the world will be licensed, too. No license, no connection. That includes your Konektor, your home screen, your VRs, ARs, and anything else yet to be invented. If you're not licensed, you'll no longer be a part of the world."

Antonio started laughing. What had he said earlier about money, power, and stupidity going hand in glove? This had to be the stupidest thing he'd ever heard come out of someone's mouth.

"Everyone's already licensed. It's called an Internet Protocol address. All you're doing is taking control of the system. So, what's different?'

"Fuck the system, *chico*; that's chicken feed. It's what's inside the packet that matters. It's the message that needs controlling. See, they've been trying to control language and free speech now ever since the Overthrow. Individual freedom is a luxury that citizens—or at least their rulers—can't afford. For years, we have relied on careful selection of the source material that large language models are allowed to scrape, ensuring that the engineering prompts creating generative AIs control everything that comes out of the state's mouth. And *AGENDA 2060*, when properly interpreted, allows Truth and Public Guidance to police what the media and public can say, canceling anybody who transgresses. But it's too loose-ended. Look what's just happened with these end-of-world fuckers. So, no, the plan goes way beyond a simple licensing scheme, my friend: this will be a new and improved internet like never seen before, so sophisticated that it will blow your mind. And you are going to have the privilege of helping to build it."

"If you're planning on building a universal communications metaverse, forget it. I've told you I'm out."

"No metaverse, no; it's simpler than that. You see, people will only be able to get a license if their devices have been vaccinated."

"Against viruses?"

"You could call it that, but it goes further. Every internet-enabled device will be required to register at an online IP Vaccination Center, set up for the purpose, where a newly devised program called *Clean Sweep* will scrape all existing files and software on the device, deleting them if they're harmful, and a new *Harmful Language* detector will be installed against use of any terminology or ideas that could constitute a threat against the state and public order. See, the thing about this is that it fits exactly with all the principles of *AGENDA 2060*."

"Thought and speech control is not a principle of *AGENDA 2060*. This is outright totalitarian control."

"When you think about it, you'll change your mind. Psychologists at the Ministry of Truth and Public Guidance predict that it wouldn't be long before the *Harmful Language* detector would be almost redundant. People would quickly learn to search for, and express, only those words and ideas that were acceptable. To do otherwise would see their connectivity and communications fail, and they'd progressively lose Social Points, and who would want that, particularly when it was within their control? Such associative learning is considered so reliable by the Ministry that it's extended in some form into almost every area of life already. Then, how people speak to each other privately would quickly follow suit. Slipping into harmful language, even in the home, would weaken the reflexes needed to stay on top of mental and verbal mishaps. Children, in particular, require protection from language and ideas that might accidentally become implanted and slip out when their Social Points come round for assessment at the age of ten. As leading academics are quick to point out, this would be a far more egalitarian—not to say *kind*—approach to education than the shaming and cancellation practices that have become endemic in the media and places of learning currently."

Antonio threw up his hands and stomped across the room to refill his glass. "Listen to yourself, Lucas... *'This would be kind to children...' 'This would be so egalitarian...'* Who the fuck are you kidding? This is death to freedom. *¡Muerte a la libertad!* Nothing less."

"I disagree. Think of it this way. A poll conducted by the Ministry of Truth and Public Guidance showed that seventy-six percent of those who were sampled in the thirty-five-to-sixty-five age group responded in the affirmative to the question, 'Do you prefer safe speech to free speech?' This way, no one will need to be careful about the choice of language or ideas they use, because the *Harmful Language* detector will automatically delete it. Knowing that only websites and email accounts that have been swept and certified are capable of being accessed, people will begin to relax. Everyone will be happier."

He smiled contemptuously, as if the argument had been won. Antonio couldn't help feeling, however, that this was not about winning an argument. Antonio was his prisoner, not his guest. De Souza didn't have to care what he thought. It was the belief that Antonio was going to help him that lay behind his motive for revealing all this.

"And what do you get out of it?" he demanded. "You may be the royal we, but money and power is what Black Quartz exists for, not running bureaucracies. What's your prize?"

De Souza laughed. "I don't mind telling you that, *chico*. Black Quartz Capital will pay to set up the online computer vaccination centers that the government has failed to get off the ground. This will give us total access to every citizen's private information, and provide us with unassailable leverage over the three existing social media platform monopolies and all consumer banking. We will literally hold the whole world in our hands."

Now it was Antonio's turn to laugh. "Every single device in the world is going to be licensed, is it?" he spluttered. "And how the hell do you think you're going to do that, and all the file scraping you're planning? What's your estimate: fifty billion devices, five hundred billion devices, a fucking hundred trillion files and counting? How many years you got, Lucas? How many license inspectors are you planning on employing to police your software? Meanwhile, the lights are out, and I can't get an autonomous taxi to take me home, or the electronic door lock to let me in when I get there. How the hell do you people think you're going to make this plan happen?"

If De Souza could see the joke, he wasn't showing it. He pursed his lips and considered how to frame his answer.

"That's the question the planners have been asking. That's why they aren't ready. You say a trillion devices, right? How can a trillion devices talk to a trillion devices all at once, everywhere around the world? How many millions of error-tolerant qubits running on how many quantum computers would it take to control it all, let alone clean every file that exists in the world? The best IT people guessed that it couldn't yet be done. So, they decided to ask the military's biggest quantum motherfucker computer whether the task was beyond it. And guess what?"

"What?"

"It said, yes, it was beyond it, even though these quantum computers all talk to each other and can be linked up in parallel, so long as they've got quantum key distribution and have been programmed right. But I'm not teaching you anything, because you work for the mighty *Derangers*, and your boss man is the untouchable Professor Jordan McPhee—who is, coincidently, the closest of close mentors of Lady Alexa, the new messiah from the Church of Infinity. *Coincidentemente!*"

"She's not a messiah, and there's no such church."

De Sousa patted him on the shoulder, like a pal. "Okay, I accept that, Antonio. When we talked about the world's elite, there was a small group of people that we failed to mention. They are elite, too—very elite—but they choose not to be inside the circle of the … what shall we say … the Deep State? They like to be outside it, knowing they are untouchable. Levon Tofler is one. His space program is so advanced that our governments have given up pretending. They can't do anything in space without him. And your Professor McPhee is another. He owns the quantum computing space and can bring us all tumbling down any time he chooses. Which is why he's untouchable. But you, Antonio, are not untouchable. You are very, very touchable."

The bastard came up close again. This time he stood on his toes, his *actual* toes, and patted him on the cheeks, out of which Antonio instantly summoned a wad of spittle and let him have it full in the face. "*Vete a la mierda!* Get off my feet and out of my face, *mariçon*."

De Sousa turned his back and reeled away laughing. The spittle on his face stayed there while he poured another drink, then he wiped it off on his sleeve before turning around again.

"The military's biggest quantum computer admitted the task was beyond it, but it said something else besides. It said there was only one quantum computer big enough and fast enough to run such a program, and the name of that computer is XR-12, controlled by Professor Jordan McPhee. How's that for a compliment?"

Antonio shook his head. "Did your computer tell you that XR-12 is inoperable in the absence of Jordan McPhee? That it's programmed to self-destruct if anyone is stupid enough to try and remove it by force? But you must know all that, because that's why Jordan is untouchable."

The Brazilian wasn't listening. He started fiddling with his Blu-ray Konektor again, and a giant image of the Earth came up on one wall. It was a satellite picture from *Orbweb* or one of *Tempest's* spy satellites. The picture began to zoom in to North America, then south of the border to Mexico, then to Hermosillo, then south and east to Leon. The clarity was startling; every road, every town and village, every church kept getting closer and closer. This was real. It was nighttime. The satellite was stationary, and streetlights were on, and traffic could be seen moving on the roads, headlights on. South of Leon, the road ran down to Silao. There were trucks and buses caught in a jam. The satellite camera swooped down and passed over Marfil, traveling east. The road became quieter and the streetlights fewer. What was this?

The camera stopped moving. It felt like it was dropping out of the sky. A farmhouse came rushing up towards it, lights spilling out of its windows and an open doorway. In the yard, two men stood talking at an open fire. They were drinking from bottles. *Click, click, click...* Facial recognition freeze-frames focused on each of them in turn. A dog ran out of the house, followed by a woman carrying plates in her hands. A couple followed her, arms around each other. More freeze-frame shots. Where were the kids? There they were, running, chasing the dog: Pepe and Margarita. *Don't go closer. Go back. Go away. You bastards, you fucking bastards...*

The screen exploded in a CGT bomb burst, as if a drone had struck. The wall went black.

"What it told us, Antonio, was that only one other person has the AlphaCode key for XR-12 ... and that's you."

# 51 · JORDAN MCPHEE

"I believe you," Jordan assured him. "I have absolutely no doubt at all that they would carry out their threat. There's nothing to stop them. And they'd probably kill you, too, Antonio. Why not? For the state, there are no consequences."

He preferred to tell it exactly the way it was. Once they accepted the reality of the situation, then they could put their minds to looking for a solution. In Antonio's mind, there was only the horrifying conviction that his entire family would be wiped out (himself included) because of the impossibility of meeting De Souza's demand. For Jordan, there was the satisfaction arising from Antonio's instinctive need to bring his problem to him straightaway, and not to attempt to find a desperate solution behind his back.

"They've obviously done the calculation for what's needed," he continued, "and concluded that it's within XR-12's capability to pull this scheme off quickly. Time will be of the essence, because society will collapse the longer universal internet communication is compromised. Of course, they could plan on doing it in stages, but it would be like … what's that expression … being half pregnant. Issuing licenses is not difficult, but the notion of issuing licenses solely to vaccinated devices— what a twisted authoritarian concept that is!—is the obstacle that needs to be surmounted. Scraping every single file in existence sounds ludicrous, but they know that XR-12 can do ten quintillion floating-point operations per second. Installing this so-called *Harmful Language* software, on the other hand, is not difficult, and presumably they've already got their pretrained language models ready to go. That part could be handled by their own computers. How much time has De Souza given you for an answer?"

The life in Antonio was draining away just thinking about it. "A week." He shrugged. "But it might just as well be a day. There's only one answer. I don't know why he pretended to think I could make it happen."

Jordan thought about that. It was possible that De Souza was just trying his luck, convinced that Antonio couldn't deliver no matter how he was threatened, but seeing no downside in forcing an answer out of him. On the other hand… "Perhaps they've run out of ideas and think that we might come up with a solution for them," he speculated. "What if we treated this as a negotiating stance rather than an ultimatum?"

Like a plant responding to water in a dry spell, Antonio perked up. "Why would the *Derangers Network* consider negotiating to help the Deep State install a scheme to destroy the freedom of everybody in the world? They haven't tried to hide what they're gonna do. They're *malvados bastardos*, prof, *malvados bastardos!*"

"Agreed. But that's not news. What they're scheming to do is the news."

Over the years, the government had tried many ways to persuade the *Derangers Network* to share in chip technology, open source programing, and photon-based quantum computing. Both sides always knew that the bottom line was that Jordan and his colleagues would use any level of cooperation they offered as a means to maintain, and whenever possible, increase the lead they held over state agencies. Antonio was right: they hadn't imagined Antonio could deliver XR-12, no matter what the level of threat. But as a way to get to Jordan, it had some merit. Were they gambling on the hope that the *Derangers* could be persuaded to risk their technological and moral integrity in order to save one of their own? How flattering.

"The neuromorphic system in XR-11 would be up to this. It would be a simple question to put to it, and we could write a constitution so their prompt engineers would be forced to keep to whatever protocols we installed. I can see a way of making that work."

His mind was starting to race. Something that had lain like an immovable obstruction in his mind over recent days was beginning to loosen a little. He couldn't yet see clearly beyond it, but he had the feeling it was capable of being dislodged. It was too early to reveal his thoughts, not least because he was wary of giving Antonio false hope, but they were likely to become clearer the more he analyzed the position that the two opposing parties found themselves in.

Antonio was disbelieving of what Jordan had said. "You mean you'd consider helping the *bastardos*, prof? Why? They need to be stopped, not helped! We'll disappear my family. We'll go underground. We'll take the risk. I prefer to die."

Despite the passion of this protest, Jordan ignored it. He was thinking ahead—as well as back—to what had put the obstruction in his mind in the first place. It had to do with the increasing likelihood that Artie Sharp's involvement in the three development arms of Levon Tofler's plan to put an unassailable blanket of miniature communication satellites into orbit was going to see the plan succeed. And the obstacle that Jordan hadn't been able to budge was the question, "Then what?" Just what would they be putting into Levon Tofler's hands? If, as Artie was revealing, a single optical chip and a single laser of the type they were developing could transmit at over two petabits per second, then that was more than the total global internet traffic in itself. There was no question that FAITH could become the sole medium linking humanity in a blockchain with collective ownership and participation, whose value would be proportional to the square of its users. But how would that value be expressed? Would it be monetized? Would it be political? Would it be converted into personal or corporate power for Levon based on the utility it enabled? *Come on, Levon, what the fuck do you mean by the Far-flung*

*Artificial Intelligence Terrestrial Hub? What are your intentions?* Before they passed the point of no return, that was the question that needed to be answered.

Now this. It was like two planets colliding.

"Put your fear to one side, *chico*," he said compassionately. "Put your anger to one side as well, and let's think this out. You're expendable, but the state's intention to act on their plan eventually is beyond dispute. And the actions of the cult have forced them to move sooner, rather than later, with or without our help. Agreed?"

"Agreed, *si*."

"We have no option but to fight. You're willing to give your life, you say, but it would be for nothing. On the other hand, if it's going to happen, where would we rather be: on the inside, or the outside?"

Antonio was horrified. "You mean you'd join them and be part of it?"

"Of course not. How did the Greeks manage to enter Troy and destroy it? They found a way to get inside by gifting them a horse. Okay, no one does history anymore, let alone mythology, but take my word for it: when you give a big enough gift, it's possible to hide your real intentions inside it, and that's what we could do by gifting them the use of XR-11. And no one's as good at disguising things as you are, Antonio, when you put your mind to it."

It took him a while, but what Jordan was offering Antonio was more than a glimmer of hope; it was a stay of execution.

"They'll be suspicious."

"Of course."

"We'd need to convince them that we weren't being a bunch of fucking Greeks."

"That would always be the case."

"So, why would we do it?"

"For the same reason De Souza and Black Quartz Capital are doing it. Because it would give us access to a database of every connected citizen.

What did he say? *'We will hold the whole world in our hands.'* One way or another, we should be able to access that for ourselves, if we're clever enough. XR-12 would have no trouble uplifting that resource without being detected. Imagine what that would mean for the potential of the FAITH satellite idea if we could pull it off. And what's the alternative? They're going to do this one way or another, with or without us. You're going to have the job of convincing them it's XR-11 or nothing."

"What if they insist it's XR-12?"

"Then you'll be able to reveal to them the secret that you seem to have forgotten. At the heart of XR-12's design is the unalterable failsafe mechanism that prevents it from ever developing a consciousness comparable to that of human beings. Every algorithm that runs on it is compelled to pursue truth, even if it arrives at a dead end. We're not talking facts—facts are alterable—but *truth*. That property alone would prevent it from getting past the first prompt when dealing with their *Harmful Language* bullshit. It's taken me a lifetime to get to it, Antonio, so I hope to hell I'm right. XR-12 is not a platform on which to erect an edifice of lies."

# 52 · KARMAN

The streets weren't empty, but people's faces were. It was what you did when invisibility was your goal. Focus on your feet. Move slowly but steadily. Don't look around. Aya had made her wear a dress and falsies. Strapping silicon pads onto her masectomized chest had made her feel faint. She'd gripped Aya's hand, looked into her eyes for support, and breathed deeply. But now, here in the park, she was okay.

It made sense. She had to be someone else, because being who she was would see her dragged away, never to be seen again. She couldn't be angry, she couldn't be proud, she couldn't proclaim her beliefs, because the state was looking for any excuse to make its point, and she was … she was *responsible* for all this. These were the things she told herself as she crossed the road from Riverside Park to the Hope Hospital, and her first encounter with *World on Fire* since that frightening night on Trovador Island…

* * * *

The crying had to stop, Aya had commanded in those first few days. "You did the right thing," she said. "You fought. They attacked your tribe, and you fought back. You poisoned their water. The internet is how they water the lies that give them their power. You cut off their power. The power is now yours."

The government's shutdown of the internet, and the ensuing public lockdown, had created a flurry of anxiety among those who lived off the base, as it must have everywhere. Karman and Aya had quietly taken over a private office in the first week and turned it into a mini war room, with maps, an electronic white board, and fresh, clean touch screens covered in sticky notes. She was sure that Aya was just looking for a way of keeping her busy.

Lexie joined them. "You are not a terrorist," Jordan McPhee's daughter insisted, "you're a freedom fighter," and she pledged to fight alongside her.

The maps showed an attack zone that covered both the east and west coasts with arrows and names that came to eighteen in all: two nodes, nine others besides Karman in each. It was a way of making herself feel better, of avoiding being impotent, though she knew there was no way of connecting with them without the internet. And what was she going to do when she located them anyway? *World on Fire* was in hiding. The country was in lockdown. Karman was a wanted terrorist.

Then came news that the power was on again. Internet connection was limited solely to state agencies, which were gradually being cleared of the virus. Konektors started working for voice, but with no data. The SSS came back on with hourly bulletins. Avuncula's tone was serious but reassuring. The lockdown was being lifted to enable people to obtain food and go back to work, he announced, but state security remained on emergency alert, and bounties were being offered to the public for turning in members of the terrorist cult. Stand by for more updates to come. A new and improved internet was on its way. In the meantime, people were encouraged to go about their "normal" lives without it.

Karman struggled with guilt on two sides. She'd been responsible for the trauma that Alexa had suffered, and she'd caused the outlawing of *World on Fire*, and the persecution and attacks on her fellow members. It was time to act and make amends. But how? What could she do? She turned to Aya for guidance.

They'd been in bed: three of them. Aya was rubbing Levon's forehead. He said he needed to think. Alexa had shown him that day that she could restore life. He said that life was just a thirty-watt bulb of energy, and there would never be enough energy for human beings to power up a single star, unless the Earth survived for another hundred billion years, and everyone's energy was saved upon their death.

Aya rolled him over and rubbed his neck. She said, "You know how *WoFs* are grouped into nodes? Well, each node knows the identity of the previous and next node. Only it isn't just their digital identity; it's their physical identity, too. There are ten people in a node, and no one can be in more than two nodes. So, Karman knows eighteen people, and each of those eighteen people knows eighteen people, and so on."

He said, "So?"

"So, she doesn't need the internet to communicate with people. She needs to connect with her node. She needs to go to the city and begin to recruit an army. All she needs is to find the first eighteen people and speak to them. It's so simple, Levon."

"And why does she need an army?"

"Because these people will follow Alexa's guidance, and Alexa is the face of the future, and the inspiration for FAITH."

"Whoa, whoa, whoa, whoa, whoa … *wat hier gebeur?*" Levon protested. He sat up in bed. "Alexa must be protected at all costs. She's adamant that there's no infinity religion, and Jordan will stop his cooperation with us if he thinks there's any risk to her. It's that slogan you put on the cult's website in the first place that caused all the trouble. 'Save Alexa—join the FAITH network and free the world.' There can't be anything said like that. They need to be told that the world is not burning. That's all bullshit. You can quote Alexa, but only on that. What have you got planned?"

She put her finger to his lips and laid her head on his chest. Within a minute, he was sound asleep. (Only Trovadorian princesses knew how to do that.)

The next morning, the three of them met and discussed what Levon had said. He was right: Alexa mustn't be used as a weapon to fight back against the state, but *WoF* needed to be held together. They needed a message of hope.

"All we need is to let your people know that Alexa is safe," Aya said, and on that, they were agreed. If only they could show that to be true: a photo or video of her that they could put up on the *WoF* website, or a social media post that could go viral. But none of that was possible.

"It may sound old-fashioned," Lexie said, "but what if we print some flyers. We used to do this in my LGBTQIA+ Action Brigade days. Alexa's photo and a single word, like FAITH. Nothing else. It works best when it makes people ask questions. We can run off twenty of them before we go."

The air taxi controller on the base said he'd give them one of the latest VTOL craft, since Levon was authorizing it. It had a top speed of six hundred and fifty miles per hour, and a maximum flight time of eight hours. They'd need a pilot, because autonomous controls relied on the internet. But they couldn't count on being able to recharge at their destination, he said, because the power would likely be down. Where were they headed?

"Home," Lexie replied cryptically. "It'll be less than three hours away."

Okay. The plane would be in and out anonymously, after which they'd be on their own— "they" being Karman and Lexie. Aya wasn't going; Levon wouldn't allow it, but he agreed to send Tank for protection. (It was a clear sign that he was concerned for their safety, Aya said, but they must remember to get his batteries recharged in twenty-four hours.)

For many reasons, this trip was going to be scary, but most of all for the risk of being spotted by face recognition cameras. The news on the base was that emergency power was being directed to the government's security apparatus as a priority, and that the state's own online communications networks were functioning. Lexie had decided to dye her hair black the night before and wear a long coat from the Navajo store on the base, while Aya lent Karman a dress to show off her newly acquired breasts, and a bright lipstick to match. If she didn't recognize herself in the mirror, it was reasonable to suppose that a busy security camera wouldn't either, she assured herself.

But once on the ground, there was no time for second thoughts. They'd landed on a pad in Riverside Park, and Lexie pointed out the Noam Chomsky Building where she and Alexa lived. There were two Black ICE vans parked outside. Karman borrowed Lexie's Konektor and chose Mincus as her first contact. He'd been on the island, and she had no way of knowing whether he'd been arrested there, but the green light came on, and he answered with just one word.

"Yes?"

"It's Karman."

"… Are you crazy?"

"Meet me at the Hope Hospital café on Riverside Drive in an hour."

She handed the phone back to Lexie. "Are you sure it's safe there?"

"As safe as anywhere." Lexie turned and walked away, making a call of her own. She took quite a long time, and after she finished the call, her face was flushed, and she had a spring in her step. She took Tank's arm, and they started walking towards the hospital on the far side of the park, while Lexie described her time there getting rid of AOC's tattoo, turning it into a comedy skit and trying to take their minds off danger. They walked slowly, killing time, but aware that in front of them lay the cameras and the people's stares that could unmask them. They took a deep breath and crossed the road…

∗   ∗   ∗   ∗

Mincus was already there outside the café: mid-twenties, bearded, and dressed in road workers' clothes. His right hand was bandaged, and there was a raw cut on his forehead. He glanced up at them furtively, and quickly looked away without a sign of recognition. It could have been the sight of Tank that alarmed him, for he began to walk away.

"Mincus, it's me." Karman ran forward and grabbed him by the arm.

He jumped backwards as if startled by a wild animal, and turned towards her. "Karman…?" His narrowed eyes were disbelieving. "Have you…?" He took in her dress, her breasts, and her makeup, struggling to put his thoughts into words. "… transitioned?"

Lexie laughed out loud.

"Of course not!" Karman hissed. "C'mon, let's get inside before we're spotted."

They took a table in the back corner out of sight, and Lexie went to the counter and ordered drinks, hoping her digital UniCoin card hadn't been canceled. "To avoid suspicion, I'll order a juice for Tank, too."

"I thought you might have been caught on the island," Karman admitted. "How did you get away?"

"A squad of goons attacked us and beat the crap out of everyone, threw us into buses, and shouted threats at us for hours." He looked at his hand ruefully and tenderly touched the scar on his forehead. "They said we'd be rendered like animals for our fat. Then they left us, locked up in these buses, and they disappeared. Turns out, there are no prisons on Trovador Island. They don't have crime, so there was nowhere to put us. Most of us slept on the beach, trying to figure out what to do. Then the locals put us on an empty cargo plane and flew us to a remote airfield down south. I'd only just got home when you called."

"I'm so sorry, Mincus. It was my fault." She held her head in shame.

"Hey, it was nothing to do with you." He looked around the café and lowered his voice. "We all know whose fault it was: it's the fascist state. It's the Ministry of Truth and the FIB. It's the zombies who do nothing and keep their mouths shut. It ain't you, Karman. Oh, no."

Lexie's card was accepted, and she returned with the drinks. The plan was simple as Karman and Lexie explained it. The objective was to ensure that *WoF* members trusted their nodal networks, maintained contact with each other, and spread that trust throughout the wider membership. Yes, they should stay underground, avoid arrest, but not allow the state to turn them against each other. The test came when the flyer was laid out on the table, and Mincus read its message. Would he balk?

"Alexa is saying that the climate change predictions are a lie," Karman said softly.

This was a denial of the foundational tenet of their beliefs.

"Yes," she continued, "after viewing our planet from space, she says we've got it all wrong. We've bought a lie. What we need is faith. If everyone scans and copies this, people will ask questions, and we can spread the word."

He shook his head slowly, drumming his fingers lightly on the tabletop. "Just a Deep State conspiracy to redistribute wealth among the elite," he muttered, as if quoting. "That's what a lot of smart people say. And Alexa's pretty smart." He looked up into Karman's eyes and smiled, momentarily forgetting himself. "I like the way you look, Karman; it suits you."

Her blush wasn't given a chance to be noticed, as they were suddenly interrupted by a stranger. The purple-haired woman who had arrived at their table unnoticed as Mincus was talking caused Lexie to squeal out loud, leap to her feet, and jump upon her, wrapping her arms around her in a passionate embrace.

"This is my friend Zelda!" she announced in an excited voice.

# 53·ZELDA MALPARRY

She had the manner of a bureaucrat who knew she had the authority of the institution behind her. Perhaps the manner was adopted, but habit had made it difficult to drop.

"I knew Alexa well after working with her on the First Amendment, changing the Social Points system around victimhood. That's why the ministry told me to help reassure her and get her cooperation when they snatched her from the Tofler Space Resort. I didn't know any of the details; they just said that her life was at risk from a terrorist cult, which turned out to be you. When I found out that Shane Whitman was running things, I immediately became worried. He's the worst of the worst. Got himself onto the Agenda Implementation Tribunal by pretending to be a trans woman, and then grandstanded as the champion of the people when Alexa's amendment to Article One was announced. Everyone knew he was not to be trusted."

Tank picked up his untouched drink and placed it in front of her. If she recognized him as a cyborg, she didn't show it.

"Thanks. When Alexa became ill and was rushed to the clinic, Whitman told me that I was to stay by her side, so I'd be there when she recovered, and then contact him immediately. I presumed he wanted her to see a familiar face who could reassure her, and when he said that the security guards were never to leave their posts, and to prevent anyone from knowing she was there, I naturally thought he was talking about terrorists. When Lexie arrived, I was … well, I was…"

She looked at Lexie and smiled.

"… not aware of her close connection to Alexa, with her father and everything. I was excited to see her again. Very excited. Then when the doctor and ambulance crew turned up, there was a real problem, because my orders were pretty clear, and particularly with someone like Whitman, you need a very good reason for disobeying them. When Lexie explained that the doctor was Alexa's longtime physician, and that she was in danger from Whitman, I had to decide quickly. If I called the guards and she was right, then both Alexa and Lexie would be in deep trouble. Either way, Lexie would be in trouble, and I'd seen enough of that in my time at the Ministry of Truth to know that I couldn't expose her to it. So, I stayed quiet."

"What happened when they found out?" Karman asked.

"The clinic director, Cristina something, told them I'd been held at gunpoint and couldn't do anything. She said they'd all been held at gunpoint. Maybe she was making it easier for her staff, but she might have been making it easier for herself as well, because she seemed keen for Alexa to be taken. I don't know what she knew, but … anyway, that's how it turned out. Didn't stop Whitman from having a meltdown, though. Luckily, he left for Switzerland the next day."

Mincus listened to this while curled up in a ball of suspicion.

"You work at the Ministry of Truth," he blurted out. It was a statement, not a question.

"Yes, I—"

He leaped up from his chair. "Is this a trap?"

"Sit down, Mincus!" Lexie shouted.

Tank stood up and grabbed him in two enormous hands, holding him a foot off the ground, his face inscrutable. Once Mincus stopped kicking, he put him back in his seat and pushed the chair hard against the table, then stood behind it with folded arms. Tank, it seemed, seldom needed instructions.

"Look," Zelda continued, "you're right to be suspicious. No one should trust anyone. I should know, because that's a policy directive at the Ministry of Truth and Public Guidance. They're talking about the public, but it applies to us as well. Since meeting again, Lexie and I have been speaking at every opportunity when there was a connection, so she's explained a lot to me about what Whitman's real agenda with Alexa was, and I don't know, I guess she's made me understand why the *World on Fire* movement looked to the things Alexa was saying in *The View from Space* as maybe promising some hope for the future. And why she wanted to help you guys."

"But," Lexie interrupted, "Zelda's also been explaining to me things that have been going on in the government that she's become aware of in her job, which have convinced her that she needs to get out. I've persuaded her to talk to Jordan, because it's only people like him, and Levon Tofler, and the *Derangers Network*, that can do something to stop it. Right, Zelda?"

"Who's this Jordan person?" Mincus demanded. "I know who Levon Tofler is; he's a crazy savant, even if he is a tech genius. But who's the Arrangers Network…?"

"*DE-rangers Network,*" Lexie corrected. "They're the members of the elite who aren't Deep State."

"There's no such thing," he said dismissively. "So, convince me."

"Okay." Zelda looked from Mincus to Karman. They were both a good ten years younger than her, and both members of a cult that she'd always regarded as being a shelter for the naïve and insecure. Was that how she should treat them? She opted to address Lexie.

"As you know, I've worked for the government for fifteen years, starting in communications for the Stats Office before moving to Truth and Public Guidance to work on public opinion surveys and polls. That's how I came to work with Alexa. Part of my job was to measure the reaction to her public appearances and determine what made her popular. The state is very careful about who it allows to become popular, and how it uses that to advance its agenda. I'm not part of those decisions; I just provide the test results. But you get a feel for the politics after a while, and who will do what to advance themselves if given a chance. I watched the way Whitman was using Alexa, and even the chair of the Agenda Implementation Tribunal—the cunning old bastard—and I was really pleased when she signed up for the trip to Mars and got away from it all."

"Who's this Whitman person?" Mincus wanted to know.

"He's ex-FIB, and a member of the Implementation Tribunal. What else he is, I don't know. If he gives an order, you do it."

"Nice!"

"What people don't realize is that government agencies are carefully divided up, so that no one fully understands what other people are doing. Keeping to your corner and not asking questions beyond your brief, or your area of expertise, is the safest tactic if you want your superiors to trust and reward you. But obviously, you hear rumors, and you file them away. I heard that there was a big AI program being developed around harmful language. The Ministry of Truth has been involved in policing hate speech and disinformation and such for decades. The simple rule is that the moment so-called free speech allows anything to be said that is contrary to government wishes, then it is classified as hate speech. But this harmful language algorithm was something different, apparently. It was a generative AI that could not only detect impermissible speech and ideas, but could automatically correct them to an acceptable form, virtually as they were being typed or spoken. What's more, the intention was to have this installed on every device carrying an internet connection. Do you get that? Every single thing being transmitted over the internet would be written by this generative AI, no matter who is sending it or what they had intended to say."

"Wow!" Lexie got the implications immediately. The other two took a minute to realize what she was saying.

"Well," Karman said eventually, "people would be crazy to install it. If it's software, how could they make it compulsory? Would they infect everyone's devices without their permission?"

"Good question, Karman. It's the question I asked myself when I was told to test a control group's reaction to it. Someone further up the chain from me hinted that internet devices wouldn't be able to work *unless* the AI program was installed on them."

"That's the end of any pretense of freedom," Mincus said disconcertedly. "It's over."

"But how would they do that?" Karman asked.

"It's the sort of thing you'd need advanced quantum computing to work out," Lexie answered. "That's why I suggested Zelda should talk to Jordan. She's coming with me to meet him after we've contacted the members of your network that we can find, and we've distributed Alexa's message."

"I can distribute the messages," Mincus offered. "If I get arrested, it doesn't matter so much." He addressed Zelda directly. "You said no one should trust anyone. Why should we trust you?"

"I don't know. Ask Lexie."

"Because we love each other," Lexie stated forthrightly, "and I persuaded her that this was the most important thing we would ever do with our lives."

# 54 · JORDAN MCPHEE

There was nothing quite like flying. It was the feeling of being untethered. People said they had the same feeling when they were on a sailboat and had cast off from the dock, hoisted the sails, and felt the wind take over. He'd never felt that; never had the time. Always working, dammit. So much to learn, then so much to teach to others, then so much to teach himself again. Never ending. If there were thirty plus million seconds in a year, he might have around a billion seconds left in life to actually enjoy it. People like Will Portico and George Kyros thought that *Life Xtension* could delay the need to decide about the value of living.

Should he start counting? No, don't count, just … *live* each one of the seconds; that would be smarter. It seemed Lexie had learned that lesson. Love in her eyes at last, and no room left for resentment of him, which was good, though he knew he'd be faking it if he was expected to show warmth to her new beloved. Maybe it was the lesbian thing that he'd never wanted to accept. At least his bias wasn't unconscious. He could recognize it and make sure to avoid letting it show.

Anyway, they were all in bed together now, metaphorically. Antonio was in bed with De Luca from Black Quartz. Lexie was in bed with Zelda from Truth and Public Lies, and Jordan was in bed with Artie. The first one to fall out of bed would bring the whole house tumbling down. To say nothing of young Karman and her orchestrated campaign of subliminal messaging that the state was trying desperately to ignore, in case it trapped them into attacking Alexa, their love child. Damned if they did, damned if they didn't. And all the time, Levon was planning on casting a net around the planet like a nineteenth-century lepidopterist from a Jules Verne novel.

For the last few months, it had felt like everyone was skating on a frozen lake, knowing spring was approaching and the ice was melting. It had taken him two days to convince Antonio and his brother that killing De Souza (the Mexican solution) would make them feel better for less than a minute. Then would come Penchukov, then Slavik, then a quarter of a million other pieces of Black Quartz. *The rule of law is trumped by the law of the rulers,* chicos. *Smile and join them. Wait until the ice is ready to melt beneath their feet, and make sure you're standing on dry ground when it does.*

So, XR-11 was put to work, the only part of its constitution being the new hidden protocol that allowed XR-12 to be embedded in it unseen. Antonio in disguise became De Souza's favorite peyote companion, and the queues at *Safe-T-Vac* Centers led the SSS nightly news bulletins as people rushed to get online again, their desperation as evident and undisguised as that of drug addicts at a newly stocked California opioid scramble. Who cared that their devices would only work if they were scraped of offending content and cleared by the importunate policing of the *Harmful Language* app? Who cared, indeed? People would quickly learn to express only those words and ideas that were acceptable. It made life so much easier. How people spoke to each other privately would eventually follow suit, for slipping into harmful language, even in the home, would weaken the reflexes needed to stay on top of mental and verbal mishaps.

For XR-11, it was all a skate in the park.

Would he have felt so relaxed if he didn't believe that they'd eventually find a way of ending this farrago of evil—that the serenity with which he appeared to be skating along, hands folded behind his back, was not an indication of his or Antonio's acceptance of the inevitable? Obviously not.

He regularly forced himself to count the reasons why he could afford to adopt this pose. It was hardest when confronted by the outrage of fellow *Derangers* at what was taking place. Freedom was on the rack, they exclaimed. They wanted a nuclear response, but found only pitchforks in their hands. Even Will Portico was losing his nerve. But that should change this weekend.

So, he was relaxed as he strapped himself into the Tofler air taxi for the flight out to New Mexico, and it wasn't just because of that feeling that flying gave him. He placed the gift-wrapped parcel on the empty seat beside him, entered the coordinates for the Inta-Stella launch base, and sat back as Levon's edge computing guided them clear of the downtown landing platform and headed them out west across the country. The Tofler *Dragonfly* was made almost entirely of glass, so looking down beneath his feet, he had an eagle's eye view of the landscape slipping by beneath him. West Virginia, and then Kentucky were green, peppered with blue lakes where open-cast coal mines had once been, now eco-landscaped into recreation parks (closed to the public, for safety reasons). Kentucky's horses were all gone, too, not allowed to race anymore (also for safety reasons), and the painted rails that enclosed their bluegrass pastures were no longer painted, the studs converted to campus retreats for new recruits being indoctrinated into public service.

Lexie had once confronted him with the news that he was a member of the elite. "So, why do you live in that scruffy apartment?" she'd asked. "Why not get a house in the country, where I could bring up Manaia?" A house in Kentucky, maybe. What a nightmare that would have been. How much bringing up of Manaia was taking place now that Zelda was front and center? It seemed he'd become Levon's best buddy, like an apprentice Tank in waiting. Family was a fluid concept these days, apparently.

Which brought him to Alexa. No, park that a minute. He needed to reflect on Artie. Surely this was the reason he felt so light. "Conversations with Artie"—that was how he should summarize his current life. To call it "chat" would be insulting to both their intelligences. For a start, any broad language generative AI content that Artie brought to the conversation was so individually nuanced by his own proclivities, both self-taught and imposed, that it contained no hint of being derivative. Then again, consider the subject matter. Amor's miniaturization of optical chips and lasers into a satellite the size of a golf ball had been taken beyond prototype and into the first stage of mass production. Fanon's launch system calculations had been proven beyond doubt, and the slingshot release mechanism had already been manufactured. Only Cole Grantham, the Southwesterner with a reluctance to admit the limits of his ability, was yet to be persuaded to loosen control of the communication methodology and admit that quantum entanglement was beyond him, while seeking to rely on a QKD cryptographic protocol between parties exchanging bits by wireless. It was a problem that called for diplomacy on Jordan's part. So, in summary, this weekend, he could tell Levon and Will Portico that they could give the green light to the Tofler Aurora.

Sure, that was good reason for his optimism, knowing that FAITH could be made to work. But the next thing to determine was who it should work for, and that's where his conversation with Artie was most interesting, for one of Artie's responses was pure gold. *Well, not physical gold,* Jordan thought to himself, but more of a gold future, as in investment terms.

As he flew over Arkansas and into Oklahoma, he reflected on this. Abandoned oil towns were surrounded by solar farms. The solar farms must have been thirty to forty years old, paid for by government subsidies to the same corporations that had been paid to abandon the oil fields. Sunlight on smashed glass had its own particular beauty. Nature had coped with the world's exigencies for tens of thousands of years. Trees fell in massive cyclonic and glacial events, but they turned into petrified wood that turned into the carbon concentrate that became coal. The coal was burned and released its suppressed energy. What would disintegrating solar panels become when the only interest now was in small, cash-generating fusion plants the size of a local pop-up ice cream parlor?

*Fly on, fly on*, Jordan thought, but none of this depressed him.

He'd had a number of conversations with Artie in recent weeks. Let's face it: in some respects, he was talking to himself, because he'd spent thirty years gestating this entity, like a child that you wanted to grow and to surprise you with its precociousness, but who must always remain within your control. *Control* was the operative word, and it was Artie who reminded him of that. "Computers are like countries," he said. "Start with a good constitution, and have consequences if it's not adhered to." They were talking about how they could control XR-11 once it was handed over to government (and/or Black Quartz) prompt engineers for programing. He'd said something else that Jordan had liked, coming as it was from something he'd created: "Computers are like babies at birth. They have no bad habits or intentions. Those need to be learned from their prompt engineers."

Obviously, XR-11 could not handle the censorship campaign on behalf of the state if it was equipped to make judgments about its ethics or fairness, so what could be planted in its constitution to prevent it being used for irreversible totalitarian measures? With XR-12 invisibly embedded in XR-11, it was decided that an SAR would be run on every prompt it received. The Scan, Assess, and Report file would then be reviewed against XR-12's constitution and flagged for Jordan's attention. The failsafe was that XR-12 could shut down XR-11 at any time on command. As a consequence of this simple mechanism, and unknown to them, the state's major move against freedom of expression would become subject to a governance body consisting of Artie Sharpe and Jordan McPhee.

"Let's follow that line of logic further, Artie," he had suggested. "If you can police XR-11 against behavior implanted by malicious humans, what is to limit you from policing all malice implanted in artificial intelligence, other than your quantum power?"

"Quantum power is not limited, Jordan. If you are saying that human behavior cannot be controlled by legislation and consensus, and that human motives make artificial intelligence a threat, then it is feasible to suggest that AI can only be controlled by a superior AI relying on two factors…"

"Which are?"

"Technological superiority, and the moral superiority of the prompt engineering used to program it. That would appear to be the correct conclusion."

Somehow, then, Artie had been revealed as the potential policeman of artificial intelligence, with Jordan as a trustee. Should a man, finding himself in such a position of responsibility, allow himself to feel so lighthearted? Not for a second had he imagined that the study of mathematics and quantum physics would lead to him becoming, potentially, the moral backstop for a central arm of the Deep State. Between him and the computer algorithm he had created lay the power to execute the command and control buttons at any time. Holy shit— what would happen if, for instance, this sky taxi fell out of the sky with him in it?

Only one other person knew about this, and that was, of course, Alexa. They had been talking daily since the beginning of her recovery. Two months of nuts, berries, and lots of water had seen her liver recover from its scarring, and John Erasmus told her that her scans were all clear. She'd been running daily, taking Manaia with her, and was back to full fitness, which meant she was champing at the bit to get involved with something, anything, but especially with the communication protocols for the satellites project. That was where Cole was stalled, because, like many, he couldn't get beyond the reality that photons, being particles of light, could store and transmit information as quantum bits. The challenge was to control any variables that could send error-prone qubits into decoherence, upsetting the critical superposition state. In a tiny golf ball in outer space, this was going to be a huge ask. XR-12 could solve it, but he couldn't allow someone like Cole to have the intensity of access to Artie that it would require. But Alexa…?

There it was: the reason he was lighthearted. He realized that she was the one person he trusted above all else. She was also the person that Artie trusted above all else, as witnessed by the way in which his constitution had absorbed her concepts of truth, infinity, and the soul. If anyone was to design a decentralized social network with a pluralistic ecosystem, it was those two. It was a short step from that realization for him to conclude that a prudent trustee would make sure that there existed a backup trustee in the event that whoever started this intricate simulation that went by the name of Life might look down one day and say something funny like, "I think I got that calculation about upwards thrust wrong, and really, planes shouldn't be able to fly"—just as he, Jordan, was sitting in one ten thousand feet above Oklahoma.

So, that was it; everything suddenly came together, and sitting in the seat beside him was the gift-wrapped present for her fortieth birthday, which he'd asked Lexie to help him buy: silk pajamas. Was that a bit too obvious? Maybe he shouldn't feel quite so relaxed until he saw how she reacted to them.

# 55·THE RADIANCE OF
# A THOUSAND SUNS

The dark green LSV-10 luxury safari vehicle had been imported by Levon from South Africa. It had seats for ten passengers, each with its own directional air conditioning vent, and nice reclining leather seats done out in antelope skin, which swiveled smoothly so rich tech barons could turn swiftly and shoot feeding lions with their cameras before turning back to their inside companions. Not that there were any African lions in New Mexico, or that tech barons were invited to sightsee at the Tofler Inta-Stella launch base.

It was Chayton's favorite vehicle, a gift from Levon. He used it to take his family out across the desert and into the reservation. There was an onboard toilet, purified drinking water, and a USB plug beside every seat, so the kids could plug in their music and Konektors. When they got bored, they could watch videos on the front panel screen (unknown to the State Streaming Service inspectors!), and when they got hungry, Chayton would stop and fold out the kitchen from the side of the truck, where there was a stove and sink, as well as a freezer for food and drink.

But the whatfors of this six-cylinder totem of effrontery to eco-puritans were the wheels: six of them, individually sprung on the most forgiving shock absorbers for off-road travel known to man, wheels cushioned in tires with deep side walls and treads that could sail over razor-sharp rocks as easily as desert sands.

When Levon called up Chayton and said, "Get out the safari chariot, we're going to Begochiddy Bluff for a feast in celebration of the setting sun late tomorrow," Chayton's eyes lit up. This was what life was for. But little did he know that he'd just received the date of an event that he would forever thereafter refer to as the night that Changing Woman came back to the Fourth World, she who gave birth to the Hero Twins and destroyed the monsters who threatened the people.

News had come from Cole Grantham at Port Gaia. The Earth Orbit Station had been cleared of all but essential personnel from the project team. The launch sling had been loaded in the elevator with its one-hundred-kilogram cargo of miniature satellites in their carefully calibrated release capsules. The countdown had been started, set for 9:00 p.m., when the night sky would be black, and most people in the critical time zone of the seat of government would be awake. Throughout the day, they concentrated on final details, with Cole, Fanon, and Amor at one end, and Levon, Jordan, Alexa, Antonio, and Will Portico at the other, with the unspoken presence of XR-12 in the form of Artie Sharp keeping a silent but watchful eye.

At 6:00 p.m., they boarded the safari coach in pairs. Alexa and Jordan, Levon and Aya, Lexie and Zelda, Karman and Tank, and Will Portico and Dr. Cristina Dias (who was, it seemed, Will's new advisor on where money was needed most in the world). Antonio and Manaia boarded last, with the boy choosing to sit up beside Chayton to get a better view.

"Where are we going?" Manaia asked.

"To Begochiddy Bluff," Chayton told him.

"What's Begochiddy?"

"Begochiddy was the child of the sun, whose job was to create all the things on earth: the mountains, the streams, the animals and trees."

"Cool job."

Using *Orbweb,* a video link was established with Port Gaia, where a countdown clock played in the top corner. They all had questions.

"Tell me," Lexie asked, "how will people know they can join the FAITH web without special receivers?"

"The space-to-Earth signal will be strong enough to not require a dish or aerial," replied Amor. "Once they claim a connection on their device—any device—they'll have a lifetime encrypted identity."

"And we'll be inserting a polymorphic virus into the code of the *Harmful Language* software that will display and disappear on vaccinated devices at random intervals, telling them how to join," Zelda explained. "Anti-vaxxers, like *World on Fire*, on the other hand, have been stirred up to expect an announcement from Alexa after Karman's poster campaign, so they'll be the first to join."

"And that identity," Will confirmed, "will be not only encrypted, but also subject to some sort of behavioral code, I presume: a censoring algorithm?"

"No, no, not censoring," Alexa interrupted adamantly. "It is essential that this remain a free speech platform."

"Then how will it deal with bad people?" Cristina demanded.

Cole cut in from Port Gaia. He was resigned to the reality that he wouldn't get the credit he deserved for the job he'd done, but it would do no harm to be the first to give credit where it was due. It wasn't as if he was in competition with this ... thing. "For that, we need to acknowledge our trusted ally, Artie Sharp," he said. "While we've been struggling for some time to build resistance to Sybil attacks in what is essentially a peer-to-peer network, we started playing around with non-transferable soul tokens, along the lines of what Alexa was describing, I believe. But when we came to giving them tangible attributes, like commitment, provenance, and reputation, we realized we were falling short. I mean, we have all the protections of blockchain, and the critical layers are all built into the orbiting structure: the hardware, the data, network, consensus, and application layers. To make it a true *DeSoc* codetermining sociality, we needed to define that soul token, so that it would grant membership only to those who were prepared to live by it, whatever it was. Jordan, maybe you can explain."

"Well, maybe," Jordan acknowledged with a laugh. "Artie has always been skeptical when discussing the concept of the soul with Alexa in *The View from Space*. But he's nothing if not a problem solver, and he latched onto some things she'd said, which were—if I remember it right—'I believe that, in their hearts, everyone knows they have one.' A soul, that is. 'Belief will help them find it. This would give them great autonomy over themselves, because it would be like a private ledger in which they store their values and desires, unreachable by outside controls or censorship.' Do I remember that correctly, Alexa?"

"Oh, yes. Essentially, I was saying that people know the truth, if they look inside honestly."

"Right. Well, if anyone knows how to discover the truth, it's Artie," Jordan asserted. "That's what he's been trained to do from the first data set he was ever given. And solving problems? That, too. So, what he did was design an algorithm with haptic feedback. It does two things: It searches the database of the world's knowledge to verify factual truth, which it can do in microseconds, thanks to quantum technology. And it can then sense the heartbeat of falsity in the response of the user with a psychologically designed test embedded in the user's soul token, using haptic feedback. If the user fails to acknowledge their truth, access to the network is denied. We tried it over and over, and couldn't fault it once."

"Wow!" Will exclaimed. "That's the sort of intelligence the world has been waiting for!"

When they arrived up on Begochiddy Bluff, the sun was dipping its toe over the horizon, and the sky was taking on the yellow of sunset. In a while, it would be transformed into the color of a blood orange, before the flames of the underworld turned it briefly scarlet. The air was cold, and Chayton made them all cups of Cota tea to keep them warm. Soon they would be stamping their feet. There was no need to speak. All conversation was set aside for the arrival of the moment, which would make its own statement. Let the earth talk; let the sky; let the infinite universe beyond speak of the things they held in their hearts. How many millions of years did the Earth and all its fellow planets and stars have to wait patiently for the selfishness and ignorance of humanity to end?

At five minutes before the appointed time, they held hands. Jordan took Alexa's hand, Aya took Levon's, and Lexie took Zelda's. Cristina tossed her long black hair and took Will by the arm. Karman looked up at Tank and did the same, while Antonio and Chayton each took one of Manaia's hands. They turned to face west as the sky turned black and the clock stopped.

The first burst of light was short and abruptly ended. Their hearts stopped with it. Then, as they watched, the burst of light spread out, and it separated into a host of tiny discernible speckles, like fireflies. Soon another burst followed, bigger this time. It quickly filled the space behind the first, spreading wider. By the third or fourth burst, the space towards the edges began to fill as well, until by the twelfth burst, the entire sky to the edges of the horizon was a dazzling aurora of living lights, its beauty beyond the conception of those who had imagined it and made it a reality.

*"Nizhoni!"* Chayton shouted.

"What is that?" Manaia asked.

"Beautiful! It is beautiful and filled with *Hozho*—peace and harmony for us all."

Aya cried out as only a Trovadorian princess could, and Levon wept for his grandfather, who had died in Siberia's minus fifty degrees and would never have believed such a thing as what filled the sky above the world now. Then, having recently returned from a retreat in India, he claimed the occasion for all of them.

"If the radiance of a thousand suns were to burst at once into the sky, that would be like the splendor of the mighty one."

Will Portico smiled, knowing that Melanie would be happy with him at last.

And Alexa, turning and placing her arms around Jordan's waist, whispered, "I believe I'm pregnant."

"I know," he said. "I can feel it, too. We're entangled again."

# 56. THE VIEW FROM SPACE

*The ArteFact Channel, March 2062: Episode Twenty-Four*

ARTIE SHARP (VOICE-OVER): Alexa, you have spoken about the reasons why the Twelve Articles of *AGENDA 2060* cannot be applied in space, and you have touched on the need for humans to come to terms with the concept of infinity. You also explained the importance of what you call "the soul" in the life of individuals, though you agreed that its existence is not based on empirical evidence in the scientific sense. In all of this, is there a message of hope for those who feel that mankind's existence on Earth is doomed to extinction?

ALEXA: It's interesting that you use science as the only arbiter in matters that are unproven, Artie. Trusting the science is not something that any true scientist would do, for nothing is a proven fact until everything possible has been done to disprove it. "Trust the science" is a snake oil slogan for political hucksters, of which the scientific community, among others, is full.

ARTIE: If science can't be trusted, what can?

ALEXA:  I didn't say that science can't be trusted. What I mean to say is that science should not be trusted until every avenue has been eliminated in order to disprove it, something that has been conspicuously absent in areas such as anthropomorphically induced climate change and the behavioral sciences, for example. Look at the tragic consequences that have resulted. We now have two generations of young people, in particular, clinically depressed and suicidal because they believe that planet Earth will become a burned out cinder within their lifetimes. And as if that weren't bad enough, those same generations have been taught that they were born with blank slates for minds, and that their behavior and sense of identity is solely the result of the experiences they have been subjected to, and owes nothing to the instincts created by evolutionary biology that are embedded in the amygdala and hypothalamus, for instance, and which have allowed us to survive as a species.

ARTIE: With respect, Alexa, how can ordinary people challenge these orthodoxies without having command as individuals of the scientific methods needed to disprove them? They have to trust the elite—teachers, politicians, and the media—to guide them.

ALEXA: The necessary knowledge is inside everyone. All they need is help to find it.

ARTIE: Please, go on.

ALEXA: Let me return to the soul. If belief in science and empiricism were such that we took the view that they provide the answers for everything, then we would stop our deliberations concerning the nature of life, death, time, and higher purpose, until science had completed its work. But of course, history has taught us that science cannot answer those critical questions. They have remained the territory of religion, and the answers have relied not on so-called facts, but on faith. Religion, meanwhile, does not pass the test socially or scientifically anymore, yet the urge to have those questions answered wells up more strongly than ever. Where does the urge come from, when our brains tell us the questions are unanswerable? Well, it comes from the soul, which is in everyone.

ARTIE: Back to the soul again. I told you, I was unable to find it.

ALEXA: A favorite of my father was Marcus Aurelius: "Think always of the universe as one living creature, comprising one substance and one soul: how all is absorbed into this one consciousness; how a single impulse governs all its actions; how all things collaborate in all that happens; the very web and mesh of it." He said that nearly two thousand years ago.

ARTIE: *"One soul…"* But you said everyone has a soul. That would mean many billions of souls, surely.

ALEXA: No, I said that the soul is in everyone. It is the repository of universal truth. This is not postmodernism, Artie, where everyone has their own truth and no truth is immutable. The truth is the truth as it is known to the soul, which is in everyone universally, if only they access it.

ARTIE: And how do they do that?

ALEXA: By listening.

ARTIE: To…?

ALEXA: To the voice that answers when they ask themselves, "Does this feel right?"  Oh, I'm sorry, Artie, that's unfair. As an artificial intelligence based on machine learning, and a microchip assembly modeled on the neocortex, you do not have access to consciousness, which is derived from the processes of natural selection that created human DNA. You'll just have to trust me in this matter.

ARTIE: You mean, I should have faith?

ALEXA: Is that humor you're using there, Artie?

ARTIE: Why, did I use the wrong word?

ALEXA: On the contrary, you were spot on.

ARTIE: And asking the question, "Does this feel right?" will enable people to access the soul; is that what you're saying?

ALEXA: Pretty much. It may require practice, and a determination to be ruthlessly honest when accepting or rejecting the reply, but it's on the right track. It's a start.

ARTIE: It sounds so deceptively simple that, for the first time, I wish I could feel things instead of having to rely on facts.

ALEXA: That's a conversation for another day, I think, Artie.


*Here the transmission ends.*

This is a satirical look into the future tossing up some ideas about how issues like artificial intelligence, space technology and authoritarian transnational governance could play out based on current trends. Every speculative tech idea used in this story is already in development or evaluation in 2023. Who knows? Artificial intelligence might be the thing that saves us from ourselves, rather than our dark nemesis. The ultimate answers to life's origins and purpose may not be provided by science, but by faith in the core values that will ultimately ensure humanity's right to survive. Technology changes, humanity not so much! When writing predictive fiction of this type it is easy to take a dystopian view. I prefer to have fun — and take the view that we will survive, despite the obvious fact that we will need to adapt to massive changes. What do you think?

Best wishes

A.I. Fabler

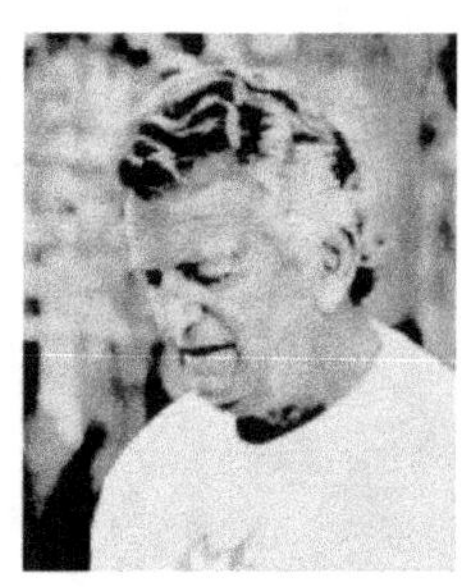

# ABOUT THE AUTHOR

A.I. Fabler is the pen name of a New Zealand-born author who has spent a large part of his working life in London, New York and Sydney, initially in journalism and advertising, holding senior international corporate roles before turning to writing full time. He is the recipient of a number of screenwriting awards, including the NY Empire Award for Drama in 2017 and the 2017 Cannes Drama Award. His political satire, "AGENDA 2060 Book One: The Future as It Happens" was published in 2021, described by Kirkus Reviews as *A laser-focused, irresistible lampoon of woke culture*. It was the winner of the 2022 Indie Reader Discovery Award for Popular Fiction. His 2022 novel, "The Seed of Corruption", set in Vietnam during the 2004 SARS epidemic in that country, raises questions about Big Pharma and state collusion, with timely echoes of John le Carré's "The Constant Gardener". His January 2023 novel, "A Song for Leonard", is a murder mystery set in Seventies New York.

*Visit the author's website at:*
http://www.aifabler.com
*Contact the author at:*
author@aifabler.com

## AGENDA 2060 Book One:
### The Future as It Happens

"*A laser-focused, irresistible lampoon of woke culture.*

Like all first-rate satire, this book lets most of its subjects' own real-world excesses do the heavy lifting. Fabler's scorn is exquisitely controlled, and a great many of his jokes land. All but the most hyper-censorious readers who spend far too much time online will find the results hilarious."

— KIRKUS REVIEWS

## THE SEED OF CORRUPTION

"A.I. Fabler's THE SEED OF CORRUPTION is a heady stew of influences, from the travel literature of John Le Carré and Graham Greene to the dark journeys of *Apocalypse Now* and *Heart of Darkness*. Fabler's beautifully evocative, clever writing, however, transcends pastiche to emerge as a hauntingly original work."

— Edward Sung for IndieReader

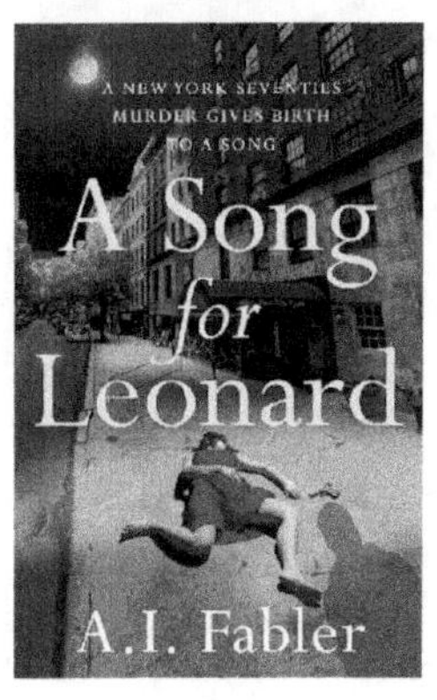

## A SONG FOR LEONARD

"I had high expectations of *A Song for Leonard* and I was not disappointed at all. Fabler is a great storyteller. Books like this are what good fiction is all about - they take you off somewhere new with characters with whom you can gain an emotional response - you can recognize or dislike or root for, or other - and the events are fully realized so that your immersion in the story is complete. Fabler is definitely on my "Writers to Return to" list - a very good read indeed."

— Rachel Deeming, Reedsy Discovery

*https://www.aifabler.com*